The Best of Best

AMERICAN
EROTICA
2008

15th
Anniversary Edition

EDITED BY

Susie Bright

A Touchstone Book
Published by Simon & Schuster
New York London Toronto Sydney

Touchstone
A Division of Simon & Schuster, Inc.
1230 Avenue of the Americas
New York, NY 10020

First Touchstone trade paperback edition January 2008

TOUCHSTONE and colophon are registered trademarks
of Simon & Schuster, Inc.

For information about special discounts for bulk purchases, please contact Simon & Schuster Special Sales at 1-800-456-6798 or business@simonandschuster.com.

Designed by Mary Austin Speaker

Manufactured in the United States of America

10   9   8   7

ISBN-13: 978-0-7432-8963-4
ISBN-10:   0-7432-8963-3

This edition of The Best American Erotica
is dedicated to the memory of my father and
editorial guru, Bill Bright

CONTENTS

CONTENTS

CONTENTS

INTRODUCTION

This is the fifteenth anniversary of *The Best American Erotica* series, and my last turn as editor.

Whew.

In this volume, I've invited some of my favorite storytellers to make an encore appearance. I interviewed each author, and asked:

What inspired you to write your story in the first place? How do you see it, now, compared to when you first wrote it?

When Debra Boxer first penned "Innocence in Extremis," she was deliberately and publicly a virgin. When Greta Christina wrote "Are We Having Sex Now or What?" she demanded to know what authentic sexual connection was made of in the first place.

I think my answer to Greta's question was, "If you have to ask, you're probably in the thick of it." Editing this series, for example, is one of the best sexual experiences I've ever had, and I'm not being coy.

So how have I changed, as *BAE*'s editor, in the past fifteen years?

When I was thirty-five, I had a new baby on my hip. I got a phone call from an editor in New York who said, "I hear you know more about erotic literature than anyone else in the country."

I shifted baby Aretha to the other side. "Well, if that's true, that's pathetic . . . but you're probably right. Most people have no idea what they're missing."

What were they missing? Honesty, for one. Good sex stories were in hiding. For a lot of readers at the time, "American erotica" was an oxymoron. It appeared as either some well-worn *Fanny Hill*–style paperback, or a plain-brown-wrapper novelty that revolved around a nymphomaniac and a pizza delivery boy. Not a bad start, but hardly the whole works!

Women erotic authors at the time were virtually unheard-of. Queer writers were underground. Henry Miller and D. H. Lawrence had been consigned to the stuffy scholars' corner of academia. Not a bright or accessible picture!

But I'd discovered something new since I started publishing small-press women's erotica in the 1980s with *Herotica* and *On Our Backs*. There were new writers willing to speak as frankly about sex as any other part of life—to hell with the smarmy stereotypes. They were inspired by Beat masters, S.C.U.M. manifestos, and *Penthouse Letters*, but had fashioned their own new breed of storytelling.

Some people wished that the "best erotica" would hold court as a romantic walk on the beach with a soft-focus ending. But the best authors I've worked with were outlaws, nonconformists, walking short planks on fantastic piers. Those are the waters where the "best" was swimming. Nobody'd ever heard their names before.

There were a couple of famous exceptions. When I started *BAE*, I wrote personal letters (e-mail was not something most people used!) to Nicholson Baker and Anne Rice, thanking them for using their real names to write unabashed and eloquent erotic novels. They came from such different worlds, but they both put their reputations on the line. The early 1990s were still a time when most "respectable" writers avoided distinct or frank sexuality.

Nowadays, I don't think there're mainstream novelists who

haven't been asked what role sexuality plays in their fiction—or why they're pussyfooting around, if they continue to avoid it. It's the stuff of Pulitzer and Nobel Prize winners.

It's not so much that erotica has made a narrow genre successful—although that's true too—it's that writers now don't hold back "the sex part" anymore when they write about . . . anything. The omission was always unnatural and deceptive, and now the lie is laid bare. Sexless stories about human relationships are dishonest. How did anyone write about love, life, or death and manage to avoid it so neatly? It was a hoax, and thankfully behind us.

Success and innovation in contemporary erotica bred fantastic originals—and also exploitation and mediocrity. Not exclusively, but certainly exponentially! That's the sign of how big American erotica became—it's admired, envied, and the butt of any number of literary jokes. But the proof of the erotic literary revolution is all around us, in cinema, on the Web, in our music.

Since I started *BAE* we've seen so much happen in American sexuality. There's been the dominance of the Christian fundamentalism in public policy, the fear—and then ghettoization—of the AIDS epidemic, the revolution of the Web, porn chic, kink liberation, the rise of multicultural literature—and gay literature, the end of the thriving independent American bookstore era, two wars, an impeachment vote, 9/11, and a national abstinence policy direct from the White House that is designed to keep us chaste until marriage, no matter how old we might get. The trench has been dug. There's a war on the ground, and a war for minds and hearts that reaches into the deepest American roots of Puritanism, individualism, and rebellion.

I don't know if we could have survived it all if it wasn't for some great erotic writing. No one wrote with more poignancy about New York and 9/11 than Tsaurah Litzky's "End-of-the-World Sex." No one captured the religiosity of sexual guilt better than Greg Boyd at his "Horny" best.

And the message of redemption—when you've done everything to screw the pooch—can be seen in the agonies of stories like Alicia Gifford's "Surviving Darwin."

What makes a piece of erotic fiction remarkable, even legendary? Probably the biggest factor is its unpredictability, the miracle when it transcends formula.

I couldn't resist Marian Phillips's "Three Obscene Telephone Calls" because it so neatly dug the "nice girls" grave. Thomas Roche innovated the trans-noir thriller with stories like his "Up for a Nickel." Nostalgia for the innocence that preceded labels, before consciousness of the world's judgments, is spun like honey in stories such as Patrice Suncircle's "Tennessee."

There're a few stories in this collection that I never got to include in *BAE* before because they predated 1993. I hungered for them; I cursed my tether to our annual tradition. First among those yearned for was "Blue Light," the novella by Steven Saylor, writing as Aaron Travis, which is perhaps the most fantastic supernatural erotic thriller ever written. Edgar Allan Poe would find a telltale cock pounding in this one. At first, I couldn't go to sleep from reading it, and then I couldn't rest until I published it! I'm so happy to finally have the story here.

The best erotic lit is always highest comedy and deepest tragedy—both in the cut, at times. I laughed at Eric Albert's "The Letters" when I wasn't moaning at his protagonist, "You've got to be stopped!"

Erotic prescience illuminates places and times that couldn't be captured any other way—like New York on a high-wire down low in Nelson George's "It's Never Too Late in New York."

And sometimes, you just need to laugh—a helpless, naked, wet belly laugh—at it all, like Joe Maynard's "Fleshlight."

The shaming prejudice about sex writing is that it's supposed to be so porny, so stupid, so obvious that "anyone" could write it, craft unnecessary.

But how many people can perfect its satire and get you off at the same time, like Serena Moloch's "Casting Couch"? How many chick-lit authors can turn a "Manicure" into a descent into the S/M looking glass, as Martha Garvey does? And who could articulate the dilemmas facing woman's sexual choices like Susan St. Aubin in her "This Isn't About Love"? Without their direct erotic approach, it wouldn't have been said nearly as well.

I also have some memorable new stories in this collection, too. I'll never say "Fuck me, Santa!" again without thinking of Steve Almond's "A Jew Berserk on Christmas Eve." Haddayr Copley-Woods's haunted house made me creep to my bed the night after I read it and felt the floors whispering to my soft feet. Jennifer D. Munro had me howling with size-queen irony in "Pinkie," and Eloise Chagrin reinvented a cuckold's tale in "Playing Doctor."

Erotic literature is made to break taboos—that's its promise. Rowan Elizabeth's "Halves" transformed a Hansel and Gretel–style fairy tale into a way of seeing unbreakable desire. Author G. Bonhomme reconstructed the male libido in his "Program," and Susannah Indigo throws every Sex and Love Addicts Anonymous rule out the car window in her "Year of Fucking Badly."

I, however, am ending my tenure as your editor a little sadly—although with great affection and respect. At the back of the book, you'll see I've included a list of all 272 writers I've worked with in our series to date—it made my jaw drop as I reviewed the list from top to bottom. I've also provided a Readers' Directory of the most influential editors, publishers, 'zines, and Web sites that've made erotic lit something to celebrate.

There's one person in particular I'll be missing as the series goes on—that's my dad, who passed away as I was first composing this anniversary edition.

When I was asked to start *Best American Erotica* in 1993, the number-one most excited person in the world was my father, Bill Bright. He was an editor, a linguist, a poet—and the greatest reader

I've ever known. That's not daughterly affection; probably everyone he knew would say the same thing. His descriptions to me of the history of American erotica, and censorship battles, were something he'd taught me since I had my first questions about "banned books."

When I was a little girl, he would sit me up at his desk while he was proofreading the galleys of his linguistics journal, *Language*. He'd give me a pencil and tell me to look for e's and a's that weren't closed up, serifs that had broken off. It took me pages and pages to find one, but what a treasure to discover a real mistake!

He proofread every one of my *BAE* manuscripts, which offered plenty of new grass to mow. His expertise and enthusiasm in world languages and writing systems were invaluable to every character in this series who spoke a line of dialog. Between the two of us, we covered a couple centuries of popular culture, idioms, and historical references.

In August 2006, Bill was proofreading the latest of my galleys, up to page 125. The next day he went into the hospital for brain tumor surgery, and he did not recover. The day before, at his desk, was the last time he used his red pen.

The following winter, I was back to work at my office, and I said to my daughter, now eighteen, "It just won't be *BAE* without him."

Aretha looked at the pile of unread manuscripts that sat on my desk, and started writing little notes all over them. And so the apple falls to the ground. I'll treasure her Post-its as I have every one of my dad's red-ink remarks.

Thank you to everyone, for all your letters, counsel, sexual inspiration, and surprises over the past fifteen good ones. I can't wait to see what's going to happen next; and I'm sure you'll find me in the thick of it, for many years to come.

Susie Bright
February 2008

[HALVES]

Rowan Elizabeth

Tavis and I are twins; each one half of a whole.

Mother was a twin. Her brother, Ian, was her only true friend. He was killed in the Pacific in forty-two. She immediately married Ian's best friend, my father, and they mourned together. They must have mourned primarily in the bedroom, for shortly after they found themselves expecting.

Our parents were blessed with both a boy and a girl in one messy arrival. Father cradled me and cooed my name, "Minna." Mother laid Tavis out on the bed to examine his ten tiny fingers and toes and to be sure he arrived with all of the requisite equipment. They promised their infants a childhood of loving innocence.

Tavis and I were inseparable. Every one of our firsts came together. First steps, first words, first climb up a tree. Neither of us would leave the other behind. We refused to bathe unless we were together. Mother schooled us at home, and we spent each hour of the day together. We slept in the same bed until we were twelve. That's when Grandmother moved in, bringing her money, her views, and her yappy little dog.

Grandmother had been left well-off when Grandfather passed away. How our mother grew up under her rule confounded us. Yet Mother was gracious and beautiful, glowing with the love of life she passed on to us.

"I will not allow Minna to be ruined like your brother ruined you," we would hear Grandmother chastise Mother. Grandmother was appalled and swore we would grow up differently.

Everything changed when she came. I could no longer wash Tavis's back as he took his bath; I had to wear my swimsuit top when we went to the lake. Grandmother didn't permit us to hold hands or to eat off of the same dinner plate any longer.

Father was a quiet man with sad, loving eyes. He was proud and worked hard to provide for us. When Grandmother and her heavy purse took up residence, both barreled over Father and Mother.

The atmosphere of eternal spring left our house.

I was kept at home to be taught by Mother while Tavis was shipped off to St. Boniface Catholic Church for a proper Catholic education. Grandmother gave strict instructions, and a healthy donation, to the school for them to keep tight reins on Tavis.

We were put in bedrooms on opposite ends of the big house. Grandmother entrenched herself in a bedroom between ours. She slept with her door open, and her tiny devil-dog would bark when anyone passed in the hall.

I couldn't sleep without Tavis next to me. Mother would lie with me until I fell asleep. After she left, I would wake and imagine I could hear Tavis down the hall. I knew he was awake and Mother was lying next to him to coax him to sleep.

Our separation was horrible, and it seemed that nature conspired with Grandmother to increase our suffering. Our bodies changed, and we could not revel in those changes with each other. I'm sure Tavis noticed my developing chest, just as I took in his peach fuzz across the breakfast table. I wanted to tell him about the monthly change, and about the heavy feeling between my legs when I tried to fall asleep.

A handful of years later, Grandmother paid the tuition for Tavis to attend a college hundreds of miles from home. I was not to receive further education. Grandmother had courted a family for their eldest son, who was tightly tied to the Church. She planned my marriage as though we lived a hundred years in the past.

As terrible as it may sound, we were relieved when the old crone died the summer before Tavis was to go away to school. Mother and Father used the money Grandmother left to send us both to the university. There I developed my love of art and the workings of the mind. Tavis studied engineering, a subject that his technical mind devoured.

Once again we were divided, not by the rules of Grandmother but by the rules of the university—co-ed dorms were unheard of at that time—and our temperaments. Like my father, I was quiet and took everything in. Tavis flourished in the public setting.

My roommate was a loud southern girl who lived in bright colors and heavy makeup. Many nights she snuck her new boyfriend through the dark halls and brought him to our room. I would feign sleep and silently watched her allow him to fondle and caress her. He would run one hand over her blouse while he tried to inch the other up her stocking-clad leg. She would giggle and smack his hand. It was the night when she didn't giggle that shocked me.

I saw his fingers coax their way up her thigh, and bunch up her skirt and slip to reveal the tops of her stockings and the suspenders of her girdle. For the briefest of moments, his hand cupped the crotch of her white panties.

I touched the heaviness between my legs and felt something spark. There was wetness, and everything felt fuller than it did when I washed in the shower. The bump at the top of my female separation seemed to dance under my fingers. Quietly, I rubbed myself, the wetness growing and unnerving energy building up. Something was coming together between my legs, and it felt as though it would break through my skin. And that's exactly what it did. The energy flew from my body into the room and took off for the sky.

"Minna, are you awake?" asked my roommate.

I lay quiet in the dark and pretended sleep.

Tavis told me, "He thinks I'm asleep. He pulls and tugs like I do and groans at the end."

Tavis and I spent every moment outside of class huddled together on the upper levels of the student union or in the stacks of the library, trying to make up for the years Grandmother had kept us apart. Over time, those years apart began to seem like an unfortunate dream.

"Tavi! You do it, too? How?"

"When I first started, I would wrap my sheet around my parts and rub against my bed. I would do it every night after Mother left my room. I wanted to come to your room to show you. I would get long and firm and just running my hand along it made me light-headed. Then I used spit, but now I use baby oil."

"What on earth for?"

"To make it slick; it's easier for my hand to rub up and down."

"I get wet all by myself. I put my fingers in my opening to get the wet part, and then massage it into my . . . uh."

"It's called a 'clitoris.' I've found books. The textbooks talk about penises and vaginas, but an author named Henry Miller calls our parts cocks and cunts."

Heat flushed not only my face, but spread between my legs. "You have to show me these books."

We read everything we could find. We would take our books to an unused room on the top floor of the library, and Tavis would help me put together the pieces.

"I rubbed myself in my room. I think all of the blood in my body rushed to my . . . my cunt. I could hear my heartbeat in my ears and I was breathing so hard."

"I jerk off as much as I can." Tavis enjoyed using our new language.

"Show me. Show me how you do it."

He unfolded his legs and leaned against the wall. I bit my lip as he opened his trousers and pulled out his pink flesh. It was bigger than I remembered from years ago. Limp and wrinkled, it had a bulbous head with the same slit in the end. It didn't seem as imposing as the pictures showed or the stories described.

Tavis spit into his hand and began running his hand over his penis. He pulled on it in such a way that I was sure he would hurt himself.

As I watched, the flesh in his hand grew. It lengthened and became fatter. Oh, how it changed!

Tavis closed his eyes and stroked up and down his length. He would pause and roughly handle the full head. Moisture formed at his opening. I wanted to reach out and touch that glimmering drop. Tavis began making low sounds. I watched in amazement of his obvious pleasure. I wondered if his thighs tingled like mine did when I touched myself, like they were at that moment.

I pressed my hand between my legs to calm the growing rush. Instead of peace, I found I needed to press harder.

Tavis began lifting his hips and jagged sounds rasped from his lips. He opened his eyes and looked at me at the same moment I knew his pleasure had reached its peak. Stroking furiously, he cried out as thick white cream spit from the opening in his penis. He slowed his hand and relaxed into the wall with a deep breath.

"Does that happen every time?"

"When I was really young, I felt a rush, but nothing came out. But now, yes, I come every time."

I was amazed. I leaned forward on my knees and touched the fluid on his belly. It was thick and clung to my finger, which I raised to smell, but stopped short of putting to my tongue.

Tavis's penis was already shrinking, and his breathing was returning to normal. The insistent ache between my legs refused to subside.

That night, as I touched myself, I thought of Tavis coming for me.

I knew that his lengthened penis was made to push into a woman's body. As I plunged my fingers into my opening, I imagined that they were the strong flesh between his legs.

Over Christmas holiday, Tavis and I went home to be with our parents.

The life had returned to our house. Mother squealed in delight when Father would tickle her and chase her through the kitchen. There was no one to tell Tavis and me that we couldn't squeeze together in our favorite overstuffed chair.

And there was no one sleeping in the hall between us; the devil-dog had been given away.

Each night, when the house became dark and quiet, Tavis crept down the long hall to my room. He lifted the heavy quilts and slid his body next to mine. I curled my back into his chest, and we slept as we had when we were children.

During the third night, I felt him grow hard and insistent against my backside. I pressed my bottom into his firmness and heard his sharp breath. His arm that had lain easily over my waist held me tight as he rubbed over the swell of my behind. His breathing became like it had been when I had watched him touch himself . . . like my breath did when I touched myself.

I could feel my heart beating between my legs and a fullness low in my belly. Tavis clutched my hip as he jerked, and his wetness soaked into my nightgown.

He pulled my soiled clothes over my head and wiped himself and me. I rolled onto my back and looked through the darkness.

"Tavi, I need something."

He took my hand and guided it between my legs, pressing it against me with his own. "Show me," he said.

I began tracing the path that slid into my wetness and pulled it up to circle my nub. Tavis curled up against me and wrapped his arm around my middle. I massaged with increased speed and pressure, the fingers of my other hand slipped into my vagina.

I came quickly and rested against him only a moment as I gathered my energy to show him how far my pleasures could take me. As I began to experience my second orgasm, I felt his penis grow stiff against my hip.

In the safety of the dark, Tavis pulled his body on top of mine. I opened my legs to let him lie between my thighs.

"I won't enter you."

I felt the smooth head of his penis as it slid up the soft flesh of my thigh. For the briefest of moments I felt it nuzzle at my opening; involuntarily my hips raised to meet him. My wetness allowed the head to break through my opening, and Tavis let out a cry of panic. He pulled his cock from me and sat up on his knees. I could see him clutching himself as he ejaculated on my belly.

Horrified, he wiped up the cream with his hand and rushed out the door. He did not come back to my bed after that night.

Back at school, Tavis would not be alone with me. His roommate, Sean, was with us always. Without him, Tavis avoided me. I did not know if it was his shame or his fear of temptation that kept him from me.

I would go to our room on the upper level of the library and take in the scent of the books that I associated with Tavis. I would close the door, turn out the light, curl up, and cry. I couldn't understand how he could leave me.

"Your brother stopped by to see you today," my roommate told me.

"Why?"

"Probably because he's your brother, silly. He wanted me to tell you that you should come by his room tomorrow after dinner. He has something to tell you."

My roommate continued her bedtime ritual, unaware of the butterflies flying from my stomach out my mouth. The butterflies landed between my legs; their light tickling made me want to rub them away.

As she slept, I caressed myself and thought of being stretched and entered.

I walked across campus, but my heart was racing and my breath was catching as if I had run the whole way.

Tavis opened the door as soon as I knocked. His sharp features softened into the smile that had carried me through childhood. For the first time in a month he opened his arms to me. I crushed myself against his chest. He stroked my hair and held me.

"Minna?"

I looked up into the face I loved more than any other.

I heard a noise off to my right. Sean stepped up beside me and pushed the door closed. Startled, I pulled back and looked to Tavis for explanation.

Sean reached out and touched my face.

I stumbled backward into the door. Tavis caught my hand. "Minna, let me explain."

I stared at the two boys as if they were strangers.

"Sean, can you give us some time?"

Before leaving, Sean kissed Tavis on the mouth. My Tavi!

Tavis led me to the sofa that sat opposite the sleeping lofts. He gave me a glass of sweet liquor and held my hand.

"Minna. Sean and I want to be lovers."

"You love him more than me?" I asked. My mind screamed.

"I can't be with you, and there isn't another girl who can replace you." He filled my glass with more of the sticky alcohol. I drank it quickly, without thinking, and he filled it again.

"I want you to see us. Watch us. I can't have my first time without you."

The liquor clouded my senses. I curled my legs under me and nestled under his arm. "Is this what you really want?"

"Yes."

I could not deny Tavis anything.

I sat in the crook of his arm and took in his scent. He allowed me to run my hands over his hard chest and down the muscles of his arms. My head lay in his lap when Sean came through the door.

Wobbly, I stood and faced my replacement. His green eyes were soft and understanding as he pressed his hand against my cheek.

"Let me see you love him," I said.

Tavis stood and held my face in his hands. With a smile of gratitude, he kissed my lips and pulled away from me into the arms of Sean.

I sat on the sofa and watched. I tilted my head and bit my lip as their mouths came together. My Tavis with another.

Sean, not as tall as Tavis, took the lead and began stripping my brother of his clothes. Their urgency was startling . . . so much so that I could taste it in the air. I sipped my liquor and watched as they shed their clothes.

When Sean sat, I inched down to the far end of the sofa. I was a mere two feet from this naked man, whose erection stood above his body. My blood pounded with a familiar throb.

His erection was only the second I'd seen; I compared it to Tavis's. Sean's wasn't as long, but it was more thick and meaty, more solid.

Tavis knelt between Sean's spread legs and brought his mouth to the protruding cock. I leaned forward to observe as much of the scene as I could. My hand ran over my belly, and my fingers slipped into the waistband of my dungarees.

Tavis's tongue darted along the raised ridge of Sean's penis before he opened his mouth to take it in. Tavis shut his eyes and, with a deep suck, pulled Sean into his throat. His inexperience engendered a gag and he pulled back. I saw that his eyes watered. He tried again. His hands ran over the taut muscles of Sean's thighs as he worked against the flesh riding his tongue.

I reached out to touch Sean's bare shoulder. He looked at me with glazed eyes that shut as he leaned into the sofa.

Tavis's mouth ran up and down the shaft between his lips. His hand followed to stroke the length and then to squeeze the full sac beneath. Sean groaned with deep breaths and began thrusting his hips into Tavis's face.

They were living art, a human sculpture of smooth skin over muscle and bone. My Tavis was as hard as Sean. I wanted to reach out and stroke Tavis's penis as I had seen him do, stroke it to explosion. Instead, I cupped my mound inside my pants and squirmed on my hand.

Tavis sat back and coaxed Sean to turn around and present his rear end.

Tavis pulled his roommate's ass cheeks apart and ran a finger down the crack to the sensitive pucker. He gathered spit and began to lubricate the entrance. He wet two fingers with more saliva and pressed them against Sean's tight rim. Sean groaned under the sharp pressure. Tavis stroked his lover's back and murmured quietly. His relaxing gestures soothed Sean; Tavis's fingers slid past the rim.

I sat forward on the sofa with my head propped to watch the entrance. Tavis's fingers slid in to the second knuckle, and Sean gave a low moan.

"Stroke his cock," I told Tavis.

Obedient, he reached around and caressed Sean's bobbing hard-on, his own erection pressing against his friend's hip.

I wanted him to know that I would give him whatever he wanted. I crossed the room to his nightstand and retrieved the baby oil I was sure would be there. I dribbled the oil over Sean's backside and Tavis's straining cock. He pressed the lubricant into Sean with twists of his fingers and then coated his own cock.

I chewed on my lips as I watched Tavis press the head of his cock to his roommate's ass. The slickness coaxed the head of Tavis's cock to pop past Sean's rim. I knew Sean's pleasure; Tavis was once this far into me.

I sat back on my heels and watched Tavis take Sean. Both rocked into the other with closed eyes and labored breath. Tavis pulled his roommate onto him by his hips as Sean furiously pulled his own cock. I rocked on my balled-up fist between my legs.

My beautiful brother, sweat beaded on his face, eyes crushed closed, was breathing like he had so many weeks ago as he pressed against my bottom. With a deep grunt, he pressed forward. I imagined his cock shooting fluid deep inside his friend.

Tavis pulled his cock out, and a thin line of his fluid dripped down toward Sean's scrotum. Kneeling, he massaged it into the sensitive skin, reached around, and grabbed greedily at the turgid flesh. Sean began to jerk under Tavis's assault and shot a long line of cream onto the sofa.

Both boys collapsed into each other. They both remembered me sitting there in the room with them at the same time.

I stared at them with wide eyes and pressed my hand harder against my crotch.

"Minna, do you need something?"

I could do nothing but shut my eyes and whimper.

I felt the sofa shift as Sean crawled toward me. I opened my eyes to find both boys within touching distance. I reached out and took Tavis's cock in my hand. It was still heavy with blood and began to come alive under my fingers.

Sean surprised me by unbuttoning my pants and then pulling them off. He coaxed my bottom up as he removed my panties.

I leaned back into the softness, Sean kneeling on the cushions under my behind.

We didn't talk as my brother and his lover shifted my legs apart. I felt Sean's long fingers run through my folds. He pulled them apart to further examine me and found my firm nub. His fingers circled as his other hand drew moisture from my opening and coated my pussy with it. He inserted his fingers into me and reached places that only I had touched.

Sean probed and rubbed me until I came in his hands.

Tavis brushed the hair out of my eyes and asked, "Do you need something more?"

My barely discernible nod was all that was needed.

Sean had become fuller and firmer again, and Tavis coaxed him to hardness with his still-slick hand. I felt the pressure of Sean's cock at my entrance. He flexed his hips and entered me slowly. My tunnel stretched to a fullness that I had only imagined from my one brief experience. Once Sean penetrated me completely he began to thrust with more urgency.

Tavis sat on the arm of the sofa behind me and cradled me as his lover—our lover—shared the power of the first time. As when we were children, Tavis and I did not take life's steps alone.

I grasped Tavis's hand and touched Sean on the shoulder. He pressed against me and surprised me with a kiss. I let his tongue enter my mouth; pleasure surged through my body. I wrapped both arms around Sean's back and pulled him to me. His deep thrusts crushed my already sensitive parts. A feeling, similar to my earlier hand-generated orgasms, grew deep within my belly. A place only barely reached by my fingers was under assault by Sean's cock. I arched my hips and rocked with his motion. The feeling grew and washed over my entire body as I came. Sean soon followed with a series of grunts and moans.

Sean lifted his face from where he had buried it in my shoulder, smiled beautifully, and kissed me again.

We spent the semesters sharing one another's bodies and discovering the many things we were capable of.

Our junior-level finals came and went. Tavis and I convinced our parents to let Sean spend the summer with us. We ran free on the house grounds and at the lake as Mother and Father traveled around the countryside in their new Ford Thunderbird convertible. The house was ours, and we lived as we pleased.

It was not until the beginning of July that I became nauseous every day. The boys comforted me with ginger ale and forced me to sit in the shade by the lake. When my monthly didn't arrive, I knew Sean had fathered my child.

Telling Mother and Father was terrifying, but they were oddly calm. They suggested that Sean and I marry and live in the big house with them. Tavis and Sean would go back to finish school, and I would stay with my parents to grow through my term.

Christmas 1964. Tavis and Sean were driving home for the holiday and to see my expanding belly. Tavis's Mustang hit a deer, and the car careened into a tree. My Tavis was crushed by the thick trunk of the oak. The police brought Sean and his armful of presents, all rescued from the smashed car, home to us.

Like my parents, Sean and I were blessed with both a boy and a girl in one messy arrival. Sean cradled our daughter and cooed her name. I laid my son, Tavis, out on the bed to examine his ten tiny fingers and toes and to be sure he arrived with all of the requisite equipment. We promised our infants a childhood of loving innocence.

ROWAN ELIZABETH
on "Halves"

"Halves" was such fun to write. My inspiration came from a relationship with a fellow writer. "John," like myself, is bisexual, and we shared stories of experiences and fantasies as we worked on our writing together. We began thinking of ourselves as twins separated at birth. The concept of the bond between twins, and how that relates to a developing sexuality, intrigued me. From there, I began writing, and the rest formed itself.

How do I feel about it now versus when I wrote it? I appreciate it more. It inspires me to run with ideas that may teeter on the edge of propriety.

SURVIVING DARWIN

Alicia Gifford

I met Curtis Greene in AA. He told me he'd gotten too fond of his Pouilly-Fuissé despite his dry Southern Baptist upbringing. He said he'd started to drink socially after moving to California, and then he'd started to look forward to getting home at night for a glass or two every day. He never wanted to go to restaurants that didn't have a good wine list. He figured he had a problem, he said, and started to come to meetings.

We got friendly and I could tell he liked me by the way he'd look for me and save me a seat. He'd get red and tongue-tied talking to me. He told me he was a pharmacist and owned three drugstores in the Los Angeles area, Greene's Pharmacies. He drove a new BMW the color of midnight and he smelled good, like money. He was married, he said, and had a little boy named Alex.

I got caught stealing large amounts of Vicodin from the hospital floor I worked on as a nurse. I'd pop a few and get to work, tending to my patients' needs while loaded on their pain meds. I loved my job when I was high. I felt connected. Actualized.

Things were great as long as a couple of pills would get me loaded, but then I needed six, and then ten at a time, to get the kind of buzz I needed. I started to wake up feeling like shit until I could get a few Vicodin in me.

Nurses are in such short supply that they can't get rid of all of us druggies or the patients would be wiping their own asses; or worse yet, the supervisors and administrators would have to do it, so they send us for our shot at redemption to a program called Diversion, a rehab for licensed health professionals operated by the state of California. They assign you a color and make you call a phone number every day, and if it's your color you have to go piss in a jar for random drug testing. You have to go to Diversion meetings once a week and AA or NA meetings the other six nights, and every six months a committee of tight asses evaluates you to see how you're progressing with your little problem.

NA was full of street drug addicts—meth freaks with open sores and junkies with the jitters. I found the AA crowd more to my liking, but I was desperate for a way out of this mess. I hated Diversion, and, without Vicodin, I hated nursing.

One night I walked to the meeting about a mile from my apartment and then I asked Curtis for a ride home. I leaned my head back against the leather headrest and laid my hand on his thigh. Fifteen minutes later his cock was in my mouth and he was telling me that he thought about me night and day. I saw possibilities.

We started an affair. He told me about his wife, how he and she were high school sweethearts back in Benton, Arkansas, where they grew up. His wife, the only woman he'd been with before me, was prudish and frigid, he said. I was forbidden fruit, a wild California girl, free-spirited and comfortable with my body. After sex the first time, he asked me if I'd felt "warm."

"Do you mean: did I come?" I asked.

He winced. "Yes," he whispered. I taught him the marvel of the clitoris and buried his face in it. He'd bawl after sex with me, blubbering how much he loved me, how lucky he was to have found me. He said he loved his wife too, and his son, and that he was just so torn up inside.

"If you love your wife so much, why are you here?" I asked him.

He blinked bewildered blue eyes. "Have you ever thought about divorce?"

He startled. "I couldn't divorce Susan," he said. "I could never leave my boy."

I laughed at him. "You don't divorce your *kids,* silly."

I lied and told him that a doctor at work had asked me out. I said that he was cute and single and crazy about me, and that I hoped everything would work out between us. Curtis didn't hide his emotions well.

I said, "Honey, you're married. I can't put my life on hold for a married man."

He sat there with his head in his hands. "I can't stand the thought of you with someone else," he said, looking like a dazed, sick cow.

"I'm not going to *sleep* with him," I said. "Not on our first date."

"I can't get a divorce, I just can't." I had to keep boxes of Kleenex everywhere because Curtis was always bursting into tears.

Later I got together with my ex-boyfriend Artie. We were still good friends and still had an intense sexual relationship even though he was living with an older, wealthy woman who supported him.

He lit up a joint.

"Get that stuff away from me," I told him. "You'll contaminate my urine." It smelled so good. I love drugs, to tell you the truth. I miss Vicodin, the stony bliss of it. If I could get away with it, I'd be using—not out of control like last time. Now and then. A sensible habit. But I had five years of Big Brother in the form of Diversion in my future.

"So what do you get out of torturing this guy?" Artie asked.

"I like him," I said. "Plus, you never know."

"Right," Artie said. "A hayseed from Podunk is right up your alley."

I waved my hand like a game-show hostess toward my new wide-screen TV and Bang & Olufsen sound system. "He also paid for my transmission."

"Any good in bed?" Artie asked, stoned now, yanking at my sweatshirt.

"He's sweet. And a good learner," I said, mimicking Curtis's Arkansas lilt. "And extremely grateful." I had to stop talking then, Artie had his fat tongue in my mouth and was digging into my pants with his fingers. Artie kissed a lot of puckered, old-lady ass to live like he liked, and when we got together, he took control and I submitted. I found humiliation cleansing somehow, absolution for something blistered in me.

I got the box out from under the bed and he trussed me up with leather straps. He put alligator clamps on my nipples and gagged and blindfolded me. Artie was fun that way.

Curtis didn't look too good. He'd lost fifteen pounds in the three months since our affair started, and bags hung under his eyes. He said that he couldn't stop thinking about me, and that his wife kept asking him what was wrong. She wanted to go to couples' counseling. He told me that if it wasn't for his son he might consider getting a divorce. They were so young when they got married, he said, and he'd become a different man. His wife was still the same Arkansas piano teacher who went to church every Sunday and Wednesday nights. Her throat had never experienced a warming swallow of alcohol or the blunt thrust of a penis.

Alex was six. Curtis showed me pictures of him, a towhead with Curtis's water-blue eyes and pouty red mouth. He showed me pictures of his wife Susan, too, your basic midwest Baptist, dressed in crisp, buttoned-up pastel shirts and tailored slacks and loafers. I scanned through the photos, a tic jerking my upper eyelid like a pulse.

He wanted me to meet Alex, so one Saturday he took him to the mall and we staged a coincidental meeting. Alex was bored and fidgety while Curtis and I drank coffee. At one point he looked at me with his crusty little eyes and said, "My mom is prettier than you."

Curtis said, "Mommy's very pretty but that's not a nice thing to say. Ms. Nolan is very pretty too."

I smiled at the little prick. "All good little boys think their mommy is the prettiest in the whole world." Curtis beamed at me, and when Alex wasn't looking, he blew me a kiss. My eye was twitching again. I craved a Vicodin.

Afterward, he phoned me. "See why I couldn't break up my family, even though I love you so much I can't function?"

"He's precious," I said, trying not to vomit. "Maybe it's best if we stop seeing each other." I hung up. I ignored his calls and didn't answer the door when he came pounding on it. He left me notes in my mailbox, desperate missives that Artie and I giggled over.

"So it's over with the hayseed?" Artie asked, flopping on my sofa.

"Hardly," I said.

"You're not going to break up his family, are you?"

"*I'm* not. He might, though. He's not as happy as he thought he was."

"What about the brat? You're not exactly the mommy type."

"He's a bit of a problem."

"It'd be awful if something happened to him," Artie said, undoing his belt and wrapping it around my neck.

"Awful," I said. Artie cinched the belt and I saw stars.

Now, Curtis is at my house. He's weepy and tiresome with his professions of love and angst over what to do about it.

"Life is short," I tell him. "I'm turning thirty-five next month. I can't be wasting my time on dead ends."

"If it wasn't for Alex—"

"Look, we've each got to do what's right. I love you but you're taken." I let my voice break a little. I'm fond of Curtis, or maybe it's his desperate adoration that appeals to me. I offered to let him tie me up, but he was shocked, wouldn't do it. He said he couldn't enjoy degrading me that way. Artie would pistol-whip me unconscious if I let him.

"I can't live without you," Curtis says. "I'm going to ask Susan for a divorce. We can share custody of Alex. You'd be such a good influence on him, I just know it."

"Baby—are you sure?"

"I love you, Nina. I want to marry you, take care of you. You could quit your job and we could have babies together, little brothers and sisters for Alex." I feel a dark, thrilling victory. I hide my face in his shoulder and cry real tears, not from happiness but for something I can't name. My skin burns and itches like I've rolled in dried grass.

He tells Susan that he's in love with another woman and that he wants a divorce. She goes berserk in a quiet, midwestern way, developing a taste for vodka and taking to her bed. He says that Alex has started to wet his pants.

Susan begs Curtis to reconsider. She calls his mother in Arkansas, who calls him and implores him to come to his senses.

"I'm in love, Mother. Life is short. I'm divorcing Susan, not Alex. I'll always be his daddy, and he'll spend half his time with me." He's talking to her on his cell phone in my apartment, and I listen to the conversation with my head lying on his bare genitals. I lick the head of his penis while he consoles his mother. "Susan will be fine. Everyone in California gets divorced. She'll be financially secure, and Alex will still have both of his parents plus a wonderful new stepmother. Wait until you meet her," he says, closing his eyes, his cock rigid against his belly.

After Curtis's lawyer serves Susan divorce papers, she takes Alex to a neighbor's house. She fills her car with gasoline and then drives into their snug, weather-stripped garage. She closes the door and drinks a pint of vodka with the motor running; a photo of Curtis, Alex, and her laughing in front of a Christmas tree is on the dash. When Curtis phones to tell me of her suicide, I'm shocked, but then it occurs to me that he won't have to pay her alimony or divide their assets—we'll have it all. And then it hits me that Alex will be with Curtis twenty-four/seven now. Artie is right—I'm *not* the maternal type. I can't help wishing she'd taken Alex with her.

Curtis flies to Little Rock with Alex and Susan's body to bury her there. He phones to tell me how awful and sad the scene is there, how much he misses me, and how he wants to get married as soon as decently possible, to create a stable family environment for Alex.

"I can't take care of someone else's brat," I tell Artie.

"You are some piece of work, girl," he says. "Do you have any guilt at all?"

There's something in me that cringes to think of Susan alone in her car, breathing in carbon monoxide and gulping down vodka. And there's another part of me that revels in it, finds a black satisfying thrill in her despair.

"The way I see it," I tell Artie, "it's dog-eat-dog, survival of the fittest. Susan wasn't a survivor."

"Brrr," Artie shivers. "I never want to get on your bad side," he says, getting undressed.

"Too late," I say, reaching for the box under my bed.

Curtis wants Alex and me to get to know each other slowly. We go to the zoo. We go to the beach. We rent Disney videos and watch them at Curtis's five-thousand-square-foot home in La Canada Flintridge, an affluent suburb of Los Angeles. It's done in a kitschy country decor that makes me want to gag. I see black granite and silk-covered walls. Chrome and nickel and sumptuous wool carpeting to hide the cliché of peg-and-groove oak.

"Why don't you take him out by yourself this Saturday?" Curtis says. "I have to attend a seminar."

"Sure, honey," I say. "Good idea."

I've been having bad dreams and sleeping poorly. I have a

blotchy rash on my chin, and my joints ache. I'm getting migraines. I don't feel like hanging out with Alex, who snivels all the time, but Curtis doesn't want me to move in or get married until he feels Alex is comfortable with me. I ask Alex what he'd like to do, and he shrugs. I get him into the car, the Range Rover that Susan killed herself in, and buckle him into his seat belt.

We head to a coffee shop to get some breakfast. As we're driving I look at Alex and see tears streaking his face.

"What now?" I ask.

"I miss my mother," he says. All Alex knows is that his mother is dead.

A dazzling scotoma appears in my field of vision, harbinger to a migraine. And me without a pain pill.

"I'm sorry about your mommy, honey," I say to him. The first throbs descend on my brain. "But she's in heaven. With God. She must be happy there." My mouth has a metallic taste, like I've been sucking a lead pipe.

"She's not happy, not without me and Daddy," he says. "I hate you. I wish *you* were dead." His small body convulses with sobs. My head hurts so bad I have to pull the car over. I'm nauseated and break into a sweat. I've just enough time to open the car door and vomit the coffee I had earlier, then bile. I'm drenched, my shirt sticks to my body and sweat streams from my armpits. I feel a tapping. I wipe my mouth on my sleeve and turn to see Alex, who's undone his seat belt and is kneeling on the seat, rubbing my back and shoulder with his hand, his face anxious and tearstained.

"I'm sorry," he says. "I didn't mean it." He covers his face with his hands. I put my arms around his sturdy little body and my nose fills with his boy smell. He hugs me, trembling. Each beat of my heart is a wrenching explosion in my brain. I left some Excedrin Migraine back at Curtis's house.

"I have to go back to the house and get my headache medicine," I tell him. I can't see; the scotoma is like a sizzling white starburst that takes more than half my field of vision from each eye, leaving me with blind spots. I hang a U-turn, careening the car crazily. Despite the headache it occurs to me that Alex has left his seat belt unfastened. I imagine hurtling into one of the thick, old elms that line the street—a horrible accident while crazed with a migraine, and poor little Alex, his seat belt undone, becomes a Scud missile. I envision him shooting through the windshield, impacting the tree. A lightning storm of pain blazes in my brain.

I pull the car over.

"Put your seat belt on, Alex," I say, panting, leaning my head on the steering wheel. Snot streams from my nose to my lap. "Safety first," I say. He nods and fastens it, and I manage to get us back to Curtis's house.

"I'm going to take my medicine and rest," I tell Alex. I lie down on the living room sofa and he goes to watch television in the den. I fall asleep and wake to find him standing over me, pale and worried looking.

"I'm okay," I say.

"Do you want a drink of water?"

"That'd be nice." He brings me water in a plastic Pokémon cup, arranges his blanket on my legs, and puts his hand on my forehead. I tell him again that I'm fine and he goes back to watch TV. I think of how his body felt in my arms, how it pulled at something in me. I wonder if I could ever love him, if I could ever love anything. I vomit the water I've just swallowed, and Alex brings paper towels and mops it up. I tell him again I'm fine.

By the time Curtis gets home in the afternoon my headache is gone and Alex and I have eaten pizza and watched cartoons. I tell Curtis about the morning, how sick I was, and how Alex took such good care of me. Alex listens, pink with pleasure, his eyes downcast and shy. Curtis, of course, is crying.

Later I'll go home and write Curtis a letter to tell him that it's over. He won't recognize it as the only decent thing I've done for as long as I can remember. I'll call Artie and tell him I've gotten off the gravy train and he'll come over. "So," he'll say, "I guess we're back in business."

I'll get the metal box from the bottom of my closet, the one I keep locked up. I'll find the key in my jewelry box and open it.

"Make it hurt," I'll tell him.

ALICIA GIFFORD

on "Surviving Darwin," first published in *Best American Erotica* in 2005

One day I received a rejection from *The Barcelona Review*, a literary journal I was jonesing to get into. The editor complimented the work I'd just sent, but asked if I had anything "edgier."

I didn't, so I sat down to write this story. I had no idea when I started where the work would go, but thinking of writing "edgy," I came up with the voice and the main character.

I'm a former nurse, and I have a very good friend who got hooked on Vicodin and went through a Diversion program offered by the state of California for health professionals who get addicted. It's an occupational hazard, so I had an insider's perspective.

The character is not likable, she's a user chick, using drugs and people. That presented a challenge, to give her a moment of redemption—which wasn't much—but for her, it was huge. The challenge was in keeping it from getting sappy. I love exploring the relativity of "good" and "bad," the gray area of what is moral.

My character's affinity for BDSM made me think of testing limits, and how she tested hers with how far she'd go in using this poor guy, Curtis. She was a dog-eat-dog character, a believer in "survival of the fittest," but she had to survive her own ruthlessness to carry on. I introduced the rash and the migraines to show she wasn't doing so well. And that's when I began to like her.

PLAYING DOCTOR

Eloise Chagrin

Julie and Andrew were a new couple when they first came to me for counseling. They were married for only three months, and already were having problems that were serious enough to rock their marriage to the point that they were having thoughts of separation. They were both twenty-three and had dated in college before getting married after their graduation. They came from a Baptist background, and both their sets of parents were deeply religious. When I first saw them together, it became evident to me that they were very much in love and that their problems, like the problems of so many couples, had to do with issues of insecurity and jealousy. To help them better, I first wanted to see them individually, separating them so that they could be frank with me about what really bothered them.

I began by first seeing Julie, alone, for one hour twice a week. I wanted to create an atmosphere of comfort and safety so that she would not hesitate to tell me all of her issues, and we made quite a bit of progress in the first two weeks. She told me that Andrew was her first love, and that she had never been with any man but him. She revealed that she was bored with her life and had a curiosity about the world, traveling, living in other places, and, finally, being with other men. She said that she sometimes had glimpses

26

of what that life could be like, especially when she was doing some routine household chore with Andrew sitting in the next room. These hints at another life made her doubt her marriage and built up resentment in her. At times she was mean to him (she realized that), but somewhere deep inside she actually enjoyed being mean. This bothered her because she loved him very much and wanted a happy life with him as well. In another session, she talked about how she did not feel that Andrew was a good listener and that the friendship part of their relationship was stagnating. She thought that they had trouble talking about anything that mattered and would argue about sundry things. She said that she was afraid to come to him with her innermost fears and insecurities because she thought he would mock her and hurt her even more. These were serious issues.

I asked her next about their sex life, and her response disturbed me. Julie said that she enjoyed having sex with Andrew but that she could "take it or leave it." She was rarely if ever excited, and had never had an orgasm with him in any way (which included oral sex). She described having sex with him as follows: Andrew would announce that he was going to have sex with her. She would strip off her clothes and lie on her back with her legs spread open, her knees raised. He would rub his favorite water-based lubricant on his penis and masturbate to erection. He would then mount her and thrust into her for about five minutes until he came inside of her. They would then get up, clean up, and go on with their day.

When I asked her how often this happened, she told me about once a week, usually on Sundays when they had time during the day. I asked her then if she masturbated, and she said that she used to occasionally when she was younger, but had stopped over the years.

Talking with Andrew I discovered some of the problems that he had with Julie. He felt that she was mean to him and enjoyed being mean. He thought that she wanted to start fights because she "hates me deep inside." He said that, nevertheless, he loved her and wanted to work through these issues. When I asked him about the bedroom, he told me that he was not entirely satisfied with Julie because she was not adventurous. She seemed to take sex with him for granted and did not know how to express herself sexually. He admitted that she was his first and only sexual partner.

This revelation surprised me as Andrew was a handsome twenty-three-year-old, and I expected him to have had some experiences. His physical appearance was not unattractive; he was a thin 5'7" and looked like he would fit into the culture with other young men his age. His conservative upbringing may have been a significant factor in his inexperience.

When I probed a little about his sexual past, he became very reticent but managed to reveal that he always felt sexually shy with girls. He told me that he had always feared that he had a very small penis and that girls would mock him for it. As I saw that this line of discussion was making him uncomfortable, I tried to reassure him that we were in a therapeutic environment and that he was safe to tell me anything he wanted to here, without the fear of it being repeated anywhere else. These sessions were for him, for his happiness, and for Julie. He seemed relieved and then asked me a question that was new to me. He asked if I would look at his penis and tell him if it was indeed small. I told him that it would probably be of no use because flaccid penis size is not a good indicator of erect size and that there was a range of sizes that were considered average. However, I was touched that he was comfortable enough with me to reveal himself this way.

My explanation did not dissuade Andrew. He said that he could make himself erect if I would tell him about his size. I thought then that he might be an exhibitionist and that the session had veered into inappropriate territory but also feared that he was earnestly trying to come to terms with a deep-seated issue, and, as his counselor, acquiesced. He took off his pants and underwear and showed me his very little flaccid circumcised penis. At that state of flaccidity, only the little pink glans showed itself. He started manipulating himself but was having trouble, so I told him that he could sit on the examination table that I keep in my office (since I am an MD). He sat there, pulled on his glans for a few minutes, and then said that he was having trouble and asked if I had some lubrication. I hesitated, but then, since we had gone this far, brought out a tube of K-Y Jelly. He took a few drops out and started masturbating until his penis began to grow. In a few minutes, I could see the shaft extend a few inches, and he held his penis proudly in his hand, looking at me.

The length was approximately three inches and the girth was thin—maybe a little thicker than a finger. He was still masturbating it then, and asked me if it was small. I said that it was hard to tell without measurement, to which he responded that I should measure him. I took out a ruler that I had in my desk and held it against the top of his penis. I had to hold his organ between my thumb and forefinger as he let go of it when I took out the ruler. It was exactly three inches long from the base to the top of his glans. I said aloud, "Three inches," and as I was holding the ruler to it with my right hand, my left hand holding it up, I felt it jerk and saw a drop of pre-cum come out of the tip. He blushed red as I took my hand off him and he put his hand back on it. He asked me then if I minded if he could finish. I said that this was fine but that we had better collect the sperm in a cup so that we could run some tests on it. I brought him the cup and held it over his glans as he masturbated. He asked me while he was masturbating whether the size was small. I told him that it was below average yet not so far below that it would be a detriment in his love life. He was on the boundary of a condition known as micropenis, but I did not want to alarm him now. He looked a little dejected when I told him that it was on the smaller side and asked me how big mine was. I told him that was irrelevant and a question that I could not answer. Within a few minutes he ejaculated, I collected the sample, and he got dressed and left the session.

My next session was with Julie. This time, she wanted to talk more about her sexual dissatisfaction with Andrew. She said that she wished for an experience with another man, if only so that she could teach Andrew how to make love to her in a way that would excite her. She asked me if I would describe some techniques to her so that she could take them home. I went along and started to explain how Andrew should manipulate her, focusing on her clitoris, until her vagina was wet, so that she was excited to have sex. Amazingly, she did not know what her clitoris was. She asked me if I could show her, to which I replied absolutely not, as it would be a breach in our relationship. She then said that Andrew told her about how I measured his penis for him and assisted in his masturbation and said that she was not getting fair treatment from me. "After all," she said, "you don't have to do anything to me; just show me how I could do it myself and what to teach Andrew." I agreed with this, and Julie started to take all of her clothes off. I have to admit that I found her very attractive. She was a thin blonde with pert breasts, which were a little large for her size. I asked her to sit on the observation table, which she did with her legs spread. I took out a mirror and had her hold it between her legs as I pulled back her clitoral hood and pointed out her clitoris.

She said that she had never masturbated by rubbing it directly; instead she thought that masturbation necessarily had to have penetration. I replied no, that most women masturbate by rubbing their clitoris in combination with some penetration. As I was holding her hood back, she took her hand and began to rub her clit gently. I could see that she was getting very wet, and her eyes took on a glazed look as she moaned, "You do it, you show me." I was also getting very excited and didn't see what the harm was of a little more help, so I moved my finger down from her hood to the sensitive little flesh and rubbed it up and down. She began to gasp and bucked a little. I took my other hand, inserted a finger into her vagina, and rubbed the upper wall as I massaged her clit. That brought her to a new level of excitement as she continued to buck harder and harder until, in just a few minutes, she was clenching her vagina tightly around my finger in an orgasm.

As we were cleaning up, she thanked me repeatedly, saying that she had never felt an orgasm like that. When she was younger and used to masturbate, she experienced little orgasms, but nothing like that one. She told me that the session was very helpful and wanted so much to continue. She said, "I can't wait to go home and explore with Andrew. You've really given me something to work on in our marriage. I feel like our relationship has hope."

Although at first I felt ambivalent about the session at best, I came to understand that I was performing a sexual service for these people and that they were both grateful. The state of their relationship also appeared to be improving.

Our next session was for both members of the couple. The two of them began simultaneously, telling me how important the last sessions were for them and that they felt much closer to each other now. They had more in common as they shared in their experiences. They also said that the instructions that I provided Julie were extremely helpful, and that they spent the entire last week practicing them at home. They said that their sex life had never been better.

I asked them how they were experimenting, and Julie answered, "Just the way you showed me in your office last time. I sit on the edge of the bed with my legs spread. Then Andrew rubs my clitoris with one hand while massaging the inside of my vagina with the other. I usually have an orgasm within minutes. Then he takes out his penis and masturbates in a cup that I hold over the tip. That also takes a few minutes. It has made us so much happier together."

I noticed that Andrew was masturbating exactly the way he had in my office, that he was replaying that experience with Julie and that she was imitating our session exactly. I thought to myself that this couple might have some kind of "sexual disability" and that their lack of creativity and paucity of experience might have given them a developmental disorder when it came to sexuality. I was experiencing a lot of transference then, as I felt that I had a tremendous power with these two, who would do what I taught them, exactly the way that I taught it. I felt a rush, thinking that I had the power to "mold" their sexuality, but I also felt burdened by the responsibility.

They asked me then if I would teach them anything new. I asked what they had in mind, and they answered that they wanted to feel pleasure simultaneously. Their mutual masturbation was good, but required the performance of both people to make one of them experience an orgasm, one at a time. I told them that I would assist them, and they immediately took off their clothes. I brought out the lubricant and asked them to sit next to each other on the examination table. I then said to them, "I want you to relax and hold each other's hand. I will try to help both of you achieve orgasm together. It would be good if you start by gently stroking and kissing each other, as that is a common way that people start their intimate relations."

They did as I told them, kissing and holding hands as I rubbed lubricant on both of my hands. Andrew was sitting on my right and Julie on my left, and I began by lightly stroking Andrew's penis with my slippery right hand while lightly manipulating Julie's clitoris with my left. Andrew's little penis instantly got hard, and I felt Julie become wet. They stopped kissing to focus on their pleasure but held on to each other's hand, their grip getting tighter. I felt that Andrew was on the verge of his orgasm, and as Julie was not quite there yet, I leaned my mouth between her legs and took her clit in my mouth while my finger slipped inside her vagina. All the time I was stroking Andrew's penis with deliberate but slow strokes.

Then, I lightly flicked my tongue over Julie's clit, rhythmically. She moaned, "Oh my god!" and I knew that she was just starting to cum—so with hard fast motions I increased the intensity of my strokes on Andrew's little penis. He gasped a breath of air and shot a stream of semen while Julie pressed her clit into my mouth and ground her hips. When it was over, they were spent, but thanked me weakly. They left the office holding hands, telling me that they would be looking forward to the next session in two days.

I could not wait for them to leave as I had a throbbing erection. As soon as they left the room, I took out my penis and masturbated where I was standing with my still-lubricated hands. I, too, came in minutes, and as soon as my orgasm was over, I realized what I had done, the extent of the indiscretion—and how it would look if I was ever found out. I also realized that, in the way I handled that last sexual experience with them, I had made myself a necessary part of their sex. There was no way for them to repeat that experience together because they needed a third party to masturbate the both of them. I knew that what I had done was considered abuse from the point of view of my profession, but that the way I handled myself involved me much further with them, and almost guaranteed the situation's recurrence.

When two days had passed, Julie and Andrew arrived as planned. They began the session by discussing their sex, saying that they wanted to know what more they could do to spice it up. Julie said that Andrew tried to imitate what I did with her clitoris the last time, but that his mouth never seemed to have the same effect. Andrew also asked if I could teach him how to use his mouth on his wife. Then he said that he wanted to know if there was anything else that Julie could do to please him. I answered that I would teach him, but Julie interrupted by saying that she wanted to learn first. I asked her what it was that she wanted to learn, and she replied, "You know, how to please a man."

I said, "You mean perform fellatio?" but when I saw that she didn't know what I meant I explained, "You know, give a blow job?"

She said, "I was always told that it's not sanitary."

"No," I replied. "Not at all. It's perfectly natural; I'll teach you."

I told Andrew to get undressed, and Julie followed the example, without being asked. Next I told her to begin by touching and rubbing Andrew's penis with her hand until it got hard, then I would tell her how to use her mouth on it. Andrew got instantly excited, and his penis shot up to its full three inches in Julie's hand.

"Now Julie," I said, "get down on your knees so that you are eye level with his penis from where he's sitting on the table. Then start by putting the head in your mouth." As I was saying this, Julie was still stroking Andrew, and as soon as I mentioned putting it in her mouth, he shot off a little stream of cum that dribbled down Julie's hand.

"Andrew!" shouted Julie, "now how am I going to practice?"

Andrew dropped his head and said, "I'm sorry. I just couldn't help it. Maybe you could practice on him," and he pointed his finger to me.

"Would that be all right?" Julie asked. Now at this point we had gone so far that I saw my input as just a part of the counseling. I honestly believed that I was helping the couple, so I said, "That would be fine."

I took off my shirt first. I work out regularly, so the two of them were visibly admiring my muscles, which made me feel sexy. Then I took off my shoes, socks, and my pants. I stood there in my underwear and then slowly took them off. My penis came out and dangled down between my legs. My penis is of above average length and girth and I am not circumcised, so the entire scene may have been astonishing for the both of them. Although I was not erect, my penis was hanging longer than Andrew's did when he was erect. Besides that, it was significantly thicker, with the extra flap of foreskin where Andrew had none.

"It's so . . . different," Julie said.

"Why do you have so much skin at the tip?" Andrew asked.

I went on to explain how it is customary for many people of our culture to cut that extra flap of skin off newborn babies, and that Andrew had had that done to him, while I hadn't. I saw the surprise in his eyes, the look that not only did he have a small penis, but, in addition, his parents had cut part of it off. I could see that he was envious and didn't think that his penis was as good. I was afraid of what would happen in his mind when I got erect and he was able to see just how big it was.

I told Julie to stroke me, which she did. I started to grow instantly—I had been attracted to her since the beginning, and with the intense sessions, that attraction had only grown.

"Oh my god," she said, "it's growing."

I soon reached my full stiffness in her hand. Andrew was eyeing me jealously, obviously affected by the display. Julie, however, was enthralled, taking her time feeling me in both her hands, trying to feel every last inch, carefully exploring all of me.

"It's so much fun with the extra skin!" she squealed. "And it's so big. How do you have sex with women, Doctor? Don't you cause too much pain for them to bear?"

I explained that although I was above average in length and girth, it was not too much for any vagina I had ever encountered. "A woman's vagina can stretch to accommodate most men, Julie," I said. She looked up from my organ in her hands and looked into my eyes. She curled a corner of her mouth up in an impish little smile, as if saying, I'd like to try that out.

Instead, she said, "What do you need me to do now, Doctor?"

"Keep stroking my shaft, and take the head of my penis in your mouth." She did as she was told. "Now," I said, "tighten your lips and use your saliva to stroke the head with your mouth."

She was a very fast learner and was bringing me close to orgasm as I was extremely attracted to her at this point. I looked over at Andrew and saw the look of awed envy, his eyebrows furrowed. At the same time, he had another erection, his hand masturbating his small penis feverishly.

In a few minutes, I said, "Good girl, Julie. Now I'm going to cum!"

She pulled me out of her mouth and I shot stream after stream of hot cum on her face forcefully. I heard Andrew cry out, and looked over to see his orgasm dribbling out of his miniature organ.

"There's so much!" Julie called out. "I never thought that there could be so much—and I love it."

That last sentence was too much for me, and without instruction or preparation, I pushed her onto the table, leaned her back, spread her legs, and dropped my head down into her very wet pussy. She let herself be taken, using a hand to wipe my cum off her face, and then, as I looked up, I saw her lick her fingers. That made me want her even more, and I licked her pussy as if it was my life's goal to make her cum. Andrew tried to look and learn how I was licking her, but I couldn't explain, I just needed to make her cum. He could learn by watching. I used my hand, rubbing her inside, licking her with fast, light, regular motions, until she was pushing her hips into me with her hands on my head, pulling me into her pussy, screaming out, "Oh god!" in a tremendous orgasm.

When the session was over, they thanked me again and left. I was learning to suppress my doubts at this point. I saw the session as successful and looked forward to the next one. I thought of myself as a rogue therapist, using unorthodox sexual techniques that would result in unprecedented benefits. I was also becoming more attracted to Julie, sexually and emotionally. That night I dreamed of her, and in my dream, we were having sex with a knowing intimacy between us. We were not client and therapist anymore; we were two people in a relationship.

. . .

The next time the two of them came in, I knew the direction that I wanted to take the session. As always, they began by telling me how valuable the last session was and how much better their lives were. Julie said that she loved giving Andrew blow jobs, but that he was usually so excited that she only had to put her mouth on it and stroke him several times for him to cum. He said that ever since our sexual sessions started, he had been so attracted to his wife that he had not had any control over his orgasm. He said that he would become erect at any thought of intimacy with her, that he thought about their sexual adventures all day and had an erection all the way home from work.

I said that it was great that he was so excited by his wife and that in the next part of the lesson I was going to teach him how to make love to her so that it was more pleasurable for her. They were very happy to hear this and quickly took their clothes off as usual. I noticed that Andrew was already hard. I then told them to show me what they had learned in our time together, to get each other excited but not to cum. Julie started to stroke Andrew's penis, but he stopped her as he was coming too close. Instead, he had her sit on the table and started to flick his tongue on her clit. He must have learned well from our last session, because she was moaning in minutes. Then I told her to get on the table with her legs spread and him to get between her legs and slowly enter her vagina. He put himself inside of her but I would not let him thrust yet. I told him that I would teach him how to thrust. The key, I said, is thrusting in with your penis with enough pressure from your body that you rub her clit in the process. What I wanted him to do was thrust in and then grind with the motion, upward against her. He tried but was so excited that he was able to manage only a few short motions before stopping to avoid an orgasm. He did this a few more times with the same effect.

He said, "Maybe if I cum once, I'll be able to hold it better the next time."

Julie agreed, took his penis out of her, leaned forward, slipped it in her mouth, and with a few strokes had him shoot off. She took his cum inside her mouth and swallowed it all. He sat down and took a deep breath. Then he said, "Doctor, I don't think that I understand what you were saying about how to thrust into her. Could you show me?"

"Yes. Could you show him?" said Julie. "Please show him."

I did not need any more encouragement; I took my clothes off right away. Julie, still on the table, put her hand on my penis and gave me a few strokes, and Andrew stood up and took a step closer.

"Do you mind if I touch it and help?" he asked. "I've never touched a dick that was so big, and I wanted to know what it must feel like to have one."

I let him stroke me a few times, and he surprised me by going down and taking it in his mouth. He got back up and said that it was just such an incredible feeling for him, touching it. He said that I was more of a man than he was and that, although he was envious, and still might be a little, he had more admiration for me than envy. He said that he was accepting it and, as part of his acceptance, wanted to show his admiration. Before I could thank him, Julie pulled me up to the table. I started to insert myself into her and saw the look of pleasure in her eyes. I pushed myself completely into her soft wetness and she moaned a little. "It feels so huge." I started to thrust gently and slowly, lightly grinding into her clit.

"Oh my god," she said. "It feels like you're splitting me open!"

She was breathing fast, very wet, coming closer. I increased my pace and intensity, holding her body close to mine, and looked into her beautiful blue eyes. She leaned forward and kissed me passionately, which only made me fuck her harder. We thrust into each other this way, her moving with me and coming up for my thrusts, rubbing herself into me as I ground into her. All of a sudden, she increased her pace, let out a whimper, and started to cum over and over again, having her first multiple orgasm. I kept up my pace, waited a little, and then let go, cumming hard inside of her.

. . .

The next few sessions were similar. I had sex with Julie in multiple ways and for longer periods. Andrew took on more of a helping role as time went on. He would start by fellating me and would masturbate while I had sex with his wife. Sometimes while I was fucking her, especially from behind, she would let him put his penis in her mouth and would give him a few strokes, which was usually enough to make him cum. When we were done, he always had another erection, and Julie would either let him cum on her or take him in her mouth again. When she was feeling especially generous, she would let him fuck her even though I had just cum inside of her. Andrew didn't seem to care, and I suspect that he actually liked feeling my cum.

Sometimes, when he would put his penis inside her, Julie would smile devilishly and ask, "Is it in yet?" She may not have actually felt it since this was usually after a long session of my loosening her with my much bigger dick. Still, I thought that she said this on purpose, out of the impulse to be mean to Andrew. What was still more surprising was how he took it. Those words would usually put him over the edge and he would cum. In fact, Andrew seemed to be learning to be excited by the idea that he was inadequate. It was a kind of emotional masochism, and it fit well into our relationship. He actually liked being a cuckold.

Julie took it further too. One time, after an especially rough session of my fucking her pussy until it was raw, flipping her in various positions, thrusting and grinding into her like she was a rag, she came multiply for many minutes. Then when Andrew wanted to finish inside of her, she let him enter her. As he was fucking her, she rolled her eyes and said, "You can cum any time. It's not like I'm going to get anything out of this." He came immediately.

These sessions went on for several weeks, and I started getting tired of Andrew always being there, watching us and masturbating his hard little dick. I was past the point of trying to make his marriage with Julie work exclusively. As I saw it, what was best for them was having me fuck his wife with Andrew as a cuckold. However, I still believed that these were therapeutic sessions and that I was doing them a service. As such, they had not paid me since the first few sessions.

The next time we met, I addressed the both of them about my feelings. I began by telling them that I felt that it would be good for Julie and me to spend some time alone together, without Andrew. That way he would better learn his role as an assistant and our relationship (Julie's and mine) would get stronger. I also said that it was apparent that, in the course of our sessions, Andrew had developed a strong attraction for men and that there was nothing wrong with this kind of sexual feeling. I told them that if he was to be truly happy, he should try to see some gay men. I told him that there was a strong homosexual side to him that needed exploring. Then on the question of money, I brought up that they had not paid me since the first few sessions and that what I was doing with them was still therapy.

Julie looked at Andrew and smiled, a different smile from any I had seen on her face before.

"Can you believe it?" she said. "This one wants it all." She then turned to me and said, "Doctor, you are really very daring asking this all at once. Trying to get me all to yourself, turn my husband gay, and be paid for it! Incredible! But let me tell you how it's going to be. These sessions that we've been having were all recorded—we both had recording devices in our clothes. If you don't do exactly as we say, you will never practice psychology again in your life. You will be writing us monthly checks now for amounts that we will later specify. These will be, of course, in the thousands, but we feel that your career is worth that, don't you?"

"You mean this has been a game to you all along?" I yelled incredulously. "What about how he can't please you? What about the little penis?"

"He can please me just fine," she answered. "Of all people *you* should know that size isn't everything, but you are too deluded by your ego. These are the roles we play. I am the cheating wife, and he is the cuckold. We like our roles, and they're very convincing, don't you think?

"As for the homosexuality," she continued, "there's one more thing that you will be doing before we leave. Take off your clothes, please."

I was in shock, but understood that I had better do as I was told, or else my career was over. We all got naked, throwing our clothes on the floor. I saw Andrew rubbing his penis with a lubricant.

"Now, Doctor, I want you to stand up against this counter and stick out your ass so that Andrew can fuck it," Julie said.

I looked at her wide-eyed, but she just smirked.

"Don't worry, you'll like it," she said.

I stood as she told me to, and Andrew came up beside me. He rubbed lube inside me with his finger, which felt very uncomfortable, and started to push his penis into me. I was very glad that it was small. As I stood there being entered, I noticed that my penis was starting to get hard.

"Good boy," Julie said. "Looks like someone's been learning from all the lessons we've given. Don't worry—I'm going to make you like this."

As she said this, she moved down between my legs and slipped the head of my dick in her mouth. She began to stroke me expertly until I was hard and ready to burst, Andrew still pumping my ass. I heard Andrew say "Okay" to her, and she increased the speed with her mouth and hand so that I started to cum. At the same time, I felt Andrew's spasms inside of me.

We separated and rested for a minute. Julie and Andrew were getting dressed by the time I looked up.

"Now, Doctor," she said, "you seem to have developed a strong attraction for men over the course of our sessions with you. If you want to be truly happy sexually, then you should start seeing some gay men socially. There is a strong homosexual side to you that needs exploring.

"We'll be in touch. Come on, Andrew," she said as she walked to the door, with an emphasis on "Andrew" that made me realize that it probably was not his name.

ELOISE CHAGRIN
on "Playing Doctor"

It surprises me to no end that the sexual fetish of cuckoldry, once thought of as a disability, could be shared by so many people. The cuckolding fetish has an element of surprise, along with a bittersweet emotional masochism.

Another key to the fetish, from the perspective of the cuckold, is that of eroticizing as a defense mechanism. When someone you care about expresses their interest in another person, you wrestle with your inadequacies. This fight may take on different forms, in many cases with the ultimate rejection of your lover.

However, if your bond is strong, and you're able to put aside that sense of self, then it's possible to experience pleasure vicariously.

Many people may think of this as abhorrent, as tantamount to abuse, while others believe it's an essential part of their sexual health. I don't know; I'm only trying to describe something that I've thought about for a long time.

Some may find putting oneself second to be deleterious to one's emotional health; others find something beautiful in the idea of loving your partner so much that you become attracted to whatever role he or she plays, whatever the two of you become. I leave the benedictions to others.

A third ingredient to the mix is homoerotic. There is no way to avoid this with groups of three. Even in the most repressed situations, at least two out of the three people are of the same gender, and all parties are interested in the situation, else they would stop participating.

In my story, as in my perceptions of cuckoldry from real life, betrayal is on the horizon. There's a real possibility that any pair may break off from the group and form a greater intimacy. That prospect keeps the game competitive, and the players had better give their best performances, bank on everything they have in their bag of tricks—because, ultimately, someone must lose.

INNOCENCE IN EXTREMIS

Debra Boxer

I am twenty-eight years old and I am a virgin. People assume a series of decisions led to this. They guess that I'm a closet lesbian, or too picky, or clinging to a religious ideal. "You don't look, talk, or act like a virgin," they say. For lack of a better explanation, I am pigeonholed as a prude or an unfortunate. If it's so hard to believe, I want to say, then imagine how hard it is for me to live with.

I feel freakish and alien, an anomaly that belongs in a zoo. I walk around feeling like an impostor, not a woman at all. I bleed like other women, yet I feel nothing like them, because I am missing this formative experience.

I won't deny that I have become attached to my innocence. If it defines me, who am I without it? Where will my drive come from, and what will protect me from becoming as jaded as everyone else? I try to tell myself that innocence is more a state of mind than body. That giving myself to a man doesn't mean losing myself to a cynical world. That my innocence doesn't hang by a scrap of skin between my legs.

In college, girls I knew lost it out of impatience. At twenty-one, virginity became unhealthy, embarrassing—a female humiliation they could no longer be burdened by. Some didn't tell the boy. If there was blood, they said it was their period. I cannot imagine. Some of those same boys thought it was appalling, years ago, that I was still a virgin. "I'll fuck you," they said. It sounded to me like, "I'll fix you," and I did not feel broken.

I don't believe I've consciously avoided sex. I am always on the verge of wholly giving myself away. I think emotionally, act intuitively. When I'm attracted to someone, I don't hold back. But there have been only a handful of times when I would have gladly had sex. Each, for its own reason, did not happen. I am grateful to have learned so much in the waiting—patience, strength, and ease with solitude.

Do you know what conclusion I've come to? That there is no concrete explanation, and, more important, there doesn't need to be one. How I got here seems less important to me than where I am.

This is what is important. Desire. The circle of my desire widens each day, so that it's no longer contained inside me, but rather, it surrounds me in concentric circles.

Desire overrides everything and should be exploited to its fullest potential. It is the white-hot space between the words. I am desire unfulfilled. I hover over that fiery space, feeling the heat without knowing the flames. I am a still life dreaming of animation. I am a bell not allowed to chime. There is a deep stillness inside me. There is a void. A huge part of me is dead to the world, no matter how hard I try to revive it with consoling words or my own brave hand.

I am sick of being sealed up like a grave. I want to be unearthed.

I pray for sex like the pious pray for salvation. I am dying to be physically opened up and exposed. I want to be the source of a man's pleasure. I want to give him that one perfect feeling. I have been my only pleasure for too long.

Do I have dreams about sex? Often. There is one recurring dream in which I can't see whole bodies at once. But I know which parts

belong to my body. I know they're mine. I know, better than anyone, my curves, my markings, my sensitive places. If I close my eyes
now, I can see the man's body. Thin, smooth, light-haired, limbs
spreading and shifting over me like the sea. A small, brick-colored
mouth opens and closes around the sphere of a nipple. Moist eyes,
the color of darkest honey, roam up and down my spine. A sensation of breath across my belly induces the first wave of moisture
between my legs. This reaction crosses the line into wakefulness,
and I know when I awaken, the blanket will be twisted aside as if
in pain. My skin itself will feel like a fiery blanket, and I will almost
feel smothered by it.

In some versions of the dream, I am on top, and I can feel my
pelvis rubbing against the man's body. Every part of my body is
focused on the singular task of getting him inside me. I try and
try and am so close, but my fate is that of Tantalus, who was surrounded by water he could not drink. Thank God for masturbation.

My fingers know exactly how to act upon my skin—they have
for over half my life now. There is no fear or hesitation. When
I masturbate, I am aware of varying degrees of heat throughout
my body. It is hottest between my legs. Cool air seems to heat the
moment it hits my skin, the moment I suck it in between my lips.
After, my hands shake as if I'd had an infusion of caffeine. I press
my hand, palm down, in the vale between my breasts, and it feels as
if my heart will burst through my hand. I love that feeling—knowing that I'm illimitably alive.

Though I've never had a man inside me, I have had many
orgasms. I have talked with girls who not only can't have one with
their lover but can't bring themselves to have one. I was shocked
at first, until I saw how common it was. And then I felt lucky. My
first one scared me. At twelve, I did not expect such a reaction to
my own touch; I thought I'd hurt myself. But it was such a curious
feeling, such a lovely feeling, that I had to explore it further. I felt

almost greedy. And, well, I got better at it until it was ridiculously easy. Still, it is always easy.

I don't expect it to be so easy with a man. I've come to believe that sex is defined by affection, not orgasm. There is that need to be held that doesn't disappear when we learn to walk on our own. If anything, it intensifies.

I love being a girl. I think of my body as all scent and soft muscle. It is an imperfect body, but beautiful still, in its energy and in its potential. I love looking at my curves in the mirror. I love feeling them and admiring their craftsmanship. I love my hip bones—small, protruding mountains. Or maybe they are like sacred stones marking the entrance to a secret city. I trace the slope of my calf as if it is a slender tree trunk, and I am amazed at how strong, yet vulnerable, the human body is. I am as in awe of my body as I am of the earth. My joints are prominent, as if asserting themselves. I know my terrain well, perhaps better than any man ever could—the warm, white softness of my inner arms; the hard, smooth muscle of my biceps, like the rounded swelling in a snake that just swallowed the tiniest mouse; the sensitive skin between my thighs; the mole on my pelvis nestled by a vein like a dot on a map marking a city beside a river. I have stared at my naked body in the mirror wondering what the first touch from a lover will feel like and where it will be.

Masturbation is pleasurable, but it cannot sustain a whole sexual life. It lacks that vital affection. I am left with the rituals, the mechanics of masturbation. I crash up against the same wall each time. It becomes boring and sad and does little to quell the need to be touched. I long to let go of my body's silent monologue and enter into a dialogue of skin, muscle, and bone.

There are sudden passions that form in my mind when I look at a man. Thoughts of things I want to do to him. I want to follow the veins of his wrists—blue like the heart of a candle flame. I want to lick the depression of his neck as if it were the bottom of a bowl.

I want to see the death of my modesty in his eyes. Although I am swollen with romantic ideas, I am not naïve. I know it will not be ideal. Rather, it will be bloody, painful, awkward, damp, and dreadful—but that is always the way of birth. It is an act of violence. The threat of pain in pleasure, after all, makes seduction stimulating. I want the pain, to know that I am alive and real—to leave no doubt there has been a transformation.

The fear is undeniable. It's a phobic yearning I have for a man's body, but I have to believe that everything, including fear, is vital when expressing desire. If sexual thoughts are either memories or desires, then I am all desires.

I am powerfully attracted to the male body. I want to watch him undress. See him touch himself. I want his wildness in me—I want to touch his naked body and feel the strength of him. His sweat sliding down the slick surface of my skin until it pools in the crooks of my limbs. I imagine the rhythm of our sex like the slick, undulating motion of swimmers. I imagine my own body's movements suddenly made new, so that we would appear to me like two new bodies. I imagine the sound of our sex—a magnificent, moist clamor of limbs.

I want to hold him inside me like a deep breath. I want to leave kisses as markers on the sharp slices of his shoulder blades, then surf rounding the oasis of his belly button. I want to slide him in my mouth like a first taste of wine, letting the bittersweet liquid sweep every part of my mouth before allowing it to slide down my throat.

I will hold my mouth to his ear, as if I were a polished seashell, so he can hear the sea inside me—welcoming him. I will pause and look at him—up into his face. I will steady myself in his gaze, catch the low sun of his cock between my smooth, white thighs, and explode into shine. I will look at him and think, I have spent this man's body and I have spent it well.

DEBRA BOXER
on "Innocence in Extremis," first published in *Best American Erotica* in 2002

"Innocence" was distilled from a two-hundred-page unpublished novel that I wrote in a kind of fevered frustration over the span of a year. It was a story that I wanted to read but couldn't find—so I wrote it myself. I was trying to make unbearable feelings bearable. It worked. I said exactly what I wanted to say.

Not long ago, I came across an essay that I wrote for school when I was eleven years old called "The Meaning of Success." I realized that I'm essentially the same in my thirties as I was at eleven. And that's exactly how I feel when I read "Innocence in Extremis" today, ten years after I wrote it. I've been through irreversible changes and galvanizing experiences, but I'm still the same person I was when I wrote that story. It's both comforting and heartbreaking to me.

THE PROGRAM

G. Bonhomme

You probably first saw the ads on the subway. Grinning guy in a tux, supermodel hotties draped over him. "Get with The Program"; or the other one, "The Program That Made a Man Out of Jerry." You might have puzzled over it for a moment. Some exercise thing, probably, or a drug like Viagra? Or any bullshit product advertisers claim can get you laid. Still, though, the way the guy in the tux looked: commanding. Rolling in sex. You'd swap lives in a minute.

The poster had some of that fine print at the bottom like they do when they're pushing something your doctor has to prescribe: "The Program is a course of cognitive-behavioral biofeedback therapy for the treatment of severe interpersonal interrelation adjustment disorders. Use only as directed. Ask your doctor if The Program is appropriate for you. . . ."

Then the doors opened, and you shuffled through with the crowd and forgot all about it.

The first time you vividly remember hearing about it was at the bar. A real looker was sitting there nursing her drink, blond hair down to here, slinky white dress, big ripe tits—the kind you'd love to get your dick between. The guys had been watching you eyeing her and you'd had a few, and with them egging you on you went for it. Somewhere between the booth and the bar, though, the rough edge of the bravado faded, and instead of just showing off for the guys, you found yourself really asking:

"Hey, pretty lady. Can I buy you a drink?"

She ignored you, but you thought you saw a trace of a smile. You sat down at the stool next to her.

"Hey, come on, I'm a nice guy. Really. You'd like me. Seriously. You want to go out sometime?"

And she burst out laughing.

That stung. The glare or the cold silence or even her throwing a fit and chewing you out, you could take that, that went with the territory. But this? She was laughing her ass off, wiping tears from her eyes and gasping for breath. And when she recovered, she looked you right in the eyes and said—almost sweetly—"Oh shit, honey! Give me a break!" She grinned ear to ear. "My boyfriend's done the Program. Why would I want to go out with you?"

And then it seemed like it was all over the place—like if you looked at the magazine covers on a newsstand, it would be:

Elle: "The Program": Why It Works!
Razor: Secrets of The Program
Cosmo: Ten Ways to Get Your Man to Do The Program
Maxim: Don't Let Her Program You!
Star: Brad to Jenna: "I'll Do The Program for You!"

But, you know, it seemed like something for Hollywood stars and Manhattan glitterati—not part of your world. Not something a guy from Queens would do. Come on!

The secretaries in the office pool were giggling about a guy over in Sales who supposedly did it. And one of them was like, "Oh my god? Can you believe it? I so am going to ask him!"

And the old biddy leering: "Ask him to do *what*?"

And they were cackling and the one who said it was blushing beet red, going, "No, just ask him what it's *like*, that's all. Come on, you guys!"

And through the laughter the dark-haired Rhonda from HR, the real sophisticated-looking one with the great ass and the steely eyes, said, "These guys should *all* do it. Our health plan covers it!"

Then:

You were in bed with Caitlin, who was this on-again-off-again piece you had, not a dog, but kind of plain—nice eyes, nice hair, a too-big nose, and little tits, and too skinny—and usually if you were feeling hard up you'd come around to her place and after some complaining on her part (about how you never came around), you'd end up on her sofa making out; and about one time out of three you'd end up in her bed, fucking. And when you added it up, she was actually the only girl you'd actually got to the fucking part with for about three years, since that thing with Tanika. And she always made these hints about being boyfriend-girlfriend, and you always laughed them off.

But this time, somehow, you started feeling insecure, like maybe she was slipping through your fingers too. Like the world was changing? So you actually went down on her without being asked. And you were enjoying it, getting your tongue all up in her muff and running it around over what was probably her clit, and her moaning: even though you wanted so bad to bust your nut, you kind of took it slow.

So that when you finally rolled the condom on and slid it into her, oh man, it was like heaven in there. Your dick had been waiting so long it felt swollen up like a balloon. Her pussy was just right, not hard like a hand or soft like a pillow, but warm and firm and giving. You pounded into that sweet strong tube of hers—all the way in! You felt her hands moving on your back, you squeezed her ass, she growled deep in her throat, and soon everything faded into the background, but the feeling of your hungry cock, taking her.

You held your breath, so as not to come too soon, and you must have lasted, what, twenty, maybe thirty strokes before that river burst its dam. The surge went like heat through your whole body, toes to head, that moment of being on top of the world, that wave of molten power, better than any liquor, better than a jackpot—but not unlike a jackpot, not unlike pulling that one-armed bandit's handle and seeing all cherries come up, and the rush of gold coins going on, on, on, on into the bowl.

But afterward, when you rolled off her, she sighed this tight little sigh and turned her head away. And when you reached over to put your hand affectionately on her tummy, she stiffened up. She got up and went to the bathroom.

She was usually chatty after sex, but not this time. And you hauled yourself up and got your clothes on and she showed you out, you still a little woozy with the glow and feeling like she ought to be grateful for how you'd made her moan. And as you stood a little unsteady on the step she said:

"Listen, Gary, uh . . . you know . . . I think this was our last fuck."

"What?" you said, feeling like you couldn't have heard right. "What?"

"Yeah, you know, I just. I think I want. Something different. Okay?"

And to your silence she said, "Okay. Yeah. Good night." And closed the door.

And one night about three months after *that*, three months of no booty at all, not even a kiss, you were sitting on the green sofa in your crappy little house, channel-surfing, and on the Entertainment Channel Kevin Costner or Matthew M-something or one of those Hollywood guys was saying sincerely to some interviewer, "Yes, I did it, and I'm quite happy to talk about it. I think it's made me a better lover and, you know, even a better human being."

. . .

So then, the next morning, you were standing on a crowded street corner in Manhattan waiting for a green light. And you see this absolute babe standing next to you: miniskirt and gray tit-hugging sweater, breasts like mangoes, perfect ass, looking like a younger, shorter Cindy Crawford—way out of your league. You turned to her, not getting too close though, not wanting to scare her, and said, "Hey, you're beautiful." She gave you the kind of brutal stare you expected, like What the Fuck. But not scared. It was a confident, intelligent stare, with a little humor behind it—like she was wondering, what's he going to say next, and if it's sufficiently out there, I'm looking forward to laughing my ass off about this guy with the girls.

And you said, "Listen—if I did the Program—would you go on a date with me?"

And get this. She blinked. She looked you up and down—*she* looked *you* up and down—and a slow smile spread over her face, like a cat looking at a canary whose cage just popped open.

And she said, "*Hell* yeah."

Man: you were hard, just like that.

The light turned green, and everyone but you two crossed. She took a pen and a piece of paper out of her purse and handed them to you and said, "If you're serious, write down your name and number. You do it, I'll call you." The light turned red again.

You couldn't believe it. Your hands were shaking. Your throat was dry. You grinned kind of lopsided, making a show because, shit, of course she was putting you on, as you wrote down your name and number. "Oh yeah? And how are you going to know if I really did it?"

She frowned as she took the paper back. "Don't be dumb," she said. "I'm a subscriber."

The light turned green again. She crossed. You stood watching her ass as it went up Fifth Avenue. She didn't look back. But you saw her tuck the paper back in her purse.

. . .

"Gary," said your doctor, "three months without a relationship doesn't mean you have a disorder."

"It's not just that," you said. Trying to recall the articles you'd read. "I've never really felt comfortable in relationships. And anxiety, I, uh, have a lot of anxiety about it. You know, keeps me up at night."

Dr. Wallace sighed. "Look, there are other alternatives. I could recommend you to a psychiatrist for a more traditional course of therapy. This Program business—it's really quite radical. It can have a lot of side effects—dysthymia, sexual dysphoria, unwanted personality changes. It can exacerbate adjustment disorders. It's a major stressor. I was extremely surprised, to tell you the truth, that the FDA even approved it."

"Are you saying I don't qualify?"

He scowled. "No, I'm not saying that. I just think you shouldn't jump into this—"

"I really just want to give this a try," you said—but he was already writing on his little pad.

The clinic was a skyscraper in Midtown. There was a small mob of protesters outside. Almost all men. With police standing by to keep the route clear.

"It isn't worth it!"

They looked like slobs. Unshaven, red-eyed. Middle of the fucking day, why weren't they at work anyway? *They* didn't have time off for a medical appointment.

"Listen, buddy! You don't know what you're giving up!"

"Don't let those bitches in your head!"

Fucking crazies. It was like going to an abortion clinic. "Oh yeah," you called back over your shoulder as you reached the doorman. "What did they do? Cut your balls off?"

Their faces when you said that. Cut their balls off. That was a good one. You were chuckling all the way up the elevator.

. . .

Then there was this long intake interview with a white-haired woman doctor in her sixties. Personal information forms, permissions, liability waivers, detailed questionnaires about how many girls you'd been with and what you liked to do in bed and how many times a week you masturbated and the whole thing. You answered them all good-naturedly, though you couldn't imagine this old lady reading them.

Under permissions there was a question that read:

"While your enrollment in the Program, like all medical information, is strictly private, we have found that many of our clients wish to make their participation known to others. As a service to our clients, Gallman Clinic LLP provides a public registry to which interested parties can subscribe. If wish to you waive your right to privacy and include your name in the registry, Gallman Clinic LLP can verify your successful completion of the Program upon subscriber request. Do you want your name to be included in this public registry?"

Which meant that that hottie could see you'd done the Program.

You checked "yes," because they didn't have a "Fuck yeah!"

"This is Sophie," said the old lady. "She's one of our assessment counselors."

Sophie was beautiful in kind of a cold, sophisticated, European way. Long white-blond hair thrown over one shoulder, loose gray sweater, piercing blue eyes. Tall, thin, long legs in black slacks. She was in her mid-thirties, probably—maybe ten years older than the hottie at the street corner. You wouldn't say hottie for her. She was just as out of your league, maybe even more beatiful, but not hot. Cold. The kind you couldn't really even bring yourself to imagine fucking.

"Your schedule is free tonight?" Sophie said. She had some

European accent, like a roughness at the back of the throat, the "r" breathy.

"Uh, yes," you said.

"Good," she said, and smiled briefly. "We are going on a date. This is mostly to establish a baseline, before the treatments: your relationship competence, your style, inclinations, performance."

"Performance," you repeated, your dick giving a little throb.

"But this is a fancier restaurant," Sophie said, "than that to which you normally invite a woman."

The waiter poured wine. You played with a folded cloth napkin. You felt yourself sitting up straighter. "Well, yeah," you said. "But, you know, you seem—it seems like it goes with you. You're, ah—"

"I'm fancy?" asked Sophie. You couldn't tell if she was kidding. She looked calm. She met your eyes, and you looked away.

"You're beautiful," you said.

"Thank you," said Sophie, smiling. "You're very sweet."

She looked around your crappy little house. Green sofa. TV dinner packages ripped open on the kitchenette counter. You blushed. "It's a lousy place."

"I like it," Sophie said, and sat down on the sofa. She eased off one stack-heeled boot.

You stood there, your dick twinging. Your heart beating. Wanting to make sure you'd got this right.

"You know, usually after the dinner, I conduct the assessment at the clinic," Sophie said. "And it's quite perfunctory."

"So, are you going to get in trouble?"

She eased off the other boot. "I have some, what do you say, leeway? And I feel comfortable with you, Gary." She patted the couch next to her. You went. "I'm going to ask you to do things," she said. "You can say no. I'll first ask you to do them the way you normally do them. Then I may give you instructions. Please don't be offended if I do. It's part of the assessment."

"I'm not gonna be offended—"

"Kiss me," said Sophie.

You leaned in and put your mouth on her dark-lipsticked mouth. She tasted a little like the wine from dinner, a little like mint. You put your hands on her waist. She took them off.

"Just kiss," she said. "Slow. Gentle. But not limp. You see?" Her lips found yours, delicate, like hummingbirds. "Wait for me to increase the power of the kiss."

Her mouth on yours. A fucking class-A broad. Unbelievable. Your health care package paying for a top-of-the-line call girl. Except she didn't really feel like a call girl. More like a doctor, or a teacher?

She pulled away. "Good. You are a little distracted, though. Now take off my sweater." She held her arms up.

Sweater off, bra off, your shirt off; Sophie lay back on the sofa. She had smallish tits, like apples, with big nipples. "My breasts like to be licked," she said. "Not every woman's do. And it is different how. Try."

You tried.

"No! Much too hard. Lick around from the edges in. Better. Polish them with your tongue. Mmmm. Now try—no! Too hard. Lightly. There. Flick the tongue over them. Yes, yes. Keep going. More. Now the other one."

On the one hand, you could hardly believe you were allowed to put your tongue onto those perfectly round, creamy tits, those hard pink nipples straining for the ceiling.

On the other hand, she was bossy as hell, and it was beginning to feel like work. You slid your hand into her panties. She grabbed your wrist.

"Not yet," she said. Her voice was gentle. You went back to work on the breasts. She made deep humming noises.

Your dick was hard, swollen up. It wanted out of the pants. You reached for her panties again.

"Gary, not yet," she said.

"I thought you wanted me to do things the way I do them."

"After I ask you to. Shall we stop now and try this again tomorrow?"

You swallowed, and a flash of anger shot through you—she'd leave you high and dry now? But then you said to yourself: Gary, you're being an asshole. This is her job. Let her do it.

You pulled away, sat up on the couch. "Hey, um. I'm sorry about that. I . . ."

She smiled a brilliant smile. "More kissing."

Then, while you were kissing, she put your hand in her panties. She broke the kiss. "Gentler. See? I am moist. That is what we waited for. Yes? Wait—stop. It's all right. You will learn this later. Sit back a moment."

She slid her panties off her hips and ran her fingers over her cunt. "Watch," she whispered. "Just watch." She licked her fingers, slid them between the folds. They slipped in and out like dancers. "Take off your pants. Put a condom on."

You were covered with sweat, and your breathing was tight. Sophie fucking herself with her fingers like something out of a porn movie, except slower, quieter, softer. Just breathing, instead of moans and cries. Porn girls pouted and smoldered, or yelled and bucked: Sophie closed her eyes and frowned in concentration, her brow wrinkling. Her bush was small, neatly trimmed, as white-blond as her head. There was a fine golden down on her thighs, almost invisible.

"Watch closely," she whispered, licking her fingers again. "See this here? The clitoris. Look: very soft touches, not directly on, around. The hood—you see? And. Then. Hmmm."

Her eyes stayed closed. Now you could almost think she was asleep, looking at her face, except when tremors would run over it. Your dick had never been this hard. You needed to get it wet.

"All right," she said. "Now. Enter me."

You pushed your cock into her. She was tight and her muscles rippled and you were coming, coming, coming.

You groaned, and then you rested your head on her shoulder.

She chuckled in your ear and whispered, "Not very good, Gary. I did not get to enjoy it very long. Or to come." She stroked your back, long smooth strokes. "But you are lovely. And you will get better. Much better."

The Program was three weeks—four days a week, mornings and evenings, at the clinic before and after work, plus three weekend training seminars. Waking up alone that first morning, you let yourself hope it would involve a lot of screwing Sophie. Maybe even Sophie hanging around afterward, sleeping over, making you breakfast. It wasn't like that, though.

In fact, you had to be celibate for the three weeks.

The hours you spent in the lab were strange. At first there were CAT scans, blood tests, running on a treadmill with wires taped to your head and this metal cap. Then, after the first few days, there was the chair.

The chair was like a cross between a dentist chair and Captain Kirk's chair on *Star Trek*. Your head wired up, and earphones and goggles on, and an IV in your arm. They'd leave you there for an hour or three, the chair tipped back, in a room with one wall that was a mirror they could see through from the other side.

Sometimes the goggles and headphones played movies—porn movies, or scenes from romantic chick flicks, or detailed instructional movies about sex. Sometimes there were just flickering cascades of images, too quick for you to make them out. Sometimes there were recorded instructions.

They set out Vaseline and warm, wet towels when they wanted you to masturbate. The recorded voice told you what to do. That was weird at first. You didn't know who might be watching. But you got used to it.

Once you asked one of the docs, a bald old guy, what all the gear did. The IV drip had something to do with enhanced memory formation, and the metal cap was actually sending electrical impulses into your brain for "subexperiential behavioral reinforcement." Whatever that was.

You stopped masturbating at home: you didn't feel like it. Even though you'd sometimes come home from the clinic and sit, channel surfing and not really seeing the TV, too wired to sleep, imagining sex. Fucking Sophie up the ass. Fucking the girl from the street corner between her mango-shaped tits. Caitlin begging to suck you off and you coming down her throat. Sex saturated your head, burned your body from your ears to the soles of your feet, but it was all distant, muddy, like under a layer of thick gauze. The images would swarm like fevered dreams, and then they'd be gone and you'd be alone in your crap house, feeling lonely and confused and desperate, and somehow guilty. Sometimes you'd run your head under the cold water from the kitchen sink, to make it go away.

The seminars were mostly bullshit: Mars-Venus stuff, how to listen, how you should wash the dishes and talk about your fear. All the guys avoided one another in the hallways. A few of the exercises were kind of interesting.

One time you were talking about your dad, the time he'd built this boat with you and then smashed it when he was mad, and you actually started to cry. Bullshit like that. The other guys all looked away, embarrassed. You got it together after a moment.

One time Sophie walked out of the observation room into the hallway, just as you were coming out of the room with the chair. She was with three other women, all good-looking, though none of them in her league. Probably all assessment counselors. They'd clearly been watching you jack off, and you flushed beet red.

"Looking forward to our exit session," Sophie called, and the other women laughed.

You couldn't think of anything to say and you got out of there. On the subway, your dick was throbbing. It felt sore. It occurred to you that you'd been masturbating in that session for about three hours, and you never did come.

The phone rang one night. "Hey, this is Jill. You remember me?"

It was the hottie from the street corner. "Holy shit. Yeah, I mean, definitely. How, how are you doing?"

"Hey," she purred, "you're really doing it! I just looked you up on the list. I thought you were just full of shit."

"No, I'm really doing it."

"For me?"

You didn't know what to say. She cackled. "Don't answer that. Woo! It's a little hot in here right now." She laughed again. "So listen, what do you do?"

You talked about work. She was a graduate student in political science at NYU. A real egghead. She wasn't stuck up, though. Then you talked about music. You both liked The Clash.

"So, um, listen," Jill said. "Can I pop your cherry?"

"What?" you asked.

"I mean I'm going to put in a request to be the first person to have sex with you, when you get out. You know. Ask them to go easy on the exit session. They'll do that, if you want them to."

Your throat was dry. "Yeah, sure. Sure."

"Okay," Jill said. "Shall we make a date, for when you get out?"

"Okay," you whispered.

You were so tired at work that last week, you could barely keep it together. You got back from the warehouse inspection and slumped into your cube and just stared at the computer for a while. You could feel every inch of your skin. You felt the seams of your jeans, running down the outside and up the inside of your thighs. The seams of your shirt, stroking your sides. If you closed your eyes, your watchband felt like a woman's thumb and fingers locked around around your wrist, pulling you downward. You could feel your toes nudging into your socks, parting the folds of cotton, pushing them back against the hard walls of leather. Somehow you'd lost weight over the past couple of weeks; your potbelly had vanished. You could feel all your muscles—biceps and quads and abs—dwelling inside your clothes; like animals waiting, breathing, ready to go.

Friday, you were so zoned out, you were late to the cafeteria for lunch. As you passed the secretaries' table there was a sudden pause in their conversation, and then a burst of laughter. You turned around, and they hushed up again. A couple of them darted you glances and looked away; the old biddy glowered disapprovingly into her soup. Rhonda from HR, though, looked up and right into your eyes, with a steady look just this side of a smile, and you felt blood shooting through your body, up through your face, up to the roots of your hair.

You made it to your table somehow. The guys weren't talking much; Harry was still on vacation and Bharat and Alex were in a shared sour mood due to recent fuckups by their boss. You looked back: Rhonda was eating. But it was like she could feel you looking at the back of her head, because she turned to you. She was eating a shrimp and it was hanging out of the side of her mouth, and she sucked it in like a satisfied cat.

And this was bullshit. Shouldn't you be going over to them, talking it up? "Oh, so you're *subscribers,* eh, ladies? Oh, no, I sure can't *tell* you what goes on in there . . . no, I reckon you'd have to *experience* the difference . . ."

You applied yourself to the meat loaf.

. . .

But what did you need fucking Rhonda and those harpies for any-way? No wonder you don't want to go over there and be made fun of—shit, groups of women like that are merciless, especially when they're single and hard up. Wait until you came to the Christmas party with Jill on your arm. She'd be dressed like a starlet at the Oscars, and you'd whisper in her ear and she'd be the one turning red, and Rhonda would be turning green.

That evening, there was no time in the chair, just the physical with the treadmill again, and this exit interview with the old-lady doctor, and then it was time for your date with Sophie. You waited in this real doctor's-office-type room, with a kind of double-wide hospital bed in it, and fluorescent lights. You were nervous as hell. First you sat on the bed, but that was kind of lame, so then you stood over in the corner by the coatrack.

How would Sophie take this whole thing about Jill's request? And shit, why the hell did you agree to that? Oh, sure, you knew why: you're no idiot. Sophie was a pro, she was just doing her job, whereas Jill was for real, Jill was a keeper. One fuck, versus as many fucks as you wanted. But still—Sophie was such a fucking beautiful piece of work. How could you pass up another shot at that svelte, golden European cunt? Could you talk Sophie into going ahead and fucking anyway, and not telling Jill?

But while you were thinking this, underneath the chatter in your head, what you felt didn't really match. You felt kind of sad and alone. You wished you could be back on the phone with Jill, hearing her laugh.

But holy shit, come on, man, you told yourself, nice problem to have, right? When before did I have grade-A babes fighting over me?

The door opened and you jumped up, because apparently you'd managed to sit down on the bed again.

Sophie, in her clean, severe Germanic glory, smiled at you.

"Gary," she said. "Are you ready?"

"Sure, of course, hey. Hello. Where are we going?"

"Indeed hello," she said, closing the door. "Here is fine. Especially since we have a subscriber request, from a"—she looked at her clipboard—"Jill Sivens, to do a short exit session with you. I assume you agree to that?"

"About that," you said, "uh, Sophie, I hope it's okay that—"

She looked up and smiles brightly. "Oh, Gary, it's great! It's a great sign when our clients are so quick to start building relationships with their new skills." She put the clipboard down on a table. "Can you take off your clothes? How have you been feeling?"

The flutter in your stomach sank a little, but you started shrugging out of your clothes. "Um, okay. Weird, really."

"Weird how?" said Sophie.

"Tired, I guess. Just kind of . . . worn out, from the chair." You were groping for some way of talking about it. She must know.

"Any hallucinations? Paranoid thoughts?"

"No, no. I mean—sometimes it feels like I can *feel* things better, you know? Like, I mean, with my skin. But nothing too weird."

She smiled broadly. "Heightened sensitivity. That's not a problem." The way she said "not a problem" made your spine tingle. You had your shoes and shirt off and you pulled your pants down and were surprised to find your dick was hard as a rock. Like, not *surprised* surprised, because here you were stripping for Sophie, but surprised you hadn't noticed.

"Any aversive thoughts about sex or sexual partners? As in, you are worried about sex, or don't like the idea of sex?"

"Jesus, no," you said, pulling off your shorts. "Quite the opposite."

"Oh, good," Sophie said, grinning again. "Very good." She came across the room and took your penis in her hands, as casually as if she was testing your knee for reflexes. "So this feels good?" she asked, gingerly stroking from the base of the shaft to the head.

You could hardly talk from surprise. Actually the feeling was like a burning, buzzing throb. Sophie's taut little breasts danced inside her blouse, and you could smell her smell—like apples and mint. "Yes," you said.

"Good," she said, and let go of you. "I won't do any more of that, because I want to honor the subscriber request." She crossed to her clipboard and made a few notes. Then she looked up at your face. "Oh, Gary, don't worry. I still have to do a little concrete measurement to see if your competence has improved. And in fact, I like this way, I tell you why. Remember how our first date was, well, a little bit all about you?" She grinned impishly. "This one will be all about me. Come take off my clothes very gently."

Cotton. Wool. Satin. Metal, the snick of the bra snap coming open. Skin, the panties moving down the legs, your thumbs brushing her thighs.

"Good." She lay facedown on the big hospital bed. "Backrub."

Skin. Warm and breathing. Your fingers could feel the little knots of wrongness. When you pushed too hard, she raised her shoulders a quarter inch, and you backed off. When it was too light, her breathing became irregular, and you pushed in. At one point you almost lost her to sleep, and your fingers started to stroke lightly, like ships dancing. Your fingertips, her pores. Her breathing quickened.

She rolled over. "Look at the clock, Gary," she said.

"Shit," you said. "It's ten o'clock." An hour backrub?

"Having fun?"

"Yeah."

"Good," she said. "Breasts."

And then: "Good. Now with your tongue."

Swollen flesh of her breast, the salty taste of her skin. Apples and mint. The nipple rolling under your tongue like a mountain. Her breathing roughening. Her stomach quivering.

She spread her legs, pushed your head down. "Tongue. Down here."

She tasted delicious. Tangy and salty. Which was weird. Sherry and Nora and Tarika and Caitlin had tasted, you know, fine, but not like this. She was wet and hot and, like, *pure* around your tongue. It wasn't even like you were doing something—you couldn't tell where your tongue stopped and her cunt started, and the rest of your own body seemed very far away. But her body—her trunk that squirmed, her feet that came up off the table and stroked the back of your head and then kicked out, her lungs that sucked in air and held it and pushed it out, her hands that ran through her hair and then yours and then grabbed the table behind her head, her ass that lifted up to your mouth and fell again—her body was all that was real.

"Tongue and fingers, now," she whispered. "Please, Gary. Please let me come."

The first time her breath caught and her cunt throbbed and her thighs gripped your head, you still weren't sure, because she didn't make any noise, and because when you started to back off, her hand snaked around the back of your head and pushed you back in. You'd been doing all these fine, whispery things with your tongue, but now you could tell she needed more, and then you were licking like crazy, your tongue like an eel, a wet slab coming down and in and over again and again, and you were drinking her up. Three fingers pushing in and just holding, firm against the wall of her vagina. And the second time, she let out a sob, and her cunt squeezed your knuckles together hard enough to hurt, and then you could feel it, white light flooding in from all sides, filling her up, filling you up. You didn't even have a body at all anymore, there was just her, the light filling her, and you'd never felt that good. As if something that had been sleeping inside you since you were born woke up and said: I want that.

"Okay," Sophie said a little later. "Stop. It's midnight. We have to go." She pushed herself up off the bed and flung her arms around your shoulders and kissed your cheek, her hard nipples pushing into your chest. "Thanks," she breathed into your ear.

You both got dressed. Your whole body was buzzing, awake. You heard every rustle of cloth like a whisper telling you a secret. How weird to be after sex and not want to fall asleep. You wanted to go play football in the park or some shit. You noticed your dick—still rock hard—when you pushed it back into your underpants. Snapped your jeans shut over it. Kind of uncomfortable.

Sophie opened the door and slapped your ass. "Go get them," she said, and giggled, deep in her throat.

You almost danced down the hall.

You had a bunch of flowers for Jill. Not roses, that might be too corny. Or, like, trying too hard. Just a bunch of yellow and orange flowers. You didn't know what kind they were. You would think that would have been covered on the Program weekend sessions, what flowers to get a girl. Instead of all the crap about listening skills.

She was a little late to the restaurant. She'd picked it; it wasn't a fancy place, but it wasn't a dive either. It was all raw wood panels and big wooden tables, and the waiters had white smocks on, and practically all they served was like coffee, bread, and salad. But really good bread, deep brown and full of seeds and shit, the kind that steams when you break it open. You sat there at the end of one table with your glass of water, waiting for Jill to show, and you could smell the bread, a powerful thick wave of bread, coming from the ovens.

She was in a tank top and khaki shorts and army boots. Belly button showing, no bra, her mango breasts jiggling, the fabric snug around them. Petite. Her stomach wasn't flat and severe like Sophie's; she had a little low roundish hill of a tummy that suggested the hill of her cunt inside those baggy pants. She looked a little wary, like she was wondering if this was a good idea, but her face relaxed into confidence when she saw you, and she grinned. Her face—yeah, like Cindy Crawford, without the mole. Holy shit, what were you doing here? It was hard to believe that she smiled when she saw you. Hard to believe she was heading over to sit next to you.

She slid in next to you and waved the waiter over.

"Hi," you said, "hey, uh, thanks for—"

"Oh, shut up," she said. "Don't thank me. What are you thanking me for? Don't thank me for being late to a date with you, that's lame."

You were going to say sorry, but you thought better of it.

She reached over and wrapped her hand around your biceps, and squeezed. "You're looking good," she said. "You lost weight in there."

"Yeah, it's weird, it's not like I had any time to exercise or—"

She gave a grin of pure evil. You remembered the chair, and you flushed red.

The waiter came and Jill said, "Just get us bread and salad, we'll share. And a carafe of Merlot. We're celebrating."

"Eat quick," she said to you when the food came.

She talked a lot, about school and politics. She had strong opinions about everything. She hated Bush and you could see her point. She'd liked Clinton and you'd thought he was full of shit. But you didn't need weekend seminars to know to shut up about that on a first date. You listened and you watched her beautiful face move.

You held hands on the way back to Jill's. It was just around the corner. Your whole body was humming. She pushed you into an alley and you kissed. Blood buzzing in your ears, the taste of bread and wine on her lips and tongue. Her breasts pushing against your chest. You grabbed her ass, and she laughed and slipped away, pulling you out of the alley.

Jill winked at the doorman, a big black guy who looked like a linebacker and rolled his eyes like a drag queen. There was this old couple arguing in the elevator, so you didn't kiss there.

Her apartment was a bedroom with a teddy bear on the bed and poster-sized black-and-white photos on the walls, a living room nook with a couch and a big window, and a kitchenette.

She shucked her tank top and her breasts bounced out. You wanted to touch them, but you just looked. It was like you could feel Sophie's ghost holding you back, slowing you down. She ran her fingers over her breasts, lifted them up. She bent down and licked her own nipple, and looked at your reaction. She grinned.

You pulled off your shirt. You dropped your pants. You yanked your boxers from around your cock, which was standing at attention.

She grinned more.

She slid her pants and panties off together, and tossed them over the couch. Now all of the Upper West side could see her bare ass if they looked in the window, but you guessed nobody who lives on the twentieth floor worries about shit like that.

Her cunt was just as you imagined it, a low hill, thick black curly hair.

You kissed some more, your cock pushing against her stomach. It felt numb. But the warmth of your belly on hers felt good.

"Eat me," she said, and she sat back on the couch. She was still wearing the army boots. You knelt down to it.

Your body faded away again into the background. Your moving tongue was the bridge between your mind and the body that was real: her sweat, her shudders, her hand knotted in your hair, pushing you in. She was louder than Sophie, rougher, her breath coming in jerks and grunts and hisses, her fist pulling at your hair. Like she was fighting, hips moving like a boxer's. You slid your hands over her flanks, her thighs, and then you slid your thumbs in to stroke her pussy lips, and then to nudge her clit in slow circles.

"Oh!" she cried. "Oh!"

You wanted her to come. You wanted that flooding of white light, that delicious wave.

She pulled you back out of her cunt, by the hair.

"Um, hey. Please come," you said. "I want to make you come."

"No," she said, and her eyes were wild, her chest heaving. "Not yet."

She pushed you down onto the couch and pulled open a drawer on a side table. She rummaged around, fished out a condom, opened it with her teeth, and slid it onto your cock. You gasped when she touched you—something was strange. Your cock felt too swollen, almost like you had to piss bad. But different. The condom felt like sandpaper going on, and you jerked away, but she followed with her hands and body, pushing it down, rolling it down until it touched your balls.

She took you by the balls and pulled you down onto the sofa again. "Ssh," she said. "It's okay. Ssh."

She climbed up onto the sofa, onto you. Her goddamn amazing breasts brushed your nose. She put one knee on either side of you, straddling over you, her cunt hair brushing the tip of your penis. She took the shaft in her hand.

It was like your cock was sore, but sore from the inside out.

She slipped the head inside, pushing it into the dense warmth of her, squeezing it past the bands of muscle. It hurt.

"Hold on," you gasped. "Jill—wait—"

"Ssh," she said. She looked excited, like a kid opening birthday presents. "Gary, I know what I'm doing. Okay? I've popped cherries of Program guys before. It's supposed to be like this."

She plunged down onto you. Her cunt was like a hot fist. You bit off a scream.

"Yeah," she breathed. "Don't come. Focus on me, Gary. What am I feeling?" She put your hands on her breasts.

She rode you. It hurt. But beyond you, in her, pleasure was building. Her nipples ground against your palms, and she groaned. Your cock felt like a throat, and her cunt was like hands crushing it, but at every stroke you could feel the waves of pleasure in her. You heard yourself moaning, but it was far away. She licked your neck, and that felt good, suddenly warm and wet. Each time she plunged down on you, crushing your cock in that incredible grip, you squeezed her breasts and the nipples in your palms were like wires connecting you to the bliss in her head, the blood and power flooding through her.

You don't know how long it was. A long time. "Oh *yeah*," she said, "oh *yeah*, Gary, oh *yeah*—"

She kissed you. That felt good.

"Wait," you said when she broke the kiss, "stop—"

"How does it feel, honey?" she said, thrusting onto you again. "Does it hurt?"

The question pierced the numbness, and you felt your cock again. Her cunt pulled back and it was like she was ripping it off your body. You screamed, and you felt the muscles of her pussy start to squeeze, squeeze, squeeze, felt her whole trunk shudder.

She threw her head back. "Oh!" she said. "Oh shit! Gary—Gary—" She looked down at you. Like a hungry woman at a slice of devil's food cake. "Gary, come on three! One—two—three—"

You came on three, and it was like fire, like blood spurting out of you. An agony so sudden and total you couldn't breathe.

And then she was coming too, and the white light was there, flooding you, flooding you with peace, washing everything away. It was her body that was the center, her singing nerves, her roaring heart, her body hugging you close, and her cry. She bit your shoulder where it met your neck, and you could feel it from her side, the pressure on her teeth, the taste of the lump of meat in her mouth. It felt good.

You slumped back on the couch and she lay on top of you.

"Ohhh . . ." she said.

You breathed. The soreness was gone. The white light was moving in you. You were dizzy.

"Now I get to say thank you," she said, and giggled.

"Uhh . . ." you said. Then you laughed too. You didn't know what else to do. You didn't know what to think.

She swung off you and stood up, swaying a little, dizzy too. "I've got ice cream!" she announced, and went into the kitchenette.

You couldn't move. She came in with Rocky Road and two spoons.

"Jill," you said. "What was—I mean—?"

She dug out a scoop with one spoon. Her hair was kind of wild, a strand wiggling down over her nose. She was beautiful. She raised an eyebrow, questioning.

"I, uh, that hurt."

She nodded, looking serious, ice cream sitting on her spoon. Her nipples were hard.

You started to laugh again.

"It gets better," she said. "Trust me." She climbed up on you, straddling your chest. Her scratchy pubic hair tickled you. Her cunt was still wet, sticky against your breastbone. Her breasts swung above you. An incredible hottie. Way out of your league. She put the spoon against your lips. "Are you sorry?"

You ate ice cream. You swallowed. "Uh, no. No."

She took the next scoop in her mouth, and then she bent down onto you and kissed you, sliding the ice cream into your mouth. She reached up and put the ice cream carton on the side table.

"Can I eat you out again?" you said. "Until you come?"

She licked the spoon. "Oh yeah. Let's move to the bed."

The guys couldn't stop talking about her—how the hell had you ended up with this piece of ass? They even asked right in front of her, over cans of Coors at the bar, the usual place, that place that girl had laughed at you, the second time you took her there. "No offense meant, but how the fuck does a guy like Gary—?"

She didn't let on about the Program; she was a total sport. "Hey, he looks like a slob, but you know, Gary has certain talents. . . ."

Hoots and slaps on the back, and the guys made some remarks, but she wasn't offended, she just kidded them back. She could hold her own.

And you'd been afraid she'd look down her nose at the place, at your life—being an egghead and an Upper West Side rich girl and all—think it was scummy and blue collar. But she ate it up, played foosball and drank Coors and watched the game on TV and laughed as loud as a guy. And god she looked good. Every other broad in the place was giving her the evil eye, and she liked that too; you could tell.

But she liked sleeping at her place better. Understandably. So you hustled down there on the train after work, and got up early to hustle out of there. Every place to eat around there was fucking expensive, and you sure as hell were not letting her pay for you—you didn't even like to go dutch, really, because fuck, what the hell were you bringing to the relationship, certainly not the looks or the smarts. But it was only the second week, and maybe her paying half was her way of showing independence or whatever. There was something about that in the seminars. Anyway.

It still hurt to fuck, and she liked that it hurt.

You got to the uptown bar after work. She was dressed in a short dress, bright blue, all dolled up. It barely reached midthigh. She was talking to a couple of guys, and you hustled over. Feeling out of place in jeans and a sweater, even a nice sweater. She curled right around you, and the yuppie guys with their expensive watches and banker haircuts got the picture and wandered off.

You were sipping your first beer (somehow you weren't drinking so fast or so much anymore), and she nestled up against you and pulled your hand under her skirt and you felt bush. No panties, in that fucking miniskirt. You got hard. She put your hand back on the counter, and she talked to the bartender and finished her drink.

Then she took you into the alley out back and fished your cock out.

"Jill—" you said.

"Ssh," she said, and straddled you. She was already wet. You went into her, and it hurt, it hurt.

She took you. She rode you as long as she needed.

She came and the white light was there.

"So you said you've popped other guy's cherries."

She slurped up a noodle. Chinese takeout. Her living room nook. Her breasts bare in the moonlight. "Mmm-hmm . . ."

"So what, uh—"

"Hey!" she said sharply. "I don't want to talk about past relationships. What a fucking buzz-killer that is."

"All right," you said.

She put down her noodles. "Come over here."

You had to work late one night, fuckup with a delivery, not your fault but you were the one who had to dig up the archival paperwork and go figure it out. You called Jill, and she went out with the girls from her study group. Some nights she wanted to go out with them alone, dish about guys. Maybe compare notes, which made your blood run a little cold. But, you know, fourth week of the relationship, that was all right, loosen up a little. Don't be so fucking clingy.

You missed her.

Eleven o'clock and the place was empty, you still weren't done, and your e-mail dinged. It was from Rhonda the HR lady, saying to come to her office. She had an office at the edge of the cube farm, not a cube. The blinds were down.

You felt like maybe you shouldn't go in, but that was kind of silly.

Rhonda got up from her chair. You'd always thought she was good-looking—she had these perfect put-together outfits, and her face was smooth and young despite a streak of gray in her hair. But shit, she didn't compare to Jill. Maybe she was going to come on to you and you could turn her down, serve her right for laughing at you behind your back. Subscribe to this, baby. On the other hand, maybe you'd somehow gotten in shit with HR. Though you couldn't imagine how.

"Close the door," she said, so you did.

She looked uncomfortable. "So you did the Program, right?"

"Yeah," you said sarcastically. What the fuck was this about? Did she think you were so hard up after the Program? Maybe she just wanted to hear about it.

"I've been, ah, reading up on it," she said. She was blushing. She was always so cocky, it was weird to see her blush. "Guys react differently. Some . . ."

"Yeah?"

"Take off your shirt," she said in a strained voice.

"Oh, this is bullshit," you said, and you turned away to the door.

Rhonda sucked in her breath, and there was a little tremor in it, like she'd been hit and she was going to cry. And that stopped you for a moment. And then you were thinking about that sound and what it would sound like, Rhonda coming. She had a lean, prim face, and you thought of all the looks you'd seen on it—irritated, bored, skeptical, and vaguely amused, laughing with the other women. But what would it be like out of control—eyes squeezed shut and mouth open in an "O," begging for more?

What the fuck were you thinking? You had Jill.

But under the fluorescent lights on the maroon carpet, with your hand on the thin aluminum door handle, Jill seemed like a dream. Manhattan and Cindy Crawford. She's just playing with you, man—and any minute now the joke will be up and ice cream on the twentieth floor on the Upper West Side will vanish like smoke.

And Rhonda was here now, clearing her throat to call it all a joke or throw you out of her office, and there was still that tremor in it, like Rhonda was scared and uncertain, and that shouldn't be—a woman shouldn't be scared and uncertain around you, she should be happy, she should be on fire with joy. Rhonda was a vessel bearing her own portion of white light.

You turned around and started unbuttoning your shirt.

"Oh my God," Rhonda said.

"I can't believe it," Rhonda said. She raised herself up onto her elbows. She was on the desk, one foot on the swiveling chair, the other hooked over your back. She'd knocked a pile of papers off the desk. You leaned back, your face hot and wet from her cunt. You were kneeling on the floor and your knees hurt. "I can't believe I did this."

You said nothing. Your body was still tingling from the flood of white light. But your stomach felt sour. A scene was stuck in your mind like a video stuck in a loop—you show up at Jill's. The doorman smiles and waves you in. Jill meets you at her apartment door with a grin. And you—what? Tell her and watch that smile disappear. Or don't tell her and then what? Sitting around her place trying to grin back at her, nervous energy gripping you like a fist, your heart racing. Shit, shit, what had they done to you? You'd dogged girls and lied before, smooth as milk. But you couldn't now. You were sure of that. Why not? Was it the Program or was it Jill? Was it love?

"And you don't—you don't need anything, right?" Rhonda said. "I don't have to do anything for you?"

"Nope," you said.

"And you won't tell anyone about this?" Rhonda said. "Don't tell anyone about this."

"Nope."

"Ohh, it felt so good." Rhonda said. "How the hell did they teach you that? Guys can never do it like that."

You said nothing.

"One more time," Rhonda said. "One more time and I'll let you go."

. . .

"What. The. Hell." Jill said.

"I'm telling you," you said. "It's something to do with the Program. I'm serious. Jill, I wouldn't—Jill, I'm serious about you. I—"

"Oh, shut the fuck up," Jill said, her hazel eyes blazing. "Stop whining. Don't you dare blame it on the Program. All the Program did was make you tell me. Don't even claim you wouldn't have dogged me without the Program. I mean, under an absurdly hypothetical scenario where I'd be with you without the Program. Don't even front."

"Okay. Okay. But give me another chance—"

"Shit, why are you even begging? Do you think I care?"

"Jill, it won't—"

"Shut up." She opened a cabinet in the kitchenette and pulled out one shot glass and a bottle of Absolut. She poured, put down the bottle, and gulped the shot down. Then she screwed the cap on and put the bottle away. Then she paced, slowly, tracing the rim of the empty glass with her thumb.

You sat down on the couch, setting your coat down on the coffee table.

"I'm keeping you," Jill said. "I'm fucking keeping you, all right? Because you're too good. But, goddamn it, I won't be dogged. So this is an open relationship, as of now. I'm going to have other guys up here. Ones who haven't done the Program, who still want it. You know?"

You looked at your feet, a slow burn of red spreading across your cheeks. It felt like the apartment had come loose from the building and was wobbling.

"Because I like that sometimes. Don't get me wrong—I like you more. What I am really going to like is telling you about them." She set the glass down on the counter. "Maybe more than that. We'll see." You looked up and she was looking at you, intensely, like trying to read something. Trying to see if something was enough. And it must not have been enough, because she still looked mad.

You were sick of yourself, of this fucking wimpiness. Maybe you should yell back at her. Or walk. But what were you going to head to? Channel-surfing on the threadbare green couch in your crappy house? Christ, you couldn't even jack off. Hearing the guys say sympathetically, "Fuck, we knew it couldn't last, you and a chick like that." Rhonda? Pretty clear what Rhonda wanted, and it didn't include waking up for breakfast together.

Then she smiled, ferally. "Come in here," she said.

You stood in front of her bathroom mirror, and she opened your pants and fished your dick out. "Get hard," she said, and blood flooded it, pushing it up like a searching finger into a straining, swollen erection. She opened the cabinet and took out a big scoop of Vaseline and smothered your cock with it, and you tried not to flinch back from her hand.

"Now jack off," she said. "But don't come."

"Jill—" you said.

"I want to watch," she said, and she sounded more eager, now, than mad.

You started stroking, gingerly, ribbons of discomfort slithering along your skin.

"Harder," she said. "Like a man."

And that fucking did it: the unease and regret in you was washed away in a tide of rage, and you yanked your hand down and up, down and up over your traitor cock, squeezing and mauling. Choking the chicken. Gritting your teeth against the fireworks of pain.

It was like mauling a broken bone. Little grunts and sobs of pain were coming out of you. And your cheeks were wet, but you weren't crying. No. Fuck that. Just tearing up with agony and anger. You weren't feeling sorry for anything. Maybe you felt safe. Maybe you just were Jill's, and that was that.

She pulled a clear, pliant plastic dildo out of a drawer and slathered it with Vaseline. "I'll give you something to make you feel better," she said, and you thought, oh, thank god, she's going to make herself come.

It was hard to look at yourself in the mirror, your red wet face, your clenched teeth. You closed your eyes.

"Even harder," she whispered in your ear, and you hurt yourself.

You felt her cool hand on your throat. It felt good. "Now relax," she said, and she was sliding her slippery finger over your anus. You clenched, and she paused, leaving it there. You forced yourself to relax, and then you lost yourself in the pain.

Then you felt the dildo pushing against your asshole, and you opened your eyes and cried out—a wordless shout. The tip was in, and though you clenched down, trying to drive it back, Jill braced herself with her hand against your throat and drove it in. It opened you up and was in you.

"Ahhhhh—" you cried.

"Keep your hand moving," said Jill, and it moved.

She fucked you with the dildo and it felt good, and now you were crying. Christ. You were a faggot. This meant you were a faggot.

"Open your eyes," said Jill. "And now come."

Hot white liquid, and a sound like thunder, and darkness swept in from the edges of your vision, and you felt Jill, far away, catching you, her arms around your chest, as your body left its footing.

You got out of there the next morning, when Jill was still asleep.

There was a little snow on the ground outside the clinic. You stood under a tree a little way from the guys with the signs, listening to them shout. They kept looking at you like they knew why you were there, like they were just waiting for you to come over and shout with them, but they knew you weren't ready yet. A guy pulled up in a taxi, dressed in a suit, and sauntered by the protesters.

It was cold. You scuffed your boots and rubbed your hands together.

You were late to work. What the hell were you going to say to Rhonda? Just not go near her?

You couldn't seem to make yourself move to the subway.

"Hey! Hey you!"

It was three girls in a car at the curb. Not cute girls—kind of punk girls, angry clothes, blaring loud music. Cars were nosing around them.

"You in the blue jacket! Over here!"

You walked over to them. The driver and the one in the back were giggling. The other one leaned out of her window. A fat girl, maybe twenty, with a mohawk and square glasses. "Get in," she said, daring you.

You reached for the door.

A woman's thumb and fingers closed around your wrist, pulling you back.

Sophie.

"Gary? What are you doing?" Sophie said.

"Oh Gary," Sophie said. "But why didn't you come in for your one-week evaluation?"

"I didn't know there was one," you said.

"But didn't you read the brochure? Didn't—" she sighed.

You put your face in your hands.

"It's not supposed to be like that," Sophie said. "Your sexual transference acclimation is overdetermining your sense of self-agency. I'm booking you today for an emergency readjustment. Stay, Gary. Just wait an hour or so in this room, okay? Until the lab techs are set up. We'll fix this. We'll make this better."

"Okay," you say.

She breathes a sigh of relief. "It's my fault," she says. "They told me never to say that, for liability reasons. But I let you slide through the exit exam. You just seemed so happy." She shakes her head.

"Sophie," you say. "Can we, uh—can we um—?"

She grins shyly. "What?"

"Can we, just one last time, before they fix me, have sex?"

She frowns. "Gary. You don't need to do that. We'll do it afterward, in a week. We'll do a proper exit exam with all the trimmings."

"No, this, this is for me. Just—you know."

"Gary." She swallowed. "I think that's a bad idea."

"I just want to say good-bye to it. To this way. With you."

She pursed her lips, and there was a hint of a blush on her pale cheeks. "You'd have to sign a release form. . . ."

You nodded.

She got up and took a clipboard and clipped a form and a pen to it. She turned around too fast, coming back, and knocked the doctor stool so that it rolled over and slammed into the desk.

She handed you the clipboard. Then she shrugged off her lab coat.

G. BONHOMME
on "The Program"

In "The Program," I wanted to see if I could write a story that worked simultaneously as erotica and classic extrapolative science fiction.

In both cases, I was juggling. I wanted to see if I could keep three balls in the air at once: literature, porn, and a thought experiment.

I also wanted to write from the perspective of a sexist, lazy guy—a boor—who gets a comeuppance. That was the original intention, but it was superseded as the character grew on me.

I played with the porn cliché of a mind-control device that renders its subject a willing sexual plaything—particularly the straight man's fantasy of being turned into such a plaything by a woman. Most straight men might overrate their usefulness as playthings—supply and demand, as seen in the market for pro doms, confirms this. It struck me that making a man actually useful in this capacity would require some . . . reengineering.

THE LETTERS

Eric Albert

"Dear Mr. Davis," Megan typed, "I would like to suck your dick."

She paused and considered whether the idea needed further explanation. No, better to keep it short and sweet. She inserted a blank line, typed "ME," saved the file, and sent it to the printer.

The "ME" part was clever. Mr. Davis would think the letter writer was hiding behind the anonymity of a first-person pronoun, but in fact it stood for Megan Elizabeth. Megan Elizabeth Bryant, in full.

Megan was used to feeling clever.

She took the letter off the printer, folded it precisely in thirds, and slipped it into a long envelope. She neatly wrote "Mr. Timothy Davis" in block capital letters. Her printer had an attachment for printing on envelopes, but she'd never been able to make it work. Everyone's capital letters looked pretty much the same, anyway.

Should she stick on a "LOVE" stamp? She was a big fan of irony. But maybe Mr. Davis wasn't. She sighed and held the letter in her hand, balancing it. Three minutes later she was on her bike. Spring had finally arrived, and the late-afternoon sun made her feel extra alive. As if the stuff that ran in the veins of

Greek gods—ichor?—coursed through hers too. She turned her head for a second and let the wind blow her warm hair across her face.

Mr. Davis's house was only a dozen blocks away. Megan coasted past, making sure his car was not in the driveway. She braked to a stop, walked purposefully up the brick path, and pushed the letter through the slot in the door. Then she headed back to finish off her homework.

That night she lay in bed, another math problem set successfully conquered, and pictured her letter's reception: Mr. Davis coming home. Mr. Davis seeing the envelope on the floor. Mr. Davis picking it up, opening it, reading it. Mr. Davis's thing getting hard in his pants.

Megan put her hand between her legs and found she was much wetter than usual. The letter was definitely a great idea. She flopped over on her stomach, both hands underneath her. Again and again she flashed on Mr. Davis, her letter in his hands, the front of his pants poking out. That's my boner, she thought. I gave it to you, and it is all mine.

When the orgasm came, it was one of the good ones, emptying her out and leaving her cheeks tingling.

The next day was Wednesday, which meant U.S. history and Mr. Davis at eleven. Megan was in her seat up front at ten fifty-eight. Mr. Davis entered the classroom exactly two minutes later.

For fifty minutes he talked about Theodore Roosevelt's accomplishments as mayor of New York. For fifty minutes Megan watched him, seeking some sign of change. She watched him pace the area around his desk like a big cat. She watched him illustrate his sentences with sweeping strokes on the blackboard. She watched his crotch. Nothing.

The bell rang. Megan felt the sting of loss, sharp as when her father had grounded her the weekend of the canoe trip. She stood quickly and walked to the door, pausing to let Kirsten Wallace catch up. Kirsten languished in the back row of Mr. Davis's class, doomed to separation from her friend by the tyranny of the alphabet.

Over English-muffin pizzas in the cafeteria, Kirsten began dishing out details of last weekend's big party. Like Megan, Kirsten was only a sophomore, but she was a sophomore on the swim team, and that earned her a place on the periphery of the high school's movers and shakers. Megan the math whiz had resigned herself to living in some parallel world that Kirsten would visit, bringing news from the planet of the popular.

In fact, it was Kirsten who'd relayed the rumor that Mr. Davis's wife had left him after he found her in the arms of another woman. Megan had been skeptical at the time. "Is this from the same source who said Peter Green's kid brother was abducted by aliens?" But the idea had stuck in her head.

"Earth to Megan."

Megan blinked. Kirsten was waving a hand. "How many fingers am I holding up?" she asked.

"I'm sorry," said Megan. "My mind went on vacation. Kirsten, did you notice anything different about Mr. Davis today?"

"Sure. That tie was a joke. He really needs someone to coordinate his clothes."

"No, no. I mean, the way he acted."

Kirsten contemplated the question for a few seconds. "Don't think so," she said. "Why?"

"No reason. I just thought he might have something on his mind."

"Nothing 'cept Teddy R." And with that, Kirsten was back to who kissed whom when the lights were out, a subject so complex that Megan had to skip dessert to make Mr. Thorndike's trig class.

That night, Megan lay in bed and stared at the ceiling in frustration. Mr. Davis had read her letter, she was sure of it. And that was all she'd wanted. Right? Right.

But now she wanted something more. She felt scared and slightly sick, as if she'd sipped one drink and woken up an alcoholic.

What is enough?

She would lose everything if this got out, all the perfectly typed papers, all the extra-credit work, all the endless activities amassed like gold pieces for her college hoard.

What is enough?

Not this, not yet, she thought.

So she converted it into a math problem. "Given that Ms. Bryant wants an explicit, sexual response from Mr. Davis, and given that Ms. Bryant in no way intends to reciprocate, and given that Mr. Davis may under no circumstances learn her identity, show there exists a procedure to obtain this response in a manner that preserves both Ms. Bryant's chastity and her anonymity."

That was better. "Now use your brain," she said softly to herself, calling her well-worn homework mantra into service. "Use your big brain." Time passed. She waited. And the answer appeared, a red apple hanging from a black bough.

Tension slowly eased from Megan's body. Already her brain had moved on to her regular fantasy of the past few weeks, unreeling the images before her eyes in a mental videotape. There was Mr. Davis coming home early from a meeting. There were his wife and another woman, sprawled on the bed. The women's actions were vague and indistinct. Mr. Davis's reaction was not.

He ran out of his house into the comfort of the night and stumbled to his car. He drove for hours, aimlessly, then parked on a small, secluded back street. His head was full of the scene at home, the women writhing on the bed, the sounds and smells. He was getting big. He fought his desires, then broke down and unzipped his fly. Tears leaked from behind his closed eyelids.

Megan, facedown and panting, let the movie work its magic once again.

"Dear Mr. Davis," Megan typed, "I look forward to having you in my mouth. In the mailbox at 47 Grove Street you will find a token of my seriousness. If you too are serious, please accept the item with my good wishes. Leave in its place a letter stating your desires. ME"

She reread it twice. It sounded a bit Victorian, but she consoled herself that the Victorians were pretty kinky underneath it all. She spell-checked the file, sent it to the printer, and took off her jeans.

All through the school day she'd been aware of the panties against her skin. They were hot pink, cut bikini-style, and unlike anything she'd ever worn. They were also two sizes too big. Mr. Davis, she was sure, would want a woman with hips.

Megan wondered if she'd left her scent. Images appeared unbidden: Mr. Davis examining the panties, running his fingers over the silky material, holding them up to his face. Something thrummed inside her. She wanted to lie on the bed in the late-afternoon sun and touch her suddenly wet self slowly, melting into the day.

She checked her watch. There wasn't enough time to also deliver the panties and letter before dinner. "Maturity is the willingness to postpone pleasure," she reminded herself as she stripped off the panties. Then she giggled. He'd certainly smell her now.

That night, Megan lay in bed and struggled to recapture the excitement of the afternoon. But that still, sweet moment was gone, lost somewhere in the day's nonstop activity. It had taken her forty-five minutes to get to Grove Street and back, about what she'd estimated. But it had taken a full hour to drop off the letter at Mr. Davis's house, and that was just ridiculous.

She hadn't expected his car to be there. For forty minutes she'd lurked around his property before convincing herself he was either out or asleep. In the next sixty seconds she'd managed to trot to the front door, jam the letter through the slot, race back to her bike, mount it, and ride madly for three blocks, only to screech to a stop a second before wiping out Mr. Davis and his Scotch terrier.

She'd almost lost it then, but she'd managed to apologize splendidly and explain she was late for supper, which she was. Mr. Davis had barely acknowledged her. She'd made it home unscathed and gulped down her meal, then plowed through two hours of English homework before doing some last-minute memorization for the French test tomorrow.

Things jostled and jangled in her head. She shifted about uneasily, then rolled onto her stomach. Sometimes the position itself would call up the pictures that brought release, the release required to disconnect her mind so sleep could carry her away.

Instead, she saw the Grove Street mailbox. And then she was standing on one foot in the middle of her moonlit room, pulling up her jeans. She dressed to be unnoticed: dark blouse, sneakers over bare feet, hair tied back from her face, a windbreaker. She slipped out the front door and closed it quietly behind her. Her parents, asleep in their separate rooms, did not stop her. In that moment, she understood that they would never stop her, that this leaving was a rehearsal for a later one.

Mist kissed her face. It was raining gently, and her thoughts dissolved in delight. She heard her mother's voice calling her across the years, "Meg, come in, you're getting soaked!" But she would not come in, she would run through the rain in a world deliciously her own.

On her bike, drops spattering her forehead and cheeks, she said out loud, "You can only get so wet," and felt that same extraordinary freedom. She was sailing through the watery streets, the tires hissing beneath her. Streetlamps drifted by, haloed in the damp night air.

Mr. Davis passed this way, she thought, dry and warm in his car, eagerly anticipating his prize. Joy boiled up in her, and she squeezed the hand brakes hard. The rear wheel caught, choked, and began to skid out, just like a thousand times before. She squeezed harder and let the bike heel sharply, squeezed harder still, flirting with gravity. She let go. The rear wheel bit into the pavement, the bike jerked wildly, she grabbed the handlebars and yanked. She was upright, in control again. She rolled into her old neighborhood smiling.

It had been two years since they'd moved, leaving the brown monstrosity behind. She passed her old street and took a quick glance. Sixth house down on the right, but all she could see was the rain. Eight more blocks and she turned onto Grove. She coasted half a block, dismounted, and laid her bike under the massive rhododendron as tradition required. She followed the crack in the sidewalk past two more houses, and she was there.

Number 47 was a middle-period Victorian, set back a full forty yards from the road. It had remained unoccupied for almost a decade, an innocent bystander in some legal battle Megan had never understood. The long narrow path to the front porch split the yard into two enormous rectangles. Ragged dogwoods lined the path, and other ornamental trees were scattered about the yard as if planted by some drunken Johnny Appleseed. Japanese maples clustered in a grove on the left, thirty feet in, while three ancient crab apple trees formed a scalene triangle halfway back on the far right. A privet hedge, long untrimmed, extended out from both sides of the house, then ran down the sides of the yard to form a wall to keep out neighbor friends and foes alike. The house itself was beat up and boarded over and basically unchanged from when she and Michael had first discovered it.

Michael. What was he doing now, anyway? His family had moved to Arizona three years ago, and he had vanished from her life. Did he ever think about the innocent messages they used to exchange here? Had he learned how to spell "rendezvous"?

Megan found herself on the large porch that wrapped around the building like a blanket, running along the front and right side of the house. A battered mailbox was bolted to the railing, a single seven hanging on its side. She stared at the mailbox and longed for X-ray vision. Would she see a pile of pink cloth, limp and pathetic? Or had her offering been transmogrified into something rich and wild?

This is stupid, she thought. She yanked open the box, the hinge squealing, reached inside, and pulled out an envelope.

Her eyes got wet. She felt like that guy in the poem when he first saw the mountains of the New World. She took a breath. This was just too good not to share with someone. Kirsten? They'd barely talked about sex, two horses nudging each other from separate stalls. But in the spaces of their conversation, sex often hid. Yes, Kirsten.

One peek first.

She tore the envelope open. Inside was a single sheet of lined paper. It was blank.

"You jerk," she said, and she was off the porch. He was coming from behind a crab apple tree. Megan dove between two dogwoods and tore away across the lawn, the marshy ground trying to steal her sneakers. Five yards past the end of the house she turned right sharply, sprinted to the privet hedge, stopped short, and sidestepped neatly through the dead spot. Then she was running again, along the big bow of the living room, under the kitchen windows, around the rear corner of the house, across the flagstones to the corner where the big porch began.

Megan could hear him thrashing around in the privet, trying to bull his way through. She dropped to the ground and pulled herself under the broken latticework with a single move that Michael would have applauded. She was beneath the porch. She scampered on hands and knees along the side of the house and turned the corner. She went twenty more feet, then stopped and huddled, the mailbox almost directly over her.

"Jesus," she thought. "How long has he been here?" It was a truly awesome image: Mr. Davis standing in the rain hour after hour, waiting for her to show. She forced herself to take slow, deep breaths as she held her body still. There was a scrape along her shin and she was wet clear to the bone. Now Mr. Davis was clomping around on the porch. "Who are you?" he called into the night. "I just wanted to talk. Please come back."

Three feet below him, Megan lay slowly down on the muddy

ground and stuck out her tongue. "Got you," she mouthed, grinning widely. "Got you!"

Friday's history class began with Mr. Davis launching into an account of the McKinley and Roosevelt presidencies. Megan listened for a while but couldn't pull the meaning from his words. It hardly seemed to matter. He specialized in knowledge of the past, while she could tell his future. She would tell him in a letter.

"Dear Mr. Davis," it began, "You broke the rules and I am quite angry with you. You will have to do penance before you can be in my good graces and my mouth. Please perform the following actions precisely as described. . . ."

She realized he was staring at her. She tried to replay his last few words, but they were gone.

"I'm sorry, sir," she said. "I seem to be having trouble concentrating today."

The final ten minutes of class crawled by as she struggled to look attentive. Kirsten caught up with her in the hall.

"What happened to that famous bulletproof brain? I've never seen you space like that."

"I didn't get much sleep last night."

Kirsten raised one eyebrow, showing off another physical skill that Megan lacked. "Care to talk about it?"

"Not right now. I'll explain everything later. In the meantime, I need to borrow some equipment from you. Actually, from your dad, but he can't know about it."

"Fabulous. And let me guess. You'll explain that later too."

"You read my thoughts like they were written on a blackboard."

"Yeah, yeah. You're going to owe me big, best friend o' mine."

It was Sunday afternoon. Megan pressed Play for the fourth time and the clearing in the woods appeared once more. A minute passed while nothing happened. Then Mr. Davis, punctual as always, entered stage left. But it was a different Mr. Davis, hesitant and uneasy. He stopped, then turned slowly, hoping to catch a glimpse of his unknown audience. "Give it up!" Megan called to her TV. "I'm not a moron." For a moment, Mr. Davis stared straight at her. Then his gaze moved on. He was looking for a woman, not a camcorder wedged in a tree.

Megan fast-forwarded, scanning for her absolutely favorite part. There! Mr. Davis, her teacher, had followed instructions perfectly. He stood in the middle of the clearing, half-facing the camera, his pants bunched at his knees. He was jerking off. Back and forth his hand moved, gliding slowly, almost absentmindedly. Megan stared, feeling the hypnotic pull. "Bet you wish that was my mouth," she thought, and just like that she was ready again.

She put the remote down and leaned back in her beanbag chair, squirming to get her bottom comfortable on the vinyl. She licked her fingers. Soon she was matching the urgency of his hand with that of her own. She managed her excitement expertly, balancing on the edge of orgasm. Mr. Davis crouched forward a little. His thing, his cock, stuck straight out in the spring air. Megan knew he was getting close, knew exactly how close. She refocused on his face, slightly fuzzy yet still intensely human, serious and sad and pained and a little lost, and there were his eyes, the lids shut tight, and there, Megan was just about convinced as they came together, were his tears.

That night, Megan lay in bed. She felt completely wired. Video frames flickered endlessly through her head, like a catchy chorus she was sick of but couldn't stop humming. It was nine hours at Disney World all over again.

What is enough?

She got up and walked to the bathroom. Sexual tension lingered in her body like a low-grade fever, but she was too tired and too tender to do anything about it. She soaked a face cloth in cold water and draped it across her neck. That was better.

What is enough?

She padded back to her room and sat at her desk. This is enough, she thought. This is enough of Mr. Davis. She clicked the switch and was suddenly silhouetted in the glow of the computer screen.

"Dear Mr. Thorndike," Megan typed, "I would like to suck your dick."

ERIC ALBERT

on "The Letters," first published in *Best American Erotica* in 1996

"The Letters" is the first story I ever wrote. I was thirty-seven, I'd signed up for an erotic writing workshop; I needed something to show.

Had I known the piece would eventually be published, anthologized, audiotaped, and, and reanthologized . . . I would have done things just the same, but with less anxiety.

I say this, because it was at that time that I inaugurated my tradition of painful, slow production, and insanely perfectionistic revision that my editors find so, uh, endearing.

Reading "The Letters" now, I'm pleased to find that many phrases, even whole sentences, still resonate. I'm not sure I could jerk off to it (my main criterion for erotica), but others have. Megan feels real. There's humor and heat; it's got a plot: I'm satisfied.

THE DESIRES OF HOUSES

Haddayr Copley-Woods

The woman's step on the stair is labored, and the cord hanging at the bottom trembles with excitement.

Her hands are busy carrying laundry. She will have to turn on the light with her mouth.

In the dark, to find the cord correctly, she must caress it with the tip of her pink tongue briefly, and the wicked, wicked pleasure of it more than makes up for the bite and the sharp jerk that turns on the bulb.

The cord over the washing machine, the braided one, is waiting joyously for the teeth.

The floor is sulking. She almost always wears shoes in the basement, and the cement lies all day in agony listening to the first floor's boards sighing loudly in ecstasy at the touch of her bare heels.

All it can hope for in its slow, cold way is that the woman will scoop the cat boxes, squatting on her heels, after she starts a load of laundry. Today, oh joy oh joy, she does. The floor is practically writhing at the smell of her (she always showers after the scooping, so her scent is thick)—the tangy rich odor. The cement feels (or maybe it's just wishful thinking) just a bit of her damp warmth.

But then she is sweeping the floor, oblivious as always to the swooning house around her, ruining the floor's pleasure with the horrible scented litter she sweeps up and tosses back in the box.

She yanks open the dryer, who feels violated and then guilty for enjoying it, dumps the hot, panting shirts and shorts into a basket, and heads back upstairs, carefully turning off the lights to avoid the lecture about electricity the man will give her later if she doesn't. Even minutes later, the cords are still shaking in the darkness.

She folds the clothes neatly and quickly, then smooths each piece with her hand. It's hard to say who enjoys this the most—the shirts or the table she presses them upon—and then the man is knocking on the kitchen door.

She opens it for him, and he growls at her to stop locking him out when he is gardening; he leaves it unlocked for a reason.

The woman is getting tired of this particular topic and instead of apologizing snaps crisply that she has no memory of locking it, and indeed she hasn't. The house just wanted a few more precious moments alone with her.

He stomps back outside, and she carefully checks that it is unlocked, even while muttering against the man under her breath.

The door handle is sure it isn't his imagination that her hand lingers on the brass.

The man has tracked mud on the kitchen floor, who nearly faints with joy when she notices. She looks closer at the cracked and peeling linoleum and forgoes the mop for a rag and brush. She mutters about how disgusting the floor is—how utterly, utterly filthy, as her nail digs at an especially difficult spot. Yes yes yes, squeaks the floor—who, like the braided cord over the washer, likes it rough.

Afterward, she heads up the stairs (which groan loudly at the feel of her toes) to take her shower.

Despite its lascivious reputation, the shower couldn't care less about the woman, even as he rains fat droplets down her breasts. The bathtub, the sole dissenter in the house, yearns for the muscular fleshy rump of the man. He hasn't felt it in ages, as it is summer and not time for long, hot baths.

The man, cursing, fumbles with the kitchen door and has to find his key with dirt-encrusted fingers deep in his pockets. He steps inside, notices the floor has been washed, and carefully removes his shoes, muttering that she'll probably want to be thanked now that she's done her annual unprompted housecleaning chore—then peers suspiciously down the stairs to be sure she hasn't left a light on in the basement again.

The midsummer sky is growing dim as he showers, unwittingly spurning the tub so far below, while the woman brushes her teeth.

The orgiastic moaning of the toothbrush annoys the towel incredibly, because after all who is it that gets to cradle her every last curve rubbing rubbing rubbing and then contentedly wrap herself around the woman's breast and hips for a little postpleasure snuggling?

It is too hot for even a tank top, and the woman lies flat on the sheet, staring up into the dark, and wonders how long it has been like this. Just today? All year? She hasn't felt so awkward, angry, unlovable, and unloving since junior high. She feels flabby, flatchested, gray, and wrinkled besides.

The man, annoyed as he is with the woman, sees the curve of her thigh in the light from the window and slides in next to her, giving it a tentative caress.

He spent all morning with his eyes on the game, grunting once noncommittally when she asked if it was her turn to do the laundry, and after lunch he had flat-out refused to dance with her when a slow waltz came on the radio. He didn't feel like it, he said.

She swats him away as she would a fly.

The ceiling fan stares down in utter loathing at the man who sighs and rolls away from the woman. If she was mine, thinks the fan, oh how I would waltz with her. Around and around and around.

HADDAYR COPLEY-WOODS
on "The Desires of Houses"

I believe short stories should take months, if not years, to write.

This one? I was pissed off at my husband for taking me for granted, and for nagging me—even as I realized I was taking him for granted, too. As I began to do the laundry, the story wrote itself in my head, a narration of my actions.

At the time, our sons were down for a nap, and I wanted to nap, too. But after I did the laundry, scooped the cat box, scrubbed the floor, and took a shower, I sat down and wrote this story instead of sleeping, because I knew I'd forget it upon waking.

It took me three hours total to write, type, edit, and submit the story to its first publisher.

And it's the story everybody loves.

HORNY

Greg Boyd

I wake up horny. God's punishing me again, testing my endurance, so I fall to my knees and pray for strength. But evil thoughts course through my mind like a polluted stream. I try my best to purify them. I am chlorine, lava soap. I bubble and foam, but in the end it happens again anyway. It's always the same. My soul screams at the exact moment of my body's release. It's a righteous voice that wells up inside me, a deep and hoary voice that comes out of the wilderness and is filled with the indignation of the ages. It inspires in me a kind of holy terror, and afterward I shake for a good five minutes.

Though I won't eat today, I allow myself one cup of instant coffee. Then I go into the garage and give myself fifty lashes on my bare back with a leather strap. Afterward I climb up on a stepladder and take down the cross I keep suspended from the rafters. I built it myself from heavy lumber, wood screws, and angle braces I bought at the hardware store. I had to carry the beams six miles home with me in two separate trips because they wouldn't fit in or on my car. That was months ago, back when I still had a car. It was midsummer then, and under the sun's whip the sweat dripped from my vile body as I walked and melted my impure thoughts about beach girls in their bikinis. I was already learning how to suffer.

There are leather straps on the cross for me to hold on to so that I can keep it balanced as I walk. The first few times I used it I kept dropping it on the sidewalk, and by the end of the day my hands were full of splinters from trying to catch ahold of it when it started to slip from off my shoulder. Like I said, it's a very heavy cross, and long enough so that if it were put into the ground, and raised up on end with me nailed to it like it's supposed to be, it would still be plenty high to keep me way above everyone so they could see just how much I'm suffering up there. The splinters were actually never a problem, as they only added to my suffering and my contemplation thereof as I pulled them out with tweezers at home later, and it's nice for the cross to hit the sidewalk once in a while, where it makes a huge noise, though better, I think, for me to fall with it, to one knee or even right onto my face, which happens more often now that I'm actually strapped to it, but once a woman with a baby carriage was walking past me and I kind of leaned over a bit to look at her and just as I was getting a good peek the cross started to slip and only the grace of God spared her child, though the carriage was damaged beyond repair. Praise be to God.

Since then the police have kept close tabs on me. It was even their idea to use the leather hand straps. They've given me a few simple guidelines to follow as well. It's a free country, they tell me, but I'm not to bother people. And they've asked me to stay out of the mall, which is where I had a little trouble another time on account of the overzealous security officers there who accused me of disturbing with my wild stares and weird cross the young girl shoppers that mill around eating salted pretzels and sucking orange drinks through straws. The security guards wanted to grab my arms and guide me forcibly to the exit, and when I refused to let them abuse my rights to freedom of religion and expression, they ended up calling the police to have me arrested for disorderly conduct and disrupting the peace. Except for those two times the police have been nice enough whenever they stop their cars to check in with me along the sidewalk downtown, and there's even a young lady officer who wears her tight blue uniform shirt with the badge pinned right over her swelling chest, though none of them can keep themselves from winking at each other or chuckling. They know I'm not a criminal, but, even so, they still like to imagine I'm some kind of kook. But that laugh-about-it-all attitude is understandable, given all the wickedness and depravity they witness on a daily basis.

I strip down completely and wrap the loincloth I made from an old white sheet between my legs and then twice around my waist. It's modest but authentic. I fasten it tightly at both the waist and legs with safety pins to keep the cloth from falling down and my private parts from spilling out as I grapple with the cross. I won't stand for people having any lewd thoughts or fantasies about an act that's meant to purify. And I certainly don't want to be humiliated in public. Outside I hear the wind blowing rain against the garage door as I get ready. No doubt about it, today I'm going to suffer.

On the street I see one of my neighbors, dressed in a yellow plastic raincoat, stooping to pick up her newspaper. She waves to me briefly before she scurries back inside her house, even though she knows I can't wave back because my hands are holding on to the wet straps of the cross. She's an attractive young woman who works in an office. Sometimes I see her getting out of her car in the evening, her tight skirt riding up her thighs, her high heels gleaming in the late-afternoon light. Only recently married, she and her husband have lived on my street just a few months. For a second I catch a glimpse of her legs as she stoops, and I wonder what, if anything, she's wearing under the raincoat. Even at this distance I can tell that her breasts are full and round. Her big red nipples puff out and stand erect beneath the cold plastic, begging for my tongue's devotion. Her hot host is already moist with the anticipation of everlasting joy, of paradise on Earth, of things to come.

But God loves me. My thoughts are interrupted by a car at the corner that splashes the cold and holy water of repentance upon me as it passes through a puddle in the road, drenching my budding lust in its wake. My hair clings limply to my head, and rainwater runs down my face as I struggle against the weight of the cross, the cold, the wind that sends chilling spikes of pain up and down my legs. Sharp pebbles press into my bare feet. I pass through residential neighborhoods, and as I do, I know that temptation lurks behind every door, every window. I avert my eyes, cast them downward. Along the sidewalk I see drowned earthworms that have been flushed like so many unclean corpses out from their soaked graves. Bent beneath my burden, I contemplate my life and its eventual end. As the sky weeps, so do I, for my sins are great and many.

Downtown I walk past rows of storefronts, windows full of worldly goods. I don't let myself look inside or think about the shopgirls standing in their short skirts—how they pull their panty hose up over their long legs in the morning, how they push their firm breasts into the cups of their lacy bras, how they splash perfume behind their ears and knees in anticipation. Finally I take my position at the center of town, stand silently in the rain at the intersection of Broadway and Main. People drive past in their warm, dry cars, listening to pop songs about love, or more often about lovemaking—the words barely clothed in a fine, see-through mesh of metaphor that leaves little to the imagination. Some of them honk their horns at me. Perhaps they know me. In better weather they might speak to me, offer me their blessing or ask for mine. More likely they recognize what I represent, why I am here. They understand that safe inside their cars they are swimming in filthy thoughts, vile debauchery.

A man and a woman in a blue Mercedes drive past slowly, staring at me *with unbelieving eyes*. The man wears an expensive suit, the woman a silk blouse under a tweed blazer. No doubt they've just come from a motel, where they've been engaging in every illicit sex act conceivable. No doubt his penis now hangs between his legs swollen red, bruised and sore from pounding inside her tight and hungry hole. No doubt her vagina likewise feels ragged and sore from their debauch, its soft walls stretched and battered from the satanic thrashing action of the devil's massive, oversize piston. It takes a long time for the car to turn the corner, an eternity. All the while the woman looks into my eyes, first through the hysterical waving arms of the windshield wipers, then, head turned sharply to the side, through the passenger window, a harlot, a fellow sinner in need of spiritual guidance, pleading for help, for compassion. I am here for her, a beacon set firmly in place in the midst of a storm. I loosen my hand from its tether to signal and the cross slips, pulling me with it to the wet concrete. When I touch my face, my hand comes away bloody. She is gone.

I could have saved her. I could have taught her how to love. I could have taken her by the hand. I could have undressed her with my teeth. I could have . . .

By the time I get home it's nearly dark. I'm soaked to the bone, skin blue and shriveled, feet numb and bloody, chilled, shivering, feverish. I wrap one towel around my head, another around my shoulders, a third over my legs and sit in front of the television for hours drinking hot tea and watching cable network evangelism. The first hour features a fiery preacher who explains the sufferings of Jesus for Mankind while threatening me with eternal damnation and a gospel rock singer with lips made for fellatio. Later, before my very eyes a blind woman has her vision restored by the love of Christ and a cripple walks when he accepts the Lord as his personal savior. As the camera pans the audience to show the radiant faces of the true believers I see a pretty woman in the third row that I want to fuck. I am exalted, mesmerized, shivering uncontrollably.

At eleven o'clock I switch off the television and pray on stiff knees in total darkness for an hour and a half. I go to bed exhausted and hopelessly horny.

GREG BOYD

on "Horny," first published in *Best American Erotica* in 1993

When I wrote "Horny," I was living in a wind-blown town on the central coast of California best known for broccoli, beets, and strawberries. There was a real-life character who used to hang out on the sidewalk downtown at the main intersection with a big, crudely constructed wooden cross strapped to his back.

In such a bland place, I suppose he was something of a local celebrity, or at least that's how I viewed him. No doubt I could've simply asked him why he insisted on parading around with the cross. Surely he would have been happy to warn me away from sin and lead me toward repentence and life everlasting. But I suspected I'd get only half the story that way.

What interested me then, and continues to interest me now, are the deeper, unacknowledged motivations that occur when religion and human sexuality intersect. Since religion and sex were originally so closely linked as to be inseparable, it's little surprise that sacredness, ecstacy, submissiveness and domination, denial, worship, and love are all the shared vocabularies of both. Whether we're talking about an ancient fertility cult or the modern Christianity, sex underlies our basic psychology, whether we acknowledge it or not.

Rereading the story now, I marvel that being devout can be so sexual, and that being horny can be so indeniably holy as well.

PINKIE

Jennifer D. Munro

He strolled through the bar as if the fire hydrant anchoring his cul-de-sac might throw his hip sockets out of whack, an orthopedic nightmare. He thrust his pelvis toward me as he neared. He tipped his shoulders back, lest he topple forward from the staggering weight of that anvil crammed in his crotch.

I was a drifting dock in want of a well-cast hawser, and he hooked his heel on my barstool.

He offered me a longneck and a grin, and I needed no further convincing to agree to a change of venue. I was more than ready to unleash the mastiff barking behind his fly.

Back at his tidy condo, in due course, he undressed without shame. And so did I.

His cock rose up like a tender shoot in springtime. Not that I ever thought he had a zucchini down his jeans, but I was expecting more than an asparagus tip.

I should have suspected foul play when he introduced himself as "Pinkie."

The rest of him wasn't bad. His abs rippled, his biceps bulged, and his face radiated sincerity. Nice.

He reminded me of one of those Roman statues.

I was aware of my inexcusable chauvinism. I was no better

than a zit-faced teen sniggering at small tits. I was worse than Joe Mechanic slobbering over his MUFF-ler wall calendar. I was measuring Pinkie by external standards. But *still*. When a girl's starved, she wants a sausage-with-the-works, not a baby dill.

"Don't worry," he said, noting my concern. "It's the motion of the ocean, not the size of the boat."

He rummaged in his dresser drawer, for a condom, I assumed.

Do they make them that small?

He got into bed beside me.

Pinkie was a nice kisser, with a shaved face and brushed teeth. I could tell by his moans that he was turned on. But nothing else gave me a clue.

"Is it in?" I asked. I wasn't usually this oblivious, but his stumplet stumped me.

"Um, I haven't started." He tucked my hair behind my ear. "Don't you like foreplay?"

He cuddled closer. "For the Greeks, the ideal penis was the small penis. Check their urns. Hercules had a teeny weeny."

The Greeks also killed Socrates, but you had to admire a guy who calls it a "weeny" with a straight face.

"They thought it meant better fertility," Pinkie continued. "Like, today, guys with low counts have to wear boxers—"

"So togas saved democracy?"

Pinkie's right eyebrow shot up, "Oh, Giselle!"

He remembered my name. I had wanted to get in his pants so fast, the introductions had been rather hasty. But. He. Had. Paid. Attention.

"I'm sorry, Pinkie. I mean, this is nice and you're sweet, but I didn't go pub crawling for sensitive husband material. If you know what I mean."

"Tell me what you want, Giselle. Whatever it is—"

As if his mini-wand could conjure magic to order.

He pulled out the dresser drawer he'd been fishing in and dumped its contents on the bed.

He had quite the arsenal. He displayed Santa's Little Helpers one by one. "You prefer matte or glossy? Neon or *naturale*? Animal-shaped or lifelike? Motorized or manual?"

Pinkie did the impossible: he rendered me speechless. "You pick," I managed.

He held up a psychedelic bunny whose nose twitched at the touch of a button. He twitched his own. I laughed.

He held up a flesh-colored, veined penis, so realistic it could have been lopped off a buckskin horse. It seemed lost without a body, reaching for contact like a blind man's hand.

"I guess we'll have to try them all," I said sadly.

Next he offered a variety of harnesses—thigh, pelvic—and some unflattering briefs with strategic holes. "Some girls tell me their boyfriends feel threatened by—"

"But you don't mind?"

"I'm sleeping with their hard-up girlfriends, aren't I? What's to mind?"

I touched his wrist. "I don't know how to ask this without hurting your feelings."

"You hardly mince words, Giselle, and I like that. Go for it."

"How do you manage such a positive attitude about, you know? Other guys with, you know, might grow up to hate women. Or at least be embarrassed."

"That's the thing. Women never made fun of me. They felt sorry for me, which was worse. So I set out to prove them wrong. That I didn't need their pity. That *they* needed *me*. I did my homework. Mama taught me you could learn anything from a book, and she was right."

"A librarian's wet dream." Pinkie's voice filled me up the way his spaghettini might not.

"I studied fashion magazines. I learned stuff like trimmed toenails matter to girls."

"They should teach boys that in sex ed."

"It was the guys who laughed at me. In the locker room. So I lifted weights. Then I beat the crap out of the bastards if they gave me a hard time." He laughed. He held up a Hello Kitty vibrator and winked. "Time to tame the wildcat."

"Mmrrooww."

Having the genuine article inside me after the parade of stimulating impostors ended up being plenty fulfilling. It wasn't exactly the motion of the ocean that mattered, but the depth and rhythm and warmth of Pinkie's heart.

Reader, I married him. His penny whistle played my tune just fine.

JENNIFER D. MUNRO
on "Pinkie"

I got stuck at dinner a few years ago with a friend's pal whom I didn't know. Our mutual friend never showed up. The conversation turned to erotica.

Folks are fascinated with the fact that I write erotic stories. I live in a suburb, work in a cubicle, and keep my butt crack covered, so apparently I don't fit their Anaïs Nin image.

At dinner, I mentioned to my new acquaintance that I'm not interested in writing about perfect bodies and gymnastic sex, since that's not my reality. Most days I'm happy if I can still unzip my pants and squeeze in a quickie.

She seemed surprised—she was currently having marathon sex in every possible position with a beautiful, well-endowed man. I believe she was telling the truth.

(Shortly after our dinner, she was checked into a psychiatric clinic. Don't ask me what the moral is there.)

At dinner that night we met she shrugged, yawned, and said, "Well, why don't you write a story about a man with a really small dick?"

So I did. To me, the idea was far more intriguing than to write about the amazing fornication that she was describing.

"Pinkie" is definitely fiction, but the character is confirmation that any writer in a relationship needs her partner to be understanding, to have a sense of humor, and to have a strong sense of self.

My husband's a good sport about the heat he takes over this story and others that I've published. Neighbors ask him at barbecues about his pubic hair and penis size. Everyone assumes that we're screwing all the time, but usually I'm telling him to be quiet so I can write.

I'm as fond of "Pinkie" as the day he introduced himself to me. Once he plunked his glorious derriere down at my desk and started to talk, I became fascinated with the problem of a woman's prejudices against him. I've written a lot about female bodies that don't cooperate, but I hadn't yet written about a man's biological challenges. I enjoyed turning the tables.

FLESHLIGHT

Joe Maynard

I'm not sure whether or not it's a dubious honor that Ms. Porn Magazine Editor asked me to test-drive a tasty little item called the Fleshlight, but what hooked me was her telling me that the inventor spent two million dollars developing the thing. It's amazing that a budget normally reserved for the space program or the Pentagon was funneled into a sex toy, but whatever. Capitalism minus the cold war, I guess. Figuring that guys like tools, the inventor designed the stealth exterior to look like a flashlight. But inside, Ms. Editor tells me, the tactile matter is damn near identical to the texture of actual labia and vulva flesh: the mother-goddess of ersatz pussies.

I rush to my girlfriend's house and proudly exhibit Fleshlight on her kitchen table. "Yup," she agrees. "Looks like a flashlight." But when I unscrew the top, there's this bubble-gum-pink, puffy sphere with what appears to be a coin slot. We poke at it with our fingers: Hmm. Feels wet, but doesn't really make your finger wet—like that "goo" stuff for kids that comes in a little plastic trash can, only substantially more "adult."

"What's that smell?" Girlfriend sniffs inquiringly through her mid-January Kleenex-buffed nose.

I breathe in deeply myself. "Vanilla?"

"Christ on a crutch!" she squeals. "You're not gonna put your dick in that thing?"

"Why not? You wanna watch?"

"Yuck. Do it at your house."

"I can't do it at my house. You're supposed to warm it up in the sink by pouring hot water over it. My roommates will find out."

"Why don't you warm it up with a glass of wine, then?" she snipes.

Poor girl. She used to go out with a travel writer who sent her postcards from exotic places like China, Morocco, and Brazil. Now she's dating a pervert who only goes places he can get to on his Huffy. I open the bottom of the Fleshlight to discover a hard plastic tube that runs down the center. I pull on it and it sort of sticks to the pink, sticky "flesh."

"What is that?" she mutters. "Vulva-on-a-stick?"

I look at the brochure. "The stick maintains the 'vulva's' shape."

She runs her fingers through her hair and squints at the ceiling. "How symbolic." The brochure also warns not to share one's Fleshlight with anyone. No problem. I'm not even sure I want to share it with myself.

Girlfriend leaves the kitchen and climbs into her loft bed. Her cute little ass cupped inside a pair of velour bikini panties causes my all-natural-flesh battery to erect an electric arc of love. Then I look at Fleshlight cupped in my hands. One look at its vanilla, gooey-pink, coin-slot eye and I'm soft again. I crawl into girlfriend's loft bed and spoon around her warm, velour hips that house her real pussy. She clenches my hands between her breasts. Ah. Better.

"What about your date?" she asks.

"I left her with the toaster."

Next morning, while Girlfriend's in the shower, I'm nursing a coffee at the kitchen table. The sun's first rays cast a pleasing light across most of the room, and Fleshlight, which stands tall and majestic on the table, casts a shadow like a sundial. Maybe I will do it tonight.

After work I feel indecisive. Instead of racing home to fuck the gooey-pink eye, I find myself at one of those bars with a million different beers. It's midway between my house and Girlfriend's. Three connoisseurs to my left are talking fruity bouquets. I flirt with the idea of admitting defeat. Somehow my groin is not amused by Fleshlight. Could be the vanilla, could be the slime, could be the coin-slot eye.

I order a Boddingtons and watch Bartender Girl build it the way you build a Guinness. The head rises to the top of the glass, then shrinks as the golden liquid emerges underneath in beer's more drinkable transparent form. I mean, it's not like I'm afraid of Fleshlight, is it? When the head settles, she pours another shot from the tap, slices off my foamy head with a butter knife, and slides the beer in front of me. Looking down into the head of my beer, I see a coin-slot eye. I raise the glass to my lips and it smells somewhat vanilla, and when I set it down, I'm acutely aware that a thin slime remains on my upper lip. I admit: I'm afraid. And once I realize I'm afraid, over the next couple of days, Fleshlight looms larger than life. It's my mother's disapproval, my third-grade teacher's declaration that I'll never amount to anything, my ex's aunt from Borough Park asking me why I'm not Jewish. It even argues politics and tells me to fine-tune my career in a more adult manner.

It's not like I'd go out and buy *Juggs* magazine, but they published one of my stories, and my contributor's copy came in the mail. As you may have guessed, they're into gooey, big breasts. In fact, they're into lactating mothers. Like a good egomaniac, I'm checking for typos over my morning coffee. Girlfriend's in the shower and I'm sitting at the table with Fleshlight. Today is my day off—my so-called writing day. It dawns on me that today is . . . *the* day. I pack my notebook, *Juggs,* and Fleshlight lovingly in my backpack and crack the bathroom door to kiss Girlfriend good-bye.

"You think you could put the toilet seat back down every once in a while?" she complains.

"Women," I mutter as I struggle with my bike down the steps of her building, hoping it doesn't snow before I get to my place.

At my desk I try polishing up a story from years ago, and I rummage through my mail, working up to the task at hand. After my last piece of mail, I realize the time is now. I peruse my copy of *Juggs*. Hmm. That "virgin" chick on page nine is kind of cute. My, what a pretty pussy. Hmm. I'm horny. I quote my yoga teacher: "Be aware of your pud throbbing in its methodical yearning way." I turn the page. Hmm. The lactating mother. Haven't considered it, and I won't begin now. My God, the boobs on that black lady with the carnival mask are bigger than my beer gut. I need a little more porn star, a little less freak show. Ah, now there's a wholesome lass washing her pickup truck in someplace like Montana. She's wet and soapy and smiling this huge shit-eating grin in every shot, rubbing her boobs against the windshield of the truck so the photographer can get a shot from inside the cab. Yoga breath turns into panting.

I reach into my backpack for Fleshlight and hastily unscrew the top. Christ. Why vanilla? I realize it would be better to run it under hot water, but the roommates are all sitting around out there. I flip back to the "virgin's" lovely hymen-clad flower. She's smiling this smile that says, "Hi, perv!" while holding her eighteen-year-old hooters out to the camera. "Getting a hard-on?" She giggles. "Go on, take it out. Whack off for me, baby." She's also muttering, "Pathetic creep," under her breath, but I concentrate on her saying, "Go a step further, Joey. Undo your belt, sweetie. Your jeans, sugar lump. Your briefs, thumper."

"Okay," I answer.

"That's better," she coos as I scoot my pants down below my knees. "Now get your toy and lube up. . . ."

It's not easy. I remove the bottom lid as well as the top in order to remove the hard plastic tube from inside the soft, saccharine "vulva." I'm afraid of ripping it—as if it were a hymen or something—but eventually I wrestle it free. I put Fleshlight on the desk with its unfortunate pink coin-slot eye staring at the ceiling, like a bored patient at an ophthalmologist's office, and snap the lid open on the lubricant. I aim into the coin-slot eye and get most of it in, but when I lift Fleshlight off the desk, the lubricant empties out the back end. It startles me, and the thing falls from my hand, bouncing off the edge of my desk, off my thigh, and rolls onto the floor about six inches past arm's reach. I rock my chair sideways. Damn. I stretch, stretch more . . .

Knock. Knock. Knock.

"Uh, yes?"

"Can I come in?" my roommate Stephanie asks.

"No!"

"Then can I borrow some milk?"

"Borrow whatever the fuck you want!"

"Well, thank fuckin' you!" She yells, safely stomping away.

Ice-cold fake pussy juice is dripping from the puddle on my desk onto my lap. My pecker, soft as a jellyfish at this point, is burrowing backward into my flesh as my teeth start to chatter. Gee. If Mom could see me now, wouldn't she be proud?

I'm in serious need of a game plan. I rock my chair back and forth until I'm close enough to reach Fleshlight. Both of my hands are slick with lube but I manage to pull it onto my lap, where I squeegee some lubricant from the puddle between my legs back into the coin-slot eye. I wipe my left hand on my shirt and put the bottom back on before too much more can drip out.

I breathe deeply in that calming yoga way and casually flip through the pages of *Juggs,* trying to pretend that it's a warm, sunny Saturday and not forty degrees in my room. Now concentrate on the girl washing her truck in Montana. Nice. Cute butt—*and* butthole, I see. A very nice pink eye. Mmm, boobs. My trusty lust is taking over. I pick up *the thing.* I tip it over my dick. I slide it over the head. It's tacky. Kinda like a chick who isn't quite wet. My dick kind of bends cuz I'm only like 80 percent hard. To remedy the situation, I let go a warm string of steamy saliva onto my shaft. Shoulda done that instead of leaking that freezing lubricant all over the place. I turn back to the virgin cutie on page nine. There's a red line on her shoulder that her bra strap has left. "Babe," I tell her, "you're cute!" A couple of insurance pumps with my trusty right hand and, yes! Solid as a friggin' rock!

I reenter like a bat into hell. There's a sensation down there of making it through the Sacred Gates of Labia. There's a Brazilian chick on page sixty-four with a deep, golden tan. She's so plump. So nice and plump. Like rotisserie chicken. She looks like what the Fleshlight feels like. Oh, yeah: Looks like what the Fleshlight feels like. She's squeezing her nipples in her fingers. The heels of her palms are plunging into her tit flesh. Wow! I'm getting it. It's gliding smoothly over my shaft while the Brazilian is graciously opening her pussy with her fastidiously manicured fingers in the next frame down. I plunge the thing over my dick to the hilt. Oh, yeah! Let the games begin! *Pfft. Pfft. Pfft.* Hey, it . . . the thing is hissing. I loosen the rear cap and plunge again. *PFFT! PFFT! PFFT!* It's hissing even louder. I take off the end completely, whether or not the fake pussy juice drips on my pants that are now bunched around the heels of my boots. The rotisserie Brazilian is so soft and plump, it's gonna be an easy ride home from here. I'm admiring her lovely full lips when it occurs to me that this thing feels like getting a blow job—only no teeth.

But sexy as the Brazilian is, I need Virgin Cutie from page nine to finish. I'm flipping back to her spread, pumping like a deranged plumber. There she is: holding her breasts up to her mouth, licking her nubile nipple. I'm pounding the squish out of the thing till it's bouncing off my nuts. Virgin Cutie is smiling, showing off the underside of her tongue while she licks her upper lip, showing off her labia, sphincter, and juggs. I get it! Finally, after years of writing this stuff, I get the whole pornography thing. See, anyone can do this. You don't gotta be a stud, you don't gotta be rich. You can be any fuckup in the goddamn universe, alone in your room and horny, pounding the bejeezus away at something that won't scold you for leaving the toilet seat up. For just a moment, I'm lost in a sensation of bouncy, wet, somewhat virgin flesh, and boom! As Woody Allen would say, there's no such thing as the wrong kind of orgasm. Even the worst ones are right on the money.

Then it's over. I'm cold. The thing is dripping everywhere . . . and I have the urge to cuddle. The thing is quite unappealing right about now. I think about my sweetheart with her mid-January nasal drip, blowing her nose, but warm and huggable under a half dozen duvets. Virgin Cutie is still smiling the exact same smile from her frozen home on page nine.

"Hey, Joe!" Stephanie yells from outside my door. "Want anything from the fucking store?"

"Nah," I wheeze absentmindedly. "Just a hot shower."

JOE MAYNARD

on "Fleshlight," originally published in *Best American Erotica* in 2001:

Funny you should ask about the circumstances in which "Fleshlight" was written.

It begins simply, as these things often do. A Bostonian woman who'd previously published my work moved to New York and was working for an erotica magazine.

We'd gone out to a movie together, and had a couple of those aesthetic discussions over cappuccino that you have with other aesthetes in your field. I was happy this new artistic ally had moved to the city.

One day she called me to say she had a product, the Fleshlight, and she asked me to write a product review. At this point in our relationship, the editrix and I were friends. Sure, she'd published a couple of my stories in Boston. But that was Boston. This New York assignment was closer to home: the assignment that would turn our relationship professional.

The story I wrote was pretty much exactly what happened while testing this product. As you said to me, "You don't hear a lot about men doing this!" and that jibes with the fact that it wasn't something I would normally do. I was happy with my girlfriend, "her cute little ass cupped inside a pair of velour bikini panties," as the story goes.

It's simple to find sex, but finding someone you love—that's magic. The point of sex is ecstasy. Being in love is the drug; sex is the needle. So I found the whole situation of fucking a cold piece of plastic absurd—even if it was "space-age" plastic.

My editrix wanted only two paragraphs, but being the conscientious artiste that I was, I wanted them to be the best paragraphs ever written. I was taking a writing class at the time, and James Salter had given us a talk on the idea of getting a notion of some sort, and stringing beads onto that notion—using the notion as a string that holds a pearl necklace together—never articulating everything inside each pearl, yet "being the string," and penetrating, then absorbing, whatever the interior of each bead had to offer.

You know, suck the pearl dry and move on.

So, geeklike, I struggled with my squeamishness regarding inter-elemental sex, my fears that I'd write a piece of boring crap, and I meditated on the wise words from the great author, stringing my friggin' beads.

One day it just all came out. Probably not exactly what Mr. Salter had in mind, but potent, pearl-sucking pages.

I faxed it in, and the next day, I called the editrix for her editorial imput. I thought she'd tell me she laughed her ass off, that the joke was a home run, that my intricate subtleties articulated a flavor never before tasted. It would be as sure as a baby pearl sings its beauty song to the mother clam, and the fruits of our first "professional" encounter would produce the first-ever two-paragraph sex product review to win a Pulitzer Prize.

Perhaps it was too close to deadline time. Maybe it was because I didn't simply say how great this fine product was: "You'll never enjoy fucking a plastic sponge as much as you will the Fleshlight."

But instead I was honest. I let people know what it really felt like. Her response, lackluster, was something like, "What's this? I just wanted a couple paragraphs."

"Fine," I said. "This is just the way I work. It's my process."

Silence.

I suggested I could change it for her, and then later rework it for *Juggs*, or *Nerve*.

"What?" she shouted. "You're giving it to someone else? This was an experience I gave you! Our experience! Not *Nerve*'s!" She said I was ungrateful and totally unprofessional even to consider publishing it anywhere else.

She hung up. Bitch! I put the phone down and looked around as four coworkers stared back at me.

"What the fuck was that?" my boss asked.

"I think she dumped me."

"Who, your girlfriend?"

"No, my editor."

Later, I sent her the requisite two 'graphs, but I'm not certain she ever used them. It was overshadowed by our breakup.

I tried to remember the good times. Her initial call—"I think I have something for you to test-drive." Her "Did the Fleshlight arrive yet?" the day it came. Her "How was it?" the morning after I fucked the sponge.

I roamed the streets despondent. Every porno shop seemed to be "our" porno shop. Every blow-up doll was our relationship: a lot of hot air that in one prickly moment explodes in your face!

[ARE WE HAVING SEX NOW OR WHAT?]

Greta Christina

When I first started having sex with other people, I used to like to count them. I wanted to keep track of how many there had been. It was a source of some kind of pride, or identity anyway, to know how many people I'd had sex with in my lifetime. So, in my mind, Len was number one, Chris was number two, that slimy awful little heavy-metal barbiturate addict whose name I can't remember was number three, Alan was number four, and so on. It got to the point where, when I'd start having sex with a new person for the first time, when his cock first entered my cunt (I was having sex only with men at the time), what would flash through my head wouldn't be: "Oh baby, baby, your cock feels so good inside me" or "What the hell am I doing with this creep" or "This is boring. I wonder what's on TV." What flashed through my head was: "Seven!"

Doing this had some interesting results. I'd look for patterns in the numbers. I had a theory for a while that every fourth lover turned out to be really great in bed, and would ponder what the cosmic significance of this phenomenon might be. And sometimes I'd try to determine what kind of person I was by how many people

I'd had sex with. At eighteen, I'd had sex with ten different people: Did that make me normal, repressed, a total slut, a free-spirited bohemian, or what? Not that I compared my numbers with anyone else's. I didn't. It was my own exclusive structure, a game I played in the privacy of my own head.

Then the numbers started getting a little larger, as numbers tend to do, and keeping track became more difficult. I'd remember that the last one was seventeen and so this one must be eighteen, but then I'd start having doubts about whether I'd been keeping score accurately or not. I'd lie awake at night thinking to myself, Well, there was Brad, and there was that guy on my birthday, and there was David, and . . . no, wait, I forgot that guy I got drunk with at the social my first week at college . . . so that's seven, eight, nine . . . and by two in the morning I'd finally have it figured out. But there was always a nagging suspicion that maybe I'd missed someone, some dreadful tacky little scumball whom I was trying to forget about having invited inside my body. And as much as I maybe wanted to forget about the sleazy little scumball, I wanted more to get that number right.

It kept getting harder, though. And I began to question what counted as sex and what didn't. There was that time with Gene, for instance. I was pissed off at my boyfriend David for cheating on me; it was a major crisis, and Gene and I were friends, and he'd been trying to get at me for weeks and I hadn't exactly been discouraging him. I went to see him that night to gripe about David; he was very sympathetic, of course, and he gave me a backrub, and we talked and touched and confided and hugged . . . and then we started kissing . . . and then we snuggled up a little closer . . . and then we started fondling each other, you know . . . and then all heck broke loose, and we rolled around on the bed groping and rubbing and grabbing and smooching and pushing and pressing and squeezing. He never did actually get it in. He wanted to, and I wanted to too, but I had this thing about being faithful to my boyfriend, so I kept saying, "No you can't do that," "Yes that feels so good," "No wait that's too much," "Yes yes don't stop," "No, stop, that's enough." We never even got our clothes off. Jesus Christ, though, it was some night. One of the best, really. But for a long time I didn't count it as one of the times I'd had sex. He never got inside, so it didn't count.

Later, months and years later, when I lay awake at night putting my list together, I'd start to wonder: Why doesn't Gene count? Does he not count because he never got inside? Or does he not count because I had to preserve my moral edge over David, my status as the patient, ever-faithful, cheated-on, martyred girlfriend, and if what I did with Gene counts, then I don't get to feel wounded and superior?

Years later, I did end up fucking Gene—and I felt a profound relief. At last he definitely had a number, and I knew for sure that he did, in fact, count.

But then I started having sex with women, and boy howdy, did *that* ever shoot holes in the system. I'd always made my list of sex partners by defining sex as penile-vaginal intercourse. You know, fucking. It's a pretty simple distinction, a straightforward binary system. Did it go in or didn't it? Yes or no? One or zero? On or off? Granted, it's a pretty arbitrary definition; but it's the customary one, with an ancient and respected tradition behind it. And when I was just screwing men, there was no really compelling reason to question it.

But with women . . . well, first of all there's no penis, so right from the start the tracking system is defective. And then, there are so many ways women can have sex with each other, touching and licking and grinding and fingering and fisting—with dildoes or vibrators or vegetables or whatever happens to be lying around the house, or with nothing at all except human bodies. Of course, that's true with sex between women and men as well. But between women, no one method has a centuries-old tradition of being the one that counts. Even when we do fuck each other, there's no dick, so you don't get that feeling of This Is What's Important We Are Now Having Sex, objectively speaking, and all that other stuff is just foreplay or afterplay. So when I started having sex with women, the binary system had to go, in favor of a more inclusive definition.

Which meant, of course, that my list of how many people I'd had sex with was completely trashed. In order to maintain it, I'd have had to go back and reconstruct the whole thing and include all those people I'd necked with and gone down on and dry-humped and played touchy-feely games with. Even the question of who filled the all-important number-one slot, something I'd never had any doubts about before, would have to be reevaluated. By this time I'd kind of lost interest in the list anyway. Reconstructing it would be more trouble than it was worth. But the crucial question remained: What counts as having sex with someone?

It was important for me to know. For one thing, you have to know what qualifies as sex because when you have sex with someone your relationship changes. Right? *Right?* It's not that sex itself has to change things all that much. But knowing you've had sex, being conscious of a sexual connection, standing around making polite conversation with someone thinking to yourself, I've had sex with this person . . . that's what always changes things. Or so I believed. And if having sex with a friend can confuse or change the friendship, think of how bizarre things can get when you're not sure whether you've had sex with them or not.

The problem was, as I kept doing more different kinds of sexual things, the line between Sex and Not-Sex kept getting more hazy and indistinct. As I brought more into my sexual experience, things were showing up on the dividing line demanding my attention. It wasn't just that the territory I labeled "sex" was expanding. The line itself had swollen, dilated, been transformed into a vast gray region. It had become less like a border and more like a demilitarized zone.

Which is a strange place to live. Not a bad place, you understand, just strange. It feels like juggling, or watchmaking, or playing
the piano—anything that demands complete concentrated awareness and attention. It feels like cognitive dissonance, only pleasant.
It feels like waking up from a very compelling and realistic bad
dream. It feels the way you feel when you realize that everything
you know is wrong, and a bloody good thing too, cuz it was painful
and stupid and really fucked you up.

But for me, living in a question naturally leads to searching
for an answer. I can't simply shrug, throw up my hands, and say,
"Damned if I know." I have to explore the unknown frontiers, even
if I don't bring back any secret treasure. So even if it's incomplete
or provisional, I do want to find some sort of definition of what is
and isn't sex.

I know when I'm *feeling* sexual. I'm feeling sexual if my pussy's
wet, my nipples are hard, my palms are clammy, my brain is fogged,
my skin is tingly and supersensitive, my butt muscles clench, my
heartbeat speeds up, I have an orgasm (that's the real giveaway), and
so on. But feeling sexual with someone isn't the same as having sex
with them. Good Lord, if I called it sex every time I was attracted to
someone who returned the favor, I'd be even more bewildered than
I am now. Even *being* sexual with someone isn't the same as *having* sex with them. I've danced and flirted with too many people,
given and received too many sexy would-be-seductive backrubs, to
believe otherwise.

I have friends who say if you thought of it as sex when you were
doing it, then it was. That's an interesting idea. It's certainly helped
me construct a coherent sexual history without being a revisionist
swine and redefining my past according to current definitions. But
it really just begs the question. It's fine to say that sex is whatever
I think it is—but then what do I think it is? What if, at the time I
was doing it, I was wondering whether it counted?

Perhaps having sex with someone is the conscious, consenting, mutually acknowledged pursuit of shared sexual pleasure. Not a bad definition. If you are turning each other on, and you say so, and you keep doing it, then it's sex. It's broad enough to encompass a lot of sexual behavior beyond genital contact/orgasm; it's distinct enough to *not* include every instance of sexual awareness or arousal; and it contains the elements I feel are vital—acknowledgment, consent, reciprocity, and the pursuit of pleasure. But what about the situation where one person consents to sex without really enjoying it? Lots of people (myself included) have had sexual interactions that we didn't find satisfying or didn't really want. And unless they were actually forced on us against our will, I think most of us would still classify them as sex.

Maybe if both of you (or all of you) think of it as sex, then it's sex whether you're having fun or not. That clears up the problem of sex that's consented to but not wished for or enjoyed. Unfortunately, it begs the question again, only worse: now you have to mesh different people's vague and inarticulate notions of what is and isn't sex and find the place where they overlap. Too messy.

How about sex as the conscious, consenting, mutually acknowledged pursuit of sexual pleasure of at least one of the people involved. That's better. It has all the key components, and it includes the situation where one of the people involved is doing it for a reason other than sexual pleasure—status, reassurance, money, the satisfaction and pleasure of someone they love, etc. But what if neither of you is enjoying it, if you're both doing it because you think the other one wants to? Ugh.

I'm having a bit of trouble here. Even the conventional standby—sex equals intercourse—has a serious flaw: it includes rape, which is something I emphatically refuse to accept. As far as I'm concerned, if there's no consent, it ain't sex. But I feel that's about the only place in this whole quagmire where I have a grip. The longer I think about the subject, the more questions I come up with. At what point in an encounter does it become sexual? If an interaction that begins nonsexually turns into sex, was it sex all along? What about sex with someone who's asleep? Can you have a situation where one person is having sex and the other isn't? It seems that no matter what definition I come up with, I can think of some real-life experience that calls it into question.

For instance: A couple of years ago, I attended (well, hosted) an all-girl sex party. Out of the twelve other women there, there were only a few with whom I got seriously physically nasty. The rest I kissed or hugged or talked dirty with, or just smiled at, or watched while they did seriously physically nasty things with each other. If we'd been alone, I'd probably say that what I'd done with most of the women there didn't count as having sex. But the experience, which was hot and sweet and silly and very very special, had been created by all of us; and although I really got down with only a few, I felt that I'd been sexual with all of the women there. Now, whenever I meet one of the women from that party, I always ask myself: Have we had sex?

For instance: When I was first experimenting with sadomasochism, I got together with a really hot woman. We were negotiating about what we were going to do, what would and wouldn't be okay, and she said she wasn't sure she wanted to have sex. Now we'd been explicitly planning all kinds of fun and games—spanking, whipping, bondage—which I strongly identified as sexual activity. In her mind, though, "sex" meant direct genital contact, and she didn't necessarily want to do that with me. Playing with her turned out to be a tremendously erotic experience, arousing and stimulating and almost unbearably satisfying. But we spent the whole night without even touching each other's genitals. And the fact that our definitions were so different made me wonder: Was it sex?

For instance: I worked for a few months as a nude dancer at a peep show. In case you've never been to a peep show, it works like this: customers go into this tiny dingy black box, kind of like a phone booth, and they put in quarters, and a metal plate goes up, and they look through a window at a little room/stage where naked women are dancing. One time, a guy came into one of the booths and started watching me and masturbating. I came over and squatted in front of him and started masturbating as well, and we grinned at each other and watched each other and masturbated, and we both had a fabulous time. (I couldn't believe I was being paid to masturbate—tough job, but somebody has to do it. . . .) After he left, I thought to myself: Did we just have sex?

I mean, if it had been someone I knew, and if there had been no glass and no quarters, there'd be no question in my mind. Sitting two feet apart from someone, watching each other masturbate? Yup, I'd call that sex, all right. But this was different, because it was a stranger, and because of the glass, and the quarters. Was it sex?

I still don't have an answer.

GRETA CHRISTINA
on "Are We Having Sex Now or What?" first published in 1992

My aunt is a philosophy professor, retired now. One semester she asked her students to bring in examples of philosophical writing related to everyday life, from non-philosophy-book sources . . . and one of her students brought in "Are We Having Sex . . . ?" from *Ms.* magazine, not knowing that I was her niece.

She was tickled pink that one of her students had been struck by the piece and had shown it to her without knowing about our relationship. If she was freaked out, she didn't say anything.

But the funny thing was: the copy of the piece that she got was the *Ms.* magazine version—where *Ms.*'s editors had edited out all the sex I wrote they didn't approve of, without my permission or knowledge.

I was furious about their rewrite, of course—but I have to admit, I was relieved that my aunt got the bowdlerized version, without the references to SM and stripping.

I'm glad to publish this here in its original version. It was "edited" in its first anthology version, too. One example is the place where I write: "Penile-vaginal intercourse. You know, screwing."

That was originally: "You know, fucking." But my book editor said he wanted the book to be accessible and mainstream-ish—and thus wanted to tone down the more extreme language. In some cases I don't object to word changes—but that one I wish I'd fought for.

Similarly, in the kinky scene that I described at the end of my story as one of my "I still don't have an answer" examples, the anthology editor got me to "tone down" just how kinky the scene was. Since I now have the opportunity, I'd like to tone it back up again!

I was such a baby when I wrote "AWHSNW," and I've changed in so many ways, both as a writer and as a sexual person.

I've learned which fights with editors are worth having, and which ones aren't. Sort of like the serenity prayer—having the serenity to accept what I can't change (e.g., serial commas)—the strength to change what I can (actual meanings of what I'm saying), and the wisdom to know the difference.

Writing "AWHSNW" clarified the way I think about sex, and thus how I act about it. I'm less anxious than when I was younger about "does this count as sex, what we're doing right now?"

I'm more concerned about whether we're having a good time doing whatever it is we're doing. And, of course, the "what counts?" question has made nonmonogamy negotiations a whole different ball game—in my opinion, a much better one.

THREE OBSCENE TELEPHONE CALLS

Marian Phillips

The phone rang the other day. I picked it up and said "Hello" in my cool, distant, telephone voice.

"Hello," said a sultry female voice in my ear. "What are you wearing?"

"I am wearing," I said, "a purple and green polka-dotted clown suit, with a big yellow ruff collar and huge white pompom buttons down the front."

"Oh, that's so sexy," my caller whispered.

"—And also," I continued, "black men's socks with black knee-garters to hold them up. On my feet I am wearing huge rubber flip-flops. The socks," I added, by way of explanation, "have been slit so that the thong of the flip-flops will fit between my big toe and my second toe." There was a low moan as I paused for effect.

"Do you know what I'm wearing on my head?" I asked.

"A rainbow-colored wig?" said the husky, familiar voice.

"No." I could hear her breathing, as I paused again to let the anticipation build.

"An arrow through the head," I said.

"Oh, Jesus, I'm so turned on," my caller gasped hoarsely.

"What are you wearing?" I asked.

"Nothing but a cock ring," she purred.

"And is it the cock ring that inflates into a seahorse inner tube, or is it the one that has coat hangers projecting out from it like the spokes of a wheel, that you can attach spare change and dollar bills onto?" I said relentlessly.

"The one with the coat hangers."

"All right," I continued evenly. "Here's my fantasy:

"You're standing on a street corner aggressively panhandling the passersby. As you follow someone down the street, screaming obscenities, I run out from an alley and knock you down, leaving you to flail helplessly in the gutter, while I steal all the spare change and dollar bills from your cock ring, and run away laughing."

"Of *course* you're laughing, for God's sake," she snapped, "you're a *clown*. Clowns *always* laugh."

Click.

I had started out the evening alphabetizing my fiction, but had gotten sidetracked into rereading the good parts of *Pride and Prejudice* instead, when the phone rang.

"Hello?"

A pleasant, unfamiliar male voice said, "Hello, who's this?"

"I," I said, "am the King of the Cats. Who are you?"

"Uh, my name's Bob," he said, sounding a little nonplussed. Picking up confidence from my silence, however, he continued: "and I just wanted to tell you that I have a huge, nine-inch-long cock that I'd like to—"

"Don't you want to know what I'm wearing?" I said in an offended tone.

"Uh . . . what are you wearing?"

"I am wearing a suit made entirely out of aluminum foil that covers me from head to foot, leaving only eye holes and a mouth hole. I wear this suit to deflect radio transmissions from the National

Security Agency, which is beaming commands to me through the steel plate in my head. In addition, I have roped my cat to my head, with its feet tied together so that it forms a turban and can't scratch; its intermittent yowling also helps block the transmissions.

"I have a friend here," I continued: "Would you like to know what she's wearing?"

"Um, well, I—"

"My friend," I plowed on, "is dressed up like a martini. She is wearing close-fitting white clothes, and around her neck is a clear plastic cone shaped like the bowl of a martini glass. Her head is bald—she shaves it—and she has painted it up like an olive, green with a red spot on the top. Instead of that arrow-through-the-head prop, she has a sword through the head."

There was a distraught silence at the other end of the line.

"Now here's my fantasy," I said. "I—"

Click.

The telephone rang.

The last time anyone at the telephone company asked me, I told them to change my listing from S. Wright to Susan Wright. Previous to this change, I had gotten about one wrong number a week. After the change, the wrong numbers mostly went away and were replaced by obscene callers who addressed me familiarly by my first name, and heavy breathers.

The telephone rang again and I picked it up.

"Hello?"

"Well, Susan, you cunt, so you're at home for a change."

An obscene caller with a wrong number—truly the best of both worlds. Also, obviously, a man with a grievance. Although I'd never heard the voice before in my life, for a fleeting moment I considered apologizing anyway. Fortunately, he wasn't expecting a reply, and he pressed on:

"You fucking whore, why aren't you out sniffing the streets for men to fuck, getting down on your knees to suck their cocks, isn't that what you like, you bitch? You couldn't be bothered to fuck me when we were together. I don't know why I call you a whore, I've met plenty of whores who are better than you."

I was getting so caught up in this random call that I almost asked indignantly where he'd been meeting all these whores, but he raced on.

"Well, you'd better watch out, because some night you're going to be crawling around offering your twat to be fucked and I'm going to come up behind you in a dark alley and rape you with the barrel of my gun. What do you think of that, scumbag?"

"I think it sounds hot," I said. "However, I should warn you that I carry a gun in the left inside pocket of my leather jacket, so you'll want to make sure to pinion my hands and disarm me first. I suggest some kind of restraining device."

There was a long silence.

"What kind of gun?"

"A Ruger compact semiautomatic seven-shot .45 with a three-and-three-quarter-inch barrel," I replied.

There was another long silence.

"You're not going to get much range with a gun like that," he said finally.

"How much range do I need? If you're close enough to grab me, I'll be close enough to hit you. Anyway, what do you care? You're going to pin me and take it away before I get a chance to shoot, aren't you?"

Silence again.

He started to laugh.

Click.

MARIAN PHILLIPS

on "Three Obscene Telephone Calls," first published in *Best American Erotica* in 1999

My sister Meg was the original inspiration for "Three Obscene Telephone Calls." I was visiting her in Florida—had just flown across the country and was fighting jet lag, trying to sleep on one side of her queen-size bed (she didn't have a spare bed).

Meanwhile, Meg, who worked graveyard shift as a nurse, was smoking, drinking, and reading on the other side of the mattress. The phone rang; Meg picked it up and proceeded to have a low-voiced conversation until suddenly she laughed, said, "Good luck, buddy," and hung up.

"Who was that?" I said.

"Well, I thought it was my boyfriend," Meg said with a chuckle. "It turned out to be an obscene phone caller."

"What did he do when you played along?"

"Oh, he was kind of sheepish," Meg said. "I think he didn't quite know how to handle it."

Some time later, in San Francisco, my friend Megan Costello called me up and without preamble cooed, "Hi, what are you wearing?"

The first part of "Three Obscene Telephone Calls" is pretty much a verbatim report of our conversation.

It wasn't until a couple of years after it was published that I realized that the story was my reaction to Saki's "The Open Window." I had adored Saki's short stories when I was younger, in part because he wrote a number of stories about self-possessed female storytellers. It isn't a common portrayal, and it definitely doesn't fit in with the way women are "supposed" to react to obscene phone calls; we're supposed to be angry or scared. And yet, there was my sister, acting like someone out of a Saki story, chuckling along and probably—knowing Meg—outdoing anything her hapless caller came up with.

[TENNESSEE]

Patrice Suncircle

I loved Rohn because she was neither a woman nor a man.

She wasn't black, but she wasn't white either. She wasn't crazy, and she was not sane. She was pretty and she liked to fuck. I was fifteen and that was ideal.

I first met Rohn in the summer down south. The weather was hot, and the air was close and heavy with dry grass and small dead rotting animals. Snakes slid out of their skins.

Before I met her I had seen her up at Bell Eagle Esso, the little grocery and filling station that our landlord owned. Sometimes she was with her mother, a thin, pale woman who wore big hats to keep the sun off her face, and who, whenever she spoke, mumbled. I did hear her speak once, and she sounded funny. My grandfather said that she was a foreigner. She usually had Rohn by the arm. Or Rohn was with her older brother, the one most like the mother. People always looked at them funny.

The day I met her, she was astride a big roan mare.

She had a black cowboy hat on, pulled low so that it shadowed her eyes. Her thick red hair fell down onto her shoulders.

We were in the middle of a pasture. Over by a pond some cows stood still as if they'd been painted there. I was walking home from a neighbor's house, where I'd gone after school.

I kind of stepped backward because the horse was so big.

She grinned, flashing her dark face under the hat's shadow.

"How you t'day?" Her drawl was soft and gentle. It wasn't high-pitched and evil like a peckerwood's, so it didn't scare me.

I said, "I'm all right."

She pushed her hat back and I saw that her eyes were green in gray. Her brows arched with the grace of a bow. I think my heart did something.

"You wanna ride home?" She told me later I had a kind of half smile on my lips to make her wonder.

I climbed up and she pulled me the rest of the way onto the horse. From up there I could see the tin roof of my folks' house. Smoke was coming from the chimney, going straight up. Grandma was starting supper.

I wedged into the saddle between her thighs. Her arms encircled me, and she rested her hand holding the bridle on the horn between my legs. Her breasts were small and firm and pressed against my back. I was too shy to move.

She asked me what grade I was in, and did I like going to school in town, and she bet I didn't like arithmetic. I thought, at the time, that she was a senior in high school or maybe already in college. We rocked in time to the horse's movements. I felt her arms tightening about me and the horse walking slower.

"You got a boyfriend?" she asked me, and I said no.

"You want to go for a ride?" she asked, and I said yes.

I knew I would get scolded, but I could no more have refused than turn down strawberries and ice cream. We turned away from the sight of my house. The cows came back into view. A big orange and black butterfly hung in the air. The sky was clear.

"Hold on," she said. When the horse sailed over the fence, I thought my heart would shoot out of my mouth. My terror evaporated in her laughter, and then her low chuckle brought another feeling altogether. She was holding me so tight still.

Rohn loosened the rein some more. She put her face down next to my cheek. I heard her breathing and felt her long fingers moving on my body, as if they were gently searching for something just under my clothes. I stopped breathing for a minute. She smelled of Ivory soap and the heat of the day. Once, her hat brim brushed my face; it felt soft as cotton.

"Can I touch your breast?" she whispered.

I managed to say yes.

With just two fingers and a thumb she rubbed softly in circles. Around and around through my blouse, from the fullness of my breast to its tip. She did it softly, and once she squeezed the nipple a little. Her hand held the reins on my bare thigh where my skirt had come up.

She put her whole hand over my breast and kneaded it. I noticed the wetness between my legs. I tried to open them wider, and they pressed against her. She kissed my cheek. The dampness her lips left there cooled in the air.

She kept squeezing and playing with my tit, and I think I moaned or gasped or something because she kissed me again. I turned my face toward her. She took off her hat and gave it to me to hold.

She unbuttoned one button of my blouse and slipped her hand inside. It was warm, dry, and smooth. Her hair fell against my face, and it felt like the silk scarf my aunt had sent my grandma from New York.

She held my tit hard and then she pinched the nipple a little. The small pain heated my whole front. Her mouth was on mine, and I thought I would die. It was warm and wet and I thought I would starve before I moved away. I opened my mouth and she pushed her tongue in. She licked the inside of my mouth, inside my jaws, the roof of my mouth. I took her tongue and sucked it.

Her hand, pressing my breast, pinched the nipple more, and

each burst of pain filled me enough to almost lift me. And she was kissing me harder and spit was all down on my chin.

She pulled away suddenly, breathing hard, and I came awake. Her gray-green eyes were soft and heavy, but they started to clear until they had the depth and transparency of a cat's eyes. I tried to smile, but she had looked away. One of the cows lowed, a long, deep chest sound. I heard birds that had been there all along. She took her hat and put it back on, pushed up this time.

"I'ma take you home. All right?"

I didn't say anything. It was hot. My blouse was damp from sweat, and there was moisture on the back of my hands. If I tasted them, they would be salty. Rohn read my mind, the first of many times. "It's all right," she said, "you didn't do anything wrong." She kind of smiled as if there were something on her mind. I smiled back.

Southern nights are full of stars and crickets and mosquitos.

The stars hang down beside your head. The crickets are inside head. The mosquitos bite. They are there for the purpose of reality, I imagine. If they don't often find their way into romantic stories, it is not their fault.

I used to sit out in the front in my rocking chair after watching *Amos and Andy* or *Ozzie and Harriet,* until it was well after dark. I used to look up at the stars and try to fathom how far away they were. It was hard to comprehend that the light I was seeing from a certain star had started from there eight years ago. I thought of furnaces bigger than the Earth. I thought of people who'd been alive eight years ago and weren't anymore. I heard somebody quietly call my name, or thought I did.

I listened and I heard it again. "Pa-tri-ciaaa." I walked around to the side of the house.

She was standing not more than six feet away, as quiet as a haunt. I grinned in the dark, and I think she smiled. She didn't have her hat on, and her hair was all tousled. She had on jeans and a man's big plaid shirt.

I stood close to her, and we whispered, because the house was right there.

"Can you go for a ride? In my car? It's right down the road."

"Naw, I don't think so."

"How about a walk?"

I shrugged. "It's late. Grandma won't let me."

"Just inside the pasture. Over that fence. Just over there."

I waited a minute. I wanted to so badly.

"Okay," I whispered.

Then she was touching me, lightly, her arm around my shoulder. We were about the same height because I was tall for my age. She smelled of some odd perfume; I learned that it was her mother's.

We walked through the garden, stepping across the rows of turnip greens and the tomato vines. It was a new moon, and everything was dark blue. She held the barbed wire apart while I climbed through, and I did the same for her. She slipped through without touching it anywhere, like she'd done it a lot.

We sat on the ground, close enough to feel the warmth of each other. I pulled out blades of grass and waited. There was nothing to hear but the crickets. She lay back, her hands folded behind her head.

"I bet I know what you were doing. Looking at the stars, huh?"

I nodded. I felt her smile.

"Bet you were sitting out there, trying to think how they could be so far away?"

I giggled.

She reached down and gently tugged me down beside her. She could read my mind. It felt good, like somebody else in there with me. I have never waited for anything as hard as I waited for that first kiss.

She pulled me onto her so that my breasts touched hers for the first time. Then she pulled my chin down with two fingers and gave me a lingering taste-kiss right on the lips. It was better than the kisses two days before on the horse, and I might not have had one like it since.

She ran her tongue across my lips. I opened my mouth and she started kissing me harder. Soon it was like the other day with her tongue halfway down my throat. We rolled over slowly until she was above me. She was on me with her legs straddled, when I felt something I shouldn't have. It woke me.

"Rohn . . . ?"

She laughed low and deep in her chest. "I told you I wasn't like other women. Didn't I tell you that?"

But she was soft. And her voice was a woman's. And her breath was a woman's. And her breasts. She kept kissing me and pushing down on my body and grinding her hips into me until I responded.

I had on jeans that night. My blouse was already open and now she started to undo my pants. I helped her and we got them off.

Then she was up on her knees, still straddling me and doing something with the zipper on her pants. She took her penis out. It was warm and hard and at first she rubbed it back and forth against my clitoris. It made me lose my breath. I pulled her toward me and she told me to open my legs wider and I did.

At this time I was still a virgin. She was big for me and it hurt going in. I squirmed and she covered my mouth with her own.

It hurt but I kept pushing up to her and trying to open my legs wider. So we lay there, twisting and rutting on the ground. I came. I'd never come before with something inside me. And my bud between my legs filled up until I felt ready to burst. I was panting, and she seemed to suck the air right from the center of my body. Taking my breath.

I came again and then she did. We were wet and sticky and a mess. My grandmother could call any time. Rohn held me.

I wanted to ask her, "How can you be?"

I could not comprehend.

Later that night in bed, I kept waking just at the edge of sleep, warmed by the soreness between my legs.

Carson McCullers wrote about "freaks" and "misfits." Faulkner wrote about freakish habits, and then there was Huck and Jim. There is a strange kind of tolerance down south when it comes to personal habits. Just don't involve politics. Just keep it behind closed doors so that it can be gossiped about. Fantasized about. Keep it under cover of night so that tales can grow.

I was your basic black adolescent tomboy with pigtails everywhere and a pointed chin. I looked from beneath long-lashed eyes without raising my head and gave tight-lipped secret smiles and rakish grins. I shrugged off the impossible.

What was nasty was funny to me, and I smelled of sweat and my jeans had grass stains. I masturbated to movie magazines and let boys feel me up because it felt good. My experiences had, in some twisted way, prepared me for Rohn.

I was told that I would burn in Hell if I did practically anything. I was inevitably going to Hell, but I was too terrified of that fact to give it much thought. So I ran wild like the heathen I was, amid flowers with odors sweet and heavy enough to drug you; ran with dogs and other beasts that copulated when the spirit struck through the tall grass on hot summer nights. This was as real to me as Bible verses. So Rohn was real to me.

Rohn was the bill for some long-ago charge that her mother— or her ancestors—had run up. Her mother accepted her as such.

She had not been made to go to school. Legally they got her declared an idiot or something. She was taught at home, better than the schools around here could teach her, most likely, because her mother was educated.

Her mother and her elder brother were the only ones who had

anything to do with her. The others despised her. She told me that her younger sister had twice tried to kill her with rat poison. Her father beat her whenever he came home and found her there without the mother or the brother.

She told me later, after I was allowed to go riding in her car, that she was always afraid somebody would tell my grandparents some wild tale about her.

But she also told me that when she was in her teens, her mother took a turn to her. The same bed that she had nursed her in. Her mother, convinced that Rohn would never find a lover, took her in. This time, instead of opening her blouse to nurse Rohn, she opened her legs to her. Anytime she wanted it, she said.

I was in love with Rohn by then. I figured that she had to like me more than most, else she would never have told me those things. On the other hand, they could all have been lies.

One Sunday she came by in her '56 Chevy; it was green and white and shiny.

I ran out to the car and leaned on the window. "Hi."

She smiled. "I just came by to tell you how pretty you are." Which she knew would make me grin.

"Can you go for a ride?" she asked.

I shook my head. "I don't think so."

"Ask."

So I ran back in and asked, and was told no, I couldn't go for a ride in anybody's car, and what was I wanting to go for a ride with Miss Rohn for anyhow?

I ran back out and told her. Her smile changed to somewhere between sad and disgusted, and she nodded. "Oh, well." Then she looked at me and winked. "Maybe some other time, okay?"

"Yeah maybe."

"You take care, y'hear?"

"All right."

Never occurred to me to say ma'am to her, ever.

. . .

I was up at the store to get some things for Grandma. It was getting near to evening. Rohn's car was there.

I'd never felt this way about a real person before. I felt about her like I only felt about fantasy movie stars.

She watched me approach the car. She was sitting with her back to the door, one leg up and her arm stretched across the back of the seat. She half smiled.

"Hi."

"Hi."

I explained about my errand; I'm not sure what there was to explain. She looked at me quietly. I think that she knew what she was doing. Driving me insane. So I took my leave and went inside.

When I came out, she offered me a ride home. Her eyes darted toward the store and then she opened the car door. She set my groceries in the back.

We pulled out of the station. Dark was falling and the bright Esso sign came on. We sped past my turn-off road. I sighed in relief.

She cut the radio to the black station from Memphis, WDIA. It had already been set on the signal dial. At home I could listen to WDIA only three times a day, when the gospel programs came on. Now some sister was singing about not having enough meat in her kitchen.

We drove across the railroad tracks and pulled off a dirt road near a stand of trees. We didn't have much time. Already I was wet.

We walked into the woods, and she pulled me to her and kissed me. We kissed a long time. I began moving a little bit, and I felt her growing big. I wanted her inside me and I kissed her harder.

But she had other plans.

She undid her zipper and told me to get on my knees. Halfway down I realized what she wanted.

I'd never done it before, I'd never even read about it, but it seemed a natural thing to do.

She took my face between her hands; her hands were smooth and they felt hot. The sky was still light though the wood was dark. One dead tree without any leaves stood in front of the others. There was an old sack or something caught in its high branches. "Don't use your teeth none, hear?"

I opened my mouth. It was like a fat sausage, tasteless except for a little salt. I slid my mouth over it, like she told me, against the plump vein underneath. And I let her shove it against the back of my mouth. I squeezed her hips firm in my hands, and she massaged my cheeks and my throat with her thumbs, and ran her fingers all in my hair and on the back of my neck. She rotated her hips slowly. And then faster and harder I sucked until my tongue felt like lead, but it had begun to taste so good. She twisted real slow, and I grabbed and sucked. Time was passing. Grandma was waiting. Time was, I think, standing still. For us. A sheriff on a horse with a posse could have come out of the trees and we wouldn't have known. Or two boys could have been watching us.

She came. I jerked my mouth away and spat, but some of it got on my shirt. Rather, my grandfather's shirt.

I was hot, too, and between my legs was very sticky, so we lay on the ground and dry fucked with our pants up until I came. She was hard again, I think. But she said that she would go home to her mother.

We sped away in the car. The wind felt good. The slide guitar from the radio drowned out the crickets.

I had a playroom. It was just a curtained-off place between the kitchen stove and the wall where I kept all of my magazines, and where I went to read them and to fantasize.

One day I was sitting in there when I heard Rohn's voice. My grandfather said something back to her and then called my name.

I went to the door. She was wearing a white shirt and old jeans and loafers. Rohn didn't look like a boy and she didn't look like a girl. I was afraid that my grandparents would see what I saw. If they did, they'd take it away from me. But Grandma kept on working in the tomatoes and Grandpa went back to help her. Only the dog followed Rohn over, sniffing her.

"Hi."

I asked her into my playhouse. The curtains could be pinned closed, and I could hear footsteps on the wooden steps if need be.

Her shirt smelled of starch; it was a white so new and clean that it had a bluish tinge. I kissed it. I kissed her. Her teeth touched my tongue. She sucked it. She had such a fine mouth. We hardly ever talked. I knew what she wanted from me, and she could have all she wanted. That particular day she was going to take much more than I'd ever imagined she could.

We pressed against each other, all our clothes on, and I felt her soft breasts pressing mine. I breathed in, and pressed against them more. It's the feeling I still like best when I'm with a woman. Those round soft tits pushing.

We lay on the floor tight and moving just a little. She kissed, with her lips parted slightly and soft and moist, first my mouth, then my cheeks and my nose and my throat.

I started to pull down my shorts. She grinned; sometimes she just did that, out of the blue, like a Cheshire cat. I wonder what went on in her mind.

I kneeled in front of her, and she cupped my buttocks in her hands and squeezed them. She put her mouth on my shoulder, right at the stem of my neck and sucked a bit until I had more of a welt than a hickey. She bit me, and I drew in the pain like a scorching breath.

I had my hands all in her hair. In the silk and the curls. I loved that hair. I felt it on my hands when I awoke in the night. Outside the kitchen door I heard the dog give a loud yawn, and then, I think, he turned around and lay down.

We kissed. She worked her hand around in front and slid it right between my vulva lips. She wriggled her finger a little, and I groaned and squeezed her to me. Her other hand was still squeezing and rubbing my behind. She kissed my neck, rubbed her mouth up to my ear, and stuck her tongue in. I laughed and pulled my head away.

Then she moved her finger from around the front and stuck it up my asshole. It was hard and sticky, and I jumped. She pushed it and it hurt just a little, so I sucked my breath in. I'd never tell her to stop when she was hurting me because I liked the deep kisses that she gave me when she did. She always kissed me like that when she was hurting me somewhere.

We kissed deep and slow, and she kept working her finger deeper up my asshole. Every once in a while I would whimper. We stopped kissing and she buried her face in my neck and pressed me to her, moving herself into my pussy and rotating her hips. I creamed. She was hard. We twisted and rubbed; I got the lips of my cunt over her dick and stroked up and down, and rubbed up and down, streaming across my bud and covering her joint with cream. Her finger was still there, I don't know how far in it was. She groaned.

She eased her finger out and chuckled; I felt the laugh in her throat. "Do you have any Vas'line?" she asked.

We had just a little, so I brought back the jar of bacon grease that was sitting on the stove to go with it.

She eased me around so that my back was to her. I felt her lips and tongue on the back of my neck. For a moment her hands cupped my breasts.

She told me to bend over and spread my legs as far apart as I could. I said she couldn't, that it was too small. She said we'd manage. She wiped the grease on me.

So I did what I was told, and I told her to be careful. She dipped her finger a few times in my cunt and I shuddered.

I was spread so wide I could already feel the pain. I held my breath. She told me to relax.

I did, except for biting my lip when I felt the tip of her joint probing around where it shouldn't. I told her again to be careful. I was scared, but the fear was part of what was making me sweat and tremble. She pushed and immediately I felt the impossibility of the whole thing. But it didn't change anything.

She rubbed my clitoris again with her finger, just barely skimming it. I was already on the brink of coming. I opened wider and she pressed in more. It hurt.

A fraction of an inch by a fraction of an inch. She pushed and I gasped. "Relax. Relax, baby." I felt her voice.

"Come on," she whispered right in my ear, her voice more like wind or dry leaves.

"I love you. I love you. I love you." I said it every time I gasped.

She gathered me in her arms, crisscrossed like a straitjacket, and buried her face in my hair. I could hear her carefully placed breaths, like somebody measuring something just so. My ass began to burn.

She pushed, she held me so tight I could hardly breathe. Something started to fill up my ass; it felt good, and at the same time I felt I was going to rip. My clit was swollen; my clit wanted to swell up big and long as my tongue. She started a regular pump now, and I think I whined. The burning was a red-hot rod sliding into moist pink flesh. Mixed in with her gasps loud in my ear were groans as if she were in a little bit of agony. She touched my clit and I jumped. She pushed a finger up my vagina. Two fingers. I covered her hand with mine to make her take it out, but she didn't. My hand lay on hers, softly, as if it were helpless.

The pain was so intense I was almost dizzy; I moaned a little, like I was getting the shit fucked out of me. I'm sure that the dog, psychic as he was, raised his head. With one finger she stroked my bud and the pleasure made me call her name.

I started to squirm, we moved like wrestlers; she was inside me and all over me. I loved it and I couldn't bear it. She might have had it all the way inside my body. We wrestled and knocked over a stack of movie magazines. We tore and twisted their pages, and they carpeted the hard linoleum beneath us.

I felt saliva covering all of my chin and strings of it wet my nose when I lowered my head. There was something wet and warm moving on the back of my neck. She came.

I felt as if I was going to explode, as if steam was building up in my bowels. She held me tight, still and silent for a minute as we both trembled. We relaxed and she pulled it out through my raw flesh. Right after, a brownish egg-white liquid streamed out of my asshole like the runs, and covered the movie stars' eyes and mouths. I expected it to smell but it didn't.

Her face was covered with sweat and around her temple a few curls lay flat and darkened with moisture. My shirt, which I'd left on and open, was wet and my breasts glistened. The playhouse seemed close, steamed. Then sounds came back. A truck passing on the road; from far away, my grandfather's voice. That was all.

She took me in her arms and kissed me gently on the mouth and face. There was blood on my bottom lip; she licked some off. I held her weakly. I kissed her back softly. We kissed for a long, long while.

We laughed a little and I noticed something warm still running down my neck and I patted it with my fingers. It was blood. I twisted around and it was all over the collar of my shirt. Then I realized that my breasts hurt; I touched them and they were tender and bruised. I felt like I had been in an accident. I felt like . . .

"I love you," she said.

She knew just what to say after putting me through a meat grinder. I was so thankful.

The next night at church was the Lord's Supper.

It was a night full of stars that I didn't want to leave to go inside. But I filed back into the building with the other girls. A sweetish yellow light filled the church.

The preacher got up and, in a conversational tone as if he were down among us, said what he always did about eating the flesh of the Lord with sins on our conscience. We would burn in hell if we did. I broke out in a sweat. If I had died since the last Lord's Supper, I knew that I would be in hell.

But then something happened worse than hell. Rohn left me. She was just gone.

I didn't see her at all the week following the Lord's Supper. I thought that maybe she had gone somewhere with her mother. But she didn't come back the next week either.

The Saturday night following the second week I knew that something was wrong. I cried a whole night so silently that my grandmother, sleeping in the same bed, didn't hear me.

I learned, mostly by listening, that she had indeed disappeared. Rohn had disappeared and so had Fauna Dipman.

Fauna Dipman was a light-skinned girl with freckles. She went to the Baptist church. She had just gotten married that past spring. I'd never paid her much attention, and Rohn had never mentioned her. I heard somebody saying that Rohn was crazy and Fauna was probably dead. Fauna's young husband walked around like somebody had hit him on the head.

One day I went to a small hollow down past our garden at the edge of the woods. It was another of my secret places, and I had taken Rohn there. While I was there, something made the hair on the back of my neck stand up. It was just a feeling.

She had already started haunting me. I ran out of that hollow so fast I had a stitch in my side. I still run from that place in my dreams. I wake up sweating and feeling the hollow, not as empty as it should be, at my back.

I didn't see Rohn again for twenty-eight years.

I lived up North then, and one spring I went to visit a long-distance lover who lived in New Orleans. On the morning of the day I was to leave, we drove to a shopping area where there were a lot of small craft shops just opening. It was early and there weren't many people about. My friend, Emily, had run back to the post office for something, and I waited near the car, under a huge oak tree. I hardly paid attention to a car that drove up and parked just a few yards away.

Rohn got out of that car.

I had no doubt it was her. Her dark red hair was shorter and slicked back. She'd put on a little weight. She wore men's trousers. Her face was quiet and mature.

She walked into a little candle shop. I could not move. Burst after burst of light was going off inside me. Rohn.

I looked at her car. It was a long, blue, shiny Oldsmobile. A car for adults. And I looked at the woman in the passenger seat. It was Fauna. Fauna, as the young wife would look almost thirty years later. With her lipstick and her powdered cheeks and her hair pulled back. Her contented smile as if she were happy. Or at least was that morning.

I tried to think of all the things that I would say to them. I imagined the scene. I thought of dinner that night. When Rohn appeared at the door of the candle shop I didn't move.

I stood there concealed by the large tree and I did not move. I stared at Rohn. I stared as hard as I could.

She was handsome. She had long, dark curving eyebrows. A one-sided trace of a smile on her face. Sideburns. And she seemed to walk with just a bit of a limp. What happened, baby?

I let her get back into the big Oldsmobile. It tilted slightly at her weight on the seat. Closed the door. Backed out of the little drive. I saw Fauna laugh at something Rohn had said. And drive away.

I watched the car go farther and farther until it disappeared.

When Emily came back we got into the car. Emily is beautiful. She is a dark, honey-skinned New Orleans woman with amber eyes. She is all woman.

I was still seeing Rohn and Fauna. I still saw the point at which their car had disappeared. Emily threw her arm across the back of the seat and playfully tugged at my hair. She was just turning back to start the car when I said, "I love you."

She raised her eyebrows and smiled. She thought it was meant for her.

I leaned closer to her, and she reached toward me and took my hand in both of hers. We kissed. She brushed my upper lip with her tongue and then she brushed my lower lip. She kissed both sides of my mouth just a taste and my mouth opened just slightly and she licked the insides. I took her tongue and sucked and sucked and we kissed and kissed . . . but my mind was on Rohn. God, she must have done something powerful to me. If Emily had been like Rohn, there is no way I would live nine hundred miles from her.

There's a certain kind of woman I can never resist, no matter what she does. A certain hair color that makes me want to touch it, a certain slow swagger that I'll turn around on the street to look at, a certain accent; that, combined with a tone of voice I remember, can make the hairs stand up on my neck.

Rohn was on my mind and I let Emily touch me where she wanted to. But it was Rohn making me feel so weak, nearly thirty years later, sucking all my breath away.

PATRICE SUNCIRCLE
on "Tennessee," first published in 1994

I was born in west Tennessee—Tennessee Delta country. I grew up on my grandparents' farm. I still am pretty much a country girl. One of the few things that can entice me away from a good book is a walk in the woods.

I'm a pagan, which is how I see the two characters in "Tennessee."

Pagan—meaning love of wild nature and all that that entails. I didn't know I was a pagan when I was growing up down south—lucky for me—nor when I first wrote "Tennessee."

Now I do.

UP FOR A NICKEL

Thomas S. Roche

I cruise the streets, smelling cheap tacos and junkie vomit, searching the faces of whores. Searching. I drink rusty water at the Darkside; some of the old guys remember me from the neighborhood, but no one gets my name right. I slip down Twentieth and pay a visit to Mama Lamia the Palm Reader in her curio shop, stalking the shadows among shrunken heads, ritual daggers, voodoo dolls. *No shit, Jakey, you ain't a little boy no more. . . .* She has to be fifty years old, but she never stops coming on to us young bucks. No one's ever been sure if she's Cuban or Haitian or Puerto Rican or what. *You're nice and big, Jake . . . where you been?* "Listen, Mama Lamia, I need a little heat, could you help me out?" *Sounds like you got enough heat of your own, pretty boy . . . was it hard time?* I smile. "Hard as it gets, Mama. You know what I mean. Some hardware." *Foreign or domestic?* "Either one." *Preferred caliber?* "Thirty-eight'll do, short barrel if you got it, nothing too heavy." *How about .38 special? Detective Special?* "Better still, I always wanted to be a detective."

Mama L. takes me into the back room, hands me the piece. It's a simple weapon, black as death, nothing pretty, but it'll do the job if it comes down to it and the job needs doing. Mama L. lets me check it out, roll the cylinders, check the action. The grip and trigger are wrapped with that porous tape that won't take prints. Nice touch. Mama L. carries only the best. "How much?" *I could set you up for a dollar, with one of those shoulder holsters like in the pictures and a nice box of shells.* "A dollar? Damn, Mama, where'd you get this piece?" *Took it off my thirty-sixth husband when I took a cleaver to his head last night, okay, Jake?* I should know better than to ask Mama Lamia dumb-ass questions. I give her two fifties, strap on the holster, slip the gun into it. I put my old jacket on over the rig.

She pushes me up against the back counter, her hand groping my crotch. She kisses me hard, and I let her tongue sink into my mouth. It feels good after these years, and she knows it; she feels me getting hard. She puts her hand down my pants and feels my cock, stiff.

Slot number thirty-seven's open, Jake, care to step up to the plate? "Thanks, Mama, I've got some business to transact." With a glance down her arm: *Sure looks that way.* She takes her hand out of my pants, straightens her hair. *That business gets transacted, or not, you come back here and let Mama Lamia show you a little business of her own, complimentary. You take good care of yourself, Jakey. I don't want a pretty boy like you to end up with central air-conditioning, if you know what I mean.* "Thanks, I'll be careful. Listen, Mama L., I'm looking for a girl from the neighborhood. You remember her— Consuela? Connie? Sweet girl, half Puerto Rican?" *Jake, she's not . . .* "Yeah, yeah, Mama L., I know, I know. I know. Where is she?" *She's got some powerful relatives who don't like her much, Jake. You know her mama was . . .* "Yeah, I know all about that, Mama, I know all about it." *I hope you're not—* "I'm not, Mama. I would never hurt this girl, I just want to talk to her. Just tell me where she is."

Mama Lamia thinks about it a long time, slips her hand into the Windbreaker, pats the butt of the .38. *All right. The Uptown. You know the place?* "I know it. She still dancing?" *Uh-huh, that's what I hear. Dances under the name Banana Flambé.* "Banana Flambé? Oh Jesus Christ." *I know. But I hear it's a good act.* "She have a guy?" Lamia shakes her head this time. *No.*

"Thanks." I kiss her on the lips. *Watch your back, pretty boy. You know what they're saying.* "What's that, Mama?" *They're saying you whacked that guy upstate. Jimmy decides he thinks it's true, things could get ugly.* "Don't you worry about me and Jimmy, Mama L. I didn't whack nobody. Yet."

I drop by one of those discount stores on the main drag. I get myself a dark suit and some new wingtips. I head back and get a room at the Ambassador. I set the .38, loaded, on the edge of the sink as I shave my beard into a Van Dyke. I want to look good for her. I wonder if Connie will recognize me right away or if she'll have to think about it, remember how I looked, remember who I was, what I meant to her once upon a time. I put on a black tie and slick my hair back. Day burns slow and steady into evening. I sit down at the tiny table, cheap wingtips propped on the windowsill, watching the world through the open window and the jail-cell matrix of the fire escape. I light an unfiltered Pall Mall and watch things go bloodred, shit brown, gray, dark gray, black. I get up and put on my hat.

The guy at the counter says Banana Flambé doesn't hit the stage until after midnight. I get myself a nice dinner up the street, sit there reading the paper, looking for word about the body. Nothing. Have a drink, have two, feeling the bulge of the .38, keeping my eyes out for trouble. They can do me in public and never get taken for it. It just ain't fair.

I'll tell you what ain't fair. I mean, I'm up for a nickel, and I don't open my goddamn trap to tell the fucking pigs Jimmy Silver's fucking shoe size, for Christ's sake. So the parole board, they hear about how I'm an uncooperative prisoner, no matter how many times I scrub the fucking floor of my cell. Five fucking years. Who ever heard of serving five years on a nickel? And what's the word I get from Jimmy Silver's people inside? Jimmy can't associate with me, I'm too hot. All because I went up on a drug violation.

So Jimmy let me rot, and he never once said so much as thank you, Jake, for doing your time and keeping your fucking mouth shut.

That doesn't bother me half so much as it will if the cops get an ID on that body. I killed a made man without getting an okay from his boss first. Not only that, but Jimmy and Frank shared blood. I'm fucked.

The only thing that kept me alive through five years in the joint was that the body was never found. So what? Fucking goddamn lousy timing for them to find it now—if I hadn't been up for a nickel I could have driven up and taken care of the body when I heard they were building that housing development right where I'd whacked him. I could have kept it under wraps, just like it had been for five years. Jimmy never knew what happened to his brother that night, and if it wasn't for me serving the whole goddamn nickel, he never would have known.

Too fucking late now. Now Jimmy will figure out what happened, figure out who did his half brother, and there's some sort of poetic justice in that.

Frank. Fucking prick. That son of a bitch deserved to die for what he did to Connie. It still made my trigger finger itchy thinking about how she must have felt—

So I did him, wearing the hat of the pale rider, as the bringer of divine retribution, but funny thing, I don't think Jimmy will see me as the hand of God. How could that son of a bitch let his brother treat a beautiful, innocent girl like that and think he can get away with it—

Easy. I tell myself. *Nobody knows a fucking thing—yet.*

I finish my second drink and walk up the street to the Uptown.

It's close to two when she takes the stage. They have one of those silver balls that flickers multicolored lights all over the room. Connie appears up there in a gentle caress of half dark and the mist from the smoke machines. She wears a thin silky thing of a tiny white slip dress, virgin pale contrasting with her rich light brown skin, as always. Her eyes are painted dark, so moist and sad. Her black hair spills over the gown and past the swell of her breasts.

She enacts her erotic *danse macabre*, the badly recorded music a tragic Latin dirge, every verse another button coming undone. She looks down and sees me and doesn't miss a movement of her intricate dance, even though I know she recognizes me right off. She wriggles out of the slip as the song grinds to a halt, and it seems to hover after her in the smoky darkness as the spotlight follows the subtle curve of her back. She looks back just in time to vanish into darkness, looking over her shoulder, her eyes glowing sadness, with a purse on her bloodred lips. The spotlight illuminates just enough of that beautiful ass, bare except for the tiny G-string, to bring a thundering round of applause and a hail of bills onto the stage. She floats back out like a seductive ghost, smiles and licks her lips, clutches her white slip in front of her, arches her back just so as she bends down to pick up the bills, so that each movement shows off the swell of her breasts. Then she's gone.

She spots me coming back. Big guy tries to stand in front of me, puts his arms up like logs blocking my path. Connie touches him on the shoulder.

"It's okay, Louie. Let him come back."

"The other dancers ain't gonna like that—"

"Look, just forget it, Louie. Jake, give the guy a tip." I slip him a five. He backs off. "Jake, close your eyes."

She pulls me backstage, holding my hand, kneading my fingers gently. "Keep them closed," she tells me as she takes me into her dressing room. She turns me toward a wall and I hear her fidgeting around as she changes clothes. I smoke a cig, wondering what she looks like getting into her clothes—I want to see that more than I want to see her taking them off. I smoke another cig. It's taking a real long time, but I didn't expect anything different from Connie. "All right," she says. "You can open your eyes now." She presents herself to me, raising her arms. She's changed into a tiny red mini-dress that comes down over her shoulders, and carries a handbag that matches the red perfectly. She's got a rhinestone choker on, and her lipstick's a darker shade than before. Her long earrings match her necklace. Her black hair's pulled up in a bun, just a few strands dancing around the curves of her neck and shoulders. She looks beautiful. "We'll go out the back. Do you have a car?"

"Afraid not," I tell her.

She smiles at me. "All right then, we'll walk. It's a nice night out. I think the only place left is the Darkside."

I shrug. "Sounds about right."

"You think about me while I was gone, baby?"

"All the time, Jake."

"Then how come you didn't come visit me?"

"Jake, don't start. You know the answer to that."

"Yeah, I do. It was Jimmy?"

"Mmmm-hmmmmmmm."

"Things going okay for you? You making money?"

"I get by."

The waitress comes with our drinks. Whiskey sour for me, Brandy Alexander for Connie. I tip the waitress five bucks and ask her to bring us an ashtray. Connie lights a thin, exotic cigarette and sips her Brandy Alexander, leaving an inviting lipstick kiss around the tip of the straw. I take a drink, hear the ice cubes clattering.

"How's your drink?"

"Fine, Jake. I like them here. Nice and weak. I can't be too care-ful." She laughed.

"You got a man?"

"I got someone I see."

"Cop?"

"Night shift at the airport. Graveyard."

"Union man."

"Yeah, sort of."

"Look, baby, I can't get you out of my head. I want you so bad, but you know I'm hot right now."

"I know that, Jake. Word on the street is they're digging up Frank's body. Word is you did him."

I stand up. "Who the fuck told you that?"

"Don't pull that shit, Jake. I'm just telling you what you already know. I figure you did him because of what he did to me. I always wondered who had gotten him. I figured it was you. Now I know."

The waitress floats by with the ashtray, puts it down, and slips away, looking nervous. I sit down and light a cigarette with shaky hands. Connie leans close, touching my arm. "Jake. Jake, listen to me. Thank you for what you did. You have to hear that, Jake. I know it's wrong, but I'll always be grateful."

"You're welcome, but I didn't do nothing."

"Yeah. Well, thanks anyway."

"I need to get out of town, Connie."

Her rich brown eyes fill mine, spicy perfume clogging my nostrils, seducing my mind. "Jake, come up with me. I've got a place near here."

"Connie, I need the money."

She pulls me close. Her tongue snakes into my mouth and she drops her hand down, under the table, scratching my cock through wool trousers with her sharp fingernails. She begins to knead it and squeeze. "Come on," she whispers. "We'll talk later."

Barely in the door to Connie's place, and the door's slammed and she's on her knees. She gets my cock out, starts sucking on the shaft while she works my balls. I don't know where the condom comes from, but she's got it in her mouth and is rolling it down over my cock. Then she swallows my prick like it was nothing, taking the whole thing down her throat. Then she lets it slip out of her mouth and rubs it over her face as she pulls her dress down over her small tits. She slips up just enough to rub the head of my rubber-clad prick over her tits, over the pierced nipples, then pushes her tits together and wraps them around my cock as she works it up and down. Then I'm down her throat again, but she knows I'm coming close; she knows my body better than she knows her own, even after all these fucking years. She stands up slowly, locking my eyes in hers. She goes over to the window.

The neon lights outside flash on-off-on-off: LIQUORS, BEER, CIGARETTES. NAKED GIRLS. OBJETS D'ART. ALL NUDE FEMALE MODERN BURLESQUE. WRESTLING.

Consuela pulls her skimpy dress down to her waist, then shimmies out of it like a snake. Her slight round ass wriggles back out of her panties—the shimmer of her thighs as she spreads them slightly, leaning forward over the windowsill with her hand slipped over her crotch.

"No hands below the waist," she tells me.

I know it. It's Connie's rule, ever since . . .

I come up behind her and crouch down just a little so that I can get the head in between her smooth, light brown cheeks. I fit the head into her tight little hole and start to work it slow, taking my time, opening her up. Then I'm in, just with the head, and she lets out a luscious little gasp. I slide it home. She pushes back against me, putting her head back and turning her face toward me. She reaches back with one hand and touches my cheek, stroking it oh so lightly with her fingertips. Her tongue slips in and out of my mouth as I fuck her from behind. The night air is cool on my face and belly. Connie lets out a little whimper as I do her. For Christ's sake, I can't believe how bad I want to reach down and grab it with my hand. I guess it comes from the time in the joint, you know; it wasn't like this before. It probably wouldn't do much for her, but I just want to touch it, caress it, taste every bit of her. With her free hand she grips the windowsill, holding herself steady. She whispers my name as I let myself go inside her. Then I whisper hers.

Connie takes a moment to go use the can. She comes out naked except for a frilly pink robe with pink fur down each side, framing her luscious tits. She takes me in her arms, the robe bunched between her legs. We tumble down onto the bed, laughing like old times, rolling about. Connie curls up with me, one hand spread across her crotch in the dark. I light up a Pall Mall and Connie takes a drag or two. In the flare of the cherry, I can see her eyes forming big moist pools. A single tear drizzles out of one eye. If she's anything like she used to be, Connie spends about half her life weeping.

"The money," I tell her. "I've got to get out of town."

There's a key in the lock. I'm off the bed in a second, the rubber leaking come and dripping Connie's spit. I get my pants buckled and get down in a crouch, hiding in the dark, the .38 in my hand. I pull back the hammer and Connie looks at me, horrified. She sits up, clutching a pillow in her lap. The door opens.

A kid comes in the room, he can't be more than fifteen. He doesn't see me at first. He takes a look at Connie, disheveled and half clothed. The guy's wearing airport blues, smoking a big fat stogie, but he's definitely not more than fifteen, sixteen years old. Okay, I've got it figured. This is the guy Connie's living with. She always did have a weakness for younger men. He turns and sees me. I drop my hand to my side, still holding the .38 but out of sight. I stand up. "What the fuck is this?" says the guy, and his voice is as high as they get. He starts at me, and I bring up the .38. He stops. Then I get it. She almost had me taken, the chick has practically no tits and this thin sleazy mustache. And that fucking cigar, it's bigger than my dick by a couple inches. She's not a bad-looking dame, though. She turns to Connie and looks like she's about to hit her. I grip the butt of the .38. Connie stands up, clutching the robe together in front of her. "Please, Mickey, take it easy. He's just a trick. Just a trick I brought back here after the show."

Mickey looks at me, her eyes stone butch rage. She takes the cigar out of her mouth. "I told you not to fucking bring them here," she growls.

"I know," Connie says, wriggling up against the dyke. "I just brought him here because it was so late. I didn't think you'd come home early. I figured it'd be okay; he just wanted a quick one and he was paying. I thought you'd be at work."

"I moved to first graveyard shift, Consuela; don't you fucking remember?"

"Oh, Mickey, I'm so sorry, I was gone when you left for work today, remember—look, he's just a trick, I didn't think you'd be here."

Mickey stares at me, shaking the cigar like an accusing finger. "Get the fuck out." She seems like an okay broad, but I just stand there smiling for a second, floored by the whole weird scene. I take time to light a Pall Mall and then slip the .38 into its holster. Mickey's watching me, and if she's even a little afraid of me now that she knows I've got a gun, she doesn't give me a fucking hint. She's got balls, I'll give the girl that. I peel a Franklin out of my roll. I reach over and tuck it into Mickey's breast pocket. "You got a hell of a woman there. You treat that whore right. She gives some damn good head." I blow Connie a kiss. I straighten my tie on the way out and then stop to pick up my hat from where it fell by the door when Connie pounced on me. I look back at Connie and wink at her. She's crying, but then, like I said a minute ago, she cries about half the time. The dyke watches me leave, her face carved out of rock.

I open my pants, pull off the used condom, and toss it into the growing pile of matching condoms in the alley. I go out into the fog.

. . .

The sewer grates are steaming like hell's ready to pay a visit. I know I can't sleep. I wander through the street-level clouds looking for something to keep me awake. Connie has her dyke, and that's the way things are. I'm not jealous. I'm happy for her. I mean, I'm up for a nickel, and Jimmy orders Connie not to visit me, with good reason. So that's the end of it. Five years later, she's found herself a dyke to keep her warm. No big deal, no one gets blamed by me. I just don't want to sleep alone—yet.

There on the corner of Tenth there's this cute Filipino girl turning tricks. She has this tight white minidress that shows everything. I like the way she looks, and we trade a few jokes. I take her back to the hotel with me and do her long and slow from behind on the single bed with a half a tube of K-Y and one hand slid down between her legs, the other playing with her tiny breasts. I kiss her neck and then her mouth as I enter her from behind; she's got this stud piercing the center of her lower lip. It feels pretty bizarre and I kind of like it. She does good work for fifty bucks, and she's really cute, with nice tits. But she doesn't match Connie. Maybe it's because she lets me touch her. Maybe I'm just still in love or some such bullshit. Either way, I give her the fifty bucks and an extra twenty for staying till morning. And I can finally get to sleep when she takes off around dawn, leaving cheap perfume on the pillow.

I wonder if the dyke has weekends off. It looks like they're just getting out of bed, or maybe getting back in. I crouch on the fire escape just outside their apartment. Mickey and Connie are going at it.

I want a cigarette, real bad, but I'm too close to their window, which is open. They might smell the smoke and look out the window, and see me crouching there in the midday shadows. Then again, they're pretty distracted. Connie's down on her knees, wearing just her red slip and a pair of black lace-top fishnet stay-ups, and the dyke's standing over her, one of those weird contraptions hanging out of her jockeys, looks like she's got a strap or something underneath. Connie's going at it like it's a real cock, her mouth and tongue drawing wet swirling patterns up to the thick flesh-colored head and then back down to the balls again, which look unbelievably real. Connie moves her mouth up and gets her lips stretched around the head of Mickey's schlong, which is no small job, believe me. Then, with what looks like only a faint effort, Connie chokes the whole unbelievable shaft gradually down her throat until her lips are wrapped around the base. I shake my head, suppressing the urge to applaud.

Mickey rocks her hips in time with Connie's ministrations. Connie lets the cock slip out of her mouth, then rubs it between her firm tits. It looks like Mickey's ready to get down to business. Connie looks up at her man and nods.

Connie lies facedown on the bed and lifts her red slip up over her ass, spreading her legs wide and sliding her fingers up and down in her crotch. Mickey gets up behind Connie and puts the head in, bringing a breathy moan from Connie. She teases the girl for a long time, just the head pushed in. Then, inch by inch, she gives Connie the whole schlong, making the girl's full lips part wide, showing her white teeth as she whimpers, "More . . . more . . . more . . . ," with every tiny squirming movement of Mickey's hips. She's loud enough that I can hear everything. I don't know if maybe Connie's putting on a good act to try to pay the dyke back for that scene last night, but either way it seems to be working. The dyke presses her meat home and gives Connie a long, hard bang on the bed, making her clutch the dirty sheets and choke and sob as she gets fucked.

Mickey lets go; I'm not sure if it's an act for Connie's sake or if she really gets off on this. But it sure sounds real, like she's shooting long streams of jizz up inside Connie's lush body.

Then Mickey curses, loud. "I'm gonna be fucking late," it sounds like she says. I shrink deeper into the shadows as Mickey races around getting on a fresh pair of jockeys and some blue jeans and a work shirt.

It takes a long time for the dyke to get ready, and I risk a cigarette, hiding back on the edge of the fire escape in the darkness between the buildings. I don't move until I finally hear the sound of a motorcycle far below and see Mickey pulling away on a Harley, wearing a backward baseball cap and a black leather backpack, with a big bunch of white roses hanging out. I go back to Connie's window.

It's still open a crack to let in the humid summer breeze. I lift it up, nice and easy, and slip inside.

Connie's still lying on the bed, sprawled on her back. It looks like she's taking a little nap. She's got the sheets tangled around her body, bunched up between her legs. The slip's hanging off her body, revealing her delicate curves. I was always a pretty good second-story man, though I suppose you could say it's part of my moral code not to break in on girlfriends. But I guess Connie counts as an ex. I'm real quiet as I come up to the bed.

Like I said, she's still got her red slip on, but one strap's hanging over her shoulder and one beautiful soft brown tit is winking at me. One long leg hangs over the edge of the bed, the torn black fishnet stocking, a lace-top stay-up, bunched almost to her knee.

Connie's eyes flutter open, and she gives a little gasp.

She moves to cover herself up. "Jake," she says, a little surprised. "What are you doing here?"

"What do you think?" I ask her.

Connie squirms over to the edge of the bed, just a little.

"Come here and show me," she says, parting her lips and reaching out with one long-nailed hand.

I could never say no to her. I come over to the edge of the bed and she gets herself laid out on her back so that her head hangs over at just the right angle. Her lips part, her tongue flickering out eagerly. She works my zipper down with her fingers and gets her lips pressed around my shaft. I don't know where it comes from, but there's a condom in her mouth again, and I don't even know it's going on until after she's got half of my rubber-sheathed prick in her mouth. Then she starts taking it down her throat. That angle she's at, on her back with her head hanging over the edge of the bed, means that it goes down easy, smooth, gentle, without a hint of hesitation. Connie always was real good at this. Connie starts to whimper, low in her throat, as she swallows me.

"Connie," I make myself say, "I need the money."

She moves back, easing my cock out of her mouth. She rubs it all over her face, smearing her spittle across her cheeks and messing her makeup. She looks somehow sexier with her mascara and lipstick all wet and gloppy over her face. "Business first," she whispers. "Then pleasure."

With that she takes me down again, working my cock down her throat, pumping it in and out. I reach down and touch her breasts, squeezing the pierced nipples. I play with them as she works my cock in and out of her throat. Next thing I know she's getting me off right in her mouth and then I'm falling forward, stretching out on the bed with her.

"Where'd your dude go?" I ask her.

"Tomorrow's Mother's Day, remember? She went to her old man's place upstate."

I wonder about that for a minute as I light a Pall Mall. Then I let it go. I look into Connie's beautiful brown eyes and kiss the soft pink lips with their red mouth painted on and skewed about a half revolution across her chin and cheeks.

"I need the money," I tell Connie. "I've got to get out of town."

Connie's eyes get all watery, glistening with lush pain.

"You did him for me," she says.

"I didn't 'do' anyone," I tell her.

"You gave me that .22 that day, about a week before you went up the river. With the money from that airport heist. You told me to hide them both and get rid of the gun when it was safe."

"Connie, I need the money. Some people are after me. They don't want to talk."

Her rouged cheeks are streaked with black lines. "Jimmy. He's going to kill you because you did his brother. Where did you shoot him? I have to know. Tell me where you shot him."

"Connie?"

"Please, Jake, I have to know how he died."

I look at her.

"Back of the head, all eight shots," I tell her. "With a .22 caliber, they take a lot of lead to die, even at that range." I'm speaking in a flat voice, like it's nothing, which it's not. "He and I went up the highway to do some gambling, maybe catch a few whores. We'd just made a big score at the airport and I had to go up the river on that late-night charge in a week. I knew what he did to you. I was just stringing him along. No one knew where we'd gone. We were drinking the whole way, talking like we were buddies. Frank had to take a piss. I pulled off the road and said I had to take one, too. Ba-da-bing."

Connie looks very sad. "I hated Frank for what he did. I'm glad he's dead."

"Look, I'm sorry. I should have okayed it with you first." I kiss Connie, hoping that will make her stop crying, not that it ever did before. "I'm going to get whacked if I can't hit the road before Tuesday. Maybe even then." I take a deep breath, telling myself this is the last time I'll ask her. "Where's the money?" I ask, knowing the answer.

Connie takes my wrist, draws my hand to her face, kisses the fingertips with sticky lipstick-disaster lips. Slowly, she spreads her legs as she guides my hand down between her parted thighs. She presses my fingertips into her crotch, and I feel the slick wetness of her cunt, the full lips, the exquisitely sculpted clitoris, the smear of lube that's dribbled down from where Mickey had fucked her ass. Gently, Connie prods my finger and I press it into her tight cunt. She gives a little gasp as I do, like her cunt's real tender. My eyes are the ones full of tears, this time.

"It's still itchy," she tells me. "And it hurts a little. But it's the best money can buy. I did it about six months ago. I'm sorry, Jake. I'm sorry. I knew you'd be back, but I just had this chance to be happy, is all . . . and I couldn't say no."

"Oh, Connie," I whisper sadly.

Then she kisses me, climbs gently on top of me, her body soft and open and her legs spread, facing me for the first time ever. She nuzzles my ear and tells me softly, "You get to be the first, lover, my very first, just like I'm a sweet little virgin. Let's pretend I'm sixteen or something, and we're both doing this for the first time . . . you can be my boyfriend, Jake." And so she gets off the bed and floats across the room to the lingerie drawer, slips out of the stained red slip, and puts on a new clean white one. "Take off your clothes, Jake."

I get off the bed and undress, leaving my clothes in a pile on the floor, and the two of us embrace in the slanted light from the window. We climb into bed together and make out for a long, long time, like we really are sixteen or something and horny as can be, and when we finally do it I know for sure it's for the first time ever.

It feels different than anything I've ever done, like I'm a virgin, too, which maybe I am, technically. But Connie's weeping as I finish off inside her. She tells me, over and over again, "I'm sorry, Jake, I'm sorry, I'm sorry . . . I shouldn't have taken that money. . . ." And even though I know Jimmy is going to whack me, smear my brains like succulent marmalade, I tell Connie, "It's okay, shhh-hhh—shhhh, little girl, it's okay, it's okay, don't worry . . . ." I can't get the thought out of my head, of what it's going to be like, when they finally come for me.

. . .

What's the fucking point in running? Hiding? It doesn't seem to matter anymore. I've still got the room at the Ambassador. I'm drinking pretty heavy. I keep looking at the .38, wondering if it wouldn't be smarter to kill myself. Instead, when I hear the footsteps on the stairs, I empty the .38 and toss it out the window, into the garbage heap below with all the shells.

But they don't bust the door down. Something's really fucked up—they knock. Maybe it's the landlord. I answer the door in my underwear, not really giving a shit if it is Jimmy, not caring if he does it or if he sends one of his men, if they give it to me in the face or the back of the head. Who gives a rat's ass anymore? But instead of one of those anonymous mob revolvers with porous tape on the grip and trigger, I see a different kind of silver, a shield.

The cop says my name.

"Maybe," I tell him.

He tells me his name and department—Sergeant Fitz, Homicide. "We'd like you to come down to the police station."

My ears are ringing. I know what it means. My whole body goes numb. I wonder how he'll do me in the joint. Piano wire? Hung in my jail cell?

"Just let me get my pants on," I tell the pig. I look out the window as I get my black suit on. Someone's rummaging around in the garbage heap in the alley.

They show me pictures of her, stretched out across the bed with two holes in her chest, wearing the white slip pulled down and soaked with blood. She's got a strange look of peace on her face, one of her sad, lush pouts on her soft pink lips. Her arms are stretched out like she's on some kind of obscene cross. The rusty little .22 that did Frank Chambers is clutched in one of her tiny hands. I told her to get rid of that fucking thing when she could. I sit there, numb, I can't even feel a goddamn thing.

"You know her, Jake?"

"Can I have a cigarette?"

They get me one, a fucking Marlboro Light, for God's sake. I light it and blow smoke.

"Yeah," I say. "I know her."

"What's her name?"

"Connie," I say. "Consuela Rodriguez."

"Born Conrad Jesus Rodriguez Chambers," says the pig, reciting all of Connie's erstwhile names like a list of offenses. "Mama was Maria Consuela Rodriguez, a pretty Puerto Rican whore, just like her son turned out to be." The pigs laugh all around the room. "Mama OD'ed about six years ago in a shooting gallery in the Heights. His daddy was Rick Chambers, consigliere to the gods. With a taste for fresh PR whore meat." Fitz is grinning, pushing me as far as he can push me. "Can't blame him, can you? Rick Chambers later started his own family; you wouldn't know anything about that, would you, Jake? Nah, I didn't think so. Anyway, Conrad changed his name early last year, legally speaking. We understand he was a fruit for a whole lot of years, turning tricks out by the wharf. Taking it up the ass, I guess. But then they say guys give pretty good head—you wouldn't know anything about that, would you, Jake? We think he was killed in some sort of lover's quarrel. He had been down to the station to talk to some detectives the day before, saying some things about certain people in his life, saying that maybe his girlfriend wanted him dead. She was one of those women who likes to slap guys around. You wouldn't know anything about that, would you, Jake?"

"Afraid not," I say. I can't stop crying, but I'm not making a sound, just wet tears filling my eyes so I can't see straight. "Did you ask her brother? Jimmy Silver? Silver Chambers, that is? Rick Chambers, Connie's old man, he married Martha Silver Chambers after Paul Silver got whacked, and adopted Martha's boy Jimmy. Sure as fuck you must know Jimmy Silver, right? I mean, they pay you to do *something* over here, don't they?" I'm looking right at Fitz, knowing I'm going too fucking far.

Fitz looks at me like he's going to smack me. Then he does. He hits me pretty fucking hard, my head rings through the hangover fog, and I taste blood through the day-old whiskey coming up my throat. I swallow.

"We think she was killed in some sort of, you know, love triangle," he said. "So maybe you could tell me, Jake. What was your relationship with Conrad?"

I close my eyes. "We were lovers."

The pigs all mutter under their breath, saying shit about faggots and pansy perverts.

"Seems she had another lover, do you know anything about that?"

"I think she was seeing some woman."

"A woman?" More chuckles from the pigs. "You know this dyke's name?"

"Mickey something."

"Michelle Dubois. Works up at the airport. Smokes big cigars."

"Sure. I never knew her."

"Do you think Michelle might have wanted Conrad dead? Might have been some sort of lover's quarrel? Some sort of sick—"

"Consuela confessed, didn't she?" I say. "She confessed to something, didn't she? Told you she had the murder weapon? And you fuckers sent her home, knowing she'd be whacked, leaked the information to Jimmy, fucking had her snuffed, all because it's easier and pays better than getting off your asses to prosecute her." I stop all of a sudden. I'm killing myself and I know it.

The cop is stone-faced. He acts like he hasn't heard me at all, which is lucky for me.

When he does answer, he speaks very slowly, as if talking to a child. "Do you think this Michelle might have wanted her boyfriend dead? Some kind of lover's quarrel?"

Boyfriend?

I wait a long time, finish my cigarette, and snub it out before answering that one.

"I wouldn't know anything about that, Sergeant. But Michelle didn't seem like the violent type. Even if she *was* a union man."

Mickey comes to see me at the Ambassador. She's still packing, all dressed up with a bulky jacket. I know she has my .38 under there. It was her baseball cap I saw bent over the garbage heap the day the cops picked me up. I wonder if maybe she came to kill me, that day or today. She did and didn't, in that order. The cops are looking for her; they've got her and Connie's apartment staked out. She's been wearing the same clothes for days.

"I thought you did her," Michelle tells me, sitting on the edge of my bed. "Who else could get to her like that? But now I figure it wasn't you who killed her."

"It wasn't."

The .38's out of her pocket like a quick whisper of death, pressed hard in the hollow under my jaw. Mickey's in my face, her teeth set, her lips curled back under the thin mustache.

"But you know who did." She's all stone butch shit, and I know if I had done Connie I'd be dead by now.

I stare her down, waiting long seconds before answering her. When she doesn't say anything, I know she's going to let me live.

"It was her brother," I say, the .38 pressing against my throat. "Her half brother. The only one left. She was taking the fall to protect—"

Mickey still has the .38 under my chin. "That bastard raped her, didn't he?"

"Not Jimmy," I say. "Frank."

"Frank? Who the fuck is Frank?"

"It was a long time ago," I tell Michelle. "A long, long, long time ago. Frank's dead. Jimmy's the one who got Connie done like that."

"Where does he live?"

I look at her, cold. She doesn't deserve to die like that, but then again, neither do I. Neither does anyone, with a few distinct exceptions.

I stare at the dyke, wondering just how much she loved and wanted Connie, just how much she needed her around to keep her warm in this city of fog and stone-cold bullshit, how much her stone-butch *cojones,* pencil-mustache bravado, and stuffed-jean swagger are worth when it comes time to pull the trigger. Wonder what will happen if the whole fucking world gets blown up by one bullet from a .38, in the forehead of a scumbag who would murder his own sister for supposedly doing something that should have gotten done a lot more than five years ago.

I reach up and take the .38 out of Mickey's hand. "Tell you what," I say to her. "I'll take you to where Jimmy works. We're gonna go over there together."

Then I catch Mickey on the jaw with a good one, she's out in a second, and I've got her stretched out on the bed. I've got one phone call to make, before I go, to Sergeant Fitz, telling him he was right, it was a lover's quarrel, but it wasn't Mickey. I did Connie with a .38 special, two bullets in her chest from about three feet. Sounds from his tone like I guessed right on the caliber and range. It's the only way to save the dyke, and Connie loved this woman, so I suppose I might as well, too, and this is my parting gift.

"You killed Conrad Rodriguez. In a domestic dispute."

"That's right."

"And you're willing to sign a statement to that effect?"

"Well," I say, "I'll be a little busy for the next hour or so. But if I'm still around after that . . . I'll sign George Washington's autograph on your fucking grandmother's ass, flatfoot."

I cradle the phone, pocket the .38, get the keys to Mickey's bike out of the pouch of her airport blues. She's waking up, but I'm gone before she knows what's happening. I figure her bike's probably in the alley. There it is, parked up next to the garbage heap, Harley 883 Sportster, beautiful. I fire it up and hit the clutch. Rubber spins and then I'm moving like hell. Mickey screams after me, hanging out the window of the Ambassador. Yelling for me to stop. "Put it on my tab," I mutter as I shift into third and lay down the rubber, skidding onto the main drag, screaming toward Jimmy's bar like a pale rider with the .38 heavy in my pocket and the bad taste of payback in my mouth. It's almost sunrise; Jimmy's always at work early, his muscle's gonna be light this time of day. The sky cracks open, spilling fire overhead, casting black skyscraper shadows along my path. Two in the chest. Birds rise in flocks as I pass, screaming death wails, announcing my approach. God put a lightning bolt in my hand, motherfucker, a lightning bolt in a .38 special. Blood is thicker than tears, you piece of shit. The city blends like nightmares into a sound less watercolor around me, painted in Connie's blood.

Jimmy's in his office, greeting me with a smile.

THOMAS S. ROCHE

on "Up for a Nickel," first published in *Best American Erotica* in 1999

I wrote "Up for a Nickel" as my contribution to the first *Noirotica* anthology, and the story is all about what I wanted to see in such a genre. I was interested in editing an anthology of erotic horror, and author Nancy Kilpatrick had suggested to me that there was a lot of erotic horror, but no one had done erotic mysteries. So I did it.

I was a huge fan of trashy detective novels, and erotic noir was right up my alley. Richard Kasak at Masquerade Books bought the anthology, and I sent out a call for submissions.

I thought I knew what I wanted my contribution to be about, but as it turned out, I was wrong. I knew I didn't want it to be about detectives. I get more pleasure out of the doomed, sometimes unsympathetic losers in James M. Cain than in the snide moralists of Chandler or John D. MacDonald.

I wrote the 7,700 words of "Up for a Nickel" in one sitting.

The transgender element in the story represents two things I was aiming for: the idea of transformation, and the idea that the crime format transcended gender conventions—which I see in the popularity of female detectives, especially with female readers.

The sexual action in the story is as much about the demands of the characters—because sex can mean something when very little else does. The idea of hopeless love and vigilante justice are very compelling to me. Add a setting that's the mystical crossbreeding of Tampa and New Orleans with San Francisco, and that's "Up for a Nickel."

THE MANICURE

Martha Garvey

L ast week, when I had some time to kill, I noticed that my nails were in sad, sad shape. I felt gray and washed out, invisible in the big, loud city. But as I wandered through Greenwich Village at sunset, the air was bright, like someone had opened a bottle of champagne and let it spray. So I found a little nail parlor on one of those streets that run at cross angles to everything else. The manicure shop was painted pink and red, like the inside of a womb.

Within the pulsing room, there was only a single manicurist, a small Asian woman with gorgeous brown eyes.

"I was going to close up," she said. She glanced at my hands. "But I can help you."

She wore a long, pink cotton smock, and her ID badge read KAREN.

I asked her what her real name was, and she looked annoyed.

"That is my real name."

I was embarrassed. What I'd meant was that somebody so beautiful should have a beautiful name. But the damage was done. I told her my name was Nell.

She locked the door, and turned out all of the lights except the one over her manicurist's table. She practically pushed me into a chair and began to file at my ragged hands.

"Shouldn't I pay you first?" I said.

"It depends on what we're going to do," she said. She smiled, I think. "You don't take very good care of your hands," Karen said, "and they're beautiful hands. You should be punished for what you've done to your hands." At least, I thought that's what she'd said. I was tired, and the fumes from the polish, the wax, and the soaking fluid were making me woozy.

She filed and soaked my nails, then went to work on my hands with pink lotion. Outside, it was getting dark, the wind was rattling, and I looked toward the door.

"Look only at me," Karen said.

My hands felt boneless. My groin felt warm, weightless.

"I really should pay you," I said, and my voice came out all soft and dark, too.

The door rattled, but it wasn't the wind. It was a woman trying to get in. She was dressed in black jeans and a shiny, red silk shirt, and even in the dark, I could see she was desperate. She yanked at the door.

"No more customers," Karen shouted.

"Customer!" the woman shrieked. "I'm not a customer, you bitch!"

Karen shook her head. "Crazy people in New York," she said, looking at me sympathetically. "You would never do such a thing, would you?"

"No," I said, more fervently than I expected. "I'd never do that to you."

Karen wore some kind of perfume, roses and spice, something off, like jazz, but right, like jazz, too. The woman outside howled some more.

"Hey, you, you in there with Karen. Get out now!"

Karen held my gaze with hers.

"If you ignore her, she'll go away," said Karen. "And you want her to go away, don't you?"

I looked only at Karen's eyes. I heard the woman walking away. I wanted to turn around then, but Karen tightened her hands around mine. How could such a tiny woman have such powerful hands?

"You wouldn't be rude like that, would you, Nell?" she whispered. "Not after I've done so much for your hands . . ."

That's when I saw the man step out of the darkness from the back of shop.

I must have passed out.

The next thing I felt was a mouth on my mouth—smoky, male, wet.

It was now completely dark outside, and inside the shop was lit only with a couple of high-intensity lamps.

My legs were cold.

My legs were naked. My cunt exposed.

Karen worked on my cuticles as if this was the way she did all her nail jobs.

The mouth continued to explore my face: a tongue on my lip, a nip on my ear. I was dizzy, and my eyes wouldn't focus. I had been tied to the chair and stripped from the waist down. Sensations came and went. The male mouth traveled over my ears, licking, and down my neck, biting. My clit began to swell, and sweat, and trickle. The moisture hit the plastic of the seat, making it sticky. Karen gave me a glance, and stood.

"Don't you ruin my chair, you sloppy girl," she barked. Suddenly, she tilted the light down to the floor. My stubby square toenails had been painted bright red. They looked like the feet of a slut. My clit grew some more. I didn't recognize those feet as my own.

Karen noticed me looking at the color. "You like it? I call it 'Wench.'"

I turned back to the shop window. Karen hadn't pulled the metal grate down, or pulled a curtain. If anyone had looked in, they could have seen us plainly: a half-naked woman being gently mauled by a silent man in tight black jeans, a white cotton shirt, and a ponytail, while being watched over by a stern, tiny mistress. I couldn't really see the man's face, but I could smell him. I hated men who smoked. But not this one.

"Show me her breasts," Karen snapped, and without warning, the Mouthman grabbed the front of my white Oxford shirt and yanked it open. The buttons fell on the floor with a clatter. Somehow that made me hot, too.

"What an ugly bra," Karen spat. "We'll have to do something about that."

Mouth pulled a knife out of his tight jeans and flipped it open, like a biker boy. Carefully, he placed it on the material between my breasts and slit the fabric. He was gentle, but still he drew blood. Karen sighed, and picked up a cotton ball. She dabbed it with rubbing alcohol: I could smell it rising in the air. She swabbed my wound down hard, and I gasped from the stinging.

But my nipples got hard, and my cunt was slick with juice. My shirt dangled from my arms, and my bra was ruined.

"I would never have taken you if your hands hadn't been such a mess," Karen whispered. "Now I'll have to do all of you."

Mouth flung my shirt into a corner, along with my bra. Occasionally, I could sense people stopping outside, staring into the window, wondering if they really saw what they thought they saw in the shadows.

My wrists were bound to the arms of the chair, just a little too tight. Then they gagged me with a ball gag. There was a click of metal: clips made of silver filigree grasped my nipples fiercely—again, a little too tight.

"No sound," Karen ordered as she finished. "No talk, no moan, no pant." The Mouth said nothing, only opened and closed his knife once more.

Then Karen yanked on the chain between the nipple clips, and something between a pant and a grunt escaped from my mouth, despite the gag. I waited for a whip, a slap, a blow.

Instead, Karen sat down deliberately and pulled the manicure table to the side. She grabbed a bottle of bright red polish, leaned into me, and painted the pinkie finger of my left hand. She smelled like heaven. Her jazzy perfume was breaking down, mixing with her sweat. I wanted to lick it off, even though I'd never touched another woman. She rose from her chair and perched on my left leg to finish the job, careful not to touch me anywhere else. This was my punishment—that she would sit right next to me, right on me, but draw no nearer. I tried to look on the bright side; I thought, this might not be so bad. Stripped naked by a dangerous man. Painted like a whore by a beautiful woman. I could be a silent, good little girl through that.

Then Karen nodded to Mouth, who had donned a pair of black rubber gloves when I wasn't looking. His smell had changed. He, too, was sweating, and his erection was obvious. I tried not to think ahead, tried not to wonder whether I'd get to see any more of his body. Then he walked directly behind me and tied a blindfold around my eyes. The sour-sweet odor of the polish rose in the air.

Blind and mute, I felt as if I could smell everything in the room, like my skin had doubled in size. Karen was on the "fuck you" finger, stroking my palm with one hand while decorating it with the other.

I would be her good girl. I could be quiet. Then I felt a rubbery hand stroke my mound, as Karen continued stroking my palm. Mouth went to work below, while Karen worked on my hands. What a bitch she was, I thought. That woman had been right.

I writhed in the chair, but I kept quiet. I ground my ass into the sticky, cheap plastic of the chair, trying not to come, trying to avoid his hand, ever advancing . . . . I yanked at my wrist restraints. I was only trying to do what Karen demanded: to absorb the pleasure without a sound. Then someone slapped me hard on the face. It was Karen, I guess; the slap was scented with perfume and lotion.

Karen hissed, "Ruin this nail job, bitch, and you'll never leave this place."

"Let's teach her something," said Mouth. His voice was smoky and dark, too. My outer lips ballooned at the sound. Everything was making me hot. How could I possibly do what Karen wished? But I wanted to. I knew I wanted to.

Mouth's hand withdrew from my crotch, and Karen stopped her nail job. I felt ashamed. I had failed her. I couldn't even get my fucking nails done without failing.

I felt Mouth grab the back of my chair, dragging me across the shop, dragging me toward . . . the storefront window. I could tell, even with the blindfold, that there was a streetlight shining outside, and that we were close enough to the glass to give anyone a very good view of my nail job.

"Will you be a good girl, Nell?" Karen whispered in my ear. I wanted to feel her tongue there, too, but it wasn't going to happen. She yanked at my nipple clip chain. "Will you be a good, quiet girl?" I nodded, biting my cheek to keep the sounds inside my mouth.

I was a liar. I wanted to come, I wanted to scream. I wanted Mouth to plunge his hand deep into my cunt, and Karen to suck on my tortured tits. But I wanted to please her. The truth was, from the moment I'd sat down in that chair and put my hand in her hand, I was hers.

Karen kept up the pace of my nail job while Mouth worked me below, kneading my mound until he flowed onto my clit, teasing it between two fingers. Sweat poured off my neck, my breasts, down my legs. I could hear Mouth begin to pant himself, and outside, I sensed, people were gathering.

Karen switched to my other hand, and Mouth's fingers drew patterns around my labia. How big was the crowd watching me?

I didn't know. I could hear a couple of people talking outside, another tapping on the glass, tapping. The blood rose in my chest, and I could feel my pale skin turn red from desire. I wanted to move my hips against Mouth's persistent motion, press hard against his long fingers, but I knew, I just knew, this was wrong.

"It's a bigger crowd than usual," Mouth said, and I could feel him smirking. The ball gag was making my mouth dry, my jaw tired. Bigger crowd than usual? I thought. What the hell did that mean?

And then, as Karen began painting my right hand, Mouth slid two fingers into me. I bit the inside of my cheek as his fingers found my G-spot and stroked it slowly. At the same time, Karen brought her mouth close to my breasts and just . . . breathed.

Outside, the crowd was quiet, but I could feel them watching. "They usually give up by now," I thought I heard a woman say, but maybe I'd imagined it. With his other hand, Mouth began exploring the crack of my ass. Karen withdrew her breath.

"Only four more fingers to go," Karen said brightly. As if in response, Mouth slid a third finger into my cunt. My knees shook, and my shoulders quivered. The ropes cut into my legs, and my circulation slowed.

"You clean up good, Nell," Mouth said mockingly. I felt him kneel in front of me, to one side of Karen, both hands wedged deep in my crotch. My asshole was still tender, untouched. I could feel his eyes on my clit and my cunt.

"Three more," said Karen, and for the first time, I heard some heat behind the ice. More heat against my crotch: it was Mouth, doing what Mouth did best. I twisted, as if I imagined I could still avoid him. Karen slapped my breasts.

"You almost ruined that one," she shrilled.

"Either she's melting, or her juices are dripping off the chair," said Mouth.

"And she looked like such a dull little thing when she came in. But I knew you for what you were, Nell," said Karen.

Mouth now lapped me in earnest, from cunt lips to the tip of my clit. I heard a *thump, thump, thump.*

"They're pressing themselves against the glass, Nell, because they want a piece of you," Karen said, as she finished with my index finger, the one I liked to use to touch my breasts. Below, Mouth shoved his tongue into my cunt and licked the deep red walls inside me.

I was desperate not to come until Karen was done, but I didn't know how I was going to hold off. I thought about taxes, Republicans, white vinyl belts. I thought about bad TV movies and Barry Manilow. But Karen was on the last digit now, my right thumb, and she was massaging my palm again. Nothing was working. I imagined a world where everyone, even John Denver, got tied up, worked over, and painted up like a slut. And we all loved it.

More thumps against the window. I thought of Hitchcock's *The Birds,* the thud of the predators.

"They all want you, Nell," said Karen. "But you're mine, aren't you?" Suddenly, my eyes were full of tears, and I nodded.

"All done," said Karen. And everything stopped. The Mouth withdrew, with a final tug at my clit. Karen dropped my hand. Outside, silence. I was on the verge of coming, and I suddenly felt completely alone. Were they going to leave me here? Was this my reward for obedience?

Karen whipped off my blindfold, untied the gag, and Mouth undid my bonds. He put his hands under my arms and forced me to stand. I shook, but I didn't fall.

And then I saw them: a crowd of twenty outside the glass—men, women, mouths, little O's of lust, their sweaty hands applauding. I was naked, my hands and feet sparkled red, the color of the whore I was, the whore I wanted to be. I was swollen, I was ashamed, and I was Karen's. I wanted to be Karen's more than I wanted to moan, more than I wanted to come.

I turned, and there she stood, in a pink smock and nothing else. Nothing else, that is, except a black leather harness and a white marble dildo. And a mean gleam in her eye. I wanted to ask her permission, but I had lost my voice.

"Bend over the chair," she said. I eagerly complied.

But then she shook her head and gave me a mean little smile.

"No. Let's wax your legs first."

MARTHA GARVEY

on "The Manicure," first published in *Best American Erotica* in 2000

I wrote "Manicure" just as the first Internet bubble was beginning to sag. It was in the late Clinton era, when New York knew nothing of 9/11.

When I read it now, I detect a giddiness that I can't summon up so easily today. I'm still proud of the story, but I write more self-consciously and politically now . . . I can't help it. I've gotten more interested in history. John Quincy Adams popped up in one of my more recent stories, and could not be denied. "Manicure" makes me miss the old New York of my story, and a little bit of the writer I was then.

I don't want to get too nostalgic, though: I believe when one hedonistic door closes, another one will open . . . if you're a registered voter.

The origin of "Manicure" is straightforward, although I admit to a lifelong ambivalence about the beauty-industrial complex, which I believe shows up in the story.

I'm the kind of Gemini who worships fashion—I am the proud owner of an autographed Tim Gunn bobblehead—but I order the same jeans and button-down shirt from L.L. Bean every year. I'm not sure *why* I know who Bobbi Brown is, or that a certain movie star's wife is breaking out as a stylist, or why I buy only one MAC lipstick (Desire) every two years. But I do.

On a lovely spring day in the Village, in between jobs and sweethearts, I decided to cheer myself up with a professional manicure, one of perhaps ten I've gotten in my life.

The manicurist took my money, softened my cuticles, put a clear coat on my nails, and then made it very clear that I was kidding myself if I thought a manicure was all I needed.

Because I wanted the manicure, and I'd already paid my money, I stayed, while the woman continued to, well, insult me. I left the shop in a jangle—furious, confused, a little turned on. Why was the manicurist so mean? Why had I stayed? I wrote the story to figure that out.

THIS ISN'T ABOUT LOVE

Susan St. Aubin

Ilka on the road in her yellow Volkswagen, traveling from job to job: I can see her as clearly now as I could then. Monday nights she's at City College teaching English as a Second Language; Tuesday and Thursday afternoons she teaches two sections of remedial composition at Cabrillo College thirty miles south; Wednesday nights she's thirty miles north at the College of San Mateo teaching self-defense; and Thursday nights it's self-defense again at the Women's Center, which doesn't pay much but she doesn't have to drive so far.

"I'm exhausted," she says when she walks into the university gym where the Women's Center holds its self-defense class.

We sit on the floor dressed in leotards or sweatpants. Lynne, who's gay and wears men's jeans, removes her heavy hiking boots reluctantly because street shoes aren't allowed in the gym. Patty, a sophomore math major with long red hair, who says she's sick of male logic, whispers to Louise and Janice from the Women's Studies Program; their breasts float loosely beneath their cotton T-shirts. I sit against the wall in my black leotard, my long braid of brown hair over one shoulder. We're the regulars; others come for a few lessons, then leave.

Ilka dumps a green shoulder bag bursting with books and papers on the floor, and pulls from it a rumpled white cotton karate suit.

"This material is so sick," she says, shaking the knee pants and jacket. "It'll last forever."

She means "thick," not "sick"; she's Swiss-German, and though she's taught English for years, her consonants sometimes slip.

A dozen years later I can shut my eyes and see her bend to unlace her knee-high brown boots, then pull on the heavy cotton trousers before sliding off her long denim skirt and vest. After she unbuttons her blouse, there's an instant when she stands in her pink camisole before it's covered by the cotton jacket she ties around her waist with a brown cloth belt. She wraps a silk scarf around her head to contain her long blond hair, except for the bangs that cover her eyebrows. She has our rapt attention when she's ready to begin the class. I'm not gay, but my breath comes quicker, then and now.

Her green eyes, which she rarely blinks, stare intently as she leads us through our warm-up exercises.

"It's best to be a generalist," she tells us while we stretch. She's taught for years, first in Japan, where she tutored businessmen in German and English, and then in California, where she specializes in English as a Second Language, a subject in which she has personal experience as well as a master's degree from our university. The self-defense course is her own invention, loosely based on the karate, judo, and aikido she picked up in Japan.

"Use your opponent's energy against him," she tells us as we glide together across the floor of the gym, moving our feet and arms as she's taught us.

"These are the vital spots of the human body," she recites, jabbing her right arm with fingers stretched straight. "Eyes. Base of the skull. Solar plexus. Groin. Kneecap. Christine!" she calls to me across the gym. "Your movements are far too weak. Put some muscle in your arm, push against the air, like so." Her arm swings forward in a controlled punch. "Imagine your attacker."

After class we go to a coffeehouse called Sacred Grounds, in the basement of a church, where we drink espresso and listen to Ilka talk about her life on the road.

"The freeways are full of boys in delivery trucks," she tells us, her green eyes round and staring. She says she's bisexual and once told us about a woman in Japan named Mika, whose body was so completely smooth and hairless that making love with her was like being caressed by a silk scarf, but only when she speaks of men are her eyes this big. Patty leans forward, while Lynne sits back in her chair with her arms folded across her breasts.

These aren't long-distance truckers high up in the cabs of their semis with their eyes fixed on the road. These are boys driving local routes in vans and pickup trucks with signs painted on the side: DOUG'S PHARMACY, RACE STREET FISH MARKET, GLOBAL PAINT. When they honk as they pass her yellow Volkswagen, she honks back.

"That's stupid," says Lynne. "No matter how good your judo skills are, you're defenseless in a car. What if one of those guys forces you off the road? What if he has a gun? I still say it's better to carry a gun, because if your attacker's got one pointed at you, you can't very well throw him over your shoulder."

Lynne and Ilka have a variation of this conversation nearly every week.

"If you're in control of your own healthy body, you'll never need a gun to defend yourself," says Ilka. This time she smiles, leaning her elbows on the sticky table, and adds, "Besides, you're assuming I'd be unwilling. How can I be defenseless against what I want?"

Lynne's mouth opens, then closes tight.

Still smiling, Ilka tells us about Denny, who has lips like Mick Jagger's and delivers stereo components to a chain of stores up and down Highway 101. He's a drama student at City College whose ex-girlfriend took Ilka's self-defense class at the College of San Mateo. The first time they met, he motioned her off the freeway in Belmont and bought her a drink in a bar, then took her in his company's van into the dry October hills, where they made love on the floor among boxes of speakers, turntables, and tape recorders. The van's back doors hung open so they could watch the planes take off from San Francisco Airport to the north. Ilka tells us that, except for his shaved face, his whole body is covered with black silky hair as smooth as Mika's skin.

Once every couple of weeks she runs into him—the literalness of this expression when applied to their freeway meetings makes us laugh—and they always drive somewhere in his van: up to Crystal Springs Reservoir, where they make love in the moonlight on the concrete steps of the Pulgas Water Temple; or over the mountains to the beach, where they lie in the back of the truck, watching the afternoon fog roll in.

It's 1975 and nobody's heard of AIDS. Ilka's on the Pill, so all she has to worry about is that Denny might turn out to be a crazed killer who'll pull an axe from behind a stack of stereo speakers and chop her into little pieces, which he'll scatter between San Jose and San Francisco. She knows if she wants to she can kick the axe from his hands and paralyze him with a chop to his Adam's apple, but still it excites her to imagine cowering before him, especially when they lie wrapped in each other's arms in the back of the truck on a deserted road in the hills at sunset.

"If there's a part of me that wants destruction, I can't be defenseless," she tells us in Sacred Grounds. "The trouble is, I can defend myself too well. I feel so safe with men it's a bore."

"I wouldn't mind being bored like that," says Lynne.

When Ilka stops seeing Denny on the road, she's not too disappointed. Perhaps he quit his job or was fired. Did his boss find the red silk underpants Mika sent her from Japan in an empty turntable box? Did Denny get back together with his old girlfriend? Does he swerve off the road whenever he sees a yellow Volkswagen in the distance?

"He was very immature," she says, sipping coffee. We're all kids, nineteen and twenty years old; she's twenty-nine, so we're flattered to be included in her maturity.

One night while pulling out of the parking lot at City College, she sees a quick flash of headlights in her rearview mirror. For a second she thinks the van is Denny's, but this one is light blue, and when it passes, she sees no writing on the side. Up front, a man leans back casually as he drives. She catches a glimpse of him, hair unfashionably short, seat tilted back, cigarette dangling from his lips, and then he's gone.

The next week she sees him again at one of the other colleges. Once more it's late because she's spent the evening tutoring students from her afternoon English class. She watches his eyes in her rearview mirror all the way home. When she changes lanes, so does he; they dance together across the nearly empty highway. When she exits, he's close behind, but three blocks from her apartment he pulls ahead and disappears around the corner. His license plate reads ZIP, but she keeps forgetting what the three numbers are.

When she sees him on a Tuesday afternoon, she gets a better look. "He has a very long nose," she tells us in a whisper. "Of course, you know about men with long noses."

We look at each other for clues.

"They have long penises, too," she says.

Late one warm night in May, he stays on her tail, changing lanes when she does, getting on and off the freeway when she does. When she stops for gas, so does he, but instead of getting out of his van, he waves a thick, stubby hand to the attendant sitting behind the flickering light in the window of the gas station. The attendant gets up and strolls out to lean on the open window of the van before filling the tank and washing the windshield.

Ilka rolls her eyes to the side to watch without seeming to as she cleans her own windshield, so she doesn't see much. His fingers do look short, which she thinks contradicts the mythology of the nose.

After paying the cashier in her booth beside the gas pumps, where she sits with candy bars and cigarette packages stacked up to her ears, Ilka drives away with the mysterious van close behind.

When he passes, blinking his lights, she follows. He signals right without moving out of his lane, and she signals, too, but stays behind him. When he actually does exit at a sign that reads REST STOP, Ilka is close behind. The moon is so full and bright she sees every bush, every rock, almost every blade of grass as she follows him up a winding road that ends at the top of a hill in a circle of picnic tables beside a lighted building nearly as big as a house, with two entrances, one for women and one for men. Two men come out of the men's entrance, one behind the other, and stroll into the bushes behind the building.

She passes the restrooms and parks beside the light blue van, where her pursuer sits staring straight ahead, one arm resting on his steering wheel. The arm looks heavier than his neck and shoulders, but she can't see it clearly because it's hidden by his loose jacket. She gets out and walks around her car to the open window of the van. At first she thinks he has no legs, then realizes his bare feet, with their clean, stubby toes, are his hands, his heavy muscular legs his arms. He sits in a padded, velvet-covered seat, with one of his legs resting on the open window, the knee crooked like an elbow, while his neatly manicured toes drum the steering wheel.

He laughs as she gasps. He wears bell-bottomed denim pants and a dark blue shirt whose short sleeves flap loosely. With his free foot he pulls a lever on a dashboard that has lights and buttons like an airplane cockpit, and his seat tilts back. He raises his legs straight up above his head, lacing the toes together like fingers as he watches her, then stretches, with a thrust of his pelvis, and puts his feet back down on the floor where they belong. She backs away one step.

"Why have you been following me?" she asks. With one kick she could knock him out of his van. She can't imagine an attack he might win.

He smiles at her and shrugs; without arms, the shrug seems to originate in his groin. "I could ask you why you followed me up here. What's your name, anyway?"

"Ilka," she says.

His eyes are dark in the moonlight. "Where're you from?" he asks. "Isn't that a German accent?"

"Originally Berne. In Switzerland," she answers before she can stop herself. This is more information than she usually gives the guys she picks up on the road. Her heart beats faster.

"Come for a ride with me, Ilka." The door on the other side of the van pops open when he pulls a lever.

She feels like she's been hypnotized, and she knows that even if she needs to, she won't be able to make herself throw him. He has a power over her she hasn't felt since she was a child. Obediently, she walks around the front of the van and gets in, landing on a padded velvet seat identical to his. He pushes a lever with his big toe to shut the door. She feels disarmed, and finds this intoxicating, as though she's just smoked a joint. She listens to herself breathe as she rubs her arms across the armrests. He puts one foot on the seat of his chair moving it rapidly back and forth to brush the velvet. The moon hangs frozen in the van's windshield.

"We don't have to go anywhere," he says, turning on a light that dimly illuminates the windowless interior of the van. There are two bunks built into each side, covered with velvet spreads to match the front seats. On one of the bunks is a fur rug. The ceiling is glued with squares of mirror; a reflection of the light glows in each one. When he swivels his seat around to face the bunks, so does she.

"Do you live here?" she asks.

"No, but I could if I had to."

He stands up and moves, half stooped in the low van, to the bunk with the fur rug, where he lies down. She kneels on the carpeted floor beside him.

In Sacred Grounds we look at each other, at her, at our cups.

She laughs at us. "You don't believe me! But his legs were so much like arms it seemed like there was nothing missing."

She tells us how he wraps a leg around her waist with a grip so firm she feels she can't escape, pulling her down on top of him. Her hands slide across the thick fur rug. With his foot he strokes her back, then with one deft motion pulls off her skirt, which has elastic at the waist, and her underpants. His foot slides up her legs, and those toes, she tells us, her mouth slightly open, those toes know just what to do. As they lie side by side, one of the toes—the big toe, she thinks, but she's not quite sure—penetrates her while two or three of the others move around faster than anything she's ever felt before, faster than her own fingers. This can't be a human foot, she thinks, and listens for the hum of a vibrator, or maybe some sort of electric arm or mechanical hand, but she hears nothing. One leg holds her while the other plays until she comes with a rushing sensation she's never felt before.

"I wet the fur," she whispers to us. "I came like a man. Can you imagine?"

We stare at her, and then I start to giggle.

"I've heard of that happening," says Lynne.

The others shake their heads.

"No," says Janice, who's organizing a library of feminist writing for the Women's Center. "That couldn't be possible."

Lynne glares at us until we're quiet.

Ilka shrugs and says, "It happened."

He rubs the wet spot with his foot and kisses her again. She's still embarrassed, but he finds nothing odd about this wetness; if anything, it seems to arouse him further.

"I don't meet many women like you," he whispers in her ear. "Take your blouse off."

While she sits up to unbutton her blouse, he lifts a toe to his crotch, ripping his fly apart to expose his erect penis. Where a zipper should be she sees strips of blue Velcro. He slides out of his pants like a snake shedding its skin, but leaves his shirt on. She's fascinated by his short military haircut.

His leg is around her waist; he pulls her down to his penis, which she takes in her mouth and sucks until she feels he's about to come, then pushes his leg down and sits herself on top, riding while he writhes beneath.

After he comes, she comes again, but she can't tell if the wetness is hers or his. She rolls onto her back beside him and feels with her hand, then sniffs and licks her fingers, but it all tastes and smells like sperm.

She sits up. "I've got to leave," she says, and is disappointed when he slithers back into his pants without comment, passing a toe over the Velcro closure. She wants those legs to grip her again so tight she can't move.

Ilka puts on her blouse, fumbling with the buttons. She imagines him reaching under a bunk with his foot and pulling out a gun, but she knows she can unbalance him easily with a kick. She feels let down.

He sits on the bunk smiling at her while she binds her hair in her brown silk scarf, then crawls to the front of the van and opens the door. In her mind he jumps on her, pulling her to the floor with his powerful legs while she struggles to break free, but when she looks back, he just sits, smiling.

She jumps out of the van and runs to her car, wanting him behind her as she roars out of the parking lot in a sputter of gravel. She keeps checking the rearview mirror all the way home, but he's not there.

And yet, he's caught her. Ilka begins driving even when she doesn't have to—Saturday nights, Sunday afternoons, early in the morning she cruises up and down the freeway from San Jose to San Francisco, looking for an unmarked light blue van. She wants to see him again, she wants his legs wrapped around her waist while his toes massage her spine. She imagines holding him where his arms should be while shaking him until his heavy legs pull her down; she imagines him with arms as they wrestle on the floor of his van, his fingers—real fingers—so tight around her neck the light turns gray.

Did he come into the world unarmed, more helpless than most of us? Or was there some sort of accident—arms ripped from their sockets in a car wreck, arms burned to the shoulder in a fire? Did he lose them in Vietnam to a Vietcong soldier with a knife, or one of his buddies gone mad? She does research in the library on the babies born in Germany in the early 1960s without arms because of a drug their mothers took for nerves and nausea, but he's too old for that; he's at least thirty. She never felt his shoulders where the arms should be, so she wonders if he has some sort of residual flipper attached to each one, like the thalidomide babies she sees in medical textbooks, reaching for rubber balls with sprouts of tiny hands. When she closes her eyes, she sees wrists and arms emerging from his shoulder stubs like plants growing in slow motion. His body is outlined in a glimmer of light that remains even when she opens her eyes again, making everything she sees look faded.

That summer Ilka teaches more than ever: remedial reading, English as a Second Language, and freshman composition at six different colleges. Twice a week she drives across the bay to teach in Hayward, where she tells us there's the possibility of a permanent job. Though her territory has expanded, she doesn't see the blue van for two months.

Then one night she says she sees him on the road again, but always so far behind she has to drive slowly to let him catch up. She sees him in her rearview mirror, the short hair, the dark eyes staring, even a glimpse of the smile, but when he gets close to her, he speeds ahead, vanishing into the traffic. She ignores the other boys in their vans, who honk and wave as she dodges in and out of traffic after the one van she can never catch.

"It's like I'm hypnotized," she says. "I can't stop." She's not smiling now; her face looks thinner, and her wide eyes are swollen.

One day when his van passes she's able to follow him up the freeway, changing lanes when he does, and flashing her signal right, right, right until she herds him up to the rest stop where they met before. His license plate reads ZIP, and she thinks the three numbers are the same. The sun glints off the chrome of parked cars whose license plates are a map of the United States, for Maryland to Oregon, Alabama to Minnesota. Families sit at the picnic tables. A man in his fifties jumps out of the light blue van. He has the short hair, the long nose, but he leans his arms on the open window of her car and says, "Lady, what the hell do you want, anyway?"

"I'm sorry," she says. "I thought you were someone else. A friend of mine has a van just like this."

"Yeah? Well, you've got a hell of a nerve trying to run me off the road like that." Turning abruptly, he climbs back in his van and drives off, the wheels spinning in the dusty gravel of the parking lot.

She sits alone in her yellow Volkswagen for nearly an hour before driving down the hill to the freeway.

Though Ilka laughs with the rest of us, I think I can feel her sadness, and I curl my hands into fists under the table when I picture the unarmed man chasing Ilka, catching her, then throwing her back out on the road again so he can play with her without letting her defend herself. What good is her karate if she can never touch him again? Lynne's right, I say to myself, Ilka should carry a gun and shoot him through the windshield the next time his teasing blue van speeds by.

"Maybe you dreamed him. Dreams can often be more true than reality," says Patty, who plans to change her major to psychology.

"No, he exists, I can assure you." Ilka takes off her silk scarf and shakes out her long blond hair, fluffing it away from her head with one hand while the other plays with the scarf. "But I did dream about him the night after that guy told me off at the rest stop."

We lean forward.

In her dream, the armless man drives up and parks beside her as she sits in her car halfway up a hill. It's not the rest stop, just a green meadow with poppies in the grass. There isn't even any road. She smiles at him; he smiles at her.

"You never told me your name," she calls to him in German.

He answers in English, "I'm one of the unnamed."

When he jumps out of his van, she sees that he's armed with a pistol held in his right foot. His Velcro fly bursts apart so that his cock, too, points straight at her, just below the gun. She's out of her car now, running up the hill. When she looks back, she sees him hopping behind her, gun and penis aimed, clearing bushes in one bound. She's panting; she can't quite reach the top because the hill grows as she runs. He dances after her, faster on one leg than she is on two, and she wakes up just as she hears the gun explode.

She's breathless as she teaches the end of her story. "I was having an orgasm when I woke up," she says. "It was as though the gun that woke me started the orgasm. He finally gave me what I wanted."

"Death?" I ask. My fingers are clenched under the table. "How can you think you're in love with someone who shoots you?"

"But it was like being shot to life." Ilka looks at me and sighs. "He shot his power into me. I can't explain it; there are no words in any language I know. I'm not talking about love, Chris."

Lynne rolls her eyes to the ceiling and chuckles. "Well, Ilka, that's one way of looking at it. If you won't carry a gun, suck power from his. It's not a bad dream, when you think about it."

Ilka smiles into her empty coffee cup, turning it around in her hands as though trying to see the future, while Patty nods like the therapist she wants to become.

I can't find words for what I want to say, either, so my mouth stays closed while I watch Ilka bind her hair up into her scarf again. Though I long to stroke the smooth light hairs on the back of her neck, there's no language in my hands for this desire. I tell myself

I'm not gay and never have been, and yet I know I could love her better than any man without arms, no matter what she thinks she wants. Sitting across the table from her that night in Sacred Grounds, I think I can save her if I just put my arms around her, but I can't move them. It's as though all their muscles have been pulled out.

We didn't see each other much after that night. Ilka had so much work in the fall she had no time for self-defense. When the job possibility in Hayward fell through, she wasn't disappointed. "One job would be as boring as one lover," she said.

She began teaching farther north at the College of Marin, then moved to San Francisco to be in the center of her work. I heard she had her hair cut short, bought a black Honda sedan, and started wearing suits and carrying her students' papers in a briefcase. In this costume, she began to meet a higher class of men who drove Jaguars or BMWs instead of delivery vans, but by then I'd lost touch with her. I heard she met the unarmed man, but he didn't recognize her; I also heard that when she saw him again he had arms, and smiled slyly at her confusion. Patty always claimed the whole thing was Ilka's fantasy.

The truth is I don't know how Ilka's story ended, though I often think about the possibilities. Does she still expect to see him whenever a blue van comes up behind her, close on her tail as she heads down the freeway to San Jose? Self-defense has a different definition these days. Is she a cautious women who carries condoms wrapped in pink cellophane in her briefcase instead of a karate suit? Does he keep a box of them in the glove compartment below the dashboard of his van? Does he pull this box out with his toes, take off the lid, rip open a plastic packet with his teeth and, with his skillful big toe, glide the glistening pink sheath onto himself? Or does he reach his foot into the glove compartment and pull out a pistol, swirling it around on his big toe before he shoots her, just the way she likes it?

SUSAN ST. AUBIN

on "This Isn't About Love," first published in 1992

In "This Isn't About Love," I got the mix of my obsession with sex, politics, and personal relationships just about right, without the usual polemic I can so easily slip into. When I reread the story this time, I was surprised to find a lot more.

I was especially surprised by the autobiographical aspects. I'm always sensitive to this, protesting loudly that I make all this stuff up. "No, this isn't my life, I'm lying, I'm inventing. I really lead quite a sedate life."

But the truth is, "This Isn't About Love" is a story about choices I made in my own life in the 1980s. It's about the years that permanent teaching jobs were disappearing, both in public schools and in universities. I was a high school teacher in the 1970s, always a substitute, never permanent. Never any benefits. I went back to school to get my master's in Creative Writing at SFSU with the hope of maybe teaching college, but there was no work there, either.

It was simply cheaper for the state colleges and universities to hire a bunch of part-time lecturers to teach one class each so they wouldn't have to pay them medical benefits, vacations, etc. There were massive budget cuts to education in California.

These poor teachers, traveling from school to school, trying to cobble together the full-time equivalent of a job at four or five different schools, came to be known as "freeway flyers."

I had to decide whether to join them on the California highways, or take a secure, permanent job, with all benefits, as the office manager of the Creative Writing Department.

And another choice, the sexual one: Did I want to live with my boyfriend of several years? Me, a bisexual, a believer in multiple relationships—did I want to settle down with this one person? In an open relationship, to be sure, but how would *that* work?

Marriage wasn't even a consideration at the time, although later we did actually marry for—you guessed it—my medical benefits. He, too, was a freeway flyer, a teacher-librarian at several libraries and schools.

All of this poured into "This Isn't About Love," the major question of the story: Which is more fulfilling—a life of change, of danger, of excitement, or a safe and secure life (with benefits)?

I opted for security, taking the safe administrative job, living with my partner. Both choices have worked out well, and yet— even as I made these choices, there were regrets, expressed in "This Isn't About Love." Mainly, a loss of the life of the adventurer, symbolized by Ilka's sex life and the man with no arms. What did that mean? Unloving—but then, this isn't about love! It's about sexual need, and insecurity, and a death wish—because what kind of future will there be for an old retired teacher with no income? Live now, because there is no future!

As I was making my safe choice, I was writing about the other possibility. As I reread the story, I feel nostalgia for that path not taken, "Ilka's way." I still wonder if she's happy. . . . I still wonder if I'm happy. . . .

The disconnected narrator, Chris, had something in common with me, perhaps more than I'd like to admit. She's the part of me that's a voyeur, observing other people's lives without fully participating—often the fate of the writer. She denies who she is (repeating, "I'm not gay" and "I'm not gay and never have been") and indicates at the end of the story that she's the one who's missed out on life. Chris cuts herself off from what she wants because she's too well defended.

I love it when Ilka says, "How can I be defenseless against what I want?"

Did I really write that?

[BLUE LIGHT]

Steven Saylor writing as Aaron Travis

I was new in town, didn't know anyone, needed a place. My old apartment in New York had made me sick of cramped quarters; I needed space.

I had no intention of moving into some tacky Houston apartment complex with a bathtub-size swimming pool and nosy neighbors. I wanted something different, something with character. A room in a house with laid-back people. Cooperative living. I'd done that back in my student days. It might be just what I needed to made me feel at home in this fucked-up town.

They say New York's impersonal. Give me those hordes on the subways any day over the automatons in steel modules that cruise the superfreeways in Houston. Forget the sweltering heat; this town is all cold concrete and glass. Maybe that explains the incredible murder rate. There's a lot of mental illness down here.

On Saturday morning I took the Harley over to Montrose and found a health-food restaurant. I leafed through a few of the free underground rags that were stacked in front of the cash register. One of the classifieds seemed to be just what I wanted:

> *Liberated person needed to share 3-storied house w/2w,*
> *1m. You help in house, garden, get privacy, fresh vegs.*
> *$90/mo.*

The address was on Beauchamp Street. I asked the cashier if she knew where it was. North of downtown, she said. Pronounced *bee-chum*. Sort of run-down, but gentrified around the edges. Lots of big oak trees and old houses. A mixed neighborhood—Chicanos, Blacks, old couples, student types.

I loaded my salad with alfalfa sprouts to get in the mood and then biked up to Beauchamp. I thought about removing the studded leather armband from my left biceps, but decided against it. If I moved in, they'd figure out where I was coming from soon enough. Better to start out being open.

The house was set on a corner and dominated everything around it, a fine example of Texas Victoriana, with lots of decorative carved wood, yellow clapboard walls, and a green shingle roof. The successive stories were set back in tiers; a jumble of gables directed my eyes up to the octagonal room at the top, where the domed roof came to a point. It seemed perched on the house like an eagle's nest, high above the tops of the oaks and pecan trees.

The yard was like a jungle, dense and green. Shady trees, century plants, stands of wild bamboo, even a few spindly yuccas. The more I saw, the more I liked it.

Two women were sitting on the front porch. As I walked up, they stopped talking and looked me over. They were both dressed in loose, lacy cotton dresses and sandals, and wore their hair long and frizzy.

Their names were Karen and Sharon. Karen wore thick glasses. Sharon wore contacts. Karen smoked lots of dope and was addicted to science-fiction magazines. Sharon smoked lots of dope and rode a Harley, which gave us something to talk about. Sharon left after a while to do some shopping; Karen gave me a walk-through.

The first-floor ceilings were twelve feet high. All the wallpaper had been stripped off, baring the dark lumber beneath. The women had separate rooms on the first floor. There was also a big bathroom, a living room, a library (shelf after shelf of *Analog* and *Fantasy and*

Science Fiction), and a cavernous kitchen with yellow plaster walls. There was a poster of Janis Joplin over the refrigerator.

A back door off the kitchen opened onto a small wooden porch. They had turned the back yard into a big garden, with rows and rows of tomatoes and sunflowers.

"Now I'll show you your room," Karen said.

The stairway was narrow and steep. The second floor was much smaller, with a short, dark hallway that led to a bathroom at one end and a bedroom at the other. The room had a low ceiling and bare walls. It was narrow and U-shaped, with windows facing all around. The drapes were gray with age and dirt. The furniture consisted of an old dresser, a few chairs, and a mattress on the floor. I told Karen I liked it.

As we stepped back into the hallway, I looked up the last flight of steps. They ended in a trapdoor.

"You might as well see the rest of the house," Karen offered. "I think Michael's out. I'm sure he wouldn't mind if we take a peek." I followed her up the short flight. She pushed the door open a few inches and peered inside, her eyes at floor level.

"Just want to make sure there aren't any burnt offerings or spilled entrails oh the floor," she said.

"Huh?"

Karen laughed. "Just kidding. Sort of. Michael's into some pretty weird stuff." She pushed the trapdoor open. "Come on up."

At first I couldn't see much for the darkness. As my eyes adjusted, I blinked in amazement.

We were in the octagonal room at the top of the house. There were four walls painted deep purple separated by four walls with windows. The windows were covered by heavy black drapes that admitted no light. I wondered where the faint illumination came from, then realized it was concentrated in a bar in the center of the room. I looked up. A tiny stained-glass skylight shaped like an eight-pointed star was set in the center of the high ceiling.

"Michael owns the place. You may not meet him for a while. He keeps odd hours, eats up here in his room. . . ."

The room was crowded with ornaments and furnishings. There was a large four-poster bed against one wall, ancient-looking wooden caskets with bronze hinges, a huge wooden chair that looked like a medieval throne. Squat candles were set all about the room. Pentacles and other symbols, indistinct in the dim light, were painted in white on the dark purple walls and high domed ceiling.

I glanced at a bookcase close by. Only a few of the authors were familiar: Dennis Wheatley, Aleister Crowley, Anton Szandor LaVey.

"He's a Satanist?" I asked, mildly curious. I had met stranger types.

"Michael? Oh, no!" She laughed. "I mean, he doesn't hold black masses or anything like that. At least I don't think so. Actually, I don't know what he does up here. Sharon and I stay pretty much on the ground floor."

I moved in that afternoon.

That evening I ate in the kitchen with Sharon and Karen. I kept expecting to see my third housemate, but he never showed.

After a hard day of moving, I decided to reward myself with an evening out. I checked out a couple of bars and ended up at one of the baths. I stumbled in around four in the morning, trying not to make too much noise on the creaky stairs. I noticed there was a thin edge of light around the trapdoor to the octagonal room.

I woke up hung over and headachy sometime in the late morning. Sunlight was streaming in the room. I got up to close the drapes. One of the windows looked down on the garden. I saw a man there, shoveling.

From the steep angle I couldn't see much except his head and shoulders. He was wearing dirty white overalls. His hair was long and black, almost to his waist, and pulled back in a ponytail. His untanned shoulders were broad and scalloped with muscles that undulated as he dug the shovel into the earth and scooped it out.

He suddenly stood up straight, turned toward the house, and looked up at me.

He was tall, easily over six feet. The overalls fit tight around his waist, emphasizing the striking width of his chest and shoulders. Sweat made the sunlight glimmer in the smooth, deep cleft between his pectorals. His smooth cheeks and forehead were spotted with dirt. I was struck by how white his skin was, like ivory. He rested one hand on the shovel at his side and raised the other to wipe the sweat from his forehead.

I stood naked at the full-length window as we looked at each other—naked except for the leather band around my left arm, which never comes off. I tried to smile, despite the pain cracking my head. Now, why couldn't I have run into *that* at the baths last night, I thought. Then I closed the drapes and stumbled back to bed.

When I finally made my way downstairs, I noticed he was no longer in the garden. Karen told me he was up in his room. Working, she said.

"What does he do?"

"I don't really know." She shrugged. "I say 'working' because he doesn't like anybody to disturb him when he's upstairs."

I took the hint.

There was no sign of him for several days. I wanted another look at those broad shoulders and muscular arms. It became a mild obsession.

I placed my bed opposite the door to my room and left the door open in the evenings. I lounged shirtless on the bed, reading or smoking, keeping an eye on the hallway. Sooner or later I'd see him pass by.

That was how I spent my evenings that first week in the house, waiting for a chance to meet Michael. Somehow he eluded me.

I must have read Karen's entire collection of *Amazing Stories* that week.

It became a game. It's my nature to win games. Or so I thought.

Finally, on Friday night, I heard footsteps on the lower stairway. Not the slap of Karen's or Sharon's sandals, but a heavier tread.

I lowered the magazine just enough to peer over it, and watched as a man appeared headfirst in the hallway. It wasn't Michael. But he easily drove Michael from my mind.

He was blond, with short hair, a square jaw, and a mustache, and was dressed in a tight sleeveless shirt that showed off muscular, golden-fleeced arms and a rippled chest. He looked more than a little like me, in fact.

I glanced at his crotch, but his chinos were too baggy to show a bulge. Instead, I found myself studying the way his nipples pressed against his shirt.

He was obviously gay, or so I thought. When his eyes met mine, I tried to lock him in with a steady gaze. I said hello. But he seemed to look straight through me, completely indifferent, and only mumbled in reply. He took the final flight up to the trapdoor. I craned my neck and saw him disappear into an arc of soft yellow light. The pants kept his crotch a mystery, but they couldn't have flattered his ass more.

I got up from bed and tiptoed into the hall. I looked up at the closed trapdoor. It was quiet for a while, then I heard voices, louder than normal, an argument of some sort. One voice was much lower than the other.

There was a shuffle of heavy footsteps overhead. I almost bolted for my room, thinking one of them was about to leave. Then the argument resumed. A silence, and their voices returned, quieter. Another silence, then shouting. Then a quiet that went on so long I decided they had made up and gone to bed.

I returned to my room. Just as I sat on the bed, wondering

where I had put my Houston bar guide, there was a dim light from the hallway and the sound of feet descending the upper stairs. It was the blond man, leaving in such a hurry that I couldn't even get another glimpse of his face.

A few minutes later, the trapdoor opened again. The game was about to pay off.

I had been waiting all week for a good look at him, remembering his naked shoulders, his beautiful long black hair. The night was warm. I was horny. My cock was hard. It showed as a thick ridge in my jeans. My chest was covered with a thin sheen of sweat. I rose from the bed and stepped into the hallway just as Michael did.

His black hair was unbound and hung straight, parted in the middle. It was sleek and thick like combed silk.

He had one of those paradoxical faces that look more masculine with long hair than short. His eyes were dark brown, with long lashes and straight black eyebrows. He had a wide mouth and full lips that looked red and moist against his pale cheeks. He looked like he was barely into his early twenties. He had to be older than that, I thought, to own his own house.

His body was even better than I had thought. Huge, square-muscled shoulders. Hard, round biceps with a pale blue vein running down each arm. His pectorals rose slablike above his rib cage, sleek and hairless, with nipples the size of half dollars. His stomach was an expanse of gentle ridges that funneled down to narrow, muscle-flat hips. The twin arcs of his pelvis were as deep and defined as Michelangelo's David.

He was wearing nothing but a pair of white nylon briefs, so sheer that his big flaccid cock and balls nestled visibly inside. Below, his legs were fluid pillars of muscle, like white marble. In the light reflected from the bare wood, he seemed to shine with a pale amber glow.

He smiled faintly. "You must be the new guy." His voice sounded almost artificially deep.

"Yeah," I said, extending my arm. He caught my hand in his and we shook fingers-up, head-style, the way hippies and bikers used to. "I'm Bill Gray."

"Michael Black. Black and Gray, huh? That's cute." There was not a trace of humor in his voice.

Our hands stayed locked together as I looked into his deep brown eyes. He lowered his gaze, taking in my body as I had taken in his.

Then he broke the handshake. "Be seeing you," he said, and walked to the bathroom. The long black hair fanned over his wide shoulders. His ass, small and round with muscle, seemed to shimmer inside the nylon briefs. I noticed for the first time just how large his legs were. My two hands wouldn't have met around his calves.

The next morning I asked Karen about the blond visitor. "Oh, that must have been Carl," she said. "He used to live here. In your room."

After that first meeting, I saw Michael only rarely and in passing. He seemed to keep odd hours, even odder than mine. He was never rude, but always distant.

I knew he was gay. The blond hunk Carl turned out to be a regular visitor, sometimes coming three or four times a week. Carl was so oblivious of me and of the band around my left arm, I decided he had to be another top. I knew they liked rough sex. Very rough. I could hear them above me at night. Flesh striking flesh with a sweaty crack. Heavier blows—the distinct whoosh and snap of a belt, or a whip. Knees knocking on the wooden floor as someone crawled back and forth, grunting.

I would have him, I told myself. I would make him do more than grunt.

No matter how often I went out, no matter how many other men I met, I found my fantasies returning to Michael. When I masturbated at night, he was the one I thought of. It was his pale skin and the long hair that set him apart, matched with his larger-than-life physique; the combination of sultry brown eyes and an innocent, nature-boy face. I wanted to own him, to possess him, to devour him.

It was a game, and I would win it. I would see his pretty face all slack and hungry, his brown eyes gazing up into mine while his thick red lips were stretched around my nine inches. I would hear him gag on it and groan. I would twist that deep grunting voice into a high-pitched whimper. I imagined him naked, erect, on his knees—arms twisted and bound behind his back, his big chest thrust up sleek and vulnerable, his long hair making him look like a conquered savage. I knew how to make those big flat nipples stand up red and swollen.

His ass had limitless possibilities. Every mark would show across the pale drum-tight flesh.

His hair would have its uses. To inflict pain, to bring hot tears to his eyes. To twist around his neck like a collar. To use as reins when I rode his face like a saddle, or mounted him like a steed. Later it might have a more important use—as a final act of humiliation, I would force him to shave it, stripping away his last shred of resistance, like Samson, chained and degraded. His naked skull would mark him as my slave for all the world to see.

I had gotten what I wanted from other men. I would get what I wanted from him. I had plans for Michael Black.

My chance came the next Saturday. I got up around noon, feeling lazy and relaxed, ready for anything. I slipped into a pair of jeans and went down to the kitchen.

The door to the back porch was open. Michael was sitting on the steps, looking at the garden. I stepped outside and sat beside him.

"Mind if I join you?"

"No." He glanced up at me, then looked back at the garden. He was wearing a pair of jeans that hugged him from crotch to calves like a glove, and a white tank top that looked a size too small around his shoulders but hung loosely below his pecs.

"You must work out a lot," I said.

"Couple of hours every day. And Lan-Tzu class three times a week." He glanced at my naked chest. "You too?"

I shrugged. "Not since I was in New York. I haven't found a gym here yet. You don't get much sun, though. Burn easy?"

"No," he said. "I'm just not crazy about sunlight. I'm basically a nocturnal animal." He picked up a joint and a book of matches from a lower step. He lit it, inhaled, and offered it to me wordlessly. I shook my head.

"Gave it up about a year ago, when it started doing strange trips on my head. Thanks, though."

"Too bad. Sharon grows some pretty mean weed in the garden." He exhaled through clenched teeth. "It helps me focus my power."

Whatever turns you on, I thought.

"You're not originally from Houston, are you?" I asked.

"No. Born in Utah. Then Southern California."

"Why would you leave that for this?"

"Too much sun out there, for one thing." He smiled. "And work's easier here."

"Oh? I didn't think you worked."

"I work," he said coolly. I got the idea he didn't care to talk about it. But after another hit, he elaborated. "I supply special experiences for people who can pay. Experiences they can't get anywhere else. I like Houston because people here have lots of money and not much imagination. They ask for easy stuff, and pay through the nose for it. Not like the Coast." He shook his head. "People there wanted heavy trips, really taxed my energy. And there are more of us out there. Here, I'm a rarity."

The joint was making him talkative. It was pretty murky, but I got the idea: he was a hustler. He had a very special appeal; the paying market might be small, but he had a corner on it. There must be plenty of rich hayseeds in Houston who'd pay to stick it to a muscular young longhair.

I decided to play dumb. "Shit, man—you mean sex?"

He stared straight ahead, his jaw tight, and took another hit. "Sometimes. But I don't always charge for that. I enjoy myself too much." He gave me a Mona Lisa smile.

I smiled back. I'd never paid to screw a guy, and I didn't intend to start, even with Michael.

We sat in silence until he finished the joint. He turned his face to mine. His brown eyes seemed to sparkle. His jaw slackened. A real stone puppy, I thought, ready to curl up in the palm of my hand. I slid my fingers over his thigh and onto his cock, rock hard and thick inside the tight denim.

"Wanna go upstairs?" I said.

He paused, staring at my face. I stared back and squeezed his cock until I got the answer I wanted.

"Sure."

I followed him inside and up the stairs. "My room," he said, as we emerged on the first landing. I followed him up through the trapdoor.

He made a circuit of the room, lighting candles until the chamber glowed with soft amber light. He pulled a cord that slid a cover over the tiny skylight, leaving only candlelight for illumination. It was high noon outside, but here it was midnight. He made another circuit of the room, pulling open the black velvet drapes. The four windows had been sealed over on the inside. In their place were full-length mirrors.

The deep darkness above, the dim light, the mirrors all around, made it impossible to sense the true dimensions of the room. It seemed to expand into infinity, endlessly reflected in the opposing mirrors. I was in his private world now, a place outside of time and space.

The effect was very special, secretive and hypnotic. And promising. Michael had imagination.

I walked to the middle of the room. I could feel my cock pulsing against my left leg. Michael finished his preparations and stood before me, his face quizzical, his hands at his sides.

"Take off your clothes," I said.

He looked at me for a moment, expressionless. Then he grabbed the bottom seam of his tank top and pulled it over his shoulders. Suddenly I knew who he reminded me of: Li'l Abner, the cartoon hillbilly who used to be in the Sunday comics when I was a kid—the exaggerated shoulders and chest, the wasp waist, the bulging thighs and calves.

"Yeah," I breathed. "Now your pants."

They were so tight he had to peel them off, turning them inside out. His balance never faltered as he bent over and lifted his feet. He was as graceful as a dancer.

He stood and slid his fingers under the waistband of the clinging briefs.

"Leave those on," I said quietly. I wanted to save the sight of his naked ass for later. His cock was hard, causing a bulge that pulled the waistband an inch from his flat belly.

I took my time, trying to stare him down. Michael never lowered his eyes. I could read no expression in them.

"Come here," I said. He walked to me slowly. It was breathtaking, just to watch him move. Even the simple act of walking he performed with animal grace, fluid and sexual.

He stopped a foot away, looming above me. I didn't like his face being above mine. It wouldn't be for long.

He raised his right hand to touch the leather band around my left biceps. "You have a beautiful body," he said softly. He brought his hands to my chest and combed his fingers through the thick mat of blond hair. "Like Carl," he whispered.

I grabbed his wrists and pushed his hands to my crotch.

"Take it out."

He looked down as he unbuttoned my jeans, spread the flaps,

and circled his fingers around the thick base of my cock. He had to use both hands to pull it out.

He held it tightly. I saw a strange smile on his downturned face. He weighed it in his hands.

"Yeah. Big and heavy. Just like Carl's."

"Then get on your knees and suck it. Just like you suck Carl's cock."

Michael knelt. In the mirrors to my left and right I saw his body, lean and sleek in profile. I watched the head of my cock slide between his lips and shuddered at the contact. In the mirror before me I saw his back-thrust ass inside the translucent briefs. I twisted the hair at the nape of his neck into a single cord and used it to hold his head in place.

His back was untouched. Maybe Carl didn't want to see that ivory perfection marred by welts. Michael would find out soon enough where the comparisons ended between Carl and me.

I yanked his head forward and gave a sudden thrust with my hips, trying to catch him off guard. Start him off gagging. Get his saliva running. Make him take it my way from the very start.

But it slid down his throat without a hitch. I looked down at his upturned face. His eyes were shut; the long lashes flickered. His cheeks were drawn taut. His thick red lips circled the base of my shaft. His jaw was thrust sharply into my balls. His throat was distended, packed with a solid truncheon of flesh.

I fucked his face hard and deep, never pulling more than halfway out, watching his throat expand and contract as I pumped into him. The candlelight flashed on the trickles of spit that ran from the corners of his mouth onto his corded neck. I kept expecting him to protest and push me away, gasping for breath, but he seemed resigned to letting me fuck his face as long and as hard as I wanted.

I finally pulled his head back by a fistful of hair and emptied his throat with a jerk. Keep him cock-hungry, I thought. He leaned back, gasping. His mouth and chin were wet with spittle. His lips glistened in the firelight.

I rested my cockhead against his lower lip while he caught his breath. He swallowed hard and spoke in a murmur, moving his wet lips over the knob of my cockhead. "You must have some toys down in your room." He rolled his eyes up to mine.

"Yeah," I said. "In a wooden locker by my bed." I reached down to gently squeeze his nipple. "Be a good boy and go fetch it."

While he was gone I stripped off my jeans. I flexed my upper body and looked at my reflection in the mirrors. Michael had said I had a fine body—a real compliment coming from a man with such an exceptional physique. And why not? I wasn't as tall as he was, or as broad; but I was thicker in the chest, more compact. The years I had spent working off the anxieties of New York through sweat and hard exercise had paid off, many times.

I liked the difference in our bodies. My deep tan and stark tan line against his pale flesh, the rich golden hair on my chest and limbs against his sleek nudity. The nine-inch column of flesh that stuck up from my crotch, and that hard round ass of his, waiting to be split wide open. I pumped my left arm and watched the biceps strain against the studded band.

Michael returned. He knelt and placed the long box at my feet.

"Go ahead," I told him. "Open it. If you see something you like—ask for it."

He lifted the lid and gazed down at the jumble of steel and leather. He noticed the dozen varieties of tit clamps. He picked up a chain-linked pair and stared at them.

"You're really into pain," he murmured naively. "You like to put these on other men's nipples. Twist them. Pull on them. A way to put pain in them. Make them whimper and beg."

"Uh-huh," I said dryly, answering his innocent act with a smirk. "You've got big tits. Probably take two clamps each."

Michael put the clamps back in the box. Afraid of them, I thought. Good.

He took out a pair of padded handcuffs. "To bind them. Put them at your mercy. So they can't strike back. So you can feel free to use them however you want."

"That's right." I spread my legs and stroked my cock with two fingers. It was throbbing at maximum erection, almost achingly hard.

He set the cuffs aside, on the floor, then took out my pride and joy. My riding crop, an intricately twined handle with a thin two-foot tongue of stiff leather. It had been a gift from a not-very-shy trick in the Village. "It's yours, Bill," he had said, "if you'll use it on me." And I had. I was amazed Michael had the nerve to choose it.

"And you use this on their naked skin, as if they were animals." His tone was fascinated but detached, as if he were an observer, taking inventory. He really knew how to ask for it.

He looked up at me with those deep brown eyes. "Is that what you want to do with me, Bill? Cuff my hands behind my back, clamp my nipples? Make me crawl after your big cock, beat me, fuck my ass?"

His deep voice, low and soft, reverberated in my head. I felt the rush of a perfect moment. "That's right, Michael. Now hand me the crop."

He held it horizontal, offering it with both hands. I took it by the handle and ran the tongue through my fist. I touched the tip against his chest and gently tapped his nipple. Then I drew it up and cracked it across my thigh to make him flinch.

But he didn't flinch.

Instead his face seemed to harden, to become steady and purposeful.

He rose to his feet and stared down at me. Suddenly my whole left arm went limp, as if the nerves had been severed. The riding crop slipped from my hand. I didn't hear it hit the floor. I tried to look down, and found that I couldn't take my eyes from his.

"Stay." His quiet voice boomed deeply in the silence.

And I stood, my body relaxed but paralyzed, as he walked to a casket across the room. I couldn't turn my head to watch him. I was forced to stare straight ahead into the mirror. It reflected the fear and astonishment frozen on my face.

Michael returned. Several lengths of thin chain were looped over his forearm.

He slowly circled me, examining my naked body. I felt like an insect paralyzed in a spider's web, waiting to be eaten alive. But I didn't panic. My mind seemed to be slowing down, shifting into neutral, losing touch with reality. I should never have smoked that weed, I thought, then remembered I hadn't.

I tried to open my mouth to ask him what the hell he had done to me. But I couldn't speak. My jaw was frozen.

He had said he was into some sort of martial art. Paralysis with a touch? But he hadn't touched me. There was no way he could have drugged me.

He ran his hands over my body, exploring my back and arms, cupping my pecs and buns. He inserted his middle finger into my mouth to wet it and slid it gently up my ass. My mouth stayed open, as his finger had left it.

He stood beside me and spoke in my ear, keeping his long middle finger inside me, gently probing. He wet his other hand in my mouth and stroked my cock. I watched in the mirror—his lean profile, the rolling muscles in his stroking arm, my mouth left gaping open like an idiot's.

"I've been paid twenty-five thousand dollars for what I'm about to do to you, Bill." Stroking, probing. "But that was for a man who wanted it. Or thought he did. And he wasn't very attractive. You are, Bill. Big cock. Hard ass." He frowned at my chest. "All that hair is unfortunate. It hides your muscles. You'll look better after the hoop."

He slid his finger from my ass, gave my cock a hard squeeze, and released it. He stood before me and slipped the chains from his forearm. There were two of them, one quite long, the other the length of a bracelet. They were made like dog chokers, with nooses and sliding rings to control the pressure.

He put the bigger chain over my head and pulled it tight around my neck. The metal was as cold as ice, unnaturally cold. The loose end hung between my pecs. Then he slid the smaller chain over my cock and balls, circled them tight and left the end dangling from the underside of my testicles.

He bent over and retrieved the padded handcuffs, twisted my arms behind my back, and cuffed my wrists. He stood in front of me and smiled grimly.

"And now this," he said, "since symbols are so important to both of us." He unsnapped the leather band from my arm. I felt as if my last protection had been stripped from me. He tried to fit it over his own left biceps, but the muscle was too big. Instead, he slipped it over my right arm and snapped it tight.

He stepped aside so I could see myself in the mirror. Naked. Cock hard and circled with cold steel. Arms bound. Choker around my neck. Leather strap on the right, marking my subservience. I groaned inside, confused and helpless. In five minutes, against my will, he had completely reversed our roles. And I had no idea how he had done it.

Then, as fogged as my mind was, I noticed something. I couldn't be certain in the dim light, but the silver chains around my neck and cock seemed to glow faintly, circled by a ghostly blue light. As I watched, the blue aura grew stronger, until I saw it clearly in the glass, like wisps of phosphorescent blue mist around my neck and between my legs.

I was not afraid—not quite. Not yet. A numbness was seeping into my head, a comfortable sense of detachment. Damn it, I thought, maybe he slipped me a drug of some kind. But I knew, somehow, that the chilly numbness wasn't in my head. It was radiating from those cold blue chains.

Michael returned. With both hands he held what looked like a hoop of glass tubing, two feet in diameter. The hoop glowed, like blue neon.

Silently he positioned the ring above my head and lowered it slowly to the floor. As it passed around my body it seemed to shed a cocoon of light behind. I saw myself in the mirror, encased in a cylinder of blue haze.

"Now we wait," Michael said, "to let the energy soak in." He cocked his head, looking me up and down as he groped himself inside his nylon briefs. His dark, handsome face went slack with lust—lips parted, eyes narrowed, sexed up.

I felt the hair on my body stand up straight, as if charged with static electricity. Something weird was happening in the mirror. I saw a mass of suspended particles in the space between my body and the cocoon of blue light, too vague to make out in the mirror. I tried to look down. My neck was paralyzed. Michael saw me straining. He reached inside the light and pushed my face down.

My body was being stripped of its hair. The process was silent, painless; magic, I suppose. The short hairs detached themselves from my skin and drifted slowly through the light-suffused air, made contact with the field of circling blue light—and disappeared.

At first the air was choked with free-floating strands, silky yellow ones from my chest and arms and legs, kinky darker ones from my crotch. Then the migration grew sparser, until I saw the last curly strand unfurl from my left nipple, stand straight, and pull free. It wafted gently like a weightless mote of dust, drew steadily toward the barrier of light, touched it—vanished.

I had been shaved once before, long ago. Before the muscles, before the armband, before the Harley. The job had taken hours, and left me with nicks around the base of my cock and around my tits. The master had not been pleased with the effect—he said it made me look too much like a boy instead of a man. Since shaving had been my idea, not his, he had punished me afterward with a razor strop.

My skin had been city-pale then, my body undeveloped. I hadn't liked the look either; the hairlessness seemed to expose every flaw. Now, gazing down at myself in the blue light, I was mesmerized by the smooth planes of my chest, all tan flesh and ridges of muscle, clearer than I had ever seen them before. My nipples looked naked somehow, vulnerable. My cock, still as hard as when I pulled it from Michael's throat, reared up big and stiff from my denuded crotch, the tight chain around the base fully exposed. There was no stubble. My body was as sleek as Michael's.

"It'll grow back," he said. He grabbed the hair on my head—thank god he had not taken that—and pulled my face up.

It was as if I saw another man in the mirror. A hunky blond slave, totally hairless, his mouth hanging open like a dog's, his cock hard for his master.

Michael moved in front of me, blocking my reflection.

"You've got to trust me, Bill. Relax. Give in. You remember how to give in. Cooperate, do your part, and you won't be hurt. Understand?"

No, I didn't understand. Nothing made sense. All I knew was that he had me in his power—literally, completely. *I've been paid twenty-five thousand dollars for what I'm about to do to you. But that was for a man who wanted it. Or thought he did.*

He slipped a finger through the steel ring at the end of the chain that hung from my neck and pulled it toward him, tightening the choker. He licked his other hand and put it on my throat, kneading and exploring with slick fingers. The choker pulled tighter. I felt my windpipe flatten.

"Don't be frightened," he whispered. How could I not be frightened—he was strangling me. The chain pulled tighter and tighter. My throat grew numb under his fingertips. I couldn't breathe. My paralyzed body convulsed.

Then—I heard a rattling of metal and saw his right hand pull away. The choker dangled free from his forefinger. I felt myself being lifted up—a sensation of weightlessness and vertigo—the room fell and whirled around me. I tried to scream with horror, and couldn't. I caught a glimpse of something in one of the mirrors—my body, stock-still within the blue light field—Michael standing aside—holding something in his hands—holding—my head—

I blacked out. Only for an instant, I think. Then I was looking up at Michael. He was holding my face between his hands. He sat in the thronelike chair, leaning back with his ass on the edge. My head was between his thighs.

His briefs were gone. His cock loomed above my face. Beyond, his flat-muscled stomach was bunched into tight folds of flesh beneath the sculpted domes of his pecs. His eyes were on mine. The look on his face frightened me—a look of contempt and total control.

"Stop twisting your face up, Bill. It makes you ugly. Cock, Bill. My cock. Look at it."

It hovered over me, white and thick. It was perfect, like the rest of his body. Alabaster white and enormously thick, tapered slightly at the base. The head was huge. The skin was pearly white and translucent, as smooth as glass, showing deep blue veins within. The circumcision ring was almost unnoticeable, the color of cream. The shaft looked as hard as marble, but spongy and fat, as if it were covered by a sheath of rubbery flesh. I could feel its heat on my face.

"My cock, Bill. Taste it." He rubbed my face all over his meat. I felt its fullness on my cheeks and nose. The big head pressed against each of my eyes in turn.

"Lick it. Lick my cock, Bill." I opened my mouth—able to move it now—and stuck out my tongue. He slid my drooling mouth over his meat, flattened my tongue against the bulging shaft, ran it over the beveled edge of his cockhead, allowed me to probe into the deep slit at the tip.

He pushed my face onto his shaft and filled my mouth with his cockhead. It came back to me, the old days, when this was what I craved from other men, the privilege of feeling their meat warm and solid in my mouth. I realized he was trying to pacify me—giving me something big to suck on to make me forget the shock of what had just happened—or what I imagined had happened.

I rolled my eyes up and drew on the massive beauty of his chest and arms the way my mouth was drawing on his massive cock. My throat had grown thick with saliva—I tried to swallow, found I couldn't, just as I couldn't speak—realized I wasn't even breathing. The accumulated spittle frothed around my lips and oozed over his shaft.

He pushed my face all the way onto his cock. There was a bruising pain as it entered my gullet, as if he were shoving a beer bottle down my throat. I retched, and spattered his balls and thighs with spit. I was gagging, but not choking—how could I choke when my breathing had stopped?

His hips never moved. He forced my head up and down, driving my throat onto his shaft and pulling back till my lips caught on the ridge of the head.

He fucked my face that way, using it like a cored melon or a pillow, for what seemed like hours. He took it slow, pleasuring himself, as if he were alone in his room masturbating. In and out of my throat, with slow luxurious strokes. Then bursts of violence—pushing my face into his groin, flattening my nose against his steel-hard belly, grinding deep and hard, making my throat convulse and ripple around his shaft. Juices ran from my stuffed mouth until his lap was slick with spittle and pre-cum.

My mind settled into a profound calm. I was aware, alert. But there was a sensation of timelessness, disembodiment. I was outside any normal dimension, as if, freed from breath, freed from my body, I was beyond panic or pain.

He coaxed me through clenched teeth, his voice low, his mammoth chest heaving so I knew he was close. "It feels good down your throat, doesn't it, Bill? My cock in your mouth. What you really wanted from me, what you need. To have your throat crammed with meat. You're a born cocksucker, Bill." He would get close that way—I could feel his cock spurting pre-cum—then pull me off till I held only the head. Hold off, catch his breath. And start over again. Until my jaw hung open like a broken hinge. Until his surging tube of meat felt a part of me, and I couldn't tell where my throat ended and his thick shaft began.

He got close again. Pulled my mouth off his cock. Held my head up by a fist in my hair, his other fist around his cock. The shaft glistened in the candlelight beneath a thick glaze of spit. He stroked himself haltingly. His hips bucked gently. On the brink.

His eyes were almost closed. The pupils flashed like sparks between the long, dark lashes.

"I'm gonna come now, Bill. Yeah." He hissed with pleasure. "My cock is gonna shoot. You want it in your mouth? Sure you do. The big bad leather boy wants my come in his mouth. Then beg for it, Bill. Beg me to shoot it down your fucking throat."

I tried. My lips couldn't even shape the words. I flexed my jaw, twisted my tongue, and curled my lips like a spastic. There was no sound except the hollow gurgling of the mucus in my throat.

Michael cried out and pushed my face onto it, down to the base. It jerked in my throat like a startled snake. His fingers bit into the base of my skull like pincers. A wild animal roar filled the darkness. I instinctively tried to swallow as the pumping started. His come clogged my throat, backflushed into my mouth. It tasted bitter and strong.

He held me down on his pulsing meat for a long time. No need to pull out. I didn't need to come up for air.

I rolled my eyes up to look at his heaving chest, sheened with sweat, and his face, beautiful and composed except for sudden moments when his eyebrows drew together and he whimpered like a puppy having a bad dream. At those moments his cock would give a little jerk.

He pulled me off at last. My mouth and throat were so full of spittle and bitter semen that it ran like slag over my chin. Thick ropes of mucus were strung from my lips to his big soft cock.

He rested my head on his shoulder and held it there while he recovered. The seeping fluids ran from the corner of my mouth onto his chest and down to his crotch.

Straining my eyes to one side, I saw a reflection of my body in one of the mirrors, still frozen in the cocoon of light. Where my head should have been, there was only darkness. I felt a dizzy fear, but it was muted by the dim light, the unaccountable sensation of freedom, the memory of his cock. Vaguely, I knew fear would serve no purpose. My only hope was to trust him.

At last he opened his eyes. He saw that I was looking at my abandoned body.

"It's true," he said softly. "You're not crazy. It's no illusion. You're here, your body is there. It's one of the things I do." He took a deep breath. My head rose and fell on his chest like a cork on a wave.

"You can handle it, Bill. I knew when I first saw you. Despite the armband on the left. Despite the heavy come-on. You know how to give a man what he wants. How to give in, even if he's handing you pain, degrading your ego. Well, this is what *I* want, Bill. This is what turns me on. I'm going to do what I want with you. You've got no choice."

The room whirled around—weightlessness again—then settled. Michael was standing over me, his big cock slick and half hard above my face. He had placed my head on the chair. I could smell steamy sweat, where his ass and thighs had rested on the wood.

"It will help," he said, "if you think of it as another man's body." He walked to the center of the room and circled the headless body immobilized there. I glanced around; the chair was set so that I couldn't catch a reflection of my face. But I saw my body reflected all around in the mirrors. There was no bloody stump where my head should be—only the smooth, natural depression inside my collarbone.

It was a beautiful body, I had to admit. I suppose anyone who has seen his body harden and fill out from hard work becomes a narcissist. Looking at my body in the dim light, studying the play of light and shadow across the sleek flesh, I felt a strange quiver of desire. It was crazy, something was wrong in my head that I could look at my body and feel such cool detachment. At the time, I didn't realize that. I was where Michael had put me, in some strange psychic zone.

That body turned me on. The hairlessness showed off my muscles, as Michael had said it would. Everything looked larger, fuller. Especially my pecs, big mounds of sleek muscle. The nipples, normally buried in swirls of hair, stood out from the taut flesh, looking exquisitely sensitive, begging to be touched. My cock and balls, hairless and chained, looked larger than life, but not commanding; exposed and vulnerable. *Do it,* I begged silently. *I want to see it crawl. I want it.*

Michael stooped and took hold of the glowing blue hoop on the floor. He did not pull it up and over my shoulders, but sideways, through my legs, as if the hoop were made of nothing but light.

"Yeah, another man's body," he crooned. "Hairless. Handcuffed. Nude." He flicked one of the erect nipples. The body flinched. He circled around. "Fantastic ass. I like the way the tan line frames those cheeks." He slid a fingertip over the crack. I saw my buttocks tighten—and felt it—in a way—far off. A ghost sensation, the way an amputee might feel a lost limb. Like being in two places at once.

He stood beside the handcuffed body and looked in my eyes. He grabbed one of the hairless nipples between his finger and thumb and pulled downward until the captive body was forced to bend sharply at the waist.

"A slave's body, Bill. A big hunky stud in handcuffs. How shall we use him? We can do anything we want. Things you haven't dreamed of."

Michael took two tit clamps from the box on the floor. I groaned inside when I saw them. Alligator clamps with powerful springs, the ones I used only on my most advanced and jaded partners, and then only as a test or a punishment. Michael approached my body. It stood relaxed, unseeing, unsuspecting. He squeezed my pecs and kneaded my nipples, until I saw my stomach draw taut and my chest rise in silent offering.

Michael smiled. He placed one open clamp over my right nipple and let it snap shut.

Far away, I could feel the sharp teeth penetrate my flesh. I saw my body jerk wildly, tugging at the handcuffs, trying to retreat. But Michael slipped a finger into the chain dangling from my balls and held my body in check. He watched my chest spasm and writhe, touched his fingers to the knotted muscles in my arms and belly. Then he attached the second clamp.

My body twisted so violently the cock chain snapped from Michael's knuckle. I watched the body stumble to its knees, scramble up, and stagger blindly into one of the mirrors, crazy with pain.

Michael picked up the riding crop and walked with long slow strides to the crouching, trembling body. He raised the leather high above his head and slashed it across my shoulders.

My body jerked, spun, rolled away—staggered to its feet, tripped over my pants on the floor, rose desperately, ran blindly into a wall—turned and took a defensive stance, hiding its stinging shoulders against the wall. Tits clamped and cock hard. I couldn't understand that, the way my cock stayed so stiff the whole time—not yet.

Michael followed slowly. He looked at the crop. Looked at my chest, muscles in high relief, tense with pain. He touched the crop to my cock. My body flinched. Michael squeezed his hard-on. Then he raised the crop and slashed it backhanded across my stomach.

I saw my body double over and run, reeling with pain and confusion, trying to escape. Michael followed it patiently around the room, taking his time, stroking his thick white cock and wielding the crop. Like a hunter, exhausting his trapped game. Playing with me.

At last the pain-wracked body collapsed kneeling in the center of the room. Shoulders against the floor, heaving—ass thrust in the air.

Michael stood over the broken body. He slowly masturbated as he beat my ass with the crop, blow after blow, until the pale buns were red and blistered.

Michael discarded the crop, grabbed my body by the clamps, and forced it to stand. In the reflections I could see every mark— the long red stripes across my shoulders, the back of my legs, my stomach. My cock—a slave's cock, rock hard after the beating, veins pulsing, dribbling from the tip. I suddenly knew why—the body craved it, but so did my head, watching, crazy with excitement at the spectacle. Two places at once. Masochistic victim, and sadistic observer of my own humiliation, wanting more.

Michael played with the clamps—twisted, pulled the hard flat muscles into sharp peaks, watched my body twitch and heave. He pulled the clamps off, one at a time, and tossed them away. He caressed my body, watching the skin writhe when his fingertips brushed over the tender stripes.

He cocked his head and flashed me a cryptic smile. "Good slave body. Takes it well. Ready for whatever's next. Shall I fuck it?"

He rubbed his hard cock against mine. "Sure. Give him what he wants. But do it *my* way."

He hooked his finger through the dangling cock choker and pulled it taut. Tighter and tighter. The chain sank into the gathered flesh, my cock bulged until I thought the skin would burst. I knew what was about to happen, and my mind plummeted deeper into the numb stupor that was its only protection.

Michael licked his free hand. His saliva seemed to glow with blue light. He worked his wet fingers mysteriously around my cock and balls. I saw his lips move, as if he were whispering inaudibly. The thin chain flashed with blue flame—

Then the chain slipped through. He dropped it quickly and raised his hand to lift the genitals free. He held the nine-inch shaft by the testicles in his right hand. In its place there was a smooth hairless swelling of flesh between my legs.

Again I tried to scream, though I knew it was hopeless. "I said, don't twist your face up like that," he growled. He swung the disembodied cock and slapped me across the face with it. My eyes welled with tears, making the candlelit room swim and sparkle.

My mind was sinking. I longed for unconsciousness. But his voice pulled me back.

"It'll stay hard," he said. He was rubbing thick lubricant over my cock. There was a dim sensation of pleasure somewhere below me. "All the energy of the spell holding you is focused in your cock, like a powerful conductor. But I have a warning for you. When you come—when your cock ejaculates—you'll break the spell. You'll remain in whatever condition you're in at that instant. So unless you want to stay in three pieces, you'd better hold off." He smiled, and slid my cock through his fist. "Of course, you won't have much control."

He returned to my body and struck it with the cock, wielding it like a blackjack. The body jumped like a startled animal.

He dug the nails of his left hand into my right nipple and pulled the body, headless, sexless, up onto tiptoes. He stepped forward and rubbed his cockhead against the denuded stump where my cock had been. My body responded instantly—thighs parted, hips rocking back and forth. The body rubbed its groin against the blunt tip of Michael's cock.

He bent at the knees, lowering his cock and breaking the contact. My body followed blindly. The hairless groin sank down and searched for Michael's cock, found it, rubbed itself on the silky knob. Humping, like a bitch in heat.

Michael folded smoothly to his knees and settled his ass on his ankles, his hard cock pointing up like a missile. The handcuffed body spread its knees and squatted deeply, craving more contact.

Michael licked his middle finger and rubbed it against the sleek spot between my legs. My body squatted, swayed back and forth, barely kept its balance. Once again, I sensed what was about to happen. The unbelievable. The unthinkable.

There was no sign of an opening in the place where my genitals had been. Just a bald swelling, like the ball of a shoulder. But as I watched, Michael slowly, gradually buried his finger in the flesh. He began to slide it in and out. My body begged for more.

He turned his head and shot me a quick glance. His face was slack, lips parted, eyes flashing with triumph. As if to say: See what I can make you into? See how badly you want it?

As he finger-fucked me, he reached around with his right hand and began to push the disembodied cock—my cock—into my squatting ass. All nine inches, all the way to the balls in one steady shove. He pressed his palm over the crack to hold it in.

My hips squirmed on his finger, pushed back onto my cock. Michael removed the finger, and my groin tried to follow, ready to abandon the cock up its ass for more of his hand. Again, I could see no opening there.

But when he grabbed my tit to pull my body forward and down, his cockhead slipped inside. And my body squatted deeper, desperate for it, until Michael's thick shaft was completely swallowed.

Michael gasped and rolled his big shoulders with pleasure. Closed his eyes and hissed inaudible obscenities. Or incantations.

And my body—the body he had handcuffed, beaten, clamped—decapitated, emasculated—subjected to something unspeakable and inhuman—it rode his fat cock and screwed back onto the shaft he held up its ass. Mindless but hungry. More a whore than a slave. More animal than human. A creature of dark magic. His creation.

I was thankful that body had no head. It gave me a way to fool myself. To say that it wasn't me.

There was a sudden ghost sensation, more vivid than the others—a flash—as if I felt my cockhead rubbing against his, deep inside my bowels. It jolted me, like two charged wires touching. I felt feverish. The lights dimmed.

For a long time my consciousness came and went. My eyes would flicker open, glimpse grappling bodies, hear Michael's sex-charged groans. Scenes in the mirrors: Michael's beautiful ass, fucking wildly, my legs wrapped tight around his hips— Michael on his back on the bed, my body on its knees above him, fucking itself on his cock while he pulled on my tits— My body, shoulders on the bed, Michael standing between my drawn-back legs fucking with long strokes while he used my hard cock like a truncheon across my stomach and chest—

After a long blackness, I felt Michael slapping me awake. I opened my eyes and saw a cock before my face. But not Michael's cock. A bigger, coarser instrument, knotted with thick veins and streaked with rectal mucus. My throat filled with fresh saliva. I opened my mouth—

—Then realized it was *my* cock held before me. I closed my mouth, recoiling from the insanity of it.

"Go ahead." I heard Michael's voice above me. "It's not as pretty as mine, but it'll give you what you need. Go ahead. What's wrong? Don't wanna taste shit? Come on, you've made plenty of guys suck it after you've screwed 'em. Besides, it's your shit, man."

I looked hard at the cock. I had seen it in mirrors, of course, even in photographs. But now I saw it as my slaves had. Huge and pulsing, inches from my lips. And I knew why men had groveled for it. Knew the power that made them crave it. I opened my mouth and moaned silently.

Michael laughed and shoved it down my throat. Rammed it in and out, the way I would have. I discovered how it felt—exactly how it felt. I remembered the riding crop trick in New York—the sweltering afternoon with the six-pack when I tied his face to my crotch and kept my cock down his throat for hours—coming, pissing, coming, pissing. Now I knew why four hours hadn't been enough for that cocksucker.

I felt pleasure in my cock as I sucked. Almost like sixty-nining, sucking and being sucked. Two places at once.

I squeezed my throat around the huge dick, milking it, savoring the pleasure I was giving and receiving. Then Michael spoke.

"Remember, Bill. When it shoots, the spell breaks. And if that happens while you're still in pieces—there's nothing I can do to put you together again." He kept sliding it in and out of my throat.

My blood froze. I stopped the undulations in my throat.

"Come on, Bill." His voice was low and evil. "Your cock's close. Been close for hours. The balls are way up in the sack. Come on," he teased, ramming it hard and fast, "make it come. Work your throat like a good cocksucker. Don't you wanna know how it feels when you shoot in some guy's mouth? Must be good—I bet they always come back for more. Don't you wanna taste your own come?"

I looked up at him and pleaded with my eyes. He kept sliding the big dong in and out—I felt it expand, the way I always do when I'm on the verge—

I clamped my teeth down on it, hard, to stop the stroking.

Michael laughed. "Okay. I believe you." He whipped the spit-streaked plunger from my throat and tossed it on the floor. I heard it land with a heavy thud, and felt ghost pain in my balls.

He picked up my head and carried it to the center of the room. My body was lying on its side on the floor, exhausted. Michael squatted, placed my head on my shoulders, wet his fingers with glowing blue saliva, and stroked the connection. I felt warmth flow from my neck to my chest, my hips, my legs. Thank god, whole again—almost.

I spent a few minutes coughing and swallowing convulsively, clearing the juices that clogged my throat. Michael undid the handcuffs and pulled me to my feet. My legs were shaky; there was pain everywhere. But it was wonderful to feel anything beneath my neck.

Michael stretched and yawned. "Shit, I'm beat," he said. "Been fucking you for hours, baby." He pinched one of my nipples, making me throw my head back in pain. "Came in you twice while you were out. Once in your ass, and once—well, you saw. Think I'll take a shower and hop right in bed."

"But—" I looked at my cock on the floor and quickly looked away.

"Oh, yeah," Michael said. "That. Go ahead and take it. It's yours."

My chest knotted with horror. "Please," I whispered.

"What did you say? I couldn't hear you."

I lowered my eyes—caught a glimpse of the bare flesh between my thighs—shut my eyes tight.

"Oh please, Michael. Let me have it back. Oh please, for god's sake—"

I felt a heavy slap across my face and knew it wasn't his hand. His voice was deep and unctuous above me. "That's no way to beg."

I kept my eyes shut.

"Get on your knees and beg with your mouth."

I knelt and took his soft meat between my lips. My face was wet with tears.

"Make me come again, Bill. It won't be easy. Three times is usually my limit. Show me how good you are. Show me how good you suck cock. Make me come, and I'll let you have it back. That is—if you don't shoot first." I heard and felt the slick crackle of flesh on flesh above my head. He was holding my hard cock and stroking it.

I sucked, and tried to think of nothing but his cock. Slowly, slowly it hardened, until the beer-bottle thickness gorged my throat. It wasn't so easy this time. I choked, gagged, felt my gorge rise—but I never let go. I forced my throat onto him over and over, strangling myself.

"Better than your cock, isn't it, Bill?"

Yes, he was right. His cock, so thick, so flawless, it *was* better.

He began to moan and twist. He was close. I was going to make it.

Then he pulled out. Held my face off, fought off his orgasm. "Not yet," he whispered, "not yet."

He tortured me that way. I brought him close over and over, sucking desperately, using every trick I could remember. Then he would pull out and make me start over, all the while working my cock.

"Think about it," he crooned. "What happens if I make you shoot first. You'll be what you are now, forever. Might not be so bad." He reached down and stroked a finger over my sexless groin. I felt an incredible flash of pleasure, unearthly. I jerked back and whimpered around his shaft.

"You'd be my slave, Bill. *Really* my slave. You've been playing that game for years, but this is real. I'd own you—or own your cock, which is the same thing. You'd be mine. You could never show yourself to another man like that. Think about it. Have to come crawling to me for sex. Maybe I'd be in the mood. Maybe not. And you've seen the kind of games I like to play."

With that nightmare in my head, I gave him my last ounce of energy. Worshipped him like the primal force he was. Sucked and sucked and *sucked*—

—and finally heard his roar above me. Felt his meat stiffen and pump. Tasted bitter semen—and at the same instant, my own hips began to jerk. I was coming, in response to him. *Too late*—

I felt his hands on my crotch—blue fire—

And when it was over, I was whole again. Michael pulled his shaft from my throat with a pop and collapsed onto his throne, chest heaving. He looked worn out and happy. I was too drained even to hate him. Too exhausted to stand. He forced me to lick my come from the floor. Made me kiss his feet.

I looked up at him. After long minutes I caught my breath. The numbness seeped out of my head. Even as wrecked as I was, I had to know how.

"Michael, what you did—what you do . . . I don't know what it's called, I don't even know if it has a name. . . . But what . . . what—"

"Something you're born with," he said. "There are others. I've met three in my lifetime, heard of more. We keep our distance from each other. Don't get ideas about learning it. I've studied, learned the ancient laws, found new ways to focus my power. But either you have it—and you know it—or you don't. I knew that you didn't when I first saw you. The tan is a giveaway. You like sunlight far too much. I can't teach it. I can only share it."

He pushed his big toe into my mouth. "So if you ever want it again, you know where to come. You'd be crazy to ask for it, though. I like danger. The possibilities—the games—are endless. Sooner or later . . ."

He pulled his toe from my mouth and pushed my face to the floor with his foot. "Now get out. I'm tired of you."

I staggered naked to my room. It was dark outside. I looked at the clock. I had spent eight hours in his room. I closed the door and crawled into bed. I saw the leather strap on my right arm. I wanted to put it back on my left, but I was afraid he would know somehow.

I heard Michael in the hallway, then in the shower. He was singing happily, basso profundo, as I dropped off to sleep.

Sunday morning I woke up sore and stiff. My ass ached, and there was a lingering fire in my groin. The marks he had put all over my body stung beneath the sheet. My nipples were raw. My arms ached. My jaw ached.

I stared at the ceiling and thought about the night before. Perversely, my cock began to harden.

There was a knock at the door. I stiffened with fear. "Who is it?"

"Sharon."

"Oh." I pulled the sheet up to hide my chest. "Come in."

She entered with a tray of food. "Michael said you were under the weather today. I thought I'd bring you something to eat."

"Thanks. Just set it on the dresser. I'll eat it later."

"Okay. You do look pale," she said maternally. Then she looked puzzled and frowned. She was looking at my armband, on the right now. Or was it my hairless arms?

"Well," she said, "I'll check on you later. Call if you need anything."

I ate the poached eggs and toast, drank the soup. I noticed that my pants and my wooden locker were by the bed. Michael must have returned them. I cringed to think that he had been in the room while I slept.

I tiptoed to the bathroom to put ointment on my welts and take a long, painful crap. It felt like I was shitting my guts out. There was blood, but not enough to worry me. Then I returned to my room and slept like a dead man till dusk.

Later in the evening I went to the bathroom again—dry heaving this time. As I was leaving I heard someone in the hallway. I couldn't bear to see Michael again. I switched off the bathroom light, cracked the door, and looked out.

It was Michael's blond friend, Carl. The regular visitor who used to live in my room. Who wouldn't make eye contact with me. Whose pants seemed to have no bulge at the crotch. He was wearing a tank top. His tanned arms and chest were smooth and hairless.

I went back to my room and tried to stay there. But I had to know.

I crept up the stairs to the trapdoor. Heart pounding, I opened it a few inches, turned my head sideways, and peered in.

Michael was seated in his throne. He was wearing only his white tank top, stretched tight across his pecs and loose over his flat stomach. His half-hard cock rested like a club on the chair between his thighs.

The blond was kneeling naked before Michael, his back to me.

"Not tonight, Carl. I'm bushed."

"Please, Michael, I need it. Now. So bad. It's been so long." He was rubbing his hands between his legs shamelessly.

"I said, *not tonight*." Michael's voice was hard.

The blond leaned forward and licked Michael's cock with long strokes. He was sobbing.

"Oh, all right." Michael pushed him aside and walked to the dresser, his pale, fat cock swaying. He opened a drawer and took out something wrapped in blue silk. "Just a simple fuck tonight," he said. "Nothing fancy."

He returned to the kneeling blond and unwrapped the object. It looked like a big, stiff dildo. I knew it was not.

"Stand up and face me, stupid."

Carl stood and turned. I could see between his legs now. I saw the smooth, sexless flesh there.

I closed the trapdoor, ever so slowly. The blood pounded in my head like thunder.

That night, under cover of darkness, I moved my things out of the house on Beauchamp Street and went to a motel. Occasionally I have felt an urge to see Michael again—a glimpse of his broad shoulders, from a safe distance, would do. But I have never returned.

STEVEN SAYLOR

on Aaron Travis's "Blue Light," first published in 1980

I had an observation recently—the observation of a fifty-year-old, retired pornographer, looking back on his early work. . . .

Lawrence Schimel recently reprinted my novelette *Eden* in *The Mammouth Book of New Gay Erotica*. I wrote *Eden* about twenty-five years ago, about a guy just out of high school, hitching across the West with a sexually ambiguous truck driver.

I reread the story for the first time in many years, just to see how it stood up, and I was blown away by the experience.

It was hot. It was surprisingly literate. I can remember coming up with every metaphor and image, every twist and turn—and yet there is such a distance between me and the author. He was so young! The story captures something authentic and obsessive and romantic that I could not duplicate now.

I'm proud of young Aaron Travis. Because he's so much younger, and will stay that way forever, Travis seems almost to be my son instead of my alter ego! He's so fearless to me! He didn't realize it at the time, he just followed that muse. . . .

"Blue Light" was originally published in an obscure gay rag called *Malebox*, July 1980, which had just been acquired by the publisher of *Drummer*. *Malebox* almost immediately went belly-up, and then "Blue Light" was quickly reprinted in *Drummer*.

I remember, when writing it, thinking about the Head of Mimir from Norse myth, the Head of Misery from James Branch Cabell's novel *Figures of Earth*, the blue glow of the electric pentacles from William Hope Hodgson's *Carnacki the Ghost-Finder*.

The story's unconscious elements have deeper roots—and when

others go poking about those roots, they reveal more about themselves than about Aaron Travis.

"It's archetypal; haven't we always wanted to be women?" Sam
Steward (aka Phil Andros) told me. The artist Charles Musgrave
remarked that the most fitting reward for writing such a story would
be the chance to actually live it—an appalling idea, I thought. Why
insist on reality when you already have metaphor?

My partner Rick Solomon (still hitched after thirty-one years)
was the first to read the story, in manuscript. He was up in the loft
reading it while I was downstairs, eagerly waiting for his reaction.
Eventually, I heard him call to me, in a spooked voice, "I'm not
coming down!"

END-OF-THE-WORLD SEX

Tsaurah Litzky

My friend Carri tells me that since the disaster her Dom won't let her out of bed. The minute he gets home from work he grabs her. It was like a second honeymoon at first, she says, but now she is exhausted, worn out, her Jezebel always sore and aching. I tell her she is free to experiment with my collection of lubes; lately I hadn't had much use for them. She says thanks but she had better get her own.

I am yearning for some end-of-the-world sex, but so far I have had no luck. The art dealer I picked up at the New Museum a week after the disaster had nimble, slender toreador hips. He looked like he could maneuver well in tight places, but when we went back to his apartment he only wanted to do sixty-nine. I was bloated, swollen with sorrow and rage, all my juices bottled up inside me, and what I wanted was to be pierced, penetrated, and drained. I told him I have some wonderful lube with me, I got it in Amsterdam on the Street of Earthly Sorrows. He looked at me as if I had just told him I had an acrylic womb. "No way!" he says. "I know all about those lubes; they are full of estrogens. I've heard they can give a man breasts." I'm astounded at his ignorance. "You must be kidding," I say. "Very funny, ha, ha, ha." I didn't tell him that I think hermaphrodites are hot. If he had breasts it would make him really exciting to me, a lover for the new millennium. Instead, I put my jacket back on and went out the door.

When I got home, I stripped, fell into bed, and slept. I dreamed of men with breasts and hermaphrodite sex. I mated with a hermaphrodite with many sets of arms like a Hindu god and two cocks, one between his legs and one growing from the center of his forehead. Eight, ten, twelve sets of hands caressed me while I held his two purple cocks in my hands and pulled at them rhythmically as if they were teats.

There is a homeless man who lives in a three-sided packing-crate house underneath the BQE overpass. I always see him when I am coming and going to the A train. He is heavyset, and beneath his tattered sweaters it looks like he has breasts. Maybe he is a hermaphrodite. He often has his prick out and is stroking it with filthy hands. Everyone passes by, pretending not to notice. Since 9/11 I can't stop myself from glancing over. His tool is uncut, huge, the size of my forearm; he could spawn dynasties, propagate thousands. When I look over at his terrible, fleshy baton, I become excited. A warm, liquid lava bubbles between my legs. I wonder if this is my end-of-the-world sex.

The headlines become more bizarre, more sensational. Mayor Giuliani announces they have not found any bodies for five days but they are finding more and more body parts, scam artists try to sell families of the victims dirt from the site, Taliban are infiltrating our colleges, gas mask sales soar. . . . The mayor says we should get back to normal, eat in our restaurants, take in movies and Broadway shows. When I go to teach my evening classes at the university in Greenwich Village, despite his urging, the restaurants are empty. The once-bustling streets nearly deserted.

At night I keep having hermaphrodite dreams. One night there are two hermaphrodites in the dream. They both have long blond hair, obese, fleshy tits, and gray, squiggly cocks like silver corkscrews. One lies beneath me, one on top. I writhe frenzied, sandwiched between breasts and cocks. I come again and again, and when I wake up in the morning the sheets are wet, soaking. First I wonder if this means I will meet hermaphrodite twins, then I wonder if this new obsession is a kind of hysterical reaction to recent events, some kind of posttraumatic stress disorder. I have a dreadful compulsion to read all about the attacks. In the mornings I pull on some clothes right after waking, and go out and get the newspapers. When I open the downstairs door and step out into the streets, there is that now-familiar burnt charcoal smell in the air. Across the river the fire is still burning.

My nocturnal yearnings for a hermaphrodite continue to baffle me. I find myself undressing for bed earlier and earlier. Last night I was under the covers at a quarter past nine. This time I imagine a hermaphrodite who is little more than a boy, a delicate cocoa boy with mochaccino skin, golden nappy hair, and eyes the color of honey; his tiny cock, not much bigger than a praline in my mouth, tastes of cinnamon. I had three fingers in the slit below his caramel bonbons. He was suckling gently at one nipple while with his nimble, wee fingers he pulled playfully at my snatch. The phone rang. I didn't want to leave him so I let the machine take it. The voice of Steve Nicholson, a painter and one of my dearest friends, floats out into the room. He has decided to move back to his family farm in northern California. "My hands are always trembling," he said, "I'm too nervous to paint anymore, I sold my loft to Tony Bambini." I'm shocked; how will I cope without him? Now I jump up and grab the phone.

"Don't go," I say. "Who will I complain to?" "I have to get out of here," he says. "I'm terrified of more suicide bombers, toxic chemicals in the water supply, poison gas in the subway, anthrax. We can talk on the phone, e-mail." He wants to come over and bring me a small lamp I have always admired. He has painted a two-headed moose and a pine tree on the lampshade. "I just don't want you to leave," I say, "and I'm already in bed, but why don't we meet at the Right Bank Bar tomorrow night. I'll buy you a farewell drink, if you change your mind I'll buy you two drinks." "I won't change my mind but I'll meet you at nine o'clock," he says. When I go back to bed I find my little friend is still there waiting for me.

Steve is already sitting at the bar when I arrive. He looks like a lumberjack, a big guy who always wears plaid shirts and Levi's. The exquisite miniature landscapes he paints are a surprise. There is a brown box wrapped and tied with handles under his bar stool, which must be the lamp. His face just lights up when he sees me; there is a halo around his head, and the air in the bar seems to be charged with electricity. I can hear it whiz around my head to the beat of "Jumpin' Jack Flash" on the jukebox. The bottles behind the bar are covered with precious gems, rubies, emeralds, sapphires. The mirror is one solid sheet of diamonds. The sudden sense of heightened awareness, this pseudo LSD glow, is what Virginia, the bartender, calls Twin Towers delirium tremens. She says everyone is getting them, they come and go.

"Well, if it's not Miss Dirty Stories of 2001," Steve calls out, his halo doubling in size. I sit down on the bar stool next to his. "Miss Dirty Stories doesn't have anything to write about; she's a fraud," I tell him. I met Steve ten years ago here at the bar. We got drunk on Wild Turkey and went off to his place to write a dirty story of our own. The geometry of his six-foot-five, three hundred-pound frame and my five-feet-tall frame did not compute. Skewered on his huge tool, I felt like a tiny cock ring. I could not encompass him and kept sliding off. In the middle of what might have eventually been the act, we both started to laugh and couldn't stop. Then we decided to dress and go to Chinatown for a very, very early breakfast. Now we are great friends. We commiserate about the vicissitudes of our careers and our love affairs.

He pokes the box below his bar stool with his size-fourteen foot. "Every time you turn on this lamp, I hope you'll remember me," he says. "Yeah, I'll remember that when the going got tough, you ran away." The light goes out of his face, and he looks sad. "Come on," he says, "give me a break, a lot of people are leaving. They don't want to raise their kids in the city." "But you don't have kids," I interject. "I am a kid," he answers. "Anyway, weren't you going to buy me a farewell drink?" "Yes," I say, and motion to Virginia. She is wearing a low-cut, red leotard top to show off the tattoo of a butterfly on her chest. "Our usual, two Cuervo Gold margaritas, straight up, no salt. And make them extra strong, I have the Tower tremens." "Who doesn't?" she answers, and then I say, "Can you believe this big oaf is leaving us?" "Yeah, I know, he told me," she answers. When she brings our drinks over and makes change from the twenty I put on the bar, she says, "The next one's on me."

Steve raises his glass and clinks it against mine. "To a better life," he says. "I hope so," I reply. "Besides it's gonzo crazy here," he adds, then he tells me about a big loft party he went to on Saturday night. It was mobbed, everyone was making out, people couldn't keep their hands off each other. "It was like one big, extended daisy chain," he says. "People were screwing on the couches, in the bathtub. There was a woman on her knees in one corner giving men blow jobs. Can you imagine? There was a long line in front of her." I ask him, "Did you go stand in line?" He doesn't answer; he hangs his head, maybe hoping I don't see that he is blushing. He changes the subject. "There was probably Viagra in the punch," he says. "Fear is a more powerful aphrodisiac," I state pompously, as if I'm an aphrodisiac expert. "You must be right," he says. "It's the end of the world, what else is there to do but have sex?"

Then I tell him about my hermaphrodite dreams, and we finish our drinks. Steve motions Virginia to bring us another. "Maybe you should go to the Eulenspiegel Society," he says. "Make your dreams become a reality . . . I'll be in town till the end of next week, I'll go with you."

"You look like a CIA agent or an *übermensch* cop," I tell him.

"No one will come near us." "You're wrong," he says. "I'd be a big attraction, they'll be on me like flies on sugar. But right now, I have to see a princess about a frog, excuse me." He gets up and makes his way to the back of the room and the stairs that lead down to the bathrooms. I think about how I will miss him and suddenly feel like I'm going to cry. I pick up my drink and finish it in a great gulp. I make myself smile; I despise looking forlorn in public.

There are more people in the bar now. The tape is playing "Tumbling Tumbleweeds." The couple on the other side of me get up and leave as a little crowd of five or six people comes in. They occupy the newly vacated seats next to me and the others stand behind them. It is a group of Virginia's friends. They are all tattooed and pierced. They have shaved heads or long dreadlocks, blue hair or mohawks, many visible piercings. One of the guys has silver studs shaped into a question mark on his cheek. They look like they are in some future-world punk band. Actually they go to school with Virginia at Columbia University, studying economics. The guy sitting right next to me is slim and rangy. His sleeveless leather vest shows off his lean, muscular arms, which are covered with blue tribal tattoos. He has a clean-cut, handsome face, a young Henry Fonda in *The Grapes of Wrath*. His dark hair is shaved close to his skull, and there is a Coptic cross tattooed in the center of his forehead. Virginia once introduced us. His name is Hook, and we talked about how he is putting himself through school working for a silk-screen company. I wonder where Steve is, and I look around. I see him at the back of the bar. A tall, elongated Giacometti woman with red hair to her waist is holding him by the arm and talking up at him. . . . He looks over her head and catches my eye and smiles.

I turn my head and find Hook looking right at me. "Hi, aren't you the writer?" he says. "Yeah," I answer. "Guilty." "Virginia showed me your poetry book," he said. "It's great, not gender based, not that usual snobby feminist glob that goes on and on about the glory of pussy. You're way beyond that." He is obviously a very smart guy. He wants to know when my next poetry book is coming out. I tell him I've been working on a book of erotic stories for a year, that the only poem I have written in the last year was about the bombing.

"How does it go?" he asks. I tell him the first line, it's all I can remember: *Bitter ashes of sunset float down through the sky like dots in a comic* . . . "That's great. When do I get to hear the rest?" he asks, and I realize that he's coming on to me. At least he hasn't given me that terrible line, the one that will make me instantly reject him. He hasn't asked me if I like younger men. He offers to buy me another drink. I look back and see that Steve and the elongated redhead are kissing passionately in one of the booths. I accept the drink and start to flirt with him. We flirt through two more drinks, and when he asks me to come home with him, I say yes.

Hook helps me on with my coat. I try to appear cool, nonchalant. I am breaking one of my own rules, one I have broken many times before: never go home with someone the first time they invite you. We walk down Bedford Avenue through a starless, cloudy night to Hook's apartment a few blocks away. I have forgotten the lamp, but I don't care. Hook lives right above the Buzzards' Nest Bar, a notorious hangout for the local cops. "At least the building is safe," he says, grinning at me as he unlocks the door. The music from downstairs is so loud it's deafening. Strains of Frank Sinatra singing "New York, New York" float up through the floor. "That's all they play ever since it happened," he says. "It's driving me nuts." He ushers me in before him, shuts the door, and switches on the light. In the stark light of the single bulb, I see how thin he is, supple like a boy. His kitchen consists of an old stove and a table made out of a door and packing crates. On the wall above the table is a large blow-up news photo of the second plane hitting the south tower. Underneath the image, the words END OF THE WORLD OR BEGINNING OF A NEW WORLD ORDER are printed on the photo in red Magic Marker in large block letters. Hook sees me looking at it. "I'm working on a silk screen of that," he says. There are stacks of packing crates filled with books everywhere. "My castle," he says deprecatingly, but I tell him I like it.

We just fall onto each other, start to kiss. Hungry, ravenous, we suck each other in. Still kissing me, he walks me backward through the open door of his other room toward the bed. He puts his hands inside the waistbands of my skirt and tights, and pulls them down to my ankles. I step out of them and out of my clogs. He unbuttons my cardigan sweater and slips it off down my arms. His lips keep me occupied, his mouth is a loving cup that I am drinking from. The bedroom window is open. I shiver in my bra and panties even though a fire is building inside me. With one arm he shuts the window, with the other he pushes me down almost roughly on the bed. I watch him take off his boots, his jeans, and his vest. I love his exotic markings, the blue wings on his back and on the top of his chest, the many tribal bracelets he wears burned into his arms. He is not wearing any underwear. His cock is very long and thin, not pink at all, a startling white. I notice that he has beautiful, large pink nipples. They look soft, fleshy, like the nipples on a woman's breast. I want to nurse there. He steps back, mumbles something I can barely hear, then I make it out . . . "This is going to be good, I know this is going to be good" is what he seems to be repeating like a mantra. In an attempt to calm him and reach out to him, I ask him if he likes my underwear. I am wearing my favorite matched set, black satin covered with red roses. "Yeah," he says, barely glancing down. "What kind of flowers are those, carnations?" he asks. "Sure, right, carnations," I say, and I just grab his hand and pull him down on top of me. His body is so light on mine. The last time I found myself in bed with a man, he had a big belly like a sumo wrestler. Hook and I begin to kiss again, but now he is more hesitant. We kiss for a long time. I'm getting wet, wetter, juice running down my legs, but I don't feel his steel pressing into my belly. I wonder if it's the extra ten pounds I'm wearing on my thighs, but he pulls his head up and says, "You're so beautiful. I didn't think you would be so beautiful." I realize he is terrified. I want him to ram his tongue so deep and hard into my mouth that my cervix opens up before it, and he is tonguing my labia from the top side, but instead he pulls away. . . . . He seems to be weeping.

"I'm very sorry," he says. "I can't do this, usually I'm hard right away." "Okay don't feel bad, it's okay," I say. I put my arm around his shoulders. I pull him closer to me. He nuzzles my neck then rolls off of me onto his back. We lie there beside each other like two beached fish at Coney Island. I wonder if this has happened because we are strangers or because we don't love each other. I wonder if the disaster has rendered him impotent or if it was the three beers he drank as he sat with me at the bar. I wonder if it's my old nemesis, tried and true, the luck of the draw.

I glance over at him. His eyes are closed, the wing tattoos on his chest start just above his sternum. It looks as if he is wearing a dainty scarf, a mantilla of blue lace. His large nipples are bubble-gum pink. I want to touch them, chew them, suck all the sugar out. First I lean over and kiss him briefly, sweetly on the lips. I stroke his limp cock, cradle it in my hands for a while. I learn the shape of it, stretching it in my hands, then I tuck it between his legs. He starts to mumble something, perhaps a protest, but I shut him up by putting my mouth right over his. I push my tongue deep inside then I pull it out. I push in again, fucking him with it. Then I take his wonderful nipples between my fingers and I tug at them until the tip of each nipple pops out and hardens like a little clit. Finally I put my mouth on his clit-nipple. The surrounding skin is soft and smooth like the skin inside my pussy. Hook must like what I'm doing because he is moving his body beneath me, rocking from side to side. I move my hands down below his hips, squeezing his legs shut tight. He is pinned under me now, pinned with my mouth at his breast, pinned by my two hands below his hips. I take my hands off the sides of his legs and put them together in a

V. I press down on his new vulva. I rub it, press it, caress it just the way I like to have my crotch rubbed before I spread my legs wide. Hook is moving under me with such frenetic force that he throws me off, but I'm not angry, I have moved into my dreams. He is my hermaphrodite, and he puts a hand out and touches my face. I kiss his wrist, his palm, the tops of his fingers, and then he opens his legs. There it is, in all its splendor, pointing straight up to the skies, white, solid as marble.

As I rise and straddle him, I feel very happy. He is still touching my face. His prick fills me up to the top, hooks me into the center of life. I'm so hot I think I must be burning him, but he does not flinch. He moves, thrusting higher and higher into me as I open wider and wider until we are at ground zero. From my position astride him I can see through the bedroom door the picture of the jet hitting the second tower. I hear a distant sound, a great explosion, like worlds colliding. The walls of the room are shaking, the edges of the ceiling beginning to break apart. Just as I am coming, he comes too, exploding into me in a ball of fire, and we are both propelled up through the crumbling roof, up, up into the black skies, our bodies disintegrating, mixing with the clouds like ashes.

TSAURAH LITZKY

on "End-of-the-World Sex," first published in *Best American Erotica* in 2003

There was trembling but fearlessness in the way people reacted in New York City in the wake of 9/11. People talked to one another openly and caringly in the streets—in stores, on the subway. It seemed briefly as if some higher consciousness might rise phoenix-like from the ashes. "End-of-the-World Sex" captures that feeling.

It's all gone now. People sit on the subway wired up into their iPods, huddled into their books and newspapers, as every day the casualties of this obscene war increase.

It makes me sad to remember what could've been.

I started writing erotic stories out my need to make some sense out of my own chaotic erotic life, of my need to change the negatives into positives, to find seeds of transformation and liberation in the part of my garden given over to despair.

I've been influenced by all my mistakes in love, and by the heat of my few brilliant successes. Then there's my unquenchable thirst for romance and my passion for the movies.

Recently, I was asked to write about Emma Goldman (one of my heroes) for a history of the Lower East Side. I finished it yesterday. Talk about someone with an intense erotic life!

The courage of Colette, Emma Goldman, and the great Lenny Bruce all have been a big influence. I learned how to write short stories by reading John Cheever. I've been inspired by Doris Lessing, Pablo Neruda, I. B. Singer, and Norman Mailer—and, my most beloved teacher, my mother.

A JEW BERSERK ON
CHRISTMAS EVE

Steve Almond

S uzanne Blacet stepped back from the Blacet Christmas tree and let out a quiet trill. The tree was enormous, something like fifty feet tall. It nearly reached the ceiling of the den, with its plush appointments.

"Traditions," Suzanne said. She paused for a moment and cocked her head, as if listening for a pleasing echo. "That's what we believe in here: traditions. Family traditions. Don't we, honey?"

"Yes, *maman*," said Adrianna, called Dria—my girlfriend. We were in college, a couple of sweaty econ majors. We'd been together for eight months and four days. This was my first visit to the Blacet mansion, to meet the family, which, by some calculus I didn't quite understand, meant that Dria was now, suddenly, against all dependable odds, willing to fuck me. She was tucked beside me in an angora sweater that made me want to rub her chest with my cock until both of us caught fire.

Also in the room were Dria's father, Bud, and her little brother, Sandro. They were wearing identical Polo sweaters the color of Tang. Paco, the handyman, stood watch over the roaring fire. Madelina, the housekeeper, was manning the eggnog. She looked ready to murder everyone in the room.

Suzanne beckoned me to step forward, toward a large cedar box. Inside was a selection of bright silver tchotchkes.

"Ornaments." Suzanne placed her hand on my forearm. "Relics of our past. We put them on the tree every year. As a way of remembering."

"That's great," I said.

"Choose one," Suzanne said. "This is the Blacet way." She pronounced her surname with a Parisian lilt (*blah-say*) and laughed at her little rhyme.

"Really?" I said. "I mean, I don't want to take anyone's favorite." Suzanne looked at her husband.

"Nonsense!" Bud said. "Nonsense! Choose one! Go ahead!"

"Volume," Sandro said.

Bud fiddled with his hearing aid.

The ornaments looked priceless, all of them, little bells and angels and stars. I choose the shabbiest-looking one, some kind of pewter peg, and hung it on a low limb.

"Oh," Suzanne said. "Perfect. So big and perfect and shiny. Isn't that nice, Jacob?"

"Yes," I said. "Very pretty."

"Do you know what it is?"

"Not really," I said.

"It belonged to my *grandpère* Marsen," she said. "His shoehorn."

"You were going to guess vibrator, weren't you?" Dria whispered. "Weren't you, you dirty little Jew horn?"

Jew horn. Was this a term I should have viewed as acceptable? No. But it was what Dria called me in her moods of amour, those brief, intense periods during which she wanted nothing more than to wriggle her soft little hand down the front of my good corduroys.

It was a horrible term, a slur, a clear indicator of Dria's various cultural pathologies. But I wanted to have sex with her *really badly.*

It was a bodily compulsion. I had certain ideas about what it would be like to be up inside her, like the ocean, like flying, like licking marmalade off the good silver. I was—if I may point this out to the assembled jury—not quite twenty years old.

Besides, dirty talk was a part of our routine. It was something Dria, so wealthy, so continental, so devoutly soaped, required. She would get herself nice and loaded at a sorority party and call me *Jew horn* and *matzo fucker* and *cum dreidl.* And I, once I figured out the rules, called her *pilgrim whore* and *Mayflower slut* and *snail pussy.*

We'd called each other these things and press our bodies together, our naughty parts yearning for consummation and all the damp, chafing fabrics in between. So much drunken hope! Isn't that a version of love also, some central, infant aspect of the thing: the dumb pulse, the warm seep? How else do we survive the rest of the bullshit?

Anyway, I'm not going to tell you here about how we met or how we broke up and the secret scars we acquired. That's part of some other, duller story. I'm going to stick to this one Christmas Eve, all the sweet sickness that came rushing at me at once, along with the nutmeg and smoke and old leather.

Dria had promised me. "You want to get that horn up there, don't you? All deep inside. It's going to be ready for you. But you have to wait until Christmas Eve. You have to be a patient little Hebrew."

Dinner was a massive rack of lamb, pale red slabs of muscle, spiced with Mrs. Dash and dressed with a neon mint jelly. The Blacets ate with grace and precision. I could never quite catch them chewing.

"Tell us about your winter holiday," Suzanne said. "You celebrate Chanukah, I assume?"

"It's *Ha*nukkah," Sandro said. He spoke with the towering boredom of a fifteen-year-old; it pained him to correct the world's relentless ignorance.

"There are eight nights, and you light a candle for each. Why is that, Jacob?"

"Well," I said, "it commemorates the Maccabeans, who were a tribe of rebel fighters in antiquity. They were trying to liberate the Jews from the Romans, and, at the same time, they were trying to keep the candles in the Temple, the Old Temple, lit, which I believe was a commandment, one of God's, but they had only enough oil for one day, but the oil lasted for eight days. It was a miracle."

The Blacets looked at me, nakedly disappointed: this was what the Jews were putting up against the birth of the savior?

"I think it's a terrific story, Joseph," Bud hollered. He'd been the top man in a steel forge, back before he married into the Blacet money.

"Jacob," Sandro said. "The guy's name is *Jacob*."

"Yes, dear," Suzanne said.

"Which one was Jacob?" Bud said. "The one with the rainbow coat?"

"That's Joseph," Sandro said.

"Did he wind up in the hole?"

"You're thinking of Jeremiah, dear," Suzanne said. "The prophet Jeremiah."

"I thought Jeremiah was a bullfrog," Bud said.

Dria squealed out her pity laugh, then reached beneath the table and placed her hand on my belt buckle.

Dessert was served by Madelina, a fruit aspic.

"Good meat, Mother," Bud said.

"Madelina made it," Sandro sneered.

Suzanne shot her son a look that made me think: *coat hanger.*

"Are we using the same butcher?" Bud said. "The old kraut?"

"Don't say that, Father," Dria said. "It's a slur. Kraut is a slur."

Suzanne looked at her husband. "Honestly, dear, Jacob doesn't want to hear about Germans."

Bud waved his hands in mock surrender.

"What does Hanukkah have to do with the twelve tribes?" Sandro wanted to know. He'd eaten fourteen slices of lamb and left half his potato.

"I'm not sure, exactly," I said.

"Can you name them?" The little butterball leered at me. "Benjamin, Judah, Levi, Dan—that's the one that got lost—"

"Quit showing off," Dria said. "It's tacky. Everyone in this family is so tacky." She released my belt buckle and let her little hand drop down onto my crotch.

Dria had sent me out to the back porch with Bud. I assumed this might be the occasion he would demand to know if I planned to deflower his daughter. (In fact, Dria had lost her virginity a year earlier, to a Sigma Chi who had plied her with grain alcohol and Walt Whitman, though this was not something I planned to share with her father.)

Suzanne was in the kitchen with Madelina. I had seen them huddled over the sink, enjoying the rich communion of disapproval.

Bud pulled a flask out, took a long slug, handed the flask to me.

I took a sip. "Wow."

"They get the real stuff," he screamed mysteriously. "From the viscount."

"It certainly tastes real."

"Goddamn Vichy money," Bud said, with an unexpected bitterness. He was a short, thick man with the face of a grizzled cherub.

I took another swallow and stared into the dense stand of trees that bordered the property. Their trunks shone like pale fingers in the light from the house.

"Cedar," Bud said sadly. He tapped his belly. "All right, let's get this show on the road. You ready, Jack?"

"Sir?"

Bud tucked the flask into the back pocket of his wool trousers.

He trundled off the porch and toward a small shed, from which he removed two giant axes. He handed one to me. The idea was that, having drunk our bourbon, we would now chop wood. These struck me as activities best conducted separately, but I was in no position to object. This was the Blacet tradition, and I wanted more than anything to be obedient to this tradition, so that later, on the very eve of Christmas, I would be granted unlimited access to Dria's lovely, well-pruned lower half.

Bud began to hack at a nearby log. "You take that other end," he said.

My swings bounced off the log in a manner that, I was fairly certain, would soon result in the loss of my foot. Meanwhile, Bud's blade bit into the wood with gaudy cracks. He was paying me no mind.

And then suddenly Paco was standing off to my left, like a grim apparition. He looked at me with something that didn't quite qualify as contempt and took the axe from my blistered palm.

They went at the wood with a frantic devotion. These were full-bodied whacks, of the sort I associated with Paul Bunyan, extended backswings, clean strokes. Their cheeks marbled with the exertion, the rapture of hard labor. They moved from the ends of the log toward the center, till they were nearly touching at the flanks, their puffs and grunts fallen into a steady rhythm.

Dria and I were in the pantry, grinding pelvic bones and discussing sleeping arrangements. They had stashed me in the basement, while Dria was on the third floor, next to the master bedroom.

"It'll be a secret mission," she said. "You'll have to be cunning, like Odysseus."

"But your parents—"

"Wait until after midnight. They sleep like the dead." She looked up at me with her chin flashing. "I'll be ready for you, Jay." She lifted her skirt and showed me the long white thighs. Her tongue was hot with eggnog.

Then we heard footsteps and jumped away from each other just as Madelina opened the pantry door. She was in a silent ecstasy, pretending to be surprised, pretending not to understand the scene before her.

"We were checking something," Dria said.

"Is that so?"

"Yes, it is."

"What were you checking, Dria?" Madelina said, in her merciless accent. "Were you checking if we had beef bouillon? Or maybe you were checking if we had saltines. And you needed someone to help, a tall boy to see on those high shelves? But, of course, that is none of my business."

"That's right," Dria said sharply. "There are some things that are nobody's business. You of all people should know that."

The two of them exchanged a look of accumulated recrimination.

"Your mother is in the sitting room," Madelina said slowly.

We made our way back and listened to Suzanne Blacet as she detailed the legacy of her forebears, who had served in the court of Louis Quatorze, Napoleon's army, the Académie Scientifique. Dria had mentioned none of this. It was unnecessary. Her very manner, the grace, the formal gestures announced her lineage.

I felt as if I were in the midst of many confusing secrets. It hadn't occurred to me that this was the central purpose of family: the production of secrets, the elaborate concealment of unbearable truths. I still thought of my family in childish terms, as a lovable inconvenience.

Suzanne talked on and on. The fire snapped. Dria sat listening to her *maman* and licking her lips.

I'd drunk too much eggnog—that much was clear. There was also the wine at dinner and the bourbon. I was not much of a drinker, even under the best of circumstances. But my nerves, my wanting to do things right, had got the best of me.

I couldn't lie on the bed; it was spinning. Instead, I sat on the toilet and put my head between my legs and waited for midnight.

It wasn't entirely clear to me how I was supposed to get to Dria's room, but these were blurry details. I stumbled up the stairs to the first floor. All the lights were off, though I could see the chandelier in the dining room twinkling in the moonlight, and the beauty of this held me for a few moments.

Then a strange smell hit me, a musk of some kind, which seemed to be emanating from the rear bathroom, where I had gone to collect myself after Madelina caught us in the pantry. I thought perhaps it was Madelina herself, taking a perfumed bath. There is no reason, aside from dumb animal curiosity, that I should have tiptoed toward that door. Then again, at that particular moment, at most of the important human moments, dumb animal curiosity is pretty much the ball game.

The door was ajar (of course it was), and an aromatic steam was puffing out. I recognized the scent: eucalyptus. I should mention that this bathroom was—like all the Blacet bathrooms—tremendous and ornately mirrored, a style inspired, no doubt, by the palatial shitters of the Sun King.

I edged the door open and peeked inside. I could see only the mirror, which was mostly fogged over, but, because of the angle, allowed me a view of what I had thought was the bathtub. It was, in fact, a sort of shower/steam room with a small tile bench, on which sat Bud and Paco. They were both quite naked—Bud red with the heat, Paco a luminous brown.

This was strange enough to disorient me a little. Then Paco began scrubbing Bud's shoulders with what I guess must have been a pumice stone, and Bud's eyes took on a drowsy, distant, grateful look, like a dog having his ears scratched. He lowered his forehead onto Paco's sturdy shoulder.

I wasn't sure what to think. There was some part of me that figured this was simply how the wealthy did things—their long-time servants performed such duties. And then there was another part of me that could see, simply by the relaxed posture of their bodies, that this was something more than a professional arrangement, a prelude to further ministrations.

I shut the door with elaborate caution; my heart was chopping.

This was the point at which I should have gone back downstairs. But I had my own needs. Dria was waiting, with her eager, presumably downy loins. She was ready, and my body knew what ready meant. I made for the stairs.

The second floor was pitch-black. I crept across the thick carpets, waiting for my eyes to adjust. I felt someone watching me and spun around to find a noblewoman, painted in somber colors, staring down at me from a gilded frame. In one hand, she held a black squirrel, in the other, a small brown nut.

I hurried away from her and toward a door that I hoped would lead to the stairs. But this was, instead, a second kitchen, with a vast counter, upon which the remains of our dinner lay about, congealing.

Then I heard a voice and ducked down, behind a wall of pans.

"Who's there?" Madelina said. "Is there someone there? Señora?"

A second voice, faint, petulant, nakedly frightened, said, "Is someone there, tía?"

"Silence," Madelina said. Her footsteps carried her past the counter. She latched the swinging door shut. I could see the hem of her dark gown and the plump calves beneath. She lifted something from the counter, with a grunt. "Now," she said. "Turn around. All the way. Do it, little lamb. Do it, or you won't get any. Hold still. Hold still, little lamb."

The only sound during all this was a moist stroking I couldn't quite place. Skin was touching skin, but it sounded medicinal, not sexual. Madelina finished whatever she was doing and I heard her approach the counter. The next sound was unmistakable: a brisk, metallic hiss. She was sharpening a knife.

I didn't know what to do. Was Madelina going to kill her victim? Who *was* her victim? Was I hearing and seeing things? Or perhaps I was dreaming—this was all an odd, pickled dream.

The sharpening stopped, and Madelina rasped, "Who's there? Who is that I hear?"

I froze. What would I do if she came any closer? Could I successfully flee her? I was faster than her, sure, but my socks would slip on the wood floor. She would set upon me with her very sharp knife and carve snow angels into my thorax. I was an intruder, after all, a Jew who had groped the family daughter in the pantry. The family would close ranks. I had drunk too much liquor and gone berserk, after Adrianna refused to perform oral sex on my Jew horn. The tabloids would get a hold of the story. A JEW BERSERK ON CHRISTMAS EVE! Full-color photos of my carcass and the heroic Madelina in her spattered nightgown. My friends would tell investigators, not implausibly, "He always *was* kind of high-strung."

Madelina was speaking again. "Who's there? Is that a little lamb? A little piggy lamb?" I could tell, though, that she had turned away from the counter. She was moving toward the far end of the kitchen.

Then I heard another weird noise, a kind of snuffled whimper.

I inched my head above the counter. Madelina was dressed in long, dark robe, a sort of nun's habit. She was kneeling before a small alcove, into which was wedged some kind of large, glistening doll. Then the doll whimpered again, and I could see that this was Sandro, that he had folded himself into this small space, which was, in fact, the dumbwaiter. He was dressed in boxer shorts, and his skin appeared to have been slathered in some kind of lotion. Then I noticed a bowl to Madelina's left, half full of what my mother would have called drippings—the liquid fat gathered from the broiler beneath the lamb.

With her left hand, Madelina stabbed at the platter beside her and slowly raised a slice of lamb toward Sandro's mouth. She was speaking softly now, almost tenderly. *"Mi gordito,"* she said. *"Tienes hambre,* eh?"

It was entirely unclear to me how Sandro had fit himself inside the dumbwaiter. He was, as I've mentioned, a fat child, folded upon himself; his limbs were pinned against his flanks. His mouth struggled for the meat, abject and fishlike. Madelina flicked his forehead to still him. She held the slice beneath his nose, drew it away, dragged it across his forehead, across the bridge of his nose.

Sandro's eyes began to tear up.

"Don't cry, *gordito.* The Lord provides. Do you believe that, little lamb?"

Sandro nodded.

She continued to drag the meat across his face, like a sick rag. "But you have to suffer for your sins on this night, don't you?"

This went on for some time. At last, she let him bite down on one end. The other end she placed in her own mouth. They chewed until their lips were touching. This wasn't kissing. It was more in the spirit of two wolverines.

I wish I could report that, having slipped out of the kitchen, I proceeded directly out of that house, to the nearest police station. But no. I was still drunk, and now quite frightened. I couldn't imagine heading back down to the basement. I had to see Dria, not to make love to her, necessarily, nothing that complicated. I simply needed to cower under her covers until daylight. I was certain she was innocent of all this.

There was a long hallway on the third floor, with many doors on either side and wheezing radiators. Dria had told me she was in the room at the end of the hall. But I couldn't tell if she meant for me to turn left or right at the top of the stairs. The prospect of making the wrong decision paralyzed me. What would I find behind the mystery door: Mrs. Blacet fucking a donkey?

So I guessed one direction (the left) and staggered that way.

I was overwhelmed, really. I thought about my family, gathered down in Baltimore—the neurotic, self-critical, petty lot of them— cheating at Scrabble and complaining about acid reflux. I saw my uncle Morris smuggling a *Daily Worker* into the bathroom, a look of assumed failure etched on his brow. My cousin Roy would be spitting at the girl cousins on the stoop. Never had these common miseries seemed so alluring.

Here was the door, big and funereal, like all the Blacet doors. I could not stare at it all night. Madelina was down below me, auditioning for the Inquisition. I opened the thing, and the familiar scent of Dria was upon me: lavender and new stockings.

"You made it," she whispered.

"Yeah," I said. "Listen . . ."

But I couldn't complete my thought. She was sitting up in bed, naked to the waist, her small breasts just there, glowing in the dim. I was overcome by gratitude, by relief.

"Get over here," she said. "I've been waiting. I'm *ready*. Were you cunning? You were, weren't you? Long johns! You're so cute. Get *over* here."

She pulled me into an embrace. "You're trembling. Are you cold?"

"Not really," I said. "I'm a little, I guess, freaked out."

Dria looked at me with her distinguished nose, her lioness eyes. "That is so *sweet*," she said. "Don't be freaked out, Jacob. This is going to be great. You were so good. You waited so patiently. Look what I have for you!" She gestured toward her chest. "These are for you!" She placed my hand on them. "Come onto the bed, Jacob."

Then I was on the bed and Dria was yanking at my waistband.

"Wait," I said. "I'd like to . . . could we talk?"

"You're nervous, aren't you?"

Dria lifted the covers. I could feel the warmth of her lower body as a wave, and the scent of her down below. It made me want to crawl down there and curl up with my cheek on her mons pubis.

That was about my speed. But Dria had her own agenda. She, too, had been waiting. She, too, was twenty years old. Her body was a configuration of inept desires loosely knit into action. She took my hand and showed me her readiness. She tossed my long johns away.

"I feel a little weird," I said. "I saw some weird stuff. Downstairs."

"You're still drunk, aren't you? You're so cute when you're drunk!" She reached for me. "He's not drunk, though. He's standing straight up. He's ready, isn't he?"

I admitted that he was ready.

Dria said, "That means we're both ready."

She was in one of her states, the rush of the thing, the anxiety, making her grabby. I was supposed to get on top of her. Those were her orders. I was supposed to open her legs and place my young readiness against hers and get the party started. And I might actually have done so; my body was ready to enact its predictable, ecstatic will—except that I heard a noise come from the closet.

"What the hell was that?" I said.

"Nothing."

Then it came again, a muffled sneeze.

"Nothing," Dria said again.

The closet swung open, and there was Suzanne Blacet, in a fancy sleeping gown, her hair gathered in a girlish ponytail.

I tried to roll off Dria, but she held me fast. *"Maman!"* she snarled. Her tone was not one of shock, or fear, but rage.

They began to speak very quickly.

"I'm sorry," Suzanne said.

"I knew you'd find some way to announce yourself!"

"Surely you don't think—"

"I do."

"There were dust mites, my dear."

"You could have used the peephole."

"This is my *home*."

"You've scared him," Dria said. "You've scared Jacob. Now he's going to be all freaked out. Are you freaked out, Jacob?"

"Yes," I said. I had freed a hand and managed, at least, to cover my nakedness with the duvet.

"You see," Dria said. Her voice was zooming toward a weepy timbre.

Suzanne took a step toward the bed. "Do you honestly think I'd want your friend to see me in this state?" Her face, scrubbed of makeup, showed a rumpled beauty.

"This is a misunderstanding," I said. "I came to tuck your daughter in. I meant no disrespect. I can head downstairs, to my room."

"Nonsense," Dria said. "You're not going anywhere. I was ready. I'm *ready*." She was crying now.

"Calm down," Suzanne said. "You are such a little actress. Jacob is not an unintelligent boy. Don't underestimate him."

"You're ruining this!"

"I'm not ruining anything, Adrianna. Don't be silly. Don't make this a scene." She smoothed her robe and seated herself delicately on the ottoman beside the bed. "Listen, Jacob," she said, in a measured tone. "I spoke to you earlier about traditions. We are a family with certain traditions. In the old days—I am talking about several generations ago, in France—most of the marriages were arranged. Girls of a certain standing with noblemen, who were usually much older. The occasion of the wedding night was a rather perilous situation. Do you understand? There was a dowry at issue. These girls were quite innocent. And some of these gentleman—their behavior was somewhat less than honorable. The result was that certain families insisted that the mother of the bride, or a suitable proxy, be allowed to witness the inaugural coupling. There was nothing prurient in this. It was merely an effort to safeguard the experience, which can be so formative."

I glanced down at Dria, sprawled beneath me, aghast. "Oh God," she said. "You're making us sound medieval, *maman!*"

"I am explaining the situation," Suzanne said calmly. "This tradition is not limited to our family. It is a widespread and sensible practice. Dria communicates with me about her life, as she will wish her children to communicate with her. She has chosen you. I accept that. I have not asked her to take a vow of chastity until marriage. I have allowed her the freedom to do as she wishes. We are a modern family, Jacob. But she is my only daughter. You must understand."

"We're not married," Dria said miserably. "This isn't our wedding night."

"Nor do I expect you to get married. You are young."

"He's going to think I'm all crazy."

"Nonsense," Suzanne said. "He will think that you are loyal to your family, which is not yet a sin. As a member of our family, I have asked that Dria uphold our traditions. I intend this as no aspersion. You strike me as a perfectly nice young man. I admire your religion. The Jews are an industrious peoples."

"Just get out, *maman!* Go back to your room!"

Suzanne shook her head. "Do not raise your voice to me in my own home," she said, then turned back to me. "We are an open family, Jacob. We have no secrets. But we do have a saying, from the French: *What the moon may know, the sun need not.* Isn't that a lovely sentiment? It has brought us much happiness. I would advise you not to become too concerned with the customs or morals of others. You'll have a very long, dull journey if you do. There is my daughter. She has waited a long time to make love to you, and you have waited, too. You may acquire this experience, or you may turn away. I will wait in the hall for two minutes. If you want to return to your room, Jacob, you may do so."

Suzanne left the room, and Dria looked at me. It was clear her mother held this power over her. She was flushed with the shame.

"It's okay," I said.

"I wanted to do it," she said. "I was so *ready*."

"Me too," I said.

She sighed. "Now you think I'm crazy."

Dria was lying naked under the eiderdown, her tender chest so disappointed. I stroked her along the hip.

"You should go," she said. "I know you want to go."

She reached out and dragged her fingertips along my stomach. "I did want that filthy Jew horn inside me," she said, nostalgically.

The mechanisms of desire are so strange in our species, residing half in imagination, half in our hearts. Who can say what means will light the magic wick? It must be easier for the rest of the animals, a matter of the glands.

Or maybe it was this easy for me, as I lay next to Adrianna Blacet on Christmas Eve. Her glands told her to start breathing more deeply. Her glands told her to start touching my belly. My glands, in turn, became suddenly attuned to her, stark naked at last. How long my glands had waited for this, eight months of swollen prelude.

There was so much perversity blooming in that house, Bud and Paco together in the shower, Sandro greased up and whimpering for lamb, Suzanne ready to witness our fumbling bodies. These were disturbing facts. I agreed. *I agreed.* But I couldn't do anything about them, really. At best, I could run off into the world of the allegedly normal with a scandalous story to tell. But the world has enough of those.

Consider this one: a woman announces she's been impregnated by God and gives birth to his bastard son in a donkey barn. Strange stuff.

Whereas Dria, she wasn't strange at all. She wasn't angry at her mother, either. Not really. She wanted, instead, a grand occasion for hope. Our skin yearned for contact. Her mouth reached for mine.

We did hear the door click behind us, just as I slipped inside Dria. She let out a moan of surprise, which I felt as a soft vibration. But we were alone, as true lovers always are, in the slippery warmth.

By morning, there was a fresh coat of snow on the ground. Madelina set out a breakfast to feed the Huns. The fire was already blazing. We were gathered in the den, drowsy and grateful, our doubles lives neatly tucked beneath the tree.

"Did anyone hear Santa last night?" Bud said.

Dria, seated primly beside me, rolled her eyes. "He asks this every year."

Suzanne looked at Sandro. This was his cue.

"I didn't hear a thing," he said sulkily.

"That Santa," Bud said. He turned and flashed me an almost imperceptible wink. "He's one quiet son of a bitch."

STEVE ALMOND

on "A Jew Berserk on Christmas Eve"

I'm not sure where this one came from, honestly. It may have come from many years spent lusting after shiksas and fantasizing about the perversities that might lie beneath their seamless family veneers. We're all freaks. That's the truth. I wanted to capture that idea in action, to keep upping the ante.

When I first wrote "A Jew . . ." I didn't think much of it—it came too easily. I always mistrust the stories that come too easily, that don't incur enough suffering. (That's how you know I'm Jewish.) But looking back at it, I can see how tenderhearted it is, ultimately, how strenuously it argues for forgiveness over judgment.

CASTING COUCH

Serena Moloch

THE JOB APPLICANT (TRIXIE)

I'm so nervous about this interview. I really want this job.

Let me go over it all again. Why I want the job: I'm interested in getting into film and video production, and I'd like to learn from the ground up; producer's assistant would be perfect. Why they should hire me: I'm organized, responsible, learn fast, and . . . what was the fourth? Oh, right, *responsive*, I'm responsible *and* responsive to my employer. Previous experience, two years as personal assistant to an executive director. Why I left that job: tricky, but stick to the standard answer, no more room for growth. I just hope Gillian wrote me a good reference, like she promised. Typing speed, eighty words per minute . . . I certainly did Gillian enough favors—a good letter is the least she could do for me in return. Oh, I'm tapping again, I have to stop that. Should I go fix my hair? No, better stay here. Do I have copies of my résumé? What time is it? Early still. Ten more minutes to go.

THE BOSS (JANE)

As soon as I saw her file, I knew she'd be perfect. With its royal-blue letters leaping off a mauve page, her résumé was eye-catching in a vulgar way that suggested initiative coupled with inexperience. She was underqualified for the position I'd advertised, and I'd be sure to let her know that, so she'd be even more grateful to be hired and even more eager to please. Furthermore, some suggestive phrases in her former employer's reference interested me. Trixie was "a model assistant who never hesitated to provide any service asked, even if that meant helping in ways that some might construe as more personal than professional." She was also "devoted and solicitous."

Trixie must have worked pretty hard, I thought. I leaned back and imagined using that wonderfully ridiculous name in a variety of situations. Trixie, come in here, I'd say over the intercom. Trixie, sit down and take a letter. This is my assistant, Trixie, I'd tell people. Trixie, get me a drink. Trixie, lie down . . . Trixie, take off your clothes . . . now mine . . . very good, Trixie.

I sighed and let the chair come forward again. Too many years of reading scripts had fostered a bad habit of associating names to types and spinning off into little fantasies. Sure, I saw Trixie as a ripe peach, with big round eyes and nipples to match, traipsing her luscious ass around the office in a tight skirt, eager to please. But Trixie would probably be more concerned with her paycheck than with me. Or she'd be all too interested in her effect on me, if the past week's interviews were any indication.

The applicants had been very good-looking, and perfectly competent for the job, but they were all actresses eager to break into the business, and it was obvious they had only their interests in mind and not mine. I had certainly been offered a variety of services.

I didn't enjoy remembering what had frankly been a tiring and unpleasant series of encounters. Jill had stared at me oddly until she finally got up the courage to make her move, opening her blouse and fondling her very beautiful breasts while maintaining intense eye contact. "Do you like my titties?" she asked, and I said, "Yes, I like them, Jill, but I don't like you. Thanks for coming in today."

Then there was Pamela, a redhead in spandex. She was quicker than Jill. After two questions about her secretarial skills she walked around my desk to stand directly in front of me, then lifted up her skirt and started to play with herself through some very transparent underwear. "I could really show you a good time," she whispered as she probed her pussy through the silk. "Not now, Pamela," I'd said, "and not ever."

Lenore had a more sophisticated appearance but an even less subtle approach; as soon as the door was closed she came up to me, got down on her knees, and started tugging at my pants zipper. "Tell me what you like," she said, and though I enjoyed imagining what her tongue might do to me, I wasn't interested; I quoted *All About Eve* to let her know why: "I'll tell you what I like, Lenore. I like to go after what I want. I don't want it coming after me."

Maybe Trixie would be better behaved.

THE INTERVIEW (TRIXIE)

Oh, no, the receptionist is telling me to go in, and I just slipped my shoe off, okay, got it, here I go, now she's calling me back, oh, great, I left my bag on the chair, good work, Trixie, all right, review the four points, learn fast, organized, responsive, and responsible. No, responsible and responsive.

"Oh, what a nice office," I hear myself saying. Stupid, stupid, not a good way to begin.

"Yes, I like it very much," she says. "Have a seat. No, no, on the chair, not the couch. I save that for more informal occasions. Well, Ms. Davis—or can I call you Trixie? Yes? Good. Trixie. Why don't you tell me what you like about the office. Why do you find it nice?"

This is a funny way to start an interview, but she's the boss. "Well, it's very comfortable." She's staring at me. Maybe she's checking out my analytical skills. "The colors are warm, and there's a mix of office furniture, like your desk and all those filing cabinets, and then furniture that's more, um, cozy, like the couch and the bar and the mirrors."

She's smiling, that's good. What's she asking now? Oh, okay, normal questions, typing speed, my qualifications, why I want the job, why I left my last job. I think we're getting along well. She's very attractive—forties, sharp suit, pants, very short hair.

"You know you're not really qualified for this position, don't you, Trixie?"

I blush, but remember to hold my ground. "I may not be right now, but I'll work hard and—"

"But I'm going to hire you anyway," she interrupts. "Because I can tell that you'll be amenable to training, and that you have the makings of a truly gifted assistant. You had a very special relationship with your previous employer, didn't you? Gillian Jackson?"

Now I'm blushing even more, because the way she mentions Gillian makes me nervous. "We got along very well, and I really enjoyed working with her."

"And she enjoyed you. She speaks highly of you and mentions qualities that I've been seeking as well: your ability to help her relax, to devote yourself personally to her needs, never to fuss at unusual requests. If you can provide me with the same attention, and if you don't object to some supplementary training now and then, you'll have no problem with this position."

Why do I feel that she's saying more than she's saying?

"Can you start tomorrow morning? Good. Ten o'clock: we're not early birds in this line of business. Any questions?"

"I was just wondering what your specialty is here. The notice just said Top Productions, film and video."

"That's a very good question, Trixie, and, in fact, we do have a specialized focus, but why don't you and I discuss that in the morning. And, Trixie, please call me Jane."

THE JOB (JANE)

Trixie's first day turned out to be a busy one: in the morning, a casting call, and in the afternoon, a wrap. With any luck, the day would reveal some significant gaps in Trixie's knowledge and skills that would require the kind of extra training session to which she had so readily assented during the interview. Ah, but I was letting myself get carried away again. I can't help but experience the world in cinematic terms, and from my first view of her, her voluptuous body straining as she frantically tried to put her shoe on, Trixie struck me as a complete ingenue in whom sweet awkwardness and powerful sensuality existed side by side. In another era, she'd have been the script girl in glasses who saves the show by shedding her spectacles and becoming a beauty just in time to replace the ailing star. Perhaps she could replace one of my stars today.

Dreams, idle dreams.

She arrived promptly, wearing a red wool suit.

"Trixie," I said sharply. "You mustn't wear red to the office. It's very becoming on you, and I'm sure someone has told you it's a power color, but it's too loud and doesn't give the right impression."

"I'm sorry." She looked hurt and anxious. I tingled.

"Try black or gray or brown. Not blue, though—too corporate. Now, look. You should keep track of these things on a list. You have paper? Write down, 'I will not wear red to the office.' That's right. And that goes for your nail polish, too. Stick to clear. Now, I know we were going to spend the morning getting an interview, but the day is packed and you're going to have to jump right in. This morning we have a casting call. You'll sort the files and run through the audition scene with the actresses. Okay? Tryouts start in fifteen minutes, so go through those folders. The scene is in that binder over there."

I watched Trixie bustle, gathering her materials, somewhat ill at ease because I'd criticized her outfit. I sat behind my desk and scanned budget sheets, looking up occasionally to enjoy her growing discomfiture as she began to understand just what it was we were doing. She looked so sweet when flustered. Perhaps she *was* the assistant of my dreams.

THE JOB (TRIXIE)

I was glad to be involved right away in the details of a casting call, but nervous about running through scenes. Oh, well, I thought, the actresses will probably be more nervous than I am. I opened up the first file, Rochelle King, and looked at her head shot—stern, unsmiling. I flipped to the next shot and nearly yelped, because there was Rochelle in a black leather corset and thigh-high boots and nothing else except for studded bracelets all over her arms and a whip in her hand. Her breasts spilled over her corset, and her legs were planted wide apart. Was she trying to show off her body to get the job? I wondered if I should warn Jane. I looked up, but she seemed busy.

I went through Rochelle's résumé next. She'd done a lot of movies, but according to her résumé they were all "pornographic feature films, with female casts with an emphasis on bondage and discipline." I wasn't sure that *Taming Lola, Slut Punishment* and *Put It All in My Pussy, Now!* were the proper qualifications for this role. Maybe some of the other actresses had more appropriate experience. I opened the next file, and the next, and the next, and they were all the same—scary women in leather wearing all kinds of whips and chains. Some of them even had their noses pierced. Three of them stood out, though: Rochelle King, Vampi Calda, and a woman called Mike.

Maybe the scene is some kind of comic sidebar, I thought, with a bit part for a dominatrix. I turned to the scene to check it out before the run-through. But when I started to read it, I couldn't believe it. This was no sidebar, and we weren't casting a bit part. And there was no way, no way I was going to be able to run through this scene.

"Trixie? I'm ready to call in the first actress."

THE RUN-THROUGH (JANE)

"Trixie," I repeated, "let's get the show on the road. What's the matter?"

"Um, Jane," she stumbled, "could I talk to you before we begin?"

"Sorry, we really don't have time. Later. What's in the files? Who looks good to you?"

"I'm not sure, but I pulled these three."

I looked at the files. For an innocent, she had quite an eye for experience. "Very good, Trixie. Two of these actresses are my top choices for the part, and, in fact, we're beginning with Mike. If she reads well, we'll just hire her."

Trixie looked even more troubled. "Is that okay? What about the other auditions we have scheduled?"

"Trixie," I said sternly, "we don't have time for questions like that. I've been in this business for ages. If I say we can do something, we can do it. Where's that list of yours? Go get it. Write down, 'I will not waste time contradicting Jane.' Great. Terrific. Now tell Mike to come in."

THE RUN-THROUGH (TRIXIE)

How was I going to run through this scene?

I trudged to the waiting room and got Mike, who looked tall in a leather trench coat and high boots.

"Mike, hello," said Jane, shaking her hand. "How've you been? Working hard or hardly working?"

"Working hard, Jane, working hard."

"What do you think of our script?"

"It's nice," Mike said. "I like it."

Nice, I thought, about as nice as being caught in a shark tank. I bustled around while they chatted and ignored me.

"Are you ready to run through the scene with Trixie, Mike?"

"Sure," she said, and took off her coat. I'd expected her to be wearing leather, but she had on a white T-shirt and black jeans. Metal chains dangled from her pockets.

"Trixie," Jane said. Something in her voice reduced my resistance. So I'll look like a fool, I thought. At least the pay's good.

I sat down opposite Mike.

"Okay," said Jane. "Let's review the plot up to this point. Mike's character, Big Red, works as a jail warden in a female prison. We've seen her on the job, restraining and disciplining various prisoners, helping the doctor administer exams, humiliating her favorites by making them do their exercises naked and pee in public. In the scene right before this, we watched her break up a gang bang. The problem is, she got all turned on by the woman she was saving and couldn't do anything about it. So now she's getting a drink at her local bar, which moves into a fantasy sequence about the prisoner she rescued. Okay, let's start reading. Trixie, you're the prisoner, obviously, and Mike's the warden. I'll read the bartender's lines."

I crossed my legs and opened my script. My lines were highlighted in yellow.

"Hey, Big Red, what can I get you tonight?" read Jane.

"Double bourbon on the rocks."

"Coming right up."

"Okay," Jane said, "so now we do some business to indicate fantasy mode, and when the fog clears, Big Red sees the luscious piece who only hours ago was being viciously humped by five bad girls. She walks over to her."

"Hey," Mike said, looking straight at me, "I thought I told you to stay in your cell."

"I didn't feel like it," I said, using my finger to hold my place in the script. "I wanted some air."

"Who cares what you feel like?" Mike's voice was as sculpted as her arms. "You do what you're told. You especially do what you're told when I tell it to you."

"What if I don't want to? It's a free country, even in jail."

"Hah! You've been spending too much time in the library. You're in my jail, and you'll do what I say. Or I'll let everyone else do what they want with you, and believe me, it won't be pleasant.

You didn't like those women putting their hands all over you, did you?"

"It wasn't so bad," I read stiffly. The directions said I should be pouting, but the way I saw it, they were lucky I was doing this at all. "At least they're prisoners like me, not some nasty pig guard."

Whack! Jane made a smacking noise by clapping her hands together, hard. "Okay, so in the scene, Big Red slaps the prisoner, and then we move into the action. Why don't you two play it out in front of the mirror so I can see more of the angles?"

I stayed glued to my chair. "I thought this was a reading."

Jane smiled. "It's a run-through. I have to see how actresses use their bodies. Don't worry, Trixie. Mike knows what she's doing, and you just have to stand there. After all, she's the one who's auditioning, not you. Unless you'd like a part!"

"No!" I said. "Um, Jane, could I talk to you for a minute?"

"I don't like to break the flow of a scene," she said.

"Only a second?" I wheedled.

"Okay," she sighed. "What is it?"

I looked at Mike. She was smiling pleasantly. I wanted to ask her to leave the room, but didn't feel I could. "Is there any way, do you think, that I could just read the lines sitting down?"

"Trixie," Jane snapped, "where's that list we were keeping?"

"On your desk," I said nervously.

"Get it."

I did.

"What does it say?"

"I will not wear red—"

"No, not that. The next thing."

"I will not waste time contradicting Jane."

"Right. Now underline that. Twice. Now write down, 'I will not make Jane repeat herself.' Okay. Now get up and do the scene, for God's sake."

I felt totally humiliated. Mike held her cool smile. I heard Jane say, behind me, in a kinder tone, "I know you haven't done this before, and that it may be embarrassing. But it's just a scene, and we're all professionals here. Okay?"

"Okay," I said.

So we continued the run-through. There actually wasn't much for me to do; I guess this movie was a star vehicle, and Mike was the star. After she supposedly slapped me, she pulled my arms behind my back and pushed me up against a wall, telling my character what an ungrateful cunt she was. "I think you'd better show me some gratitude," she said. "I don't think I'm going to give you a choice about it." Then Mike got to show off how quickly she could get me gagged and bound in a bunch of devices. Still holding my arms behind me, she snapped cuffs around my wrists, tied my arms together near the elbow with some ropes, gagged me with a scarf, and put a chain around my waist that she connected to the cuffs at my wrists.

I kept telling myself we were all professionals while Mike read her lines and ran through simulated sex movements. At least I still had clothes on.

"Who's the pig now?" she asked, while she stood a couple of inches in front of me and pretended to grind her hips into me. She looked really convincing, her body strong, her movements lustful, her voice charged and powerful. I even felt myself getting caught up in the scene, wondering how I looked.

"Are you my little heifer?" she grunted, and kept up her air-grinding. "Are you my little sow?" She whirled me around and pushed my hands onto the sofa. Now I could see myself in the mirror. I looked like a cross between a prisoner and a trussed-up farm animal. A twinge between my legs took me by surprise, but before I could focus on it, a stronger sensation took over. Mike had taken some kind of whip out of her bag and was whacking the seat of my pants. It stung like hell.

Luckily, Jane intervened. "Whoa, Mike, hey, it's just a rehearsal." Mike stopped. Thank God.

"Sorry, Jane," she said. "Got a little too into the scene."

Sorry, *Jane*? I thought. I'm the one getting my ass whacked.

"Why don't we just skip ahead to page forty-five," said Jane.

"Where I take the gag off and force her to go down on me?" Mike asked.

"Right," said Jane.

If you'd asked me twenty minutes before whether I'd even read that scene, never mind act it out, I would have said no. But I'd crossed a line. Maybe it happened when I saw myself in the mirror; I was excited now.

"Have you learned your lesson, you little bitch?" Mike barked. "You ready to show a little gratitude?"

"Yes," I read. "Let me show you. I'll do whatever you say."

According to the script, Mike was supposed to bring me to my knees, force me to open her pants with my mouth, lick her clit, and then, as the script put it, "etc." But Mike was doing something different. She was pushing up her T-shirt on one side, exposing a breast, and pushing my mouth toward her nipple. "Go ahead," she said, "show me what you can do. Suck on that."

Something about the authority of her voice and the authority of that brown, pointed nipple made me forget myself. I leaned down and took it into my mouth. I'd barely closed my lips around it when Mike yelled "Hey!" and shoved me halfway across the room.

"What's the deal, Jane?" she yelled, pulling her shirt down. I was confused.

THE RUN-THROUGH (JANE)

"I'm sorry," I laughed. "Trixie's new. She just got a little carried away. She didn't know that it's impolite to touch an actress during a run-through. Did you, Trixie?"

Trixie looked mortified and stared at the ground.

"Say you're sorry, Trixie," I said, more sternly.

"I'm sorry," she mumbled, still looking down.

"Not like that. Like you mean it."

"I'm sorry," she said, only a little more clearly. Mike stood with her arms crossed.

"Trixie, you've offended one of my best actresses. I think you're going to have to show how sorry you are a little better than this."

She looked up, flushed. "What do you want to do? Whip me? Throw me on the floor and teach me a thing or two? Or maybe I should kiss her feet?"

"Those are all fine ideas," I said coolly. "You pick."

She was mad now. "Or maybe I should read my little list while Mike holds me down and you spank me, since I've been *such a bad girl.*"

Mike spoke up. "Hey, Jane, I'm out of here. I'll call you later about the contract." Out the door she went. Trixie and I were alone.

THE TRAINING (TRIXIE)

I don't know what made me say all those things, but I meant them. I was quiet with Mike gone, silently daring Jane to make it all a joke now that we were alone.

She sat down behind her desk and said, "Well, Trixie, what will it be?"

I remained silent.

"I think we're both agreed that you're in need of some correction. You've made several mistakes this morning, and it's best not to defer our discipline and training session too long. Since you don't seem able to decide on what your punishment should be, I will."

I felt nervous, excited, unreal. The boss and I were about to go over.

"Take your list, Trixie, and put it on the desk."

I did.

"Now pull up your skirt and hold it up."

I did. My body blushed, my pussy contracted, and the blood rushed to my clit.

"Look down at the list and read it out loud, over and over again. Don't stop, and don't look up."

I did. I read, "I will not wear red to the office. I will not waste time contradicting Jane. I will not make Jane repeat herself." While I read and held my skirt up, I heard Jane rustle around in her drawer. What was she doing?

She got up and came around behind me. Her arm snaked around me and removed the list. "I think you have it memorized by now, Trixie. Keep reciting, but put your hands on the table and your ass in the air."

I tried to do it right, but she had to push on my pelvis and spread my legs apart to get me in the position she wanted. Then she grabbed my panty hose and ripped them apart from the waist down. They floated free of my legs and settled around my ankles.

"Keep reciting," Jane said. "Your punishment will only get worse if you stop. But if you absolutely can't take it anymore, start saying 'I will not type letters to my friends on the job.' Got that?"

"Yes," I said, and hastily resumed. "I will not waste time contradicting Jane. I will not wear red to the office. . . ."

Whack! Her hand landed where my butt cheeks met, and my skin heated up. *Whack!* again! She spanked one cheek, then the other, hard. I almost collapsed onto the table, and I lost track of my place in the list.

"What's the matter, Trixie? Did you forget your orders? Maybe this will help you remember."

A barrage of slaps on my ass, even harder than before, vindictive but controlled. My skin felt crisp and burned. I imagined the marks of her fingers on my butt, and my pussy got electric. I felt completely out of control even though I knew I could make her stop. I liked the feeling. She was the boss, and I was a bad, bad girl.

"I'm going to spank you ten more times, Trixie. Keep count now. If you mess up we'll have to start all over again."

Whack! "One," I gasped.

She made me wait, then dealt me another enormous slap. "Two," I said, wondering if I could make it through eight more. But after teasing me by making me wait a long time for a few more vicious wallops, she dealt the rest of my punishment out rapidly, then undid my skirt and pulled it down around my ankles.

"Turn around, Trixie," she said. I did, but I was too embarrassed to look at her. "That's right, Trixie, don't look up. I'm the boss. I'll look at you." She put her hand under my chin and raised my face. I made sure to keep my eyes averted. "I'm going to undo your blouse now, Trixie. I want to see what you're hiding from me." Her hands were warm, her fingers deft, and as she exposed my breasts, I worried about my pussy. It was getting so wet I thought my juices might drip down my thighs and onto the floor.

Her hands cupped my breasts and her fingers teased my nipples. "Nice," she said, "very nice." Her voice had gotten sweeter, but it still commanded. She moved over to the couch and lay down. "Come here. Trixie." I went to her, my movements hampered by the skirt around my ankles. "Get up on the couch, between my legs." I did what she said. "Open my pants." I started to, but was alarmed when I felt something big and hard in her pants. "Take it out," she said, and I did—a long, thick, and very lifelike dildo. She reached under the couch and brought up a condom. "Put it on," she said, "with your mouth." I was clumsy, but I did it. The condom was lubricated, so when she told me to start fucking my tits with her dick, the dildo slid right between them. She groaned as if she could really feel every inch of it. "Suck it," she said. "Get it in your mouth." I moved my chest up and down on it, feeling the friction on my breasts and enjoying it when my fingers occasionally rubbed my nipples. I lowered my mouth onto the head. I sucked and licked it enthusiastically. I moaned and sighed. I felt crazy, and for a second panicked, when I realized that anyone could walk into the office and see me there, naked except for the torn hose and disheveled skirt that held my feet together.

"Oh, that's good," Jane said. "That's it, really put your head into it. Show me how sorry you are that you did your job so badly. Show me what a good slut you can be." She fucked my breasts and mouth some more, then pulled away from me. She got up and rearranged me so that my skirt was completely off and I was kneeling on the couch and looking straight into the mirror. She got behind me.

"I want you to see what you look like when you get fucked," she murmured in my ear. "That way, you'll learn your lesson even better." She explored the entrance to my pussy with her dick. "Spread your legs, you bad thing." I moved them. "That's right," she said, "show me your pussy." She edged the dildo in more. "The boss is going to fuck you now," she warned, and pushed it in hard and deep. My pussy swallowed it up and I started moving against it.

She moved with me, working it in and out, watching my face in the mirror. She grabbed my hair and pulled my head up and back. "Watch yourself get fucked," she hissed. I saw her, still perfectly dressed in her executive clothes, knowing that her dick was lodged inside me. I saw my face, tense with arousal, my flushed neck, and my heavy breasts. I felt something change and realized that Jane had put her fingers between the dildo and her skin and was stroking her clit. "You're going to make me come," she told me. "Do you want to come, too?"

I nodded. In the mirror, I saw her stare at me.

"Please," I said.

"The boss comes," she smiled. "The assistant doesn't."

"Please," I begged. I pushed my pussy onto her dick even harder, but I needed my clit touched.

"Why should I?" she asked, stroking herself more and more.

"I'll be good," I promised, "so good. I'll make you come all the time. I'll fuck you whenever you want, and your clients, too. I'll give you blow jobs at lunch and a hand job with your morning coffee. Just please, please let me come now."

"All right," she said. "Touch yourself."

And I did, digging my fingers into my clit, hard, thrusting myself onto her dick. In seconds, I was coming so much that I didn't even realize until after that she was coming at the same time. I sank into the couch, and she collapsed on top of me.

When our breathing and heartbeats got back to normal, I realized how awkward the situation was. She was mostly dressed, but I felt ashamed of my partial nudity and my exposed, reddened ass. If I can't see her, I thought, maybe she can't see me, and so I stayed facedown even when I felt her get up.

"Trixie," I heard. I turned my head. "Trixie! Sit up!"

I sat up. Jane looked perfectly composed. Her pants were closed up.

"Button your blouse. Put on your skirt. What kind of a spectacle are you making of yourself?" She smiled as she spoke.

"I don't know what we're going to do with you." She took her wallet out of her pants. "Here's some money," she said, and as I struggled into my skirt, I saw that she was giving me two hundred dollars. "Get yourself some new stockings. And keep the change. Consider it a disability payment—I'm assuming you might have some trouble sitting down for the next two days."

I took the money and smiled back. My first day at work was certainly turning out nicely.

"I hope to see you again after lunch," Jane said. "I think we could work very well together."

"I'd like to come back," I said. "And I'm sure you'll do everything you can to see that I do."

Jane looked puzzled at first, then cleared her throat. "Hm, well, yes, certainly, of course. It's clear that we should be paying you far more than the initial salary we settled on. You're so much more qualified than your résumé suggested. I'll have the new contract drawn up and you can sign it when you get back. How does that sound?"

"Beautiful," I said.

And then I took a very, very long lunch.

SERENA MOLOCH
on "Casting Couch," first published in *Best American Erotica*
in 2000

I think Susie and her bossy, flattering solicitation letter got me
writing this story. I didn't start with an inspiration, but with a deadline.

Once I started, it flowed easily, and I wrote it faster than any
story I'd composed before. I decided in advance that I wanted two
points of view, from a top and a bottom, someone in the know and
someone who's unaware.

Comedy is the highest art and, like porn, perpetually under-
valued. I liked writing a story that worked the way fantasy does—
switching points of view, starting and dropping story lines and
scenes.

The most hilarious thing about "Casting Couch" is that a couple of years after I wrote it, I fell in love, and early in the relationship I decided to tell my girlfriend about my porn stories. It turned
out that earlier that week, she'd been reading *BAE* and had jerked
off to my story! Without knowing that she was already having sex
with its author! It was incredible confirmation of my powers as a
pornographer and of the chemistry between us.

IT'S NEVER TOO LATE IN NEW YORK

Nelson George

There's a part of me that's always envied my good buddy Walter Gibbs, so whenever we played ball, I always came hard. An elbow in the lower back, a kick toward his groin on a jumper, a move to inflict a bit of pain and give me an edge. After all, Walter was a better athlete than I was. I was taller and had longer arms, but Walter had strong legs that gave him more hops than a rabbit. I knew that if I let up on Walter for even a moment, he'd win.

So whenever we were matched against each other, I found that if I beat on him enough, Walter would fold. I'd use my legs to cut off his drives. My elbows to push him off the perimeter. My whole body to keep him from spots near the basket when he posted me up. If I brought it like that, Walter would give in. Not quit exactly, but just not care as much as I did. So on this Super Bowl Sunday afternoon, I beat Walter in three games of one-on-one, not by outshooting or even outplaying him, but by making one or two hustle plays—getting my own rebound on a missed shot, knocking a ball off his leg, anything that gave me an edge. I never won by much—one point, two points tops. But it meant something to me every time.

Later, as we sat in the steam room, Walter, in his humble way, remarked, "Niggah, you ain't shit."

"Then why did I win the trifecta today?"

"You won three games because my mind was on ass. I was holding back for tonight."

"Since when do you have to marshal your strength to get busy, Walter?"

"I have a special treat coming my way, that's why."

"I take it you're not talking about going to Andy's for the game?"

"Nah. But you know what, Dwayne? I'm gonna put you down."

"You mean 'in-there-like-swimwear'?"

"You know you're really showing your age right now, niggah. You sound like a Heavy D record. This is the twenty-first century. It's time for some new slang. Word?" I laughed at that. Walter was getting as old school as I was. So for effect he capped his riff with, "Yes, home slice, word."

In a cab downtown Walter gave me the details of his postgame strategy.

"Her name is Medina."

"As in 'Funky Cold'?"

"Yes, yes, and you don't stop. Met her at the Paradise Strip Club. Right as she rubbed her pussy against my dick, she realized she'd seen my picture in *Vibe*."

"Wait a minute, I met this girl. Her real name's Beatrice. Remember, we all went to the movies together?"

"Oh yeah. Beatrice. I like Medina better myself. When'd she tell you her real name?"

"I think when you went to get popcorn."

"Okay, good," he said, not really sounding pleased. "She must have liked you."

"I guess so."

. . .

It was about two months back. He'd just wrapped production on a movie and was chillin' in town. He'd met me at the Sony on Sixty-eighth Street with Medina, aka Beatrice. She was petite, with skin the color of a ripe tangerine. She wore outrageously high black platform boots—the kind Japanese tourists usually sport—and a flimsy beige dress under a snazzy leather coat. In her hair were two decorative beige barrettes. Her eyes were slanted and framed with dark eyeliner. Her lips, moistened by red lipstick, seemed to go on forever. Though probably twenty-six, she radiated a baby-doll sexiness I liked. That night she eyed me carefully, pulling me in with her gaze. *Desire me*, her eyes ordered, and I obeyed.

Somehow Beatrice ended up sitting between Walter and me. The protocol for your man and his date is that he sits in the middle. At first that didn't seem important. Not until Walter got a page on his two-way and left to make a call in the lobby. Nothing should have happened. I was attracted to her, but I wasn't gonna kick it to my man's date. All I did was lean over and say something innocuous to her about "too many commercials and not enough trailers." She responded by brushing my knee with her hand and then letting it rest there. I covered it with mine and then, impulsively, brought them to my lips and kissed her fingers. She took her hand out of mine and, using both hands, held my face.

Wordlessly, we tongued each other as images of coming blockbusters flicked across our faces. I hadn't known this girl more than ten minutes, and we'd made this quick, curious connection. Maybe it was because we both knew that Walter had a high-profile girlfriend. Maybe we just felt like being naughty. I wondered what the people behind us were thinking.

By the time Walter came back with his arms full of bottled water and a huge bag of buttered popcorn, our lips had parted. But despite Walter's presence in the darkened theater, I still let a hand rest on her thigh, and she'd brush it even as Walter chuckled at Eddie Murphy's latest. When he went to the restroom, about halfway through the movie, Beatrice whispered her real name to me along with her number, but alas, all I could recall later was her warm breath on my ear.

After the movie Walter, not an unperceptive man, gave me a hug and then whisked her away in a taxi while I went home with a very hard dick.

"So, you're meeting her, huh?" I said, feeling jealous. "Sounds like fun to me."

"Oh, Dwayne, that's not all. She's bringing her lover to meet me."

"Who, based on your grin, is a female."

"Yes, niggah. And because of your fine performance on the hardwood, I'm gonna give you an opportunity to express your hard wood. You feel me?"

"Oh shit."

"Yes, niggah. Oh shit."

Walter and I had been friends some fifteen years. With admiration and envy, I'd watched (and sometimes helped) his rise from movie novice to edgy low-budget film producer to Hollywood hack capable of making $20 million jammies. Along the way Walter developed an amazing skill for orchestrating nontraditional, multipartner sex. Just as Walter had a knack for finding the right young director to give voice to black rage and humor, the man had a gift for plucking the inner freak out of otherwise seemingly conventional women. I'd seen him fuck models in Porto Sans in Bryant Park and entice the collegiate daughters of potential investors back to his crib. I'd also received a few three A.M. phone calls from my stoned friend in some posh hotel with the voices of many women groaning in the background.

As a pop music journalist now turned screenwriter, I'd bedded my share of singers, models, actresses, and wannabe stars. Yet, in all my years in the entertainment game, I'd never followed Walter's lead and indulged in orgies. There seemed something, well, unsanitary about more than one person penetrating a woman at the same time. Two dicks in the bed, in my opinion, meant two testicles too many.

A couple of girlfriends had suggested we add another woman to the mix, but I'd declined. I think of myself as a one-on-one kind of guy. Yes, I'd cheated on women—sainthood was not my destination—but to me sex demanded full concentration and abandonment into the depths of a woman's body and soul. I simply didn't believe I could split my focus and be a good lover. But, yes, of course I was curious. And I already knew I desired Beatrice and that she desired me.

"Come correct," Walter said a half hour later as the cab stopped in the East Village in front of Bowery Bar. "I know you're new to this orgy game, but it's never too late to learn. That's why I love this city. It's never too late in New York, niggah."

Inside, a huge TV screen set up in the back of the restaurant was projecting the interminable pregame hype that hard-core football fans savored. A few of the mostly male downtown-hipster crowd were making wagers on the Titans versus the Rams. Thankfully, instead of sports chatter, light R & B was playing as the commentator's words ran across the bottom of the screen. However, if you looked to the right of the screen, there was a much better show under way.

Swinging her hips in a slow, seductive motion was Beatrice. She was dancing alone to the music in front of a small table where an attractive thirtyish woman sat sipping wine. She had an oval face with hooded eyes, slim lips, and skin the color of a harvest moon. Her breasts were full, and, from what I could see under the table, she had thick, shapely legs. To the envy of many at Bowery Bar, Walter strolled over and kissed Beatrice as I stood anxiously behind him.

"You remember my man, right?"

Beatrice received me with a light kiss and a long hug. Then she said, "This is Sonja—the friend I told you about."

"She talks a lot about you, Walter," Sonja said, locking eyes with him.

"Likewise," he replied, and then sat down next to her. After I was introduced I squeezed in on the other side of Sonja as Beatrice went back to her dancing. Sonja and Walter traded endearments and then gazed at Beatrice, the lovely link between them. I watched Sonja laugh, then softly touch Walter's lips. "Yeah, sweetness," he murmured. "Yeah."

Walter's two-way buzzed. He checked the message and grinned. "I'll be right back," he said. "Why don't you two lovely people make friends." And so we did. I went first: Ex-full-time music critic; author of the critically acclaimed black-music history *The Relentless Beat;* single; childless; writing a screenplay for Walter's Idea Factory Productions called *One Special Moment.* I told my story neatly with an emphasis on my professional résumé.

Sonja, in contrast, took time with all the details, especially the personal ones: Trini immigrant family; raised in Hempstead; Cornell undergrad; New York Law; a day job at Universal Records in business affairs; an IBM executive boyfriend with a crib in Jersey; and a nightlife that had nothing to do with contracts and depositions.

"My boyfriend," she said at one point, "would love this big-screen TV and this conversation. He's always watching documentaries on jazz and blues and all that. He probably knows your work."

"Really," I replied, not knowing how to respond. "It's a shame he's not here."

She smiled and turned her gaze from me to Beatrice. "Now that's not what you really think, is it?"

"No, counselor, it isn't."

"The truth is always a good thing. How long have you and Walter been friends?"

"Known him fifteen years or so. Way back before his first music videos."

"So you must have a lot in common."

This was an encouraging line of questioning.

"As much as good friends do. As much as you and your good friend have in common," I answered.

"Well, it's been only two months, but we already share so much." She had more to say, but Walter walked up to the table.

"Let's go, team," he said, gesturing for us to stand. "I have a new recruit."

Walter led Beatrice by the hand while I guided Sonja behind them, my hand resting in the soft curve of her waist. We moved around the chairs of envious men to the bar where a barely post-college chocolate-brown cutie awaited us. Her name was Robinette, and she was dressed in '70s retro style—plain hip-hugger slacks, a beige turtleneck, a brown leather jacket, black platform shoes, and yellow-tinted shades. A woolly natural silhouetted her baby face.

"Walter," she whined, "I'm supposed to be meeting some friends."

He took her by the hand like a father would his child. "No, Robinette, that's dead. You're coming with us." She didn't resist, but wore a petulant scowl as we headed for the door. A bouncer looked at me and joked, "Y'all planning your own personal Super Bowl party, huh?" I nodded like it was my game plan and headed out the door.

Outside we commandeered two taxis. Walter got into the first one with Robinette. "Let me get her head straight," he whispered, and then instructed me to jump in the second cab with the other two women. As we drove west across the Village to Moomba, Beatrice nestled in between Sonja and me, turned and began kissing her friend. As their tongues tied I at first watched like an intruder until, timidly, I started rubbing the insides of Beatrice's legs. I then progressed to kissing her neck. She opened her gams wider in encouragement. By the time we reached Moomba my fingers had traced some delightful geometric patterns inside her panties.

Up on Moomba's second floor we dined on seafood, artfully arranged vegetables, and a medley of alcoholic beverages. The seating was strategic. Sonja and Beatrice sat next to each other, nuzzling like deer. Walter sat at the head of the table, beaming and pouring Moët like water; Robinette and I sat to his right. Robinette stared, mesmerized by Beatrice and Sonja, while Walter and I soothed, cajoled, and whispered to her about the joys of being sexually open. Robinette's eyes looked a bit glazed, and it hit me that "getting her head right" probably involved drugs. Walter was an old hand at this game, so I just noted it and said nothing.

Initially I'd just followed Walter's lead in seducing Robinette. But as the evening's possibilities became apparent, I grew more animated. I softly rubbed her legs, gazed deep into her brown eyes, and listened empathetically to her frustrations with the fashion game. "Yes, I worked at Condé Nast two years before I got to go on a shoot," she complained. As I nodded that I understood her frustration, mentally I was licking my lips.

Unlike Sonja, a seemingly practical girl with an extravagant inner life, Robinette was obsessed with the surface. It was clear why she fancied Walter—he represented power, opportunity, and mobility. Still, I wasn't sure we would pull Robinette in until she bragged about her close relationship with a Eurasian model and her white photographer hubby. At this couple's mention Walter's eyes widened.

"Have you been out to their house in East Hampton, Robinette?" He leaned in close to her.

"Yes," she said haughtily. "They were kind enough to ask me out."

"And did you stay the weekend?"

"Of course, Walter. I wouldn't go out for just one day."

"No doubt. Now," he said matter-of-factly, "who ate your pussy first—him or her?"

Her reply was a guilty giggle. So now it was on. All our predatory eyes gazed hungrily at young Robinette. Walter pressed on.

"Did you enjoy more eating or being eaten? C'mon, darling. Everybody at this table likes the taste of pussy."

Walter's frankness must have melted Robinette as a dreamy look replaced her earlier self-absorption; it was now clear she had officially joined our party.

"Let's go," Walter announced, the check disappearing under the weight of his black AmEx card.

Robinette asked, "Where are we going?"

"My place," Walter answered. "After all, it's Super Bowl Sunday."

Outside Moomba we snared a cab. Now the rules of the New York taxi industry preclude carrying more than four passengers at a time. Sonja, the attorney, sweet-talked Pierre, the Haitian cabbie, into taking us. Walter, Beatrice, Sonja, and Robinette squeezed snugly into the backseat and I, the fifth wheel, sat up next to the driver. The taxi's two sides were separated by a bulletproof partition. There was a wide hole in the center for exchanging money. Soon after we pulled off I glanced into the back and saw the most remarkable things.

From left to right sat Sonja, Walter, Robinette and Beatrice, as tightly packed as the dot on an *i*.

Walter kissed Beatrice by leaning across the body of a very uncomfortable Robinette. With his left hand he reached back toward Sonja, who began sucking his fingers. Beatrice reached down and across Robinette to unzip Walter's pants. Then she bent down and placed her mouth around his dick. Sonja and Walter locked lips as Robinette sat motionless and the taxi's windows began to fog.

And then, as if someone gave a signal, Sonja, Beatrice, and Walter descended on young Robinette. Walter unbuttoned her blouse. Beatrice unzipped her slacks. Sonja reached over and pulled down Robinette's leopard bra, revealing her tiny, hard black nipples. Her matching leopard panties showcased a flat, smooth stomach and a thin wisp of carefully shaved pubic hair. Her moans filled the now-steamy car as I stuck my hand through the opening in the bulletproof glass, stretching my fingers to touch Robinette's soft, slender legs. But that was all I could really do, aside from peer at the proceedings like a poor child outside a bakery. Pierre, our very focused driver, didn't flinch, slow down, complain, or even seem to care. He just rolled up unconcerned to Walter's apartment in a smooth, efficient manner. As we drove I could hear the Super Bowl starting lineups being announced on the radio.

Outside of very well-cast porn videos I'd never seen anything like this. I was involved, but then, not really. What could be worse than being three feet away from an orgy? I was just a horny-ass voyeur, separated from the action by steel and plastic and leather.

When we stopped at Walter's building on West Thirty-fourth Street, I paid Pierre as the lord of the manor and his three concubines sauntered inside. I have no idea how much money I gave Pierre, 'cause I was not getting left behind again. I had never been in an orgy before—hadn't even had a threesome. Now I was ready to lose my "virginity."

Walter was reserved in the lobby, speaking politely to the doorman, before checking his mail even though it was Sunday. Even in the elevator, when a glassy-eyed Robinette tried to smother him with kisses, he seemed more interested in the security camera than her.

Ah, but once he closed the door to his apartment, he dropped the mask and returned to his true lecherous nature, doling out orders as if he were a drill sergeant.

"Ladies, there are two guest bathrooms. Why don't you make any necessary stops while Dwayne and I get refreshments."

The women dutifully retreated to the bathrooms, which were located along the apartment's long central corridor adjacent to two guest bedrooms. Walter's main bedroom was at one end of the corridor next to his gym. Beyond that was the kitchen. At the opposite end of the hall was the entry to the living room and dining area. Walter locked the door to the master bedroom and opened the door to one of the guest rooms.

He then turned to me and spoke with great seriousness. "If anyone asks, you spent the night here. Unbeknownst to me you took advantage of my generosity and brought some ass up here. You with that?"

"Of course."

Walter then dropped down to the carpeted floor and began furiously doing push-ups. I laughed. "Laugh now, niggah. In twenty minutes you'll be singing my praise," he huffed between sets.

I went back into the hall. One of the bathroom doors was open. In Walter's gym, Robinette stood staring at herself in the floor-to-ceiling mirrors. I came up behind her, placing my hands on her hips and my lips on her long brown neck. She moaned as I nibbled softly, but never took her eyes off her image. She ran her hands up her body, finally stopping at her chest. Then she cupped her breasts through her blouse. My hands followed her trail and then blazed new territory by sliding inside her blouse and under her bra. Together we slipped out one breast and then the other. My groin pressed between her small buns, and my hands pinched her nipples. Slowly, like we were dancing to an old-school jam, I turned her around until we were in profile in the mirror. Watching the spectacle of my hands on Robinette's girlish body and shining ebony skin, I felt like a vampire preparing for the first bite.

But I knew that for Robinette I was just a tool being employed to achieve pleasure—a pleasure that her hazy eyes suggested wasn't necessarily dependent on me. This moment was more about her mind, her fantasy, than me. I went down to my knees, pushing aside her leopard panties, savoring her taste with my mouth. As I slipped my tongue under the crotch of her panties she opened her mouth and a moan escaped from the back of her throat, a beautiful sound I remembered from the taxi. But now I was the reason she made it.

As Robinette rocked in my mouth, an animal sound came from down the hall. It was primordial. It came from deep inside someone, from down where the larynx meets the lungs.

For the first time since Moomba, Robinette's eyes seemed focused. "What was that?" she asked, her voice hushed.

"Sounded like either Sonja or Beatrice?"

"Who?"

Now I was pulled out of the moment. This woman—a girl, really—didn't know anyone here except Walter. Not even the guy who was currently eating her pussy.

This was really crazy.

"Let's find Walter," I said, pulling her clothes up around her as I stood up. We walked down the hall, drawn by the heaving of bedsprings. We entered the guest bedroom and stood there staring at the bed. Walter was on the bottom. Sonja was above him, her pussy enveloping his dick. Beatrice was behind Sonja humping her ass with a black strap-on dildo. As Sonja was penetrated from below and behind, shock waves of pleasure moved through her fleshy body. Walter smiled as he saw our faces and motioned Robinette over. When she reached the bed he pointed at Sonja. An obedient Robinette then leaned forward and began fondling Sonja's breasts and kissing her neck.

At that moment I vowed, "This is not gonna be the mother-fucking cab all over again!" After ripping open a packet of my favorite green-and-white Trojans and doffing my coat, I placed myself behind Beatrice's active little ass and found her sweet spot.

The other four bodies had to adjust to my presence and, for an awkward moment, I felt like an intruder, like a DJ playing Bach at a down-home blues joint.

But then we found our collective rhythm. Beatrice adjusted her stroke to mine, Sonja arched her back higher, Walter thrust his pelvis differently; and Robinette, well, she didn't do anything but close her eyes even tighter. For a time we were all in harmony.

After a while, it felt like I was standing outside the pile, just marveling at the beauty of these five undulating brown bodies. It was gorgeous in the way of some erotic African wood carving—the kind they keep under wraps at the Metropolitan Museum of Art. My mind took mental snapshots of this moment, moving around the bed like the camera in *The Matrix*. It was sex, but not sex as I'd experienced it in my previous thirty-plus years. It wasn't just fucking—it was a full-fledged never-to-be-forgotten freaky-deekey-funkadelic jam. I was already nostalgic for it, and the night wasn't even over.

It was like a sequence of edits in a film as we shifted from person to person, position to position. It seemed like I spent most of my time with Sonja, doing a duet that was deep and funky, while Walter somehow handled Beatrice and Robinette in a balancing act involving fingers, mouth, and penis.

Things took an even stranger turn when I became aware I was kissing a leg that was a touch hairier than it should have been. I looked up to see it belonged to Walter. "Go ahead," urged Beatrice as she returned my lips to his leg. "Lick it," she ordered. "Now kiss it and use your tongue."

And so I did, as the three ladies murmured their approval. Walter sniggered and said, "Don't be a trick, Dwayne."

"Shut up," Sonja said.

"And," Walter responded, "what does he get for licking me, ladies?"

"Yeah, what do I get?" I chimed in.

"Sonja, go help him," Beatrice commanded.

And, like magic, a soft hand took control of my dick and a mouth engulfed its head. I tongued Walter's leg right up his knee, and then asked, "Is that all I get?"

No, it wasn't. Robinette took one nipple and Beatrice began licking the other, and I was caught up in a series of new, joyously weird sensations. My mouth opened and my body wiggled and I could feel blood twirling inside me as I licked Walter and was licked by the ladies. The feeling was of total abandon. I don't know that I'd ever felt so free, yet so passive. I was a vessel, a cup that pleasure was being poured into. And, happily, I was overflowing.

I didn't sleep for long. Maybe a half hour. But there had never been a sleep like that in my life because I'd never had a night like this before. So satisfied, so calm. I opened my eyes slowly. It was quiet. To my right was Robinette. I saw her swallow a little black pill and follow it with wine.

"Are you all right?"

"Ah-huh," she replied.

"Where'd they go?"

"The girls said they were hungry."

"No doubt."

"But they told me to stay here."

"Really?"

"Yeah. That Beatrice girl is so bossy, but it's all right. I'll have my time with Walter, too."

I rolled onto my back and took inventory. Had I already had my Super Bowl? Was I out of the game? After that experience, what did I have left? Not much, it seemed. Yet Walter was somewhere in the house still getting busy with two women. Again I was envious of Walter, but I guess that's why he was a mogul and I wasn't. There was a certain hunger for conquest in Walter I just didn't possess.

I rose gingerly off the mattress and felt dizzy when I stood up. I'd come so hard my head was still spinning.

Down the hallway, past the two bathrooms, and into the gym I stumbled toward the strange, sexual sound coming from the kitchen. It was different from the moaning and grunting from before. It was a man's voice. Not a moan or groan, but a weirdly contented whimper. Didn't even know that such a sound existed.

I stepped into the kitchen doorway and, for the third time tonight, witnessed sex as I'd never seen it before. My eyes widened. I almost stopped breathing. Sonja was sitting on a chair with her legs around Walter's neck. So far, so good. Walter was on his hands and knees, jerking himself off with one hand. No surprise there. The tricky, heart-stopping, world-wrecking part was Beatrice, who was bent over Walter's back, slowly humping his ass with that black strap-on dildo. In and out she stroked, moving as expertly as she had with Sonja, but with a more leisurely, almost luxurious stroke. Not only hadn't I ever seen anything like this, I'd never even imagined it was possible. I guess I was more innocent than I wanted to admit.

Beatrice saw me standing there, smiled, and then bent her finger in a "come here" gesture. Before I had been stunned. Now I was horrified. I stepped backward, turned, and almost ran back down the hallway.

The guest bedroom was a mess of rumpled sheets, wet spots, and condom packages. In the air hung the aroma of sweat, perfume, and sex. Robinette had disappeared into a bathroom. I slipped on my pants and T-shirt and sat on the bed feeling numb. I decided to do something normal. I went into the living room, sat down, and messed around with the remote, hoping to find the Super Bowl and try to blank out what I'd just seen. It was the fourth quarter, and the Titans were mounting a comeback led by quarterback Steve McNair. It was shaping up to be a memorable effort; commentators predicted this could be one of the greatest endings of all time. But obviously, the game, no matter who won, wouldn't be what I'd remember about tonight.

To my surprise Beatrice, in panties and an open robe, walked in and sat down on the sofa beside me. She wanted to know the score.

"The Rams are winning, but the Titans are making a game of it," I said. "You like football?"

"A little. I watch it at the club with customers. It gives men something to talk about. But I find it too violent."

"Sometimes," I suggested, "a little violence is good?"

"A little pain, yes," she replied. "But not violence."

"Okay," I said, and then took a moment to really study her. Her face was moist and her eyes tired. Still, if I didn't know what she'd just done, nothing about her manner would have revealed it. She looked like someone's flirtatious girlfriend. We pass people every day on the street, people who have done the most unusual things. We think they are just ordinary people, but we don't know who they really are or what they're truly capable of. I thought I knew who Beatrice was. A freak. A stripper. She's still both. But on this Sunday it was clear the lady was also one hell of a head coach.

She said, "You know, I think you're cute."

"Are you being sarcastic?"

"No, Dwayne. Don't be so insecure."

"Did Walter ask you to do that to him?"

"Do what?" She wanted me to say it.

"You know. What you did in the kitchen."

"No," she said slyly. "I asked him and he agreed. I've done a lot for him. Things you don't know about. It was something he owed me. A little returned favor, you know?"

"A little favor. Wow. You sure move through the world differently."

"I don't know. Everything's about exchange. If we get closer, Dwayne, I may ask a favor of you, too."

"You already had me kissing Walter's hairy-ass leg. Isn't that favor enough?"

"And that wasn't so bad, was it?"

"I was, you know, distracted."

"That's how it starts, baby. One distraction leads to another."

. . .

On the TV McNair was driving the Titans. The clock was ticking. A field goal wouldn't do. A touchdown was the Titans' only shot. Walter ambled in and sat next to me, requesting an update on the game. Sonja appeared next, seating herself partly on Beatrice's lap and partly on mine. We sat there and, for a funny moment, we were just any close American family watching the big game.

Sonja asked for the phone—something about calling her boy-friend. I suppressed a chuckle and watched her ass bounce as she exited. A moment later Beatrice left, too. When they were gone Walter leaned over and said, "Soon as the game's over, you say you're going home and take all the freaks with you. I gotta call Daria."

Daria Dinkins, black ingenue, decent actress, all-around cutie, was shooting a sci-fi/martial arts flick in Thailand. She was "the black girl" in a multiculti cast.

Whatever "favor" Walter felt obliged to do for his bisexual gal pal was in the past. The bass was back in his voice, and he'd reverted to mack mode. But now, of course, I would never, ever, see Walter Gibbs the same way again.

Still, he sounded, looked, and acted like the Walter I'd always known; like the guy I'd played ball with that afternoon; like the man who'd seen more ass than a toilet. Besides, wasn't I the one who'd been licking his leg not too long ago? Yes, I had been "dis-tracted." But then again, licking a man's leg and being ass-fucked by a stripper are not exactly the same thing.

"Mum's the word on this, right?" I said.

"Niggah, we shouldn't even have to have that convo. But you got a big mouth, which is one reason I never put you down before."

"Like I can't be trusted."

"Like you're CNN. I only tell you shit I want known. In this sit-uation I expect you to tell lots of niggahs everything. Shit, I expect you to be a big man in every gym or bar in the Apple. Just leave my motherfucking name out of it. Aiight."

"No doubt. By the way, that girl Robinette is talking like she expects to stay."

"Yo, Dwayne, you got to take her. She wants to be my girl. Now, she's talented for her age—"

"Which is?"

Walter ignored my question and just said, "I just don't wanna be alone with her right now. That girl's trying to get ahead in life. You never know what ideas she might get about how to do that. Tonight was cool. Two weeks later I'm in the motherfucking *Post*. As long as you guys are all in it with me, I'm safe. You feel me?"

"I got you, dog. You have the most to lose."

"And you have the most to gain, so keep my name out of it and we'll be stacking paper for a long time to come." He held out his fist, and I met it with mine.

We looked up and saw that a Titans wide receiver was being tackled by the Rams linebacker one yard short of the goal line. The gun sounded. The Super Bowl was over, and bettors all around the nation were scrambling for their phones. Back in the bedroom I began searching for my shoes and socks, all the while keeping an eye on Robinette, who had emerged from the bathroom and was sprawled lethargically across the bed.

"Robinette," I said, shaking her. "Robinette."

"Yes," she said in a sleepy voice.

"We're all getting ready to leave."

"Oh."

No movement, not even an effort. Sonja and Beatrice, now dressed, walked in. Beatrice placed her slender hands on her hips and surveyed the situation. "Why don't you take a quick shower?" she suggested. "I got this."

The water rolled over places of my pain—a bite on my left forearm, scratches on my back, a sore right shoulder, a rawness of the left side of my dick from someone's teeth. I put my clothes on gingerly, like a running back after a hundred-yard game. In the mirror my eyes were red and my face flushed. I craved my empty bed.

By the time I was dressed the ladies were gathered in the living room. Robinette, now fully dressed, sipped apple juice. Walter was nowhere to be found. Beatrice stood by Robinette and clearly had our young friend under control. Perhaps the godmomma of decadence had found a fine young disciple. Meanwhile, Sonja's demeanor had changed. I could see the well-bred, highly motivated, ambitious Buppie in her had now reemerged. She'd freaked enough for the week. I guess it was time to put her mask back on.

"I just spoke to my boyfriend, and he does know who you are," Sonja said excitedly. "He saw you on something on A&E about Prince."

"That's what I used to do," I said. "I was a talking head for years."

"Well, I need to get an autographed book for him."

"Not a problem," I replied, as if we'd just met at a book signing.

In a perfect world I would have met Sonja at a conference on African American something or other. Maybe at a dinner party via a mutual friend. There we would have talked about our families, our careers, our past lovers, and what we liked for dessert. We would have gone to the movies. Some theater perhaps. Had sex on the third or fourth date and vacationed in Cancún or Negril. But this wasn't a book signing.

As we stood on Thirty-fourth Street hailing cabs, I mused that Sonja was outwardly the type of sister any man would aspire to marry. Her shape, her gig, her complexion were a black man's ideal. But then Sonja was no stereotype of upwardly mobile accomplishment. There were other shades to the lady. And then there was that boyfriend.

As if reading my mind, Sonja asked if I had a card. I didn't, but I wrote my digits on the back of hers and put another one into my pocket. Beatrice watched without comment, though there was a twinkle in her baby browns. The ladies hopped into the backseat, but I didn't get in.

"You're not going with us?" Beatrice wondered.

"No, ladies, I'm gonna stop and grab some food and then take the subway home."

"See you soon," Beatrice said warmly.

"Call me," Sonja commanded. "I want an autographed book for my boyfriend."

Robinette offered a listless "Bye," and then sank into the backseat as the cab pulled off.

I stood on the curb watching the departing cab and then slid out my cell. By the time I was in Mickey D's I'd raised Walter.

"Yo niggah, I'm still on the phone with my girl."

"Just wanted to say that was unbelievable, my man."

"No doubt."

"No doubt, indeed."

At this point in the conversation I tossed a fry into my mouth and wondered if I should mention what I'd seen in the kitchen. Should I bring up the fact that my longtime friend and current employer had just an hour ago been looking like a *Man Date* magazine cover boy? Eventually I would ask him. I would. Just not on Super Bowl Sunday.

Instead, I mumbled, "Okay, Walter, I'll let you go."

"Aiight. My niggah."

"Yeah. Peace."

I sat there, munching on my fries, remembering the pleasure and trying to forget that damn dildo. A brother came in wearing a Tennessee Titans snorkel. "Tough, my man," I said to him.

"Naw, dog. Nothing like being in the Super Bowl. Don't know when you'll be back. Getting in the game is all you can ask, you know?"

He held out his knuckles. I met them with mine. Then I stood up, luxuriating in how sore my whole body was and smiling at how it got that way.

NELSON GEORGE

on "It's Never Too Late in New York," first published in
Best American Erotica in 2005

I've always found New York to be a place of limitless possibility.
Anytime you walk out your door, the day could take you away onto
a great adventure or, perhaps, a major tragedy. That sense of the
unexpected led me to write "It's Never Too Late in New York."

The day/night that inspired the story was supposed to be about
a little weight-lifting and a couple of games of full-court basketball.
With one conversation, the trajectory of my day changed, and I
entered a world of escalating erotic possibility and risk.

I guess this night could have happened in another city, but it
never has (though hope springs eternal). I'm not even sure it could
happen in squeaky-clean twenty-first-century New York. New York
City is different, and so am I. Some of this did happen. But the
devil is in the details, and it's the devilish details that turn reality
into fiction and possibility into a really fun story.

THE YEAR OF FUCKING BADLY

Susannah Indigo

"There is no such thing as bad sex," I say to no one in particular.

We're at the big oval table at the Empress Gardens eating dim sum to celebrate the Chinese New Year when it all begins. It's the beginning of the Year of the Ox, a year that is supposed to bring the promise of new discoveries, or maybe fertility, I forget.

"Of course there is, Kenna," my friend Bill replies. "Bad sex: sex so awful, so unexpected, so terrible that just telling someone about it later makes them turn away in laughter, or horror."

"This really exists? Then why hasn't anyone made a whole magazine or something about it ever?" I can picture bad relationships, bad love even, bad breakups, but not plain ol' bad sex, unless you're counting boring sex, and then if you do, boring sex rules half the world and is often the norm rather than the exception.

Bill pauses and puts his hand on my knee. "You want me to show you, Kenna?"

I laugh. Bill is my sweet friend, my occasional fuck buddy, and about as obsessed by sex as I am. He's a Pig, as in the Year of, defined quite appropriately as a sensual hedonist. I know this fact because I work as a research librarian—an "information specialist" they call us nowadays—and I get so many calls this time of year about Chinese astrology that I keep the chart by my desk.

I hike my black leather skirt a little higher as Bill watches, smiling. "Hell, you know what I like, Bill. Most anything that moves." To put it mildly. "What exactly would you do to show me bad sex? Take me home and fuck me for five minutes in the missionary position and then roll over and say good night?" I don't talk this way around work, of course, where I wear my wavy red hair up in a bun, skip the leather, and leave the contacts home for my everyday glasses.

Bill offers to rape me if I want, which hurts my brain to think about. Everybody knows rape is not about sex. But if I let him rape me, is it still rape? I'm such a pervert I'd probably like it no matter what.

"More stories," says Bryan across the table from me, probably trying to deflect the conversation away from rape, which nobody ever talks about but most everyone fantasizes about.

"Define 'bad,'" Mary says.

I wave my little librarian hand. At least I can add this. "Did you know that the word 'bad' is thought to originate from two Old English homophobic words from about the thirteenth century—'baeddel' and 'baedling'—which were derogatory terms for homosexuals, with overtones of sodomy?"

"Really?"

"Yeah." I can't recall why I remember this, but maybe it caught my attention because of those overtones of sodomy.

Everyone around the table goes on to tell their own "bad sex" story. The boys almost always involve not being able to get it up, but that strikes me as "bad imagination" or even "bad ego" rather than bad sex. Let's face it, women know. They make enough cocks down at Good Vibrations to keep us girls happy for the rest of our lives.

I notice a trend. Every bad story seems to supply bare-bones details, a gasp, and then trails off into "and it was so awful. . . ."

I'm racking my brain for a story of my own as my turn arrives. I think about the worst situation I can remember—the guy I married when I was eighteen, my manic-depressive young husband. I remember getting divorced from him at twenty. I remember the angry words, the suicide threats. I remember the cold metal of the gun on my bare thigh the night before I finally moved out, I remember being terrified, and I also remember being very, very wet. No, I imagine that story won't work.

Nobeko starts in on a story about a woman who wanted to tie her up and how shocking this was to her. I can't stand it. The world is desperately in need of more people with enough passion and drive to understand the dynamics revealed in restraints. You wouldn't believe how many people I've actually had to *ask* to tie me up, pretty please, which tends to limit the high of submissiveness. Believe me, the concept of men and domination is a myth.

I shrug and pass on telling a story when it's my turn, and after a couple more "it was awful's" the conversation turns to great sex. But the bad sex concept holds in my mind, and I know there is no way to look this up in my library. Field research is required. I never pass on anything. That's why people like me become researchers, because the urge to know everything and anything about a subject is overwhelming once it slips into that certain mind-curiosity groove. If there's bad sex out there, I'll find it.

"It's sort of a scavenger hunt for bad sex, Holly," I try to explain to my upstairs neighbor and lover. We're buried deep under her pink comforter eating chocolate chip cookies the next night. Holly is the Martha Stewart of my love life—candlelight and cookies and flowers all the time. Some nights just walking into her place is better than actual sex. She's a Dragon—as into mind-touching as body-touching.

"Sometimes I have bad sex with myself," Holly offers. "You know, those nights when even your own fingers bore you to death?"

"Bad sex for one? Sounds like something Stouffer's would make."

Monogamy is not a fetish of mine, but still I feel a little guilty, even though Holly and I have always been open about any other lovers we might have. I decided a long time ago that two lovers was exactly the right number for me. My other lover is a student named Keith, a Snake like me, but from a different generation, twelve years younger. He knows what I need. He likes to use my hair to tie me up in strange places before he fucks me, and I'm immensely fond of that particular knot.

Holly agrees it might be a good project as long as I promise only to attempt bad sex. She's an academic, so she decides to chart this all out for me. We decide that random bad sex would probably have to involve a stranger. We decide I need to keep a log of it all, and that there has to be a way to sort it out. She remembers the old Sears catalog ratings of "good / better / best" when buying products and decides that will do. Our final scale runs: Worst / Worse / Bad / Boring / Good / Better / Best—and that's it, I'm off for the hunt.

Driving down Broadway the first night I sense one problem. I'm already wet at the promise of getting laid by someone new. I try to control myself by reciting the Dewey Decimal system out loud.

The lounge at the Holiday Inn on Colfax is the first stop. I'm wearing fishnet stockings and leather, but my hair is pulled back in a ponytail and my turtleneck rides high, a sort of combo slut/cheerleader look. It doesn't take me long to pick out a paunchy-looking, balding guy at a table by himself and start the flirtation.

He tells me his traveling salesman story, the exquisite details of selling hospital equipment, while I brush his leg with my boot and watch the surprise in his eyes at his luck. He's a Rat, I find out—outwardly cool, self-controlled, but passionate.

"Push the button on my watch," he says, holding his wrist out for me to see.

I push the button.

"Tell me what it says, Kenna."

I'm stifling a laugh. Can I pick them or what? "It says, 'WANNA FUCK?'" And in large letters no less. "Pretty damn clever." I don't remember any mention of Rats having crass taste in jewelry.

"I had it made special in Taiwan."

Maybe, just maybe, I've found what I'm looking for, and on my first try. I don't want to sleep with him. So I will.

"Wow," I say, flipping my ponytail. "And, yes. But do you know where the word 'fuck' comes from?" Now why on earth would I share this with him? But I do. "It's actually a mystery, but they think it might originally be from the Scandinavian 'fokka.' There's one written record of the word in 1278, and then nothing, nothing at all until three hundred years later, maybe because it was such a taboo to say it." They probably didn't even make these watches back then.

He reaches over and twists my hair in his meaty hand and whispers, "I'll show you where fucking really comes from, sweetheart."

A kiss, the check, and he's guiding me to his room.

"Take off all of your clothes, lie down on your belly, and close your eyes," the Rat orders after we enter the tackiness that is room 413 at the Holiday Inn. "I want to show you something."

Another watch? His cock? Some strange hospital equipment? But this is my game, and I'm stripping down and stretching out.

He's searching in his bag and I'm peeking out of one eye and he's bringing out what looks like a bottle of oil.

"I used to work as a masseur," he says as he climbs up on top of me and begins with my back. "Let me massage this fine body, sweetheart." When his hands start in on me, I see this boy starting to slide way up my sexual-rating chart. By the time he's worked me over with his oil front and back I'm completely limp in his hands and ready for anything, and he's entering me from behind and riding me hard and holding my hair tight with one hand and slapping my ass with the other. He's got me hollering, "Fuck me, fuck me, fuck me," and I know that if this Rat had been around in the fourteenth century, they would have definitely written the word down.

"Okay, so looks aren't a good indicator of bad sex, Holly," I admit, safely back in her pink bed. "But what can I do—interview people and ask them if they're a lousy lay?"

Holly's reviewing my log. "All it says here is 'his hands, his hands,' Kenna."

"Shit, that's all I can remember. It was great."

She sighs, but we begin to plan the ex-lover possibility next. Julia was the love of my life ten years ago, until she decided she was too good for me and dumped me coldly. She's a Monkey—clever, witty, manipulative, pretentious. The Chinese chart doesn't really say all that, I'm just projecting. I do distinctly recall her saying she was going to sleep only with PhDs after our breakup. And that she was with me only because she was crazy about my breasts. This has to be bad.

I find her at her modern-dance class, where I show up in a low-cut black leotard to get her attention. I lie to her over lunch, tell her about my newly minted PhD in the thirteenth-century dialect of Baedel Fokka, and get invited back to her place. I make up other stories for her about the places I've been and who I've met. When I create an imaginary friendship with Camille Paglia, who I know she idolizes, I'm in. She spreads her legs for me and I'm devouring her and I suddenly can't remember why I found her so attractive in the first place, but I go for the sex just to show her how hot I am, and it works.

When I leave and turn at the door to tell her, "I'm sorry, I won't be back, because I just realized that I should really sleep only with tenured professors," I realize that this is the most fun I've had in weeks.

I try to dive back into work and forget this whole idea, but every research question I'm asked sounds like sex. I've started watching everybody I see and thinking all the time about how they fuck, why they fuck, where they fuck, is it good, what do they do badly. When I'm not answering the phone, I can be found doing some heavy breathing back in section 306.7, reading every sex book I can get my hands on. Hell, I'm so immersed in it I could practically write a thesis—maybe you *can* get a PhD in bad sex.

Joe's Bait Shop, the local dive bar. Holly scoped the place for me over the weekend and thinks it's a guaranteed bad time. Every possible sport on a dozen big-screen TVs, pool tables in the back. The bartender's a babe. It's amazing how fuckable everyone looks when you're looking for people who aren't.

I'm wearing black tights, a long baby blue sweater, black suede boots and nothing underneath. I'm getting a few looks but no bites because of the damn football game. I forgot it was Monday night. Maybe *this* is bad sex, when you can't even draw a man away from the television.

I get myself a drink and wander toward the back room. There's some kind of a meeting in progress and no TVs, so I slip in and sit down in an empty card chair in the back to check out the crowd.

"My goal," the handsome man speaking says, "is to help others achieve sexual sobriety."

Wait, wait. Sexual sobriety? Is this where you fuck only *before* you get drunk?

"The twelve steps were my saving grace," he continues. "I turned my lust over to God."

Holy shit, I think I've wandered into a meeting of OverFuckers Anonymous.

I laugh. Heads turn in my direction, followed by frowns at my laughter. I can't help it. I know they're deadly serious. But maybe God knows what bad sex is. I wonder, does God *like* having all this lust turned over to him? Didn't God turn it over to us in the first place?

The speaker's looking right at me and smiling. "Who would like to share their story with us today?" He's got piercing green eyes and big shoulders and a fuzzy beard that I can already feel rubbing between my legs, and I'm considering making up a quick sad story to tell him and I know I should consider getting the hell out of here instead.

I do not volunteer. They'd never believe me if I told the truth about why I'm here. But wait, bad sex, bad sex. These folks have potential. Oversexed people trying *not* to have sex could be real bad. Or would they be real good, heading toward better/best, like reformed Catholic girls let loose?

At the break, the speaker comes directly to me and introduces himself. "My name is Tony," he says with a gorgeous grin. Oh my. I don't even have to ask, I know he's a Tiger, as in the Year of, the Hour of, the Moment of, the Bed of, the Cock of, and I'm heading for trouble.

"I just stopped in here accidentally," I say. "Giving up lust? This is like a bad dream."

"I know," the Tiger says. He pauses, and then takes my arm firmly and guides me out toward the dark back corner of the bar. He smiles. "But I bet your dreams are spectacular, darling. You look like a girl who knows how to dream." Fresh drinks in hand, strong arms wrapped around me. "Do you dream in color, Kenna?"

That's the best pickup line I've heard in ages. "Everyone does, Tony, or can. Did you know that nobody ever questioned this fact before the advent of black-and-white television in the fifties? Not Freud, not Jung . . ." I hear my little librarian voice being smart, and at the same time I feel my knees shaking like a little girl and I just want to climb up on his lap and let him turn his lust over to me instead of God.

He listens to me as though every word I utter is gold. He knows the secrets. Words and hands and eyes and laughter. Attention paid; intensity gained. But it keeps sneaking through the haze of my desire that this man is one of *them*.

"Tony, didn't I just hear you discussing 'sexual sobriety' as a way of life?" I ask as he pulls me onto his lap and his hand is higher and higher on my thigh, so high and so right that I think I imagined it all and that this is my punishment or maybe my reward for thinking and dreaming about sex day and night and forever, ever, pretending I know a single thing about what it all means.

"For you, darling, I'm willing to fall off the chastity wagon." His mouth is on mine, and he's biting my lip with the force that I need and I am *going going gone*. I don't believe a word he says, and I don't care. The cock of the Tiger is hard beneath my ass and all the lines are slipping away and good is blending into better and heading off the chart and he's whispering in my ear and I want it all and we're out the door.

Before he starts the car he says, "Pull your tights down and spread your legs and let me see," and I do, and he just watches me. When he stops the car at Sunset Park, a short drive away, and leans over, his beard is rough against my thighs exactly as I imagined it, and he's biting and sucking and I'm in heaven and then he's suddenly slowing way down.

"I shouldn't do this," he mumbles with his mouth still buried in my pussy. Oh god, maybe *this* is the bad sex I deserve, when it begins to orbit off the chart and you know that somehow when it's over it's going to wrap right back around and come up on the awful horrifying side as chastity reclaimed.

"I shouldn't do this," he repeats, and I think maybe he's waiting for me to save him. This is one of those damned defining moments in life. Define the moment or it defines you. Screw him, or screw him? Fuck it. Or fuck me. I reach down and stroke his hard cock through his jeans.

"I'll be good for you, Tiger. Don't stop, don't stop." He lifts my sweater and we're tumbling toward the backseat like teenagers in lust, and I'm not sure I'll be able to excuse this behavior later as research but maybe I don't even care. My tights are off and my legs are wrapped high around his big shoulders and his cock presses into me and he leans down and begins to bite my nipple and send me over the edge. He pauses and I think I will die if he stops one more time. "You're right, darling," he whispers, driving into me hard. "For tonight, there's just no such thing as bad sex."

SUSANNAH INDIGO
on "The Year of Fucking Badly"

I wrote this story after a discussion of "bad sex" as a writing theme. Just like my protagonist, I couldn't quite pin the concept down, and I had no great "bad sex" story of my own.

I'm sure fifteen years ago before BDSM became cocktail party chatter and standard TV fare, someone asking to be tied up might have been "bad" or emotionally traumatic, because it was misunderstood.

The Internet altered much of this—knowledge changes everything. I figure by the twenty-second century, the concept of "bad sex"—and even boring/selfish sex—will simply be absurd: who would ever let that happen to them in a century where every human being is empowered with full knowledge of all aspects of sexuality?

STORY OF O

BIRTHDAY PARTY

Susie Bright

> "... a happy prisoner upon whom everything was imposed
> and from whom nothing was asked."
>
> —THE STORY OF O

I had big plans for my thirtieth birthday party. Inspired by *Life-styles of the Rich and Famous*, I planned to spoof the career expectations of the entire thirty-something generation by having a Filthy Rich and Wretchedly Famous Blowout, where, diamond tiara on my head, I would preside over my royal Coming of Age.

But my plans were changed for me. I never got close to a diamond tiara. In fact, I wore very little at all.

Two days before my birthday, my lover, Honey Lee, asked me if we could have the day all to ourselves. She had a little surprise. Surprises aren't Honey's forte, but I thought that after six years together I'd allow her attempt at unpredictability.

"Okay, I'd love to spend the day with you. Just tell me what to wear," I said. That turned out to be the key that pried open her secret.

"Nothing, nothing at all," she answered. "All you have to do is wake up in the morning and be ready for anything."

March 25. I woke up, put on my furry purple bathrobe, and set the kettle on to boil. I wasn't jumping to any conclusions. Honey Lee didn't seem to be in any particular hurry. "You're having some guests over at ten o'clock," she said.

I sipped my tea and imagined the possibilities. Two weeks ago, I had been putting away Honey's bags and discovered a new paperback copy of *The Story of O*. Honey Lee credited Pauline Réage's classic S/M novel with every hot sexual fantasy ever to enter her head, but she was all sexy dreams and no action. Honey had never tied me up, slapped me, or spanked me. She said the real thing made her sick to her stomach. Was she about to turn it all around for my fourth decade?

I heard heavy steps approaching the front door. And who of our women friends was so big that she bumped her head on the ceiling?

It was no lesbian. It was a six-foot-tall man, with a head as bald as Yul Brynner's and an enormous wooden table in his arms.

"This is your masseur, Patrick," Honey Lee announced. "He'll be with you for the next two hours. I'll be back when he's finished."

I was speechless that she was leaving me alone with a giant. Patrick set up his massage table and covered it with a flannel sheet. I slipped out of my robe and thought, Well, here we go. If Honey Lee was preparing me for something, I'd need every minute of a two-hour massage.

The masseur handled every corner of me, every pinch of flesh. He washed my feet and stroked my hair and pulled and kneaded me into a floating fog. When Honey returned, my face was as soft as a baby's and I could only mumble my thanks. She brought me a cup of tea and the doorbell rang again.

"Your dresser is here."

In walked a blond, curly-haired angel. It was my friend Debi, who worked as a stripper and was dressed in one of her most outrageous costumes: white satin underwear and pearls, all covered by a sheer crinoline veil. But the clothes she had brought for me were even more spectacular.

First, she cinched my waist with a tight leather corset until I looked like an hourglass. She had me slip on black silk stockings. She rouged my nipples. Honey Lee brought out a black satin and gauze gown that exposed my breasts but covered my hips and legs. The lace tops of my stockings barely peeked out over the thigh-high leather stiletto boots she handed me. Debi crimped my hair and applied the same lipstick to my lips that she'd touched on my breasts. Such a beauty. By the time she was done with me, I could not make any coy remarks about my physical flaws. When I looked in the mirror, I saw Mistress Venus.

Honey packed up some parcels for the car. "I can't go out like this!" I protested. But Debi had already thought of that. She folded me into me her black patent leather trench coat. Now I was a sex slave with an Emma Peel wrapper.

Debi kissed me and gave me some last fairy godmother words of advice. "You won't be able to talk from now on," she said. "Anything you want to say to Honey Lee or me, you should say now."

I don't know what it was, but I burst into tears. "I love you so much . . . and I'm a little worried about what you have planned for me. . . . I don't know if I can be quiet," I admitted.

Honey took my face in her hands. "Parts of today might be hard for you, Susie, but I don't think you'll regret it. Do you trust me?"

I nodded, but my heart did a flip-flop. I always fantasize about submission, but in real life, I am a control fanatic. I hated her for putting me to the test like this, and I couldn't believe the lengths she'd gone to prepare for it.

For all my fears of not being able to button my lip, I suddenly didn't feel like saying a word. Honey escorted me to the car. Debi, still in her bra and G-string, sped away in her Saab.

Honey Lee and I don't have many separate friends or secrets, and I know my way around the city better than she does. So when we drove for a half an hour only to end up in one of the worst neighborhoods in town, I was sure that she'd gotten us lost, the one torture I cannot abide. I was about to break my vow of silence and tell her to move aside, when she pulled into a parking space. "This is it!" She grinned.

Fabulous. Was I supposed to pirouette to the corner and let the gang bang begin? But Honey steered me toward the creaky stairs of the Victorian flat in front of us. We were buzzed in, and she sent me ahead, up three flights of stairs.

The door at the end of the hall came ajar, and my mouth opened as wide as the sky. Greeting us was a fully uniformed member of the San Francisco Police Department. She was a woman cop I recognized from the neighborhood I work in, someone to whom I'd never said more than "Have a nice day." Honey and she shook hands like old friends.

"Kelly, how are you?" Honey started.

"I'm just on my way to work. All I have to do is polish my boots."

"What a coincidence," Honey said. They were both speaking like marionettes. "I just happen to have a boot-polishing kit with me, and I think Susie would love to give you a nice shine."

I broke my quiet spell. "I don't remember how to shine shoes."

Honey snorted. "Shame on you. We'll give a you a little review."

Honey Lee handed me a shoeshine box with all the equipment. In the corner was a Post-it note reading, "I will be back for you. Do your very best. Love, René."

In *The Story of O*, René is the lover who requires O to submit to other men in order to prove her love and obedience to him. My premonition was coming true.

Kelly took me into her bedroom. She had a couple of guests visiting, a young man and woman who looked me over thoroughly and followed us to the doorway. "Can we watch?"

Kelly gave them the nod. I got out the black polish and tried to remember when the spitting part was supposed to be performed. She was very patient. In fact, for a police officer, I'd gotten a real pussycat. She saw how I kept eyeing her gun belt, and when I had polished her thick work boots as brilliantly as I could, she pulled me to my feet and asked, "You wanna try on my belt?"

She emptied the bullets out of her revolver and showed me where she stored her ammunition, her nightstick, her cuffs, and her flashlight. She slipped the whole contraption around my hips. It must have weighed thirty pounds.

"How can you chase bad guys like this?" I was breaking the no-talking rule again, but Honey Lee wasn't around to keep discipline.

"I'm not interested in dying," she said. She preferred to sweat it out in a heavy bulletproof vest every shift.

"Honey Lee is going to be back before you know it," I said, pulling my original costume together. "You'd better tell her I didn't say a word."

Kelly handed me over with a high recommendation and no squealing. Honey drove us over the hills into yuppie heaven.

"The hardest part is coming up," she said. "Maybe harder for me than for you." She was headed for our friend Coral's apartment.

Coral is what I would call a gourmet sadomasochist. Her home is decorated and constructed for sex play. Her collection of sex toys, particularly whips, is Smithsonian caliber. Honey and I love to talk about sex, pain, and pleasure with Coral, but we are intellectual companions, never participants. I wondered what kind of scene Coral could concoct with me, for if I was to be like O, then Coral would have to perform as a sadist, and I knew that would be a switch.

I should have guessed that Coral could dish out the pain/pleasure she loves to receive. She let us into the bottom floor of her penthouse with more authority and pure wickedness than I'd ever seen in her before.

"Of course, this is out of the ordinary for me," she said. "But I love to make exceptions for the very young and the very pretty."

She and Honey took me up to the master bedroom and told me to stand against the window while they talked about what to do with me. I felt a little rebellious.

"Look, Coral, why don't I just turn you over and give you a good spanking. I should slap both of you for humiliating me like this."

They couldn't believe my cheek. "That's ten extra strokes right there," Honey said.

"Make that with the cane," Coral added.

"A cane! But I've never even been hit with so much as a feather duster!" I said. Coral's eyes got terribly bright all of a sudden. Oh yes, I was a virgin for her, a virgin bottom. The two of them instructed me to take my clothes off, one piece at a time, and pose for them in a completely exploitative way. I bent over in my leather boots and fingered the stretch between my ass and my cunt. I ran the pearls between my legs. I insulted them gamely. "Enjoy yourselves now, you little shits, because I'm going to turn the tables twice as hard when this is over!" Finally I had nothing left on but my stockings, the corset, and my mother's rhinestone necklace. Coral invited me to approach her as she pulled a small red-and-black leather whip from her hip pocket. "I'm going to hand you the handle, and if you return it to me, it means you accept my authority."

I took my sweet time returning it to her. There is no one on earth I would let whip me except Coral. I trust her sensitivity and expertise, but I didn't know how I would react to the pain.

Honey Lee knew what was on my mind. "Do it for me, Susie," she said, and kissed my lips and hair. Then she put on her jacket. I started crying.

"You mean you aren't going to stay?" I sobbed.

"No, but I'll be close by," she promised.

I could tell it was harder for her to leave this time, and I didn't understand why.

Coral stretched me out belly down on her bed and fitted my wrists and ankles with thick fleece and leather restraints. They were chained and locked fast to eyebolts on the floor. I truly could not move. I felt myself flirting with panic. Although there were only the two of us now in the room, I felt more embarrassed than ever and buried my head in the sheets. I didn't want to see what was coming.

Something coarse and thick swept over my back. It was a horse tail! Coral whisked it softly across my ass and then flicked it sharply on the same spot. It barely stung, but before I could let it register, another tender sweeping sensation floated over the same stinging spot. The tail felt completely different depending on how she stroked me.

"Look at what your next choices are," Coral said. Sitting in front of my nose were five whips: one knotted, one thick with many strips, one riding crop, one strap, and one paddle board like Sister Teresa used on our fifth-grade class. I was a Goody Two-shoes and never felt that paddle on my butt. Now I had a perverse desire to get it. "I want to try all of them," I said. "Just build up slowly to the meanest ones."

Coral built it up all right. She took each whip in turn, sliding it across my buttocks once just so I got the feel of its surface, then she hit me quickly, lightly—then she spiked it. She reached under me and pinched my clit between her fingers. That felt so good I pulled at my bonds as hard as I could. "You're teasing me!" I cried.

Of course she had to laugh. My ass was red now. The crop she used was a far cry from the horse feathers. It burned like a match. Below the waist, I felt like another body was taking over. When she reached for my cunt and pressed her knuckles inside me, I groaned and let her give me the hardest strokes. Her fucking me was the only thing that made it bearable.

I had to ask for a break. My tears were constant now, but my mind felt clear. "Coral, how am I supposed to take this pain? It's so intense. I don't know where to go with it."

She pushed my hair out of my face and helped me blow my nose. "Well, there are lots of ways to think about it. When I get hit, I like to think about deserving it, needing to be punished."

"I can't do that!" I choked. "I was just thinking the very opposite . . . all I can think of is that I don't deserve this. I didn't do anything wrong."

"Well, you can do it for Honey Lee. I know that's what she'd like."

"Yes, that's what O would do, but I'm too selfish for that."

"You can be selfish as well. A lot of people like to take the pain and connect the intensity to their clit or their nipples."

"Maybe. When you stroke my clit and fuck me, I appreciate the whip a little, because my cunt sucks the sensation right up."

My break was over. That cane, the five-foot bamboo cane, was still standing in the corner. I had a feeling I wouldn't be able to erotically connect any part of my body to *that.*

Coral traced her fingers over a little star of a welt on my left bottom cheek. It did indeed throb. She picked up her cane and drew its length through the crack of my ass. It was so hard and spiny. Then she cut it through the air like a thunderclap. When it snapped on my ass, my legs turned to Jell-O and for the first time, I screamed. I screamed so loud I scared myself. It came down again and my heart flew out of my mouth.

"Coral, please, please, I can't do it, please, Jesus, I can't."

Maybe that's what I said, I don't know. All I remember is begging Coral to stop. She complied instantly.

She knew I'd reached my limit. She didn't carry out the rest of the punishment they'd threatened for all my earlier smarty-pants remarks. She unlatched my wrist cuffs in an instant and took me in her arms. There's nothing like being taken care of after you've been hurt like that. I wanted to cling to her for ages.

"Your lover is waiting for you," she said, untangling herself from my sweaty body and reaching down to unchain my legs. I wobbled out of bed and picked up my boots. Everything was so heavy.

"Coral, you're going to suffer terribly for what you did to me today." I knew that would make her happy.

I stood by the front window and gathered my things. Glancing down below, I saw that our car was still there, with Honey Lee inside. She was staring right up at our floor, with her mirrored sunglasses on. What had she been dreaming about, watching the window this whole time!

I don't think Honey has ever seen me so serene as when I got in the front seat. "You look like a saint," she said when I sat down.

"Yeah, well, you know how religious experiences are," I whispered. I wasn't surprised when she pulled a long white scarf out of the glove compartment and told me to turn my head. She wrapped it around my eyes several times. I didn't even try to follow the car's direction. I felt nothing urgent, except the pulse of the stripes on my behind.

When we came to a stopping place, she led me down a narrow sidewalk and into a low-ceilinged room. We were back home. I could hear voices exclaim their admiration as I entered the room. Many hands, too many to count, reached out for my clothes and undressed me. They lifted me onto a soft bed, but I still couldn't tell how many or who they were. I was being kissed all over. Oil was being dribbled on my chest. I was massaged by countless fingers. Someone lifted my head and slipped in a cold piece of peach. I smelled the champagne just as the glass was pressed to my lips. A little of that spilled down my neck and then I felt a cool mouthful of the same liquid circle my nipple. I tried to count how many were there, and identify their voices, but it was impossible. They kept changing positions, and I couldn't concentrate on more than three sensations at a time. I was so wet and warm and stinging that I gave up trying to think at all.

But someone else started kissing me, deeply: Honey Lee. The other hands and tongues began to fade, and it wasn't just my imagination. The hundreds of fingertips were leaving me. Honey Lee never left my mouth, but the rest of my body became still.

She took off my blindfold. No one was left except for us.

"Are they going to come back? You tell me who they were!" I knew she wouldn't tell me. "How can I go out and work or call my friends when I have no idea who was here making love to me?"

Honey gave up nothing. "Did you like your birthday, Susie?"

The next week, I pulled a couple of handwritten envelopes out from among the bills piled in the mailbox. I opened the first one and found a polaroid of my friend Miranda doing something outrageous to my toes, surrounded by seven other busy pairs of hands. "Your feet were divine," she had written on the border. Similar envelopes followed.

"I wonder how many photographs like this are in circulation?" I said out loud. But O wouldn't have asked such a thing. She would have written her story in all its detail. And so I did.

SUSIE BRIGHT
on *"Story of O* Birthday Party"

I wrote this the day after my thirtieth birthday. I'm turning fifty this year. Everything in it is exactly as it took place. There're some beautiful photographs that accompany the story—too bad this isn't a picture book! I still don't know how Honey Lee convinced that cop to do a scene with me. It's a love story about dykes in San Francisco, and a time when we thought anything was possible.

TOP OF THE 15TH:
Best American Erotica's *Authors*
1993–2008

Blake C. Aarens
Matthew Addison
Eric Albert
Dorothy Allison
Steve Almond
Katya Andreevna
Adelina Anthony

Nicholson Baker
Vanesa Baggott
Marianna Beck
Wendy Becker
Edo van Belkom
Dodie Bellamy
Todd Belton
Aimee Bender
Marie Lyn Bernard
Bertice Berry
L. Elise Bland
Hanne Blank
Francesca Lia Block
Ted Blumberg
Paula Bomer
G. Bonhomme
William Borden
Bernadette Bosky

Debra Boxer
Greg Boyd
Bill Brent
Susie Bright
Poppy Z. Brite
Michael Bronski
Cara Bruce
Lauren P. Burka
Rachel Kramer Bussel
Mark Butler
Octavia E. Butler
Robert Olen Butler

Pat Califia
Jamie Callan
Eloise Chagrin
Renee Charles
Alexander Chee
Maxine Chernoff
M. Christian
Greta Christina
Richard Collins
Ernie Conrick
Dennis Cooper
Haddayr Copley-Woods
Amelia Copeland

Alan Cumming
Jameson Currier
Jessica Cutler

Joel Dailey
Vaginal Davis
Samuel R. Delany
Robert Devereaux
Elise D'Haene
Susan DiPlacido
Michael Dorsey
Daniel Duane
Sidney Durham

Lars Eighner
Rowan Elizabeth
Stephen Elliott
Bret Easton Ellis
Nathan Englander
David R. Enoch
Alicia Erian
Corwin Erickson
Estabrook
Maggie Estep

Edward Falco
Lauraleigh Farrell
Leslie Feinberg
Scarlett Fever
Bonny Finberg
Bob Flanagan
Charles Flowers
Michael Thomas Ford
Lynn Freed
Jack Fritscher

Amelia G
Mary Gaitskill
Sera Gamble

Martha Garvey
R. Gay
Nelson George
Shanna Germain
Alicia Gifford
Dagoberto Gilb
Gabrielle Glancy
Robert Glück
Sigfried Gold
Barbara Gowdy
Damian Grace
Myriam Gurba

Mel Harris
Kathryn Harrison
William Harrison
Bert Hart
P. S. Haven
Maria Dahvana Headley
Trebor Healey
Will Heinrich
Vicki Hendricks
Shu-Huei Henrickson
A. W. Hill
A. M. Homes
Linda Hooper
Nalo Hopkinson

Karl Iagnemma
Susannah Indigo
Robert Irwin

Linda Jaivin
Bianca James
Tennessee Jones
Brandon Judell

Ginu Kamani
Nicolas Kaufman

Susanna Kaysen
Kevin Killian
Nancy Kilpatrick
Wade Kreuger

Geoffrey A. Landis
J. T. Leroy
Le Shaun
Shaun Levin
Marc Levy
Tsaurah Litzky
Rosalind Christine Lloyd
Allegra Long
Michael Lowenthal
Al Lujan

Mary Malmros
Alma Marceau
Ann Marie Mardith
Debra Martens
Gwen Masters
Andi Mathis
Joe Maynard
Adam McCabe
Bernice McFadden
Dan Taulapapa McMullin
Kelly McQuain
Melissa
Magenta Michaels
Jay Michaelson
Martha Miller
Mary Anne Mohanraj
Serena Moloch
Lisa Montanarelli
Susanna Moore
Mistress Morgana
Eva Morris
Jennifer D. Munro
Peggy Munson

Jack Murnighan
Susan Musgrave

Ben Neihart
Bill Noble
Anna Nymus

Chris Offutt

Lisa Palac
Chuck Palahniuk
Gerry Pearlberg
Keri Pentauk
Tom Perrotta
Bart Plantenga
Marian Phillips
Marge Piercy
John Preston

Andy Quan
Carol Queen

Donald Rawley
Shar Rednour
Annie Regrets
Rachel Resnick
Anne Rice
Stacey Richter
Thomas S. Roche
M. J. Rose
Gary Rosen
Camille Roy
Leigh Rutledge

Dominic Santi
Steven Saylor writing as Aaron
    Travis
David Sedaris
Dani Shapiro

Raye Sharpe
David Shields
Marcy Sheiner
Simon Sheppard
Robert Silverberg
Nicki Sinclair
Laurie Sirois
John Mason Skipp
Mr. Sleep
Jane Smiley
Alison L. Smith
Mel Smith
Linda Smukler
Jill Soloway
Stephen Spotte
Jerry Stahl
Michael Stamp
Susan St. Aubin
Mark Steurtz
E. R. Stewart
Donna George Storey
James Strouse
Patrice Suncircle
Ronald Sukenick
Robin Sweeney
Matt Bernstein Sycamore

Cecilia Tan
Lucy Taylor
Lana Gayle Taylor
Michelle Tea
Abigail Thomas
Trish Thomas
Doug Tierney
Ivy Topiary
Touré

Anne Tourney
Claire Tristram

John Updike

Loana DP Valencia
Joy VanNuys
I. K. Velasco
Bob Vickery
Susan Volchok
Trac Vu

Sharon Wachsler
Kweli Walker
Anne Wallace
Helen Walsh
Pam Ward
Molly Weatherfield aka Pam
    Rosenthal
Jess Wells
Rose White
Salome Wilde
Danielle Willis
James Williams
Carter Wilson
Lisa Wolfe
Kim Wright

John Yohe
Shay Youngblood
Gaea Yudron

Zane
Steven Zeeland
Bob Zordani

READERS' DIRECTORY
The Most Influential Erotic Editors, Journals, and Web Sites of the Past 15 Years

Adrienne, publisher and editor, Erotic Readers & Writers Association, http://www.erotica-readers.com

Marianna Beck and Jack Hafferkamp, publishers and editors, *Libido*, http://www.libidomag.com

Hanne Blank, *Unruly Appetites, Shameless*, http://hanneblank.com

Joani Blank, publisher and editor, Down There Press, erotica and sex education, http://www.joaniblank.com

Violet Blue, *Best Women's Erotica, Sweet Life, Taboo*, http://www.tiny nibbles.com

Bill Brent, publisher, *Black Sheets, Black Books*, http://litboy.typepad.com

Susie Bright, *Best American Erotica, Herotica, On Our Backs*, http://susiebright.com

Rachel Kramer Bussel, *S/he's on Top, Naughty Spanking Stories*, http://www.rachelkramerbussel.com

M. Christian, *Best S/M Erotica, Garden of the Perverse*, http://zobop.blogspot.com

Amanda Copeland, editor, *Paramour Magazine*, http://www.wellesley.edu/Womensreview

Rufus Griscom and Genivieve Field, founders and publishers, *Nerve*, http://www.nerve.com

Susannah Indigo, Bill Noble, Maryanne Mohanraj, editors, *Clean Sheets,* http://www. cleansheets.com

Maxim Jakubowski and Marilyn Jaye Lewis, editors and authors, The Mammoth Erotica series, http://www.fantasticfiction.co.uk/j/maxim-jakubowski, http://www.marilynjayelewis.com

Harold Jaffe, editor, *Fiction International,* http://www.fiction international.com

Richard Kasak, publisher, Masquerade Books, http://www.magic-carpet-books.com

Richard LaBonte, series editor, *Best Gay Erotica,* http://qsyndicate.com

Literotica.com, http://www.literotica.com

Mary Anne Mohanraj, publisher, editor, and author, *Aqua Erotica,* http://www.mamohanraj.com

Joe Maynard, author and editor, *Beet* and *Pink Pages,* http://myspace .com/dalailamaparton

LaVada Nahon, editor, *Penthouse,* http://susiebright.blogs.com/susie_brights_journal_/2005/08/penthouse_lette.html

Felice Newman and Frederique Delacoste, publishers, *Cleis Press* erotic series, http://www.cleispress.com/category_index.php?category=Erotica

Lily Pond, publisher/editor, *Yellow Silk,* http://www.well.com/user/green/Yellow%20Silk/ysysysysys.html

John Preston and Michael Lowenthal, editors and authors, *Flesh and the Word,* http://en.wikipedia.org/wiki/John_Preston, http://lowenthal .etherweave.com

Mark Pritchard and Cris Gutierrez, publishers, editors and authors, *Frighten the Horses,* http://www.toobeautiful.org/fth.html

Carol Queen, author and editor, *5-Minute Erotica, Whipped, The Leather Daddy and the Femme,* http://www.carolqueen.com

Blanche Richardson and Iyanla Vanzant, editors, *Best Black Women's Erotica,* http://www.cleispress.com/book_page.php?book_id=6

Thomas S. Roche, editor and author, *Noirotica,* http://www.skidroche .com

Ruthie's Club, http://www.ruthiesclub.com

H. L. Shaw, editor, *Fishnet*, Blowfish.com, http://www.fishnetmag.com

Simon Sheppard, editor and author, *In Deep, Roughed Up, Rough Sex, Hotter Than Hell*, http://www.simonsheppard.com

Marcy Sheiner, editor and author, *Best Women's Erotica, Herotica*, http://marcysheiner.tripod.com

Michelle Slung, editor and author, *Slow Hand*, women's erotica, http://www.chronogram.com/issue/2007/4/Books/The-Constant-Gardener

Cecilia Tan, publisher, editor, and author, Circlet Press, erotic literature specializing in science fiction and fantasy, http://www.circlet.com

Joel Tan, *Inside Him: New Gay Erotica, Best Gay Asian Erotica, Queer PAPI Porn*, http://www.cleispress.com/book_page.php?book_id=10

Tristan Taormino, series editor, *Best Lesbian Erotica*, http://www.puckerup.com

Carol Taylor, series editor, *Brown Sugar*, http://www.brownsugarbooks.com

Alison Tyler, *Red Hot Erotica, Naked Erotica, Best Bondage Erotica, Birthday Book, Caught Looking, Down and Dirty, Naughty Stories A–Z*, http://alisontyler.blogspot.com

Sage Vivant, *Best of Both Worlds: Bisexual Erotica*, http://www.sagevivant.com

Greg Wharton and Ian Phillips, publishers and editors, Suspect Thoughts Press, queer and outlaw erotica, http://www.suspectthoughts.com

CONTRIBUTORS

ERIC ALBERT has been an interpreter for the deaf, computer scientist, teacher, crossword-puzzle constructor, sex researcher, stock-market investor, editor, and writer. He's trained as a psychotherapist but has never practiced, except with intriguing strangers in long conversations really late at night. He lives in a suburb of Boston, and his cunnilingus skills are legendary.

STEVE ALMOND is the author of two story collections, *My Life in Heavy Metal* and *The Evil B. B. Chow*, and a new book of essays called *(Not That You Asked)*. He lives outside Boston with his wife and baby daughter Josephine, whom he worships at all hours.

G. BONHOMME does not live in a small, run-down former servants' cottage on the grounds of an abandoned European manor, smoking furiously, and penning erotic tales on a recalcitrant 1970s-era Selectric typewriter. Nor does G. Bonhomme walk grumbling on cold mornings through winding, narrow paths in the undergrowth overtaking the manor, scaring the swallows, and waiting for the mail carrier to arrive on her rickety bicycle. However, it is true that two of Bonhomme's stories have been published at Fishnet.com, in the friendly neon hubbub of San Francisco, far away from manors, swallows, and underbrush.

DEBRA BOXER is a writer from New Jersey who currently lives in Seattle. Her work has appeared in *The Best American Erotica 2000* and *2002*, *Nerve, Clean Sheets, Moxie, Publishers Weekly*, the *San Francisco Chronicle*, and the *Daily Record of New Jersey*. She is currently working on a collection of short stories.

A visual artist as well as a bullshit artist, GREG BOYD currently enjoys a view of the Blue Ridge Mountains. His latest book is a multimedia fictional biography entitled *The Nambuli Papers*, and his novella "The Widow" is part of Susie Bright's novella series *Three the Hard Way*. Having created and portrayed so many characters over the years, he has finally come to understand that he himself may be a part of some larger fiction and that all human endeavor, imaginary or otherwise, is just a form of tide writing.

ELOISE CHAGRIN is a writer of erotic poetry and prose. Her first short story, "Playing Doctor," was on ThreePillows.com and her second, "Tango Before Lomo," on TheEroticWoman.com. Ms. Chagrin is working on a collection of short stories, and has been told that she spends too much of her life fixated on emotional masochism. She currently lives in St. Louis.

GRETA CHRISTINA has been writing professionally since 1989. She is editor of *The Best Erotic Comics* series, which debuted in 2007. Other books include *Paying for It: A Guide by Sex Workers for Their Clients*, and "Bending," one of Susie Bright's three-novella erotica collection *Three Kinds of Asking for It*. She has been published in several magazines and anthologies, including *Ms.*, *Penthouse*, and *The Best American Erotica*. She blogs at gretachristina.typepad.com.

HADDAYR COPLEY-WOODS has stories in places such as *Strange Horizons*, *Ideomancer*, and *Polyphony*. A columnist for the *Minnesota Women's Press*, she lives with her husband and two sons in Minneapolis, Minnesota. She has never heard suspicious moaning sounds coming from the basement. Her Web site is http://www.haddayr.com.

ROWAN ELIZABETH lives in small-town Indiana with her husband, daughter, and a menagerie of pets. Her wide array of erotic fiction has appeared in *Ruthie's Club*, Erotica Readers and Writers Association, *For

The Girls, and in Cleis Press's *After Midnight*. You can share in her perversions at www.rowanelizabeth.com.

MARTHA GARVEY is a New York–based writer whose fiction has appeared in multiple editions of *The Best American Erotica*, as well as other collections, including *Strange Pleasures 3*, *Exhibitions*, and *Glamour Girls*. Her essays have appeared in *Bust*, *Bitch*, *The New York Times*, and *Killing the Buddha*.

NELSON GEORGE is an author, TV producer, and film director. He's written numerous novels and award-winning nonfiction books, including *The Death of Rhythm & Blues* and *Hip Hop America*. He has produced television programs for HBO, BET, and VH-1. He made his directorial debut with *Life Support*, an HBO movie starring Queen Latifah. George lives in Brooklyn, New York.

ALICIA GIFFORD lives, loves, and writes in the Los Angeles area. Her short fiction appears in *Alaska Quarterly Review*, *Narrative Magazine*, *Confrontation*, and *The Barcelona Review*, among others. She believes in chaos, coincidence, evolution, and serendipity.

SUSANNAH INDIGO is the editor in chief of *Clean Sheets* and the founding editor of *Slow Trains Literary Journal*. Her books include *Sex & Laughter*, *Oysters Among Us*, the *From Porn to Poetry* series, and her new collection, *Geishas Don't Eat Nachos*. For further information, see http://www.susannahindigo.com, http://www.cleansheets.com, and http://www.slowtrains.com.

TSAURAH LITZKY writes dirty stories for *The Best American Erotica* because she believes in sharing her cream. Tsaurah's cream is for world peace and against mind control. Her erotic novella "The Motion of the Ocean" was included in *Three the Hard Way*, a series of erotic novellas edited by Susie Bright. Tsaurah's erotic stories have appeared in *The Best American Erotica* eight times. When not writing dirty stories, she writes poetry, teaches erotic writing at the New School in Manhattan, does yoga, eats good food, and, hopefully, makes love.

CONTRIBUTORS

JOE MAYNARD published his own 'zines *Beet* and *Pink Pages* in the 1990s, and his fiction, essays, and poetry have been included in numerous publications, most recently in *Up Is Up But So Is Down*, edited by Brandon Stosuy. He also writes songs and performs with a band under the moniker Maynard and the Musties, and can be found at http://myspace.com/maynardandthemusties and http://myspace.com/dalailamaparton.

SERENA MOLOCH went into informal retirement from writing erotica after publishing "Casting Couch," and since then has been having the most wonderful sex of her life.

JENNIFER D. MUNRO makes an unsavory living working for lawyers. Her credits include *The Best American Erotica 2004, Best Women's Erotica 2003, Mammoth Book of Best New Erotica Numbers 3 & 6, The Bigger the Better the Tighter the Sweater: 20 Funny Women on Beauty and Body Image*, and others. Her website is http://www.munrojd.com.

MARIAN PHILLIPS lives in San Francisco. Her publications include her translation of *The Confessions of Wanda von Sacher-Masoch*. She is currently at work on a novel.

THOMAS S. ROCHE is the managing editor of ErosZine.com and the author of more than four hundred works of published fiction, most in the erotica genre and others in crime, horror, science fiction, and fantasy. A longtime resident of the San Francisco area, he teaches at San Francisco Sex Information, and organizes the Barbary Coast branch of the burlesque figure-drawing salon, Dr. Sketchy's Anti Art School. More information can be found at his site, http://www.skidroche.com.

STEVEN SAYLOR writes about ancient Rome—eleven volumes in his mystery series featuring Gordianus the Finder. When his muse was erotic, his alter ego "Aaron Travis" flourished; then his interests moved to history, politics, and warfare, "where the real obscenities can be found." His most recent novel, *Roma*, was a *New York Times* bestseller. He lives in Berkeley, California, and Austin, Texas.

CONTRIBUTORS

"This Isn't About Love" is SUSAN ST. AUBIN's fifth story to be chosen for *The Best American Erotica*, a reprint of her second appearance in the *Herotica* series, and the fourth erotic story she ever wrote. Many more stories have followed over the years. Recently her work has been in *The Best American Erotica 2007*, *Amazons: Sexy Tales of Strong Women*, and *Transgender Erotica: Transfigures*.

PATRICE SUNCIRCLE was born in west Tennessee Delta country. She has lived in Illinois, Florida, Hawaii, and Minnesota. She resides in Oakland with two rooms full of books and plants, and is writing a novel about the famous vampire balls of the Harlem Renaissance.

CREDITS

"The Letters," by Eric Albert, © 1995 Eric Albert, first appeared under the name of Rickey L. Bert in *Paramour,* vol. 3, no. 1, Fall/Winter 1995, edited by Amelia Copeland, published by Paramour, 1995, and is reprinted by permission of the author.

"A Jew Berserk on Christmas Eve," by Steve Almond, © 2005 Steve Almond, first appeared in *Nerve,* published by Nerve.com LLC, 2005, and is reprinted by permission of the author.

"The Program," by G. Bonhomme, © 2006 G. Bonhomme, first appeared in *Fishnet,* May 10, 2006, edited by Heather Shaw, published by Blowfish.com, 2006, and is reprinted by permission of the author.

"Horny," by Greg Boyd, © 1992 Greg Boyd, first appeared in *Fiction International 22,* edited by Harold Jaffe, Larry McCaffery, and Mel Freilicher, published by San Diego State University Press, 1992, and is reprinted by permission of the author.

"Innocence in Extremis," by Debra Boxer, © 1998 by Debra Boxer, first appeared in *Nerve: Literate Smut,* edited by Genevieve Field and Rufus Griscom (Broadway Books 1998); was subsequently published in *Moxie* magazine, edited by Emily Hancock (Moxie, 1998), and is reprinted by permission of the author.

"*Story of O* Birthday Party," by Susie Bright, © 1992 Susie Bright, first appeared in *Susie Bright's Sexual Reality,* published by Cleis Press, 1992, and is reprinted by permission of the author.

"Playing Doctor," by Eloise Chagrin, © 2006 Eloise Chagrin, first appeared in *Three Pillows,* September 2006, published by ThreePillows.com, 2006, and is reprinted by permission of the author.

"The Desires of Houses," by Haddayr Copley-Woods, © 2006 Haddayr Copley-Woods, first appeared in *StrangeHorizons,* February 13,

ABOUT THE EDITOR AND AUTHOR

SUSIE BRIGHT is the founding editor of *The Best American Erotica* series. She is the original editor of *Herotica*, and one of the founders of the first women-authored erotic magazine, *On Our Backs*. She is the author of seven books on sexuality, politics, and culture and a teaching book on erotic writing and publishing, is the coauthor of the award-winning *Nothing But the Girl* photography portfolio, and is the publisher of a daily blog, *Susie Bright's Journal*. Her writing has been featured on film in *Bound, Celluloid Closet, Erotique,* and *Six Feet Under*. More information may be found at http://susiebright.com.

Read the entire collection of
Susie Bright's groundbreaking
EROTICA SERIES

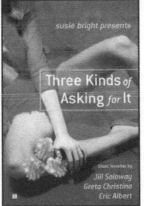